PRAISE FO~~R~~
THE WO~~RK~~

'Lee's debut novel is like Caoilinn Hughes' *The Orchid and the Wasp* meets Andrew Lipstein's *Last Resort*. A smart, sexy page-turner, *The Work* cleverly traces the flow of cultural capital in the international art world, bringing sizzle and romance to the age-old tension of art versus commerce.' **Madeleine Gray, author of *Green Dot***

'Well this is annoying. Bri Lee—whose nonfiction debut *Eggshell Skull* revealed a fine mind and a stout heart—turns out to be a brilliant novelist as well. This novel isn't just good; it's superb. Assured, and powerful, and intelligent, and very, VERY hard to put down. Bri Lee has an established knack of articulating human confusion, pain and the cracks that open up in the systems we design to govern ourselves. And in *The Work*, she brings all her thrilling intelligence and her journalist's eye to the art world, and its awkward historic dicta about who gets to make art, and how badly they can behave while they're making it. Also it's a love story. And a story about growing up in the country and moving to the city, observed with a perfect degree of spiky tenderness. I consumed it in a passion.' **Annabel Crabb, journalist, broadcaster and author of *The Wife Drought***

'Bri Lee has an uncanny, remarkable and refreshing way of drawing you in quickly. By the first chapter, I felt like I personally knew the characters and was LIVING the moments with them. Bri's style of writing is comfortable even during uncomfortable moments in the story. Work, power, passion, intimacy and vulnerabilities collide, and best of all, SMUT!!!!!!!!!!!!!!!!!!!' **Flex Mami, author of *The Success Experiment***

'An ambitious and meticulously modern fable about art, sex, money, power and the perils of self-curation.' **Gina Rushton, author of** *The Most Important Job in the World*

'What is art and who gets to make it, champion it, sell it, buy it? A fresh and compelling answer to timeless questions. Urgent, sexy and deliciously cynical, *The Work* interrogates the unholy marriage of art and capitalism.' **Neela Janakiramanan, author of** *The Registrar*

'Pacy, racy and high-octane, *The Work* delves into the volatile world of contemporary art, forcefully exposing it as a bedfellow to the world of high finance.' **Caoilinn Hughes, author of** *The Wild Laughter*

'A thoroughly modern love story, *The Work is* Rooney-esque in how it handles the collision of our ideals, our ambition and our feelings. A brilliant meditation on the gap between the person we wish to be and who we actually are. I was completely gripped.' **Bridie Jabour, author of** *Trivial Grievances*

'Bri Lee the novelist has *arrived*. Provocative, precocious and utterly gripping, this is the kind of novel that has everyone at book club talking over one another. Without an ounce of banality, Bri Lee perfectly skewers the millennial woman's "career or family" conundrum. As formidable as it is tender: a brilliantly told long-distance love affair.' **Jamila Rizvi, author of** *Work. Love. Body.*

'*The Work* is a punchy, pacey and powerful interrogation of the politics of love and art. Bri Lee writes sex like Sally Rooney and critiques capitalism and privilege like Bri Lee. I couldn't stop reading this daring and dazzling book.' **Paige Clark, author of** *She Is Haunted*

'A completely exhilarating, powerful, mesmerising novel, filled with ALL my favourite things: sex, art and New York City. This is a searing story about artistic labour, ambition and the endlessly exhausting pursuits of our ideal self. I already knew Lee to be an exceptional writer. Now, I know she is also an exceptional novelist.' **Jessie Tu, author of** *A Lonely Girl is a Dangerous Thing*

'*The Work* is a glamorous and dirty capitalist fever dream, highlighting the individualistic tensions and ambitions rife within the art world. This dynamic novel is complex, opulent and horny.' **Ella Baxter, author of** *New Animal*

'Smart, witty and super steamy, *The Work* oozes intelligence and pulses with energy. I devoured it!' **Emily Maguire, author of** *Love Objects*

'Bombastic, libidinal, and even vulgar, *The Work* hurtles the reader through bright lights, big cities, and even bigger questions about art and life—all the while beating with a warm Queensland heart.' **Jessica Stanley, author of** *A Great Hope*

'About exclusions and inclusions, old and new art and the spoken—and unspoken—rules governing privilege and class, *The Work* covers so much ground impressively without being laboured or weighty. I've long admired Bri Lee's non-fiction and investigative writing but her fiction work is wholly its own—I couldn't put it down.' **Zara Wong, journalist**

'Scorching, self-scouring: a young woman finds her steel and learns to wield it.' **Helen Garner**

'Just finished this in tears, full of admiration. Bri Lee's story of standing up for herself and braving a biased, underfunded, incompetent legal system to demand justice is beautifully written, tender and powerful. Accompanying Lee through her transformation from a frightened girl into a blazingly formidable adult—whose courage comes from her determination to stand up for all women—was moving, gut-churning, and ultimately triumphant. I punched the air when I finished. RESPECT.' **Charlotte Wood, author of *Stone Yard Devotional* and *The Natural Way of Things***

'An important story, beautifully told.' **Julia Baird**

'Half the people I know are reading this or have just finished and with good reason. Confronting, tough and very, very necessary. Thanks for holding your nerve, @bri.e.lee.' **Emily Maguire, author of *Love Objects***

'Brutal, brave and utterly compelling, Bri Lee's extraordinary memoir shines a light on the humanity and complexity of our justice system and the limitless courage victims of crime must summon in a legal process stacked against them at every turn. In the age of #MeToo, *Eggshell Skull* is a prescient personal account of a young woman's fierce and unflinching battle against her abuser. I can't remember a book I devoured with such intensity, nor one that moved me so profoundly.' **Rebecca Starford, author of *The Imitator* and co-founder of *Kill Your Darlings***

'Just wow @brieloiselee. *Eggshell Skull* is extraordinary. Vulnerable, moving and ever so wise. Huge congratulations.' **Tracey Spicer, AM**

'I loved *Eggshell Skull*. It is grim, intense but utterly triumphant. Congratulations.' **Jane Caro, author and public education advocate**

'If you have ever uttered the phrase "there's no such thing as a rape culture", you need to read this book. If you believe that "women lie all the time" just to get revenge or out of guilt over sex, you need to read this book. If you think men are being unfairly accused by women and that the system is predisposed against them "because feminism", you need to read this book.' **Clementine Ford, author of *Fight Like A Girl* and *I Don't***

'Lee walks a precarious line with incredible control, is never exploitative or voyeuristic, and remains frank and articulate . . . Above all, Lee is simply a good writer. She tells her story with remarkable empathy, vulnerability and clever, even humorous, prose . . . *Eggshell Skull* will leave you feeling triumphant and crushed. Sitting at my kitchen table after reading the final page, I put it down and cried.' ***Good Reading***

'Lee's story has the addictive quality of any car crash in slow motion. She has a talent for making the often dreary practice of law seem electric with weirdness and submerged drama, and a particular flair for the one-liner. We should feel gratitude and optimism that women of talent and intelligence are writing brave, self-aware, excoriating books such as these.' ***The Australian***

'A searing exposé of the unacknowledged wankiness in our most revered ideas and structures, imbued with Bri's unmistakable unflinching self-examination.' **Alice Pung, author of** *Unpolished Gem* **and** *Laurinda*

'Bri Lee is that most wonderful of writers: she uses language in the service of thinking. *Who Gets to be Smart* is an electric thrill of a book. Lee takes the very idea of intelligence and pokes at it, turns it over and reshapes it so that we might be unshackled from our worst instincts. The writing is impeccable and driven by a delicious curiosity. Though the subject can often become disturbing in its implications, I took a distinct pleasure in reading every line.' **Rick Morton, author of** *A Hundred Years of Dirt* **and** *My Year of Living Vulnerably*

'A fascinating, eye-opening and sometimes hurtful reminder that we have a lot of unlearning to do. This book was a sharp wake-up call, asking me to reflect on who I personally regarded as smart, and why. Or worse, who I regarded as dumb. Also got me thinking, why do humans go out of their way to create wiiiildly subjective reasons as to why our particular views and our approach to life makes us smarter than others?' **Lillian Ahenkan/Flex Mami, author of** *The Success Experiment*

'Once I started reading, I couldn't put it down! Bri Lee brilliantly explores the criss-crossing of money, power and colonialism with notions of knowledge, education and smartness. She does this with heart while fearlessly delving into her own insecurities and assumptions, challenging me to do the same.' **Senator Mehreen Faruqi**

'I love how this book's mood starts out with genuine humility, turns fiery, and finally emerges into a bright clear light. It is essential reading for anyone who suspects that "intelligence" is not a fixed, objective quantity but a sophisticated con job. It left me full of hope.' **Malcolm Knox, author of *Bluebird* and *Truth is Trouble***

'What is so very impressive about Lee's book are the precision and clarity of her arguments, and also the elegance and attentiveness of her prose. I was absorbed by *Who Gets to be Smart* from the first page. This is debate and questioning done with absolute verve, with eloquence and generosity.' **Christos Tsiolkas, author of *The In-Between* and *The Slap***

'Intriguing and vital examination of contemporary elitism and how privilege determines who lucks out in the game of education and its associated opportunities for life.' **Liz Allen, author of *The Future of Us***

Bri Lee is the multi-award-winning author of *Eggshell Skull*, *Beauty* and *Who Gets to be Smart*. Her journalism, essays, and short stories have been published widely, and she is the creator and editor of *News & Reviews*. *The Work* is Bri's debut novel.

BRI LEE

THE WORK

ALLEN&UNWIN
SYDNEY·MELBOURNE·AUCKLAND·LONDON

First published in 2024

Allen & Unwin
Cammeraygal Country
83 Alexander Street
Crows Nest NSW 2065
Australia
Phone: (61 2) 8425 0100
Email: info@allenandunwin.com
Web: www.allenandunwin.com

Allen & Unwin acknowledges the Traditional Owners of the Country on which we live and work. We pay our respects to all Aboriginal and Torres Strait Islander Elders, past and present.

A catalogue record for this book is available from the National Library of Australia

ISBN 978 1 76106 939 0

Set in 13.2/17 pt Garamond Premier Pro by Bookhouse, Sydney
Printed and bound in Australia by the Opus Group

10 9 8 7 6

MIX
Paper | Supporting responsible forestry
FSC® C001695

The paper in this book is FSC® certified. FSC® promotes environmentally responsible, socially beneficial and economically viable management of the world's forests.

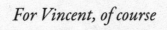

For Vincent, of course

1

THEY SIGNED MOMA'S ACQUISITION CONTRACT and got drunk to celebrate. By the end of the second bottle, Lally felt like she was flying. You really could mix business and pleasure. You really could make money and art.

'Come here,' Joseph said to her, putting his flute down and pulling her to him.

They'd been dancing across her small living room, knocking down lamps. She was breaking her own rule—never sleep with your artists—but this was different. She had feelings for him. That hadn't happened in a long time. 'Shall we consummate it?' Lally grinned and kissed him.

He reached around her head and took out the hairclip, throwing it onto the couch, and her brown waves fell down past her shoulders. At first he was stroking her hair, but then his kiss got harder and he pulled it. She made a noise.

'Yes?' he asked.

'Yes.'

'Yes what?'

'Yes please.'

He turned her around and pushed her towards the bedroom. She pulled her dress up and over her head, felt his hand on her back, pushing her forward over the mattress, pulling down her underwear. All the lights on, all the blinds open. There were hundreds of other apartments lit up outside across East 12th Street, and she looked out at them as she touched herself, listening to the clink of his belt buckle, startling at his hand grabbing the place where her thighs met her hips. She turned around to face him, and he looked disappointed for a millisecond before she opened her legs and reached up for him.

'Do you like my nice apartment?' she asked.

He responded by going all the way in.

'Do you like my nice wine?'

He reached up and pulled the hair at the back of her neck again.

'I'm gonna make you rich, Rivera.'

He sped up. 'How rich?'

She laughed. 'Rich enough to make whatever art you want, do whatever you want.'

'Do whatever I want?' He slowed down again and looked at her.

She met his gaze. 'Whatever you want.'

He pulled out and grabbed at her hips, pushing her onto her knees and pulling her back to the edge of the bed. She knew he wouldn't come until she had. He knew she liked it hard sometimes, especially when she was in a chatty mood. They'd been here just enough times to flick each other's switches. Not enough times to be sure what might happen next.

Lally let her head drop forward and savoured the moment. One of his hands was leveraging her, the other was . . . where? About to smack her? She felt pleasure rippling through her just thinking about it. She'd ride him and look out these windows.

At the snow falling. At the miracle of a good day at work and a good fuck. A light came on in the distance outside. She watched it, wondering if maybe she was into voyeurism somehow, listening to the smacking of his skin on hers. But actually the light wasn't like the others. She tried to focus her eyes. The light wasn't from another apartment at all. The light in the window was a reflection of something in the room. The light was coming from right behind her, from the phone Joseph was holding, in his free hand, pointing down at her naked body.

Lally froze, trying to understand. Maybe she'd just drunk too much and was mixed up. But then she watched his reflection in terrible slow motion as he noticed she no longer had her back arched for him, and he followed her gaze out, and their eyes met in the reflection of the window.

'What the—' she started, moving forward up the bed.

His laughter cut her off. 'Just a little something for later.'

She turned to face him, pushing through the powerful drive to freeze on the spot, grabbing a pillow to cover herself. 'What!'

'You said whatever I want. It's just for me.' He moved towards her.

She screamed. 'Don't!' She couldn't formulate more than that. The shock of it. Her pulse.

'Woah.'

'Don't you come near me!'

'Lally, calm down.'

'Fuck you!'

'It's okay.' Joseph moved slowly towards her again and she scrambled off the side of the bed, still holding the pillow in front of her.

'I'll delete it,' he said, making a show of deleting the file then tossing the phone onto the bed. 'There.'

'Get out,' she ordered.

'Oh, come on now,' he said, acting hurt, his erection still strong. 'You're drunk, just take a deep breath.' He reached for her arm and she smacked his hand away, hard. 'Jesus!'

'How could you do that!' she yelled.

'Do what?' he yelled back, his arms out like a baller appealing an umpire.

She didn't say the second half: *How could you do that to me when I liked you?* She couldn't explain it through the hyperventilation. Couldn't understand how he didn't understand. Didn't he understand? She was sweating, a lot. He wasn't. He was walking over to the bottle of champagne on the side table, bringing it straight to his mouth, tipping it up and gulping it down until it was done. Then he wiped his mouth with the back of his hand and dropped the empty bottle onto the mattress.

'Get out.'

'Oh, come on, we're having a good time, let's—'

'Get out.'

'Lally . . .' He moved towards her and she flinched away, grabbing his phone where he'd left it.

'Get out!' she screamed again, still not able to formulate much else. Brain still flatlining. She held the phone up between them.

'What are you doing?'

'Get—' she keyed 9-1-1, the tone of the numbers instantly recognisable, and hovered her thumb over the little green phone symbol—'out.'

'The police!' He laughed, maniacally. 'For what?'

'For an aggressive Mexican working on a tourist visa, you piece of shit.'

His face turned nasty then, and his dick went limp nice and quick. She watched him gather his dirty work clothes, tripping as he tried to pull up his pants, all the while she was holding the pin in the grenade in her hand. He was mumbling cruel things in Spanish, banging the bathroom door open to find his shirt, and then when he'd gathered it all and made for the door, he froze. Lally saw the wave of panic cross over his body.

'Lally, come on.' He reached for her again.

She started crying when she saw his face. He had realised he'd made a mistake. Maybe he would say he was sorry. He could hold her. He could make some promises. Breathing in deeply, finally, the panic began to subside and a glimmer of the possibility of survival appeared. The phone was so heavy in her hand, the temptation to drop it was enormous. The temptation to drop all of it . . . Her chest heaved as she looked to him, wanting so badly for this to not be a serious thing. They would both feel better if it wasn't a serious thing. They could go back to the track they were on, of being together for real, not just for work.

He placed his hand on her forearm so gently then, and she let him take the phone from her and put it on the table. 'See,' he said, using his other hand to wipe her cheek, giving her a gentle smile. 'I told you,' he whispered, 'just calm down. Nothing's wrong.'

She screamed and slapped him across the face, and when he stumbled back, stunned, she shoved him as hard as she could in the chest, and he caught his foot in the leg of a chair at the dining table, falling backward. 'Get out! Get out! Get out!'

'You crazy bitch!'

'This crazy bitch is cancelling your show, motherfucker! I will sink you! Sink! You!'

He grabbed his wallet from where it sat in a little dish with hers, then yanked the door open and stormed out. *Crazy fucking bitch!* she heard him yell in the stairwell.

She tried taking deep breaths but could only pant. Her hands wouldn't stop shaking. His shoes still sat by the side of the couch where he'd kicked them off. He'd left without them, in the snow, and she worried for his feet, then worried more that he would come back for them. It was enough to un-anchor her. She went to the bottom drawer of the kitchen cabinet, ripping a trash bag off the roll, and went room by room. Every thing of his he'd left there in the weeks of them getting closer went into the bag, and she put it by the door with another bag of actual rubbish.

The rest of the night shat on by. She called Gen, who came over and helped take care of things. They went around the apartment, scouring it for any evidence of him. They changed the sheets. Gen put Lally in a hot shower.

'I didn't tell you,' Lally said to Gen, stepping over the side of the tub. 'I was . . . God, this sounds so fucking stupid—'

'You liked him,' Gen said.

Lally nodded and cried.

'I've just had an excellent idea,' Gen said, leaving the bathroom and returning with Joseph's phone, which she held out under the water until the screen showed a technicoloured freak-out and shut off.

When Lally got out, Gen poured them both tequilas.

She gestured to the garbage bags. 'Do you want to send this stuff back to him, or is it going in the trash?'

'Trash.'

'Good girl.'

They did their shots and poured two more.

2

PAT HEARD EMILY'S SOFT ONE-TWO knock on his heavy maple office door. 'Come in.'

'I've got a walk-in for you.'

'Oh, sure.'

She lowered her voice. 'New money.'

He smiled and shrugged. 'Great, send him in.'

Any commissions were better than no commissions. He'd been at Osborne's Sydney office almost a month and it hadn't been a strong start. This was his first-ever walk-in. So far he'd only been sent out to do appraisals and to assist with on-site auctions. He'd had no problem with those because he could prepare. A walk-in would require thinking on his feet and he wasn't so confident with that.

Em's voice came through the doorway a beat before she and another woman appeared. A bolt of recognition shot into Pat's guts.

'Ms Bauer, this is Patrick, our junior associate.'

'Thank you.' He paused to smile at Em, so that Sophie Bauer would have to make the first move towards him and set the tone.

He certainly remembered her, but there was a solid chance she wouldn't remember him.

Em backed out of the room with her hand on the brass knob.

'Patrick, call me Sophie.' She was smiling, holding out a hand. Gold bangles tinkled on her tiny wrist.

'Sophie it is,' he said, shaking her hand. 'Please have a seat.'

The woman who sat in front of Pat looked even more cosmetically enhanced than when he'd last seen her, about a decade earlier. Life had clearly been generous to Sophie, but perhaps not kind. As she described her impending divorce from Gregory, and explained that she had things she needed to sell, the blanks were filled in. Pat had gone to school with Gregory's sons—Sophie's stepsons. He'd been to their Mosman home. Laughed at the jokes Rory made about her getting stuck in the washing machine. They'd made bets on whether Sophie's tits were fake. Pat must have only seen her a few times. She wasn't one for school pick-ups. He didn't even know what line of work Gregory had been in. 'Business', no doubt. A lot of the boys' dads were just 'businessmen' or 'bankers'.

'Stuff like this,' Sophie said, reaching into her fine leather handbag and pulling out a filigreed mantel clock. She plonked it unceremoniously onto his tooled leather desk. 'I hate this old stuff, but it belongs to the family, so my lawyer says it's in the "shared asset" class and I'm entitled to half.'

Pat picked up the clock. 'Ah . . . the filigree work is good,' he said, focusing on what he did know rather than the horological acreage he didn't. 'Does it run?'

'Does it run?' She stared at him. 'Does it have to? Isn't it old enough to just be, you know, an antique?'

Pat laughed. 'I'd have to confer with a colleague, but you're right, it's old enough to be of value despite the condition of the internal mechanism.' He started pointing out features and asked her a question about provenance, but she was looking at her phone.

'Aren't you supposed to know that stuff? Or figure it out?' Sophie was eyeing him with a little wariness now. 'Anyway, the important thing is: can you sell it?'

'I'm sure I can.'

'Wonderful!' She sent a message then stood up. 'I'll come back in a week then? What do you think? A few thousand? Maybe five?'

'Ah . . .' Pat rose and walked around his desk to open the door for her. He didn't know how everything at Osborne worked yet, but he knew they didn't work like this.

She paused in the doorway and looked at him, putting her left hand on his bicep. 'I've got a house full of this stuff, Patrick. I was expecting to talk to someone more senior, but Emily said you're just new here and I wanna give you a red-hot go.' She squeezed his arm. 'I'll be back next week, and if you've got some good news for me, maybe we can make some money. How does that sound?'

He nodded. 'That sounds great.'

'But hush-hush, yes?'

'Sure.'

'Good boy.'

Sophie was gone as quickly and bafflingly as she had arrived. Pat remained standing at his office door with his hands on his hips, getting some oxygen in. What the fuck was that all about? She mustn't have recognised him or she would've said something. He returned to the computer at his desk, now graced with a mantel clock, and did a quick search online. His suspicions were immediately confirmed: Gregory Bauer's independent financial consultancy had gone under. Pat's heart started racing. This was a big, big fish. Sophie had given Pat a chance to prove his capabilities, and Pat would swallow his distaste for Sophie's clunky manoeuvre, because if his quick assessment of the situation was correct, he was about to sign a client who might bring in five times his annual salary. An embarrassing divorce. A need to liquidate assets without attracting too much attention. Everyone knew the Mosman mansion with the view was the Bauers', and their 'little getaway at Byron' had been featured in *Vogue Living* the year before, so it would be too humiliating to sell that. The Bauer family was up shit creek, and their significant arts and antiquities collection would be their only paddle.

He swung by Rory's bakery just before the sun rose the next morning. It was an artisanal place in Surry Hills where the croissants drove chicks nuts. The downside was that Rory's working day started at four thirty in the morning. Pat had a little stool in the corner of the poky kitchen. Sometimes after a big night he would get a cab straight to the bakery and sit in the corner talking shit while Rory worked, scoffing any slightly malformed goods that came out of the oven.

'A little sugar for my sweet,' Pat said, slapping Rory's shoulder and dropping a baggy on the counter.

'Oh, you shouldn't have!' Rory replied, retrieving his salt-measuring tool from the pocket of his apron. 'What's the occasion?'

'I need some information,' Pat said, lowering himself onto his stool in the corner, and they both laughed. 'Seriously, though— what do you remember about the Bauer family?'

Rory made a raspberry noise. 'I'm still mates with Dan. Chris was two years older than us but only one grade above, because he was so slow.'

'Yeah, yeah, I meant their house. What do you remember about their house?'

'The "media room"'—Rory made quote marks with his fingers—'and later on, when we were at uni, the parties.' He brought the spoon to his nose and snorted the little mound, flicking his fingers on the sides of his nostrils then rinsing them under the tap before turning back to his trays. Everything in Rory's work went by trays. Tray trolleys lined the walls. Oven trays and display trays and pastry trays and pie trays. He was about to take the morning's first batch of croissants out of the main oven: four trays of twelve.

'I didn't go to those parties. What do you remember seeing in the house?'

'Their stepmum hating all the schoolgirls vomiting in the bathroom,' he laughed.

'The art, I mean,' Pat clarified.

'Come on, that's more your field, isn't it?'

'Were there sculptures, do you think? Or any particularly big paintings?'

'Mmm, there was that awkward family photo with Chris and Dan's mum in it that their dad liked and their stepmum hated.' Then he grinned and raised his eyebrows at Pat. 'Remember their stepmum?'

'Focus!'

'Okay, sorry. Focus! I once snuck a girl into the master bedroom—remember Lindy?—and saw a huge photograph of a naked lady in black and white above the bed. I remember thinking it was the most boring kinky thing I'd ever seen.'

A buzzer went off and Rory snapped to the oven's attention. The next bit was Pat's favourite: when Rory pulled hard on the large silver latch to open the oven, the steam that plumed out filled the tight space with the smell of whatever had been baked. This time it was buttery pastry.

'What else?' Pat pushed.

'Once when Gregory was drunk he showed me his study and it had one of those green glass and brass lamps and an old globe. Like a wannabe James Bond den or something, so funny. All the clichéd shit.'

'Yes, more! What clichéd shit?'

Rory fished the baggy out of the front pocket of his black apron and took another tiny bump then squeezed his eyes shut, rolling his hands in a tumbling motion as if he could physically will the momentum of his own memories to return. 'Oh, man.' He started laughing. 'Hunting dogs—like, that old British style with men with shotguns over their shoulders and servants holding ducks by their feet.'

Pat laughed at that too. 'I don't think that guy ever held a gun in his life.'

'Or a duck! Oh, dude,' Rory brought his hands down and looked straight at Pat, his pupils positively lunar. 'I think they have a Warhol.'

'Bullshit.'

'It's small, but I saw it.'

'I shouldn't have given you that coke first.'

'Didn't I tell you?'

'I would fucking remember that.' Pat wasn't laughing. 'If you'd told me something like that I would remember it.'

'Don't be mad, dude.' Rory went back to his work. 'It's not a big deal to me.'

'What was it? Where was it?'

'Dining room. I remember it looked a bit weird because it was kind of small, but they'd given it this gigantic frame, and it was the only thing on a huge wall the length of the table—like, *look at our painting*, and the upholstery on the dining chairs and the flowers and the vase on the table all matched it.'

'Matched what?'

'The colours in the painting. I don't know anything about art, but even I knew this was cringe. These fat red tulips to match the soup can.'

'It was a soup can? You're sure?'

'Honestly, dude, I know the soup cans and the Marilyns. I don't think I would've known it was a Warhol if it was something else.'

Pat whipped his phone out and Rory went back to painting trays of raw *pains au chocolat* with egg yolk.

'They bounce back like a nice fat arse, don't you think?' Rory grinned, giving one a gentle spank and dipping the brush back into the bowl. 'You gonna tell me what's up?'

'Just a minute.' Pat was giddy. 'No soup cans have sold—in Australia, at least—in the last decade. I reckon they must still have it.'

'They'd have to redecorate the whole fucking room if they sold it.'

'Gimme a bump,' Pat said, excited.

Rory threw him the baggy and spoon.

'Sophie came to see me at work,' Pat explained, sorting himself out. 'Didn't know it was me. They're selling. Family's in trouble. They want it kept quiet.'

'And you want to sell their fancy shit so the poor little Pat inside you feels good again?'

'Wow, fuck you too, lol.' Pat threw Rory's spoon at him, but he caught it. 'And no. It's just that if I can swing this I'll probably get off probation. Landing big clients is how you get promoted.'

As Rory nodded, the buzzer went off, and he did the dance again, did another bump, and Pat noticed that outside the sun had almost risen.

'Want me to pop these on the counter?' he said.

'That'd be great, thanks, mate,' Rory called back over the sound of the trays clashing again from oven to trolley. 'By the way, one of the boys bought a ticket for the ten-year reunion but now he can't come. You want it?'

The school fucking reunion. He'd joked to Rory months ago that he couldn't afford a ticket. But perhaps Dan would be there. And now Pat had the inside scoop. There might be a little schadenfreude on the menu, and he hadn't even had to orchestrate it.

'Beauty, sure,' Pat said.

Some early customers were starting to line up outside the front doors.

'I'll leave you to it.' Pat tapped Rory's shoulder and nodded to the waiting customers before heading to the back door.

'See ya!'

———

Pat waited for the bus home, his buzz turning to anxiety. The people around him who stepped on when it arrived were all fresh and in exercise gear. One woman with a great figure and a high ponytail had celery sticking out the top of a green bag. *Low balance!* the card scanner screamed at him as he tapped on.

His place in Darlinghurst was barely fifteen minutes away. The wood on the sash window beside his front door was rotting and the overhead light was out again. Had it been a mistake to sign a twelve-month lease when he had a six-month probation period on his new job? Undoubtedly. He could be fired at any time with no notice, and if he was, he was totally fucked. But something inside him couldn't handle looking down the barrel of another four-bro share house in Enmore. For a start, it was way harder to convince girls to come back. But more than that, he had a sense that after all this time he'd surely paid his dues. All those kilometres on the dial, doing the rounds for the shit-tier auction houses in the Inner West. All the so-called 'estate sales' that were eighty per cent second-hand furniture superstore trash. Enough. Landing the Osborne gig had made him so high with hope and relief he lost his senses. The Darlinghurst apartment was forty per cent of his weekly pay, and yeah, maybe it had been a mistake, but the mistake was made. If he could just get off probation so many of his stresses would evaporate.

He flopped down onto the swivel chair near his small desk and flipped through the photos he'd taken of Sophie's clock. It was a beautiful little object. There were worse mistakes to waste your money on. Then again, anything old called to Pat. In high school it was history. Everything was so learnable, so know-able. Things from the past rarely changed. Apart from the odd paleontological revelation, or an exciting new underwater find, textbooks were reliable. Once you had the dates of the French revolutions memorised, they would never up and change on you. Names were literally carved in stone. With enough study, Pat felt, he could bring it all under his control, hold all the necessary information in his mind and never have to amend it or grapple to problem-solve from an unexpected upset. That's why the Osborne gig was such a dream. Old art was all this and more. The movements of politics and the movements of aesthetics.

Rarely was the Osborne world view upset by anything at all. If he could secure his place there then he'd never have to be upset by anything either. And it offered instant recognition. To introduce himself at parties, to meet new people, girls, whatever. He was fit and he fucked enough women to shrug off gay jokes from the boys, and once that was out of the way, all people were left with was the impression that Pat had money and taste, and was smart enough to work for people who had even more of both.

Nobody else knew his base salary was so low. Once he was off probation he'd make a decent kick from independently acquired sales clients, but even then the trouble with working for a place like Osborne was that very few new clients walked in the door who didn't already know of, and want, one of the seniors. The seniors owed each other countless favours and tips, and they all shared their buyer profiles and helped each other out of tight international spots. The women roped in clients from gala dinners and Opera Australia board meetings. The men did their best work on the golfing greens. The only people Pat knew who were under forty and had crazy cash were different kinds of dealers. There was no way he could find a buyer who would pay top price for the clock, with no provenance, in four business days.

Beside his old laptop a clunky porcelain spaniel sat looking at him with its head cocked to one side. Tufts of kitsch grass came up beside his paws and he wore a handsome red collar. The money bank had come with him all the way from the antique store in Esk, through boarding school, and had somehow survived the turbulence of several share houses.

'Show me what you got, Buster,' he said, tipping the heavy reservoir upside down, removing a crumbling cork plug from where the dog's arsehole would be, and sticking his two fingers up inside. Coins and notes spilled out over the desktop. He felt better while he was counting it, but then again also much sadder when he finished and it totalled less than three hundred bucks. For a long time he'd promised himself he'd start saving for a real dog once he got a real job. Or, rather, saving to move to an apartment building where dogs were allowed, maybe with a dog park nearby. It was his dream, to have a dog. It would be medium-sized and it would run with him and he would teach it to play dead when he held his fingers in a gun shape and said, 'Bang!' Renting in Sydney made him feel like an idiot child. Only pocket money left over, not allowed the things you wanted.

His phone lit up: *MUM is calling*. He watched it ring out. There was no way he could talk to her now, when he was this anxious. She'd sniff it on him and then she'd be anxious too about him living in the city 'alone', and they'd have that conversation for the fiftieth time and it always ended badly, with him saying, 'You sent me here,' and her saying, 'I thought you'd come back.' The phone went dark and a notification popped up saying there was no voicemail. He exhaled and swiped back to the clock pictures.

A hot shower and a wank was normally enough to put him straight to sleep, but the sun kept rising after the old one-two didn't work. Every time he thought he'd made a decision to buy the clock himself he'd get afraid and feel guilty, or he'd decide to play it safe and have the sense that he was missing a grand and obvious opportunity.

3

LALLY PUSHED AGAINST THE HEAVY glass and went out front to pick up a few stray exhibition flyers people had dropped. GALLERY LALLY the frosting read, split across the double doors, sans serif font to draw attention to the repeating angles of the letters. She was proud to stand out front with it still lit up, like a beacon to the street outside. The success of the opening night had made it all worth it. *All* of it. She closed her eyes and tilted her head back, relishing the freezing air. Her personal situation with Joseph Rivera had been a colourful, ill-advised detour. Probably every gallerist learned the hard way sooner or later not to fuck their artists. Just a rookie error. That was what minimal significance she would allow him. He was not entitled to any greater emotional space and certainly no more of her extremely valuable time. She was not going to feel sad about his death. Under no circumstances would she 'miss him'.

Inside, the installation flowed from one corner, like lava bubbling up. As though a hoarder had vomited up all manner of things. A great big beast sitting underneath this part of town, spewing junk through the gap in the tectonic plates her gallery sat directly above. Large objects—a rattan chair, a steel ladder, an old streetlamp—erupted from that spot at the far end, and cylindrical things—promotional pens, a tampon applicator, a dinner roll—seemed to have been splattered up onto the walls near the eruption point. Then the ripples began: an undulation of objects creating waves and clear flowing lines, spreading over almost two-thirds of the floor space. Where the floor met the walls the things—cups, phone chargers, a dildo—had somehow been sliced perfectly to curl up and against the right angles, so that when the viewer closed their eyelids just a little, or saw the work from any kind of distance or angle, it really was lapping like water.

'Has he painted it all?' she'd overheard someone ask at the opening.

'I don't know. It doesn't look like there's paint. It's all still kind of dirty.'

'But it's blue.'

'I know. I don't know.'

The colour the artist had gone for was 'fucked ocean', *Artforum* reported online the day after the media preview. Something you wished was real blue but undeniably was not. Every single person who knew how Rivera had created that blue had signed a non-disclosure agreement. Except for Lally, of course. The artist had trusted her. She had trusted the artist. The thought brought an onrush of memories and she raised a hand to the glass window to steady herself. Her sweaty print left a mark beside the hundreds of other smudges. She always had the glass cleaned before an opening, and if things had gone well, it would be filthy like this by the end of the big night. It was always a good sign when people hung around on the sidewalk out the front of the show, when they dressed for it and took photos.

Things had gone especially perfectly throughout this opening night. The view of the work was best from where Lally was standing. Just outside the gallery's windows the viewer would think they could see the art clearly, but the glass inevitably softened their perceptions just enough to complete the water-like effect of the work. She hadn't even needed to explain that stroke of genius. One of the younger freelance journalists mentioned it in her own online journal and the word spread.

As a curator, Lally has the ability to think outside the square—even the square of her own gallery. What a comment on the inaccessibility of this world, what a statement of self-awareness that does not at all detract from the work being shown. Rubbish turned into art, locked away from the regular public who created it, elevated by virtue of being presented in a clean space. The levels of irony and meaning lap over each other in waves.

Lally had liked that. She'd made a note of the young critic's name.

She went back inside. Her slightly wired state told her to lock the door behind her. How dare he make her fearful of her beloved Chelsea streets? These were more hers than they had ever been his. She had given him these streets, this space. She had made him with this show. Her, the Midas of the independent modern art scene, and him, with those filthy fucking fingernails from all that posing fucking 'fossicking' around the shoreline.

Walking over to the edge of the work, Lally stretched the toe of her pointed boot out and kicked at it. A broken remote control budged a little, and a small disc-shaped object came away at the edge, scooting across the polished concrete floor, returning to its normal colours when removed from the installation. She should have panicked. Tiny movements like this could upset the careful ecosystem of the in-built lights. The installation had been meticulously photographed as soon as it was completed in situ, but if someone from the buyer's side noticed any anomalies they wouldn't raise the matter with her for fear of word getting out that the work had been compromised and their investment tainted. They all patted each other's backs and asses like that. Praise could be showered upon a work by a critic or editor who happened to be the husband or lover of the assistant to the acquisitions team of the major gallery which had already made a deal with the curator to buy the work. They all clinked flutes and cackled. Sometimes the artists knew, sometimes they didn't. It depended a little on their talent and mostly on their temperament. Ego and all that. So tiresome.

Now the opening was over she'd have to turn up to work for the next six weeks cooing over the departed 'genius'. It would be impossible to hide her complicated disdain, even though her routine was so polished. Usually, the weeks after opening meant hustling for sales, but that was all done and dusted. The obvious answer was to bump Leah up from intern to assistant. She'd love that. Good, good. Leah had been wonderful too, staying right through the night, tidying and monitoring the social media flow, until Lally had shooed her away a little after three. This was a great idea. Perfect timing.

Lally gathered her things. The quiet time straight after a show night had always felt sacred to her. That mixture of achievement and ambition realised. Pride, happiness, reflection enhanced by solitude. Whatever was tainting this moment wasn't her fault. She had done everything right. Worked as hard as ever. Delivered on every little detail.

'Ready to roll?' Gen emerged from the hidden bathroom, wiping her hands, and stopped when she saw Lally's face. 'Are you okay? Scratch that. I know you're not okay. I can't even make you feel better by telling you how fantastic the show was, because it was him, but I want you to know that, regardless of him, *you* nailed tonight.'

'Yeah?'

'Fuck yeah. Come on, Lally. People were talking about you as much as they were talking about the fucking art. You've hit your motherfucking stride. This "sapling" idea of yours, to promote emerging artists, they love it—but it's also just genuinely exciting and you're doing a good thing, and you're doing the good thing so fucking well!'

'Yeah.' Lally nodded.

'Now, why are we still here with his dump? Let's go.'

'It's not a dump.'

'It is a dump. In the truest and most metaphorical sense of the word, Lally. It is literal garbage and a shit thing. You're the brilliant one here. Now, let's go.'

'He was a shit thing, that doesn't mean his art is.'

'Oh god, don't you fucking start that separationist shit with me!' They'd had this argument so many times it was now almost satirical.

Gen jostled Lally towards the door. 'Let me take you home.'

'Are you staying at mine tonight?' Lally asked, locking up behind them.

'Yeah, I have to be at the clinic at nine,' Gen replied. 'I'm not getting on the five just to sleep for three hours.'

'Shit. Are you going to be sober?'

Gen waved down a taxi. 'Yeah, yeah, I stopped drinking at midnight.'

'Liar. I popped that Dom at one.'

'I stopped drinking at one.'

'Lucky your patients are dogs.'

'How dare you!' Gen opened her mouth wide with fake outrage and recited the clinic's jingle as they got into the cab. 'At East Village *Vet* every *pet* is a member of the family.'

'So those poodles are genetically snobby?'

'Tsk, tsk, Lally—you run a gallery in Chelsea, you'd better be careful with the "s" word.'

The cab took them along Lafayette Street towards Lally's East Village apartment. It was quiet on East 12th Street, but at either end Second and Third Avenues still showed signs of life. It was February, not the best time of year in New York, but the day had been unusually warm. People had shed their puffers, and NPR got a climate change expert on the afternoon show to explain that they were all doomed but they might as well enjoy it.

Gen was gone by the time Lally got out of bed later that morning to begin her post-opening ritual. She made herself a pour-over and sat at her small, round dining table, scrolling through the messages and notifications and tags, taking note of who needed replies or follow-ups. It was windy outside but the sun was bright again, streaming through the two large windows, the heavy calico curtains fully drawn back. Lally felt a delicious sense of normalcy, a semblance of control returning, like wheels mercifully clicking back into tracks.

A text from her mother made her smile. It had come through at eleven thirty the night before. Estelle must have sent it as soon as she finished the second dinner service. *Congratulations from me and Gary. Dinner please!* There were missed calls from pseudo friends asking if she was coming out for drinks after, voicemails from journalists who hadn't been at the media preview asking for an interview slot. Emails with simple inquiries were forwarded directly to Leah. Lally didn't have personal social media profiles, and Leah managed the Gallery Lally accounts, but Lally kept an eye on it all. She never posted images of herself anywhere for the same reason she went to the local Y even though she could afford Equinox. In everyone's rush to brand themselves they gave it all away. Lally was playing the long game, and the long game didn't involve broadcasting her information everywhere. The long game was about maintaining a little mystery. Letting admirers populate their imaginings of her life with their own wildest desires. Forcing a wedge of nebulous space between her image and her real self.

'Leah, what are you doing for the next six weeks?' Lally asked loudly, smiling, pushing open the gallery doors.

Leah had some excellent percussive music playing. Unpredictable but chill.

'Ah . . .'

'Trick question! Do you want to be the assistant manager and earn proper money and come here every day?'

Lally saw her protégé's mouth drop open.

'Yes?'

'Don't put question marks at the ends of your sentences, Leah.'

'Yes!'

'Fantastic!'

'Thank you.' Leah was grinning now.

'We'll put the details in writing after all this'—Lally gestured at the installation—'is dealt with.'

Leah was dressed all in black, of course, but today's outfit had a faintly militaristic edge, utilitarian pants and boots offset by hot pink lipstick. Having an Asian American with a pixie cut on the desk was a very good look for the gallery.

Lally remembered clearly the first time they'd met.

'I think you're going to grow,' Leah had said to her boldly, after one of Lally's first shows, 'and you might not need an assistant now, but you will, and I want to be that assistant.'

Initially, Lally had been put off by her presumptuousness. In this new world order, girls like Leah seemed to draw from unending wells of self-confidence. But then Lally spotted the tiny tremor in Leah's outstretched hand, giving away the terror hidden beneath her defiant stare and uptilted chin. Leah had the look figured out and had none of the bullshit 'influencer' aspirations shared by ninety per cent of Parsons graduates. It also helped having a younger eye around the place. Lally had taken the leap of opening her gallery the year she turned thirty, but even that was ancient compared to Leah's twenty-two. New independent magazines opened and closed, new bars opened and closed. Lingo and terminology for groups and identities morphed rapidly. This was New York City: it belonged to the young in spirit and the old in money.

A knock on the glass interrupted them. It was Curtis Davidson, the head of MoMA's acquisitions team.

'Lally,' he said, opening his arms as though for a hug, but then placing his hands on her shoulders instead and giving each cheek an air kiss. Curtis wielded monumental power in the independent gallery scene, representing the illustrious, gilded, establishment-approved pot at the end of the indie rainbow. He clearly enjoyed wielding this power over Lally, but he was also a genuine art encyclopaedia and a queer cinema academic. Curtis's eyes moved from Lally's face, passed over Leah altogether, and settled on the work with something like lust.

'Twenty-seven,' he said, shaking his head and tucking his sunglasses into the breast pocket of his jacket. 'So young to have this maturity of concept and simplicity of execution.'

The two women listened closely even though he was quoting from his own column in the weekend paper, published after the media preview.

'Tragic.'

'Almost a cliché, really,' Lally said.

Both Curtis and Leah turned to look at her, shocked, but she didn't elaborate.

'That's right, I suppose,' Curtis conceded. 'He was a true artist. The pride of the talented and the insecurity of the outsider. The mania. The drugs. You know, everybody's asking if it was an accident or not.'

'And now you're asking too?' Lally looked Curtis square in the face, but he simply raised his eyebrows. She shrugged. 'Who knows?'

'Well, anyway, I'm here to start the conversation about transport specifics,' Curtis said, switching to business mode. 'Obviously we have ownership of the piece from end-of-business on the final Friday of the show. We want to get our people here first thing Saturday.'

'Have they signed NDAs?' Lally asked.

'Not yet, but I'm on it,' Curtis assured her. 'Can we discuss—'

'Actually, Curtis,' Lally interrupted, 'I'm going to hand you over to Leah. She'll be managing the gallery for the rest of this exhibition.'

Leah extended her hand for Curtis to shake. He responded as though he'd received a little static shock and looked at it for a moment before taking it.

'Well, a pleasure, Leah,' he said, before turning back to Lally. 'You're off to the Bahamas with all my money, I suppose?'

'You mean MoMA's money?'

Curtis waved her off with his manicured hand. 'I suppose Señor Rivera can't use it. The proceeds of his one big, final work. That's a clever little contract of yours, isn't it, Lally?'

'I'm a clever little girl, Curtis,' she replied, and they all smiled.

Lally left them to it and hailed a cab, shooting off emails all the way home. There was one name she had long been determined to secure: Chuck Farr. A controversial and mercurial portraitist whose work she'd first encountered when she was still at art school. It hooked her back then—his determination to 'abandon the paintbrush'—and had continued to challenge her over the years as she interned and worked her way up other galleries' ladders. An artist who only ever did portraits but who was, in fact, face blind. An artist who used paints but not brushes. Photo-realism but never plain photography. A male artist whose work mostly featured men, playing with the male-on-male gaze. It hit that sweet spot in Lally's aesthetic–intellectual interior. Farr was already represented, but there were rumours going around that there had been a huge falling-out between him and his current gallery. Over what? Lally didn't care. Against her better judgement she'd been keeping her November exhibition slot open for him on his manager's promise to 'consider it'. Now, with the MoMA acquisition public, it was time to strike.

Hi Eric, she wrote, *I'm sure you've seen the news. I've got journalists eating out of my hands right now. Would Farr consider it a good time to confirm a November show?*

Whether or not Farr came on board, the MoMA money was enough to confirm the final Saplings Program choice for the year. Olivia Hernandez, an emerging performance artist Lally knew to be flat broke, would be thrilled. *Green light for December*, Lally wrote to her in a text.

Lally had used her unexpected inheritance to pay for twenty-four months' rent on the Chelsea space. Her dad would have turned in his grave, a thought that thrilled Lally. Angry man in life, angry man even in death. The two years was her landing strip, and Lally had bled, sweated and cried for it all, and it had worked. She had announced the Saplings Program at the beginning of this, her third year. It had always been a part of her vision and she could finally afford it. A brand-new emerging artist each season, usually young and diverse. The Saplings Program kept her ahead of the curve. Fresh blood and fresh sweat and fresh tears. That's what the market hungered for, and that's what she'd give them. The contract stipulated that in return for being exhibited as part of Gallery Lally's Saplings Program, the curator would be paid with one piece of art, of her choosing, from the show. It removed the financial barrier for young artists to exhibit, it meant Lally had a real stake in choosing the best shows to put on, and it also meant her personal collection was growing steadily in both size and worth. The Saplings Program was symbiosis in action. A nod from Gallery Lally was everything a young artist could want, increasing their critical regard and the value of their work, and they did whatever Lally asked, bent to her will, which she sometimes disguised as whim, and she traded on their talents and exciting new visions. Four shows a year, just like the seasons, and Joseph had been winter. No matter how busy she kept herself, she still got that sinking feeling when her mind brushed against him.

Back up in her apartment, she poured herself a large glass of wine, put some Nina Simone on her stereo, and cried. She cried with exhaustion and the embarrassment at being tricked. It had been the best sex she'd had in years. Until it was the worst. He wasn't a gentle or generous lover. He was more determined than anything, and that determination made him incredibly communicative. Most men were so silent it was annoying. Joseph's questions weren't 'dirty talk', which Lally despised because guys always made it infantilising and creepy. He'd ask, 'Do you like this? Do you want more of that?' Even remembering it made her pulse quicken. Sometimes they'd be eating a meal and he would ask, 'Do you like it?', meaning the food, and she'd get wet. He had the slim muscularity of a hungry artist who did sculpture and physical works. He was always kind of dirty. Her favourite thing was to shower with him—to wash him, really: an extended foreplay, because Lally stipulated he couldn't touch her until he was clean. She remembered scrubbing his nails with a brush under the hot water as he grew hard, shampoo suds from his unrinsed hair pouring down over her nipples as he leaned in and kissed her neck. 'Come on,' he'd said. 'Please.'

Her art was her life was her gallery was her heart, and he'd stumbled into the middle of it all and come and shat and pissed and overdosed, and she'd never be able to have the last word or show him what he'd done to her, or go on to be the best gallery in the city without him and completely sink him as revenge. He was dead now, but it didn't feel good like revenge. In the movies, when people died that was the end of the revenge arc. This felt unfinished. No big exhale. Worst of all, she missed him, and she wasn't allowed to. The official report was that he had been almost clean, like he told her, and that going back to a previous dose was the classic relapser's mistake. If you filmed yourself fucking someone without their consent did you deserve to choke on your own vomit? She might have said 'yes' that night, but now she just felt confused and sad. It was strange to think that at the moment he died she had become properly rich. Nobody knew that after they'd signed the contract with MoMA, between the first and second bottles of champagne, she had offered to let him keep the installation and he had said, 'Thank you.' Lally would take that piece of information to her grave. Not even because of the money, but because it betrayed how much she'd given to him. How much she'd compromised for him. How much she'd felt for him. The exchange for keeping this secret was also keeping the secret that he was a complete asshole. Curtis would make sure Joseph Rivera became a 'name', and her gallery would have its taste-making status confirmed. Everybody in the scene working together to make names and money.

It was true that she had been attracted to his scrawny youth and genius. Was it so unfair to accuse him of being attracted to her power? Perhaps that had been their unique fusion. They had a good balance and togetherness in art, and the sex had upset things. Men could never do both.

4

'PAT, YOUR TEN AM IS here.' Em buzzed through to him.

He hadn't been able to find a buyer. 'I need five minutes.'

'No worries.'

Pat walked down the short, wood-panelled corridor to the ivory-tiled bathroom. His hands were shaking as he flipped the lock on the stall and pulled his phone out to check his bank balance again, as though it could've changed in the past half-hour. Just under a thousand in the everyday account and less than six in his savings. The credit card was in case he needed to get back home in a hurry, or for any other freak scenarios. Was this a freak scenario? He ran his hands through his hair, grazing his fingertips past the too-short sides from last week's visit to Just Cuts. Thirty seconds to make a decision.

Nobody in the family was sick. He'd finally paid off his orthodontics debts. It wasn't so long since he'd done the two-minute-noodle diet at university; he could do it again. Was this incredibly stupid, though? He'd never be able to onsell the piece without revealing his unprofessional conduct in purchasing directly from a client without them knowing. People in big business podcasts always talked about taking risks, but they were always the people whose risks turned out to be smart moves. Pat worried he was not like the men in the podcasts. He was not rich. The small amount of money he'd be taking a slightly-too-risky risk with happened to be *all* of his money.

Someone entered the cubicle beside his so he fumbled with his belt buckle, flushed the loo, and stepped out to rinse his hands. When the sound of the flush died down, he heard the man swear and sigh, struggling to dribble out a tiny bit of piss. Probably Martin or Arthur. It hadn't occurred to Pat that he should be grateful to be able to piss when he pleased and not when he didn't. Not even thirty yet. He regarded his own face in the mirror and stood up straight. If you don't say 'fuck it' at least once before you're thirty, when are you gonna?

He stretched his head to the left and right, cracking his neck, then flexed each arm once to get the blood pumping. The gym was an expense he fought hard to justify, going at least three times a week. Part of it was for the apps. At five eleven, Pat was literally 'average' height and couldn't afford not to be fit if he wanted to fuck. But it was also for work. The bodies of the rich—he had noticed immediately, going from a dusty town to a sparkling city—were more obvious the less they were clothed. The Eastern Suburbs kids genuinely thought McDonald's tasted bad and enjoyed outdoor activities like rock climbing and sailing. They walked dogs in beautiful parks where it was both safe and relaxing to do so. Part of the deep well of entitlement the Osborne crowd carried around with them came from their health and stratospheric life expectancy. Sickness was supposed to be the great leveller, but tell that to someone who had to drive five hours to get to Ipswich for dialysis, compared to his new boss Josephine whose 'brave fight' against an early-detected breast cancer saw her spend more time with the reconstructive surgeon than the oncologist. According to the gossip, at least. Pat had nasty thoughts about that. His own mother's 'scare', as the family called it, had upended all their lives. Pat had flown home and missed exams for his first year of uni. Health and fitness was the most important part of Pat's disguise, and he worked hard to maintain it. So yes, he would pass Sophie's stupid little test. He would pass it, and he would take their money.

He returned to his office and buzzed through to Em that he was ready to see his client.

'Sophie! Great to see you, and perfect timing.' Pat extended his hand for a firm shake. 'A client of mine can't wait to get their hands on this clock. It's a done deal. I just need you to sign some paperwork.'

She had gigantic Gucci sunglasses pushed up onto her head, keeping her blonde-ish waves off her extraordinarily smooth forehead. 'I knew you could do it, Patrick.'

He couldn't figure out if her tone was patronising or provocative. Both?

'I've brought pictures,' she said, passing him several A4 pages with what were clearly phone snaps and dot points listing 'artist' and 'date' underneath. The font was some kind of gothic serif situation—a cringe-inducing attempt to formalise an embarrassingly amateur display of potentially high-value works.

'Fantastic,' Pat said, reaching for the pages without looking closely at them. That would be an hours-long thrill, an indulgence he would take his time undressing, preferably with a drink in hand.

'You'll have to come over to the house and see them in person, though,' she said, not letting the pages go.

Their eye contact over the desk extended a moment too long.

'Oh, sure, of course,' he said, nodding, the image of agreeableness, and received the papers.

'What's your mobile number?' Sophie asked, pulling her phone out of her bag as she sat back.

He recited it, a little startled, and a moment later his pocket vibrated. When he retrieved his phone he saw a text of a smiling emoji and a kissing-face emoji from an unknown number.

After some mandatory polite small talk, he persuaded Sophie to leave by swearing to visit her at home within a fortnight. Then finally Pat was back in his office, taking deep breaths, preparing himself for what the pages might contain. He started flipping and felt himself go light-headed. It was more than he could have imagined. The Warhol was there, and in the same absurdly gigantic frame Rory had described. There were two separate 'Boyd' paintings. No first names were given, but the dates and styles told Pat they were probably by Arthur and Mary. Neither of them were particularly strong pieces, but the Boyd name alone guaranteed a sale. Some landscapes too. If he weren't still on probation the commission from this estate would have been a deposit on an apartment. It was definitely enough to get him a proper employment contract. The English hunting work from Gregory's study was on the final page but was missing the artist's name and year, possibly it had been printed on a final sheet that Sophie had accidentally left in a printer tray somewhere. Pat held the piece of paper close, trying to discern detail in the cheap inkjet print. It was oil, early 1800s, pheasants not ducks, and beagles. He put the pages down, euphoria coursing through him. Taking a punt on the clock had been the right call. It had brought him a leap closer to a dog. He felt high. High as a fucking kite.

Ducking into the bathroom again, running a small plastic comb through his hair, he practised how he'd present himself to the boss and began the short walk to the other side of the building. It was amazing how even after just ten metres of hallway east to west the values of the works on the walls accumulated zeroes. In the midpoint of the corridor, a huge, top-heavy Ming dynasty vase erupting with white agapanthus sat on a small Georgian card table inlaid with ivory figures. Just walking past the arrangement made him nervous. The walk from reception to Josephine's office was designed to both impress and intimidate. Pat had to put on his big boy pants even to bring Josephine's face to mind. The wall across from the door to her office displayed one of Robert Mapplethorpe's gigantic phallic black-and-white lily photographs. It was impossible to speak to the woman and depart without the sensation that something in your inner ear had been upset, and you were doomed to spend the rest of your day off balance. Pat took a deep breath, rolled his shoulders back, and knocked.

'Come in,' a voice commanded from the other side.

He entered.

'Patrick,' Josephine said, sounding surprised. She'd been leaning over her desk, but now stood up straight and still. A fat string of pearls sat tight at her neck. 'This must either be very good or very bad.'

'Well, it's not bad,' he said with a cheeky smile.

It didn't work.

He approached the desk and handed her Sophie's printouts. They worked. Normally Josephine moved her body with great economy and poise, but as she took her time with the pages, her attention fully engaged, Pat saw her shift her weight between her high-heeled feet.

He waited, minutes passing.

Josephine's eyes narrowed when she looked up at him. 'Where on earth did you find this collection?'

'A walk-in,' he said with a shrug.

'You're telling me someone walked in with this'—she flicked the pages with her long nails and he tried not to flinch at the loud crack—'and trusted you to handle it?' She made no effort to conceal her scepticism.

'I went to school with the client's son,' Pat replied. Kind of true.

'My, my.' She raised her eyebrows but seemed to accept this. 'Take a seat,' she directed, but stayed standing herself.

'Thank you.' He'd never been invited to sit in Josephine's office before.

She flipped backward and forward through the images, pausing on some and speeding past others. Her arms were sinewy. There was a single pen on the desk and he strongly suspected it was not merely gold-coloured.

'It's a weak Boyd, but a Boyd's a Boyd,' she said. 'And that hunt—that's your territory, if I'm not mistaken?'

'It is, yes. I'd say an Aiken, or similar.'

'You'd say?' She looked at him from under mean brows and he felt himself spontaneously perspire.

'The lady just left the building. I came straight to you.'

She nodded, but then put the pages down, out of her hands entirely, and leaned forward on the desk. He tried to keep his face neutral.

'Don't bullshit me, Patrick. Where is this art from and why is it yours to sell?'

'A divorce. Liquidating assets quietly. It's true that I went to her son's school. Well, her stepson.'

'So what's not true?'

He faltered. 'I already bought the first piece from her myself. A clock, nothing special. It was a test. She doesn't want it to get out that the family are selling all their stuff'—he couldn't stop the words tumbling out—'but she only gave me a week and I couldn't find a buyer and—'

Josephine raised her hands to stop him. 'So you gambled?'

'I gambled.'

A moment of silence passed. Finally, Josephine said, 'You're not going to be able to find the best buyers for this motley mix—not if we can't list the pieces for public auction.'

'No.'

She looked straight down at him. 'I don't like irresponsible young men, Patrick, but I do like this much money.'

'I understand.'

'You won't make a commission on this estate, which I consider fair, since we're going to need help from the rest of the team to move the stock. Do you agree?'

He knew it wasn't fair, but it also wasn't a question. 'Yes.'

'If it goes well, we could gross seven figures. If it goes well, you'll be off probation. Deal? Just say yes please, and thank you.' And for the first time, she smiled.

'Yes please and thank you,' he replied, and Josephine extended her hand, so he stood up and shook it.

'Good boy. Now, what are you doing in March?'

'Next month?'

She didn't dignify this with a response.

'Nothing?'

She picked up her phone and punched some numbers. 'Al!' Her voice was positively chirpy. 'Can you swing by my office? Yes, now. Wonderful, thank you.'

Pat smiled at her and clasped his hands together in his lap. He had no idea what the fuck was happening now. She continued looking through the pages for an agonising few minutes of sweaty silence. Eventually a soft knock sounded.

'Al, lovely, come in, have a seat,' she said, and promptly explained their exciting predicament to the senior associate.

Albert looked about the same age as Pat's father, though a life of outdoor labour had brutalised Pat's father's skin, which meant Al, with the help of Sydney's finest dermatologists, could have been anywhere between fifty-five and eighty-five.

'Al has clients with appetites for high value post-war pieces, and he's heading over to the Armory Show in New York next month to shore up his connections there. With the Australian dollar so weak and your new client's need for privacy, you're going to accompany him and assist him. Convince the Yanks they're snapping up secret bargains.'

'What?'

'Don't worry.' Al reached out and patted his arm. 'I don't bite.'

'You're obviously not my first preference to go,' Josephine told Pat. 'Usually Erin goes with Al, but apparently it's her child's birthday or something and she's refusing to travel.'

'I'll do my best,' Pat declared, aiming for confidence, sounding like a boy scout.

'This will be your, what, tenth Armory, Al?' Josephine's voice was warm as she addressed Al, then turned cold as she said to Pat, 'This is an incredible learning opportunity for you.'

'I understand. Thank you.'

'Most of these fairs are just great opportunities for a lot of people to be in the same place at the same time,' Al said, standing up to leave. 'We've heard rumours that the government is about to ramp up a new Australia–America soft diplomacy initiative that might see funding flow to galleries with strong bilateral representation. My clients here need that information before the general public has it so they can manage their storerooms accordingly. And if it's true we need to come home with a shopping list of names. We'll shake a lot of hands, show everyone a good time. Ten days or so plus transit.'

'Good, good,' Josephine said, waving them out.

In the hallway Al kept talking. 'Go to Emily and get the travel reimbursement forms arranged. Start on your visa paperwork today too.'

'Got it.' Reimbursement meant he'd have to get another credit card. But the trip was only for a couple of weeks. Then pay day a fortnight after his return. He could probably borrow it all then pay it back within the fifty-five-day interest-free period.

Al lowered his voice. 'Tell me, Pat, how does someone of such youthful stature come to work here at Osborne? I'd presumed you had some kind of an in with Josephine, but I can see now that's not the case.'

'A few flukes in a row, I suppose,' Pat replied honestly. 'I was the only male to graduate from Sydney Uni with an art history master's in my year, and I was at this old boys' college event a few months ago and met an old boy who turned out to be Malcolm.'

'What timing.'

'I know. He must have been on the lookout for a protégé right before his retirement. I mean, I was invited that night because I tied with a girl for valedictorian the year before, first-class honours.'

'Of course.' Al nodded.

'But we were drinking, and the Banksy stunt had just happened.'

'Oh, the October shredding?'

'Yeah. Malcolm was on the phone to the London office. In a bit of a panic about it, to be honest, and I'd had a few beers, and I just said to him, sort of as a joke, "You should just say it's been newly completed and double the price," and then he called London back, and boom, it was in their press release, *Girl with Balloon* was now called *Love is in the Bin*, and boom, I had a job.'

Josephine hadn't been thrilled by Malcolm's unorthodox recruiting style, Pat remembered uncomfortably.

'Remarkable,' Al said, and turned to leave. 'Give me a ring if you have any questions about the New York trip.'

Pat found Em at her desk. 'New York!' she said when she saw him coming. 'Jealous!'

'News travels fast,' he said.

She got up and went to a filing cabinet nearby, pulling out two different sheets and laying them on the desk. 'This is for actual travel reimbursements, like flights and accommodation, and this other one is for expenses. The main thing about the expenses category is that you need to be able to allocate a client name to the expense—and depending on the calibre of the client, you can claim pretty much anything.'

'Wow. Anything?'

'I've seen some freaky shit.'

'Like what?'

'Once there was an eleven-thousand-dollar expense to a company called Hollywood Catering in Kings Cross, allocated to a major account.'

'Right.'

'Hotel massages all the time. When I'd only just started here there was a super-high charge for a hotel's in-room movies on an expense account, so I thought I'd do some helpful follow-up—you know, check the figures and ask for the titles. The hotel manager called me and yelled that the films were of a private nature and he couldn't possibly betray the confidences of his guests. All the usual pathetic, freaky old men crap.'

'I'll make sure to pay for my own massages in cash then,' he said, and she laughed.

'You heading off now?' Em asked when they were done.

Pat sensed an opportunity. He had been planning to stay back and work late but wanted the elevator ride down with her. 'Yeah, you?'

She nodded.

'Let me grab my briefcase.'

Em had a slight lankiness to her. She wasn't just slim, she was skinny, scrawny maybe, in a way Pat noticed other women noticing. She had blonde hair and he didn't know exactly how long it was because every single day without fail it was in a bun at the base of her neck. He learned from an offhand reference she'd made once that she'd done ballet all her life, and then Pat found himself thumbing through brochures for what was on at the Opera House. She mostly wore pants and heels. Crazily high heels. When she wore the heels she was taller than him, but he felt sure if he was ever around when she took them off, he'd be just that tiny bit taller than her. For a few weeks they'd been chatting in the mornings when they arrived, and they'd get each other coffees during the day, and for the last few days they'd been lingering to discuss things after stepping out of the elevator on the way home. Pat had found himself looking forward to seeing her each the morning, which had started to make him nervous around her. The previous Friday afternoon he'd made clear headway when he discovered the history of auctioneers was the topic of her master's thesis. When he met her by the elevator to go down he picked that conversation up where they'd left off, asking her what she'd found in her research.

On the ground floor Pat's heart did a little dip-down, knowing they'd split to go their respective ways home. She turned towards him, still talking, but he interrupted.

'Can I buy you a drink?' he asked.

She shifted her weight and made direct eye contact with him, pausing for a moment. Then, without moderating her voice at all, totally chill, she asked, 'Do you eat pussy, Pat?'

His eyes widened involuntarily, his brains scrambled. 'Um, yeah?' He could feel his face going red. 'I mean, absolutely,' he added, louder. It was impossible to remain calm, let alone cool, and simultaneously convey the requisite enthusiasm. His blood was pumping, a little of it to his cock too. God, she was stunning. How had he not noticed how strong her eyebrows were? And so keen. Exhilarating.

'Me too,' she replied with a short nod, matter-of-fact.

He recognised the expression on her face. It was the one she used when the older men came through the office and they didn't realise she was condescending to them. It took him a moment, then he barked out a laugh. Was that relief flooding through his body or embarrassment? He put his hands on his hips and smiled. 'I'd still love to buy you a drink.'

She smiled too. 'Wonderful.'

After the two rounds of drinks he couldn't really afford to buy for a girl he would never actually date, he got the bus home, took the clock out and placed it on his desk beside Buster. It was like a sort of wealth grenade. Money made money. Pat had always known that, in a sort of academic, hypothetical sense, but here he was. Finally, maybe, making some money. So what the fuck was up with the anxiety still sitting there in his guts? He tried to focus on the picture he'd taken of the hunt he'd need to identify. The horses, mid-gallop, had the kind of stretched leanness typical of Aiken. It would be absurd to try to make any assessments based on the colour because it could have been so distorted by the low-quality ink. Sometimes Aiken's clouds were a bit dodgy like these ones. Could be a good sign.

His mind wandered again, back to the uneasiness that never left him. It was the same trouble with being sent to boarding school on a scholarship. If you didn't perform you'd lose your new home. Someone could whip the rug out at any moment. The terror of an unexpected bus trip back up north had always weaved in and out of his dorm room nightmares. Somehow in these horrors he turned up at his parents' house and their surprise turned to rage then resignation as they realised he'd squandered his great opportunity. The wankers at school had used better food as a reward for good grades or good behaviour. It enraged him that things he had to work so hard for—new footy shoes, or a DVD for dorm movie night—could simply be bought by other parents then brought to school by the day boys. They would just shrug about it. He struggled to get dates because of his stupid curfews and residency rules, while his mates got to finger the netball girls at semi-formal afterparties. When he returned home for summer after year twelve, waiting for the exam results, he learned from his mother that of course he'd had a kind of bank account with the school, for the shoes and for tuckshop.

'But they wouldn't let me use it!' Pat was livid. The stress of finals had not yet seeped out of his veins. His skin was bad in the Queensland humidity. Everything made him furious.

'You got the shoes, you had your tuckshop—you did fencing, for Christ's sake! What are you complaining about?'

They were taking clothes in off the line, and his mum was throwing the perished plastic pegs into the old wicker basket, never missing.

'I mean they wouldn't let me choose! I had to work for it!' he said, realising a moment too late how this sounded.

'Oh, Patty Pie.' Kel's voice had a nastiness to it as she paused to look at him. 'You had to work for money . . .'

'I mean I didn't know that I could have anything nice unless I studied so hard.'

'You're a student! Studying is your job!'

They argued on until she held up a hand and said, 'Enough!' and thrust the basket into his stomach. He dumped it in the laundry and stormed off to his boiling-hot room.

A week later, when he got his good results, she cried. 'And aren't you glad you went to that school? Now you can go out into the world and do anything you want.' His mum's face was all wet against his chest as she hugged him, but he felt robbed, like his school, which had made him dance like a monkey on eggshells, was getting all the credit.

It had coalesced in him that summer—the pride and resentment, the boredom of his home town, the distance from his siblings, the separation from his mates who were at schoolies and the envy at them having sex—into a kind of driving truth. He needed enough money to have a place of his own and a bed he couldn't be kicked from, and he needed to be in among it all in the city. In a strangely ironic, circular way, the Bauer estate would be Pat's ticket up and out. He would sell their assets and get his employment contract, and he would move to a new place and get a dog.

5

THE WALLS OF HER APARTMENT were antique white, much warmer than the gallery's. It kept things homey. Four large photos by Diane Arbus hung around the living and dining area, all different shots from Queens in the 1980s. Once or twice a year Lally made a trip to her storage space and swapped the art. She'd only just done that at Christmas, but it would be nice to replace the works sooner rather than later. Make things fresh-to-the-eye again. She'd been toying with the idea of getting her Eames reupholstered. That could be fun. Yes. Tomorrow, after visiting her mother, she'd go pick some new works, take them to the framer's, then swing by the Garment District and pick out a new fabric to match. Having money was excellent.

Just as she was about to shut her laptop an email came through from Farr's people. It had a subject line but no body: *November confirmed. Portraiture. Send contract.*

Lally screamed. This was it. The MoMA acquisition was the public-facing metric of her gallery having 'made it', but programming Farr was her personal one. She'd been watching his work develop over the years, loving each of his shows more and more, quietly wondering if her own career was progressing too. Now she knew for sure. An established artist she admired profoundly had judged her his equal. She looked out the window and breathed deeply. How much she had toiled over the years. How much she had sacrificed while everyone else partied their twenties away. Now there really was no doubt in her mind: it had all been worthwhile. It was impossible not to think of her father. And Rivera. The strange repetition of the two situations. The way men in her life brought her so much pain and so much capital.

When Lally's parents met in 1977, Estelle was running away from a fucked-up family situation in the country. Her folks had a bloodline obsession, but it was obvious Estelle's only brother was gay, so all the perpetuation pressures were redirected to her. Finishing school, debutante, the whole package. Then a fit Italian–American firefighter strode into her life and swept her off her feet—literally, they would go dancing for hours—and made all the promises young men do. In New York she'd get whatever job she wanted. Earn her own money. Sure, go to cooking school. Antony lived in a big house just outside Manhattan where they'd have a garden she could grow food in. Et cetera, sigh, et cetera. The pictures from their first few years in Queens were amazing, with all the outfits and the parties as the 1970s became the 1980s.

The problems grew slowly at first. Antony was hit by a falling beam and lost some mobility on his left side. After that the problems grew faster, accompanied by drinking and painkillers and depression. He was one of two boys. Antony's brother could still mow his own lawn, he had a good Catholic wife, and that wife was pumping out good Catholic kids. Estelle's folks had cut ties. She had been 'too much' for them and then she was 'too much' for her new family too. Lally came along in 1986. The birth of a girl was apparently only a minor setback for Antony once Estelle promised him they would 'try again'.

It was difficult for Lally to reconcile the happy memories of her early childhood with what came later. She had barely spoken to her father for several years by the time he died. On her birthdays she would receive a card with *To My Little Angel* written at the top and *Dad* written at the bottom. Hallmark had to do all the emotional heavy lifting in between. She responded in kind with cards for Father's Day and Christmas, mostly to keep the peace for her mother's benefit. Lally had ceased in-person contact with her dad the second time he'd yelled at her for 'taking' Estelle away from him, slamming an open palm down on his dining table. He got old quickly after that, and died at the family home in Flushing. The silver lining was that he wasn't around to vote in 2016. And he obviously hadn't expected to die when he did because he hadn't made a will, so everything went to Lally automatically, and it was far more than she or Estelle had expected. Antony had assets he hadn't told either of them about.

So here she was again. Another terrible man who, despite his best efforts, had made her rich. Lally texted her mom: *Looking forward to tomorrow. I'm bringing champagne.* They had a standing weekly lunch arrangement, Monday being the only day they both had off each week. She considered emailing Leah, getting to work immediately on the Farr contract, but paused. Lally took a breath. She put her phone down. It was Sunday. Sunday and Monday were the two days when the gallery was closed. Nothing would be done until Tuesday anyway. Why not let this be her delicious private secret until then? A secret little spark in her heart.

It was only a half-hour cab ride uptown and across the Queensboro Bridge from Lally's apartment to her mom's place. The area had gentrified rapidly over the last decade, which was lucky for Estelle, with her restaurant going upmarket and thriving. Lally's cab idled at some lights beside the sign for *Little Angels Montessori*. She winced.

Nonna's house had always been full of cousins and cooking, and when you gave Nonna a kiss she would give you a quarter. Antony was always bragging to her aunts and uncles about how well Lally did at school. At Christmas everyone stood around while she played 'Silent Night' on her violin—the only one among the cousins with such an instrument—then they all clapped and her dad swooped her up into his arms and said he would put her on top of the tree in the middle of the living room because she was his little angel.

According to Estelle, Antony never hit her. It didn't matter to Lally whether or not this was true, because if you're afraid your husband is going to hit you, and you're shrinking yourself down to a pinprick, does it matter whether or not the blow lands? He belittled Estelle in front of people, eventually even in front of Lally. He said she was getting ugly in her old age. He said her voice sounded stupid, and he would shush her if she spoke in public. Lally's early childhood memories of happiness were littered with details she'd spend the rest of her life interrogating for signs of her mother's misery. After Lally was born, Estelle wasn't allowed to go back to work, so she didn't have her own money. Antony used her financial dependence against her, treating her like a child. When Lally was in college she asked her mother why she and Antony hadn't had more children. Estelle told her the story of how she'd waited until Antony had gone away with his family to Palermo for a fortnight then took a jar of emergency cash she had literally buried in their back garden, went to a woman in Koreatown and had her tubes tied in secret.

There had been two or three painful years when Lally was annoyed at Estelle for not just leaving. Lally didn't like to think about that time, or the times she was kind to her dad in front of her mom, just to play at being a happy family.

The cab pulled up in front of Estelle's apartment building, and Lally debated with herself whether she would try to explain the Rivera situation. There was an implicit agreement between them, forged early in Lally's college years, that she would only mention a man if it was 'serious'. But her mother was one of the only people who might appreciate the situation. A man's death leading to a life-changing amount of money. How it felt like receiving a paycheck for the work of enduring their cruelty. How you went in loops: *I'm glad he's gone, I didn't kill him, what does that mean, does this money come with strings, is this money dirty, is all money, is it real freedom if it is bought* . . .

The elevator bell rang. It was a familiar sound. She'd been here before. She'd made it work last time, and she could make it work for her this time too. That was the answer. When some cunt's passing offered to fast-track you a few rungs up the ladder of life, you didn't look a dead gift horse in the mouth.

Gary opened the front door and they hugged. 'Come in, come in,' he said. 'Your mom is in the kitchen.'

'Of course,' Lally replied, handing the bottle to him, kicking her heels off and hanging her coat and handbag on their overflowing hall rack. Gary had arrived a year before Estelle's Michelin star. He was hired for front-of-house but then grew into Estelle's life in a way Lally didn't even realise was love, but of course clearly was, as soon as you thought about what two adults might do when they didn't have to prove or perform anymore. It helped that he was a widower. At first Lally had dismissed him as a pushover. That was before she understood that sorrow turned some men soft rather than hard, and that soft might sometimes be better.

Lally went through the small dining area and into the kitchen, where Estelle was washing her hands.

'So what's this about champagne?' Estelle leaned in for a hug and kiss.

'Some news,' Lally said. 'I sold the work from the last exhibition—the installation, the big one, by the artist who died. I sold it to MoMA for a huge amount of money.'

'Hey!' Gary called out, clapping his hands together.

Estelle gasped. 'Congratulations! Oh, that's so wonderful. You work so hard. You deserve this.'

'A *lot* of money,' Lally repeated. 'I paid off most of the apartment, and there's some to spare, and I'm going to put it back into the gallery.'

Estelle's eyes grew wide and Gary's mouth fell open, then they both cheered.

Estelle put her hands on Lally's shoulders, and they looked at each other for a long time. 'I am so very proud of you, gorgeous. I knew you would be this good.'

Gary came over and put his arms around both of them, drawing them into a gentle family hug.

'Bubbles, then!' he declared.

'Yes!' Estelle said, turning to get glasses from the overhead cabinets. 'We'll have a toast.'

The cork popped, making them all start, and they laughed.

'To Lally,' Estelle said, as they held their flutes up. 'Our unstoppable girl.'

Lally felt tears coming to her eyes and she closed them as she took a sip. Yes, that would be it. Unstoppable.

Later, after a feast and a long chat, Estelle walked Lally to the front door, then rode down with her in the elevator. 'Make sure you take this slowly,' her mother warned. 'I'm just thinking of your migraines. You know what happens when you go too hard and don't rest.'

'Yeah, yeah.' Lally brushed her off, but she'd been thinking the same thing. 'I've got my pills with me all the time.'

'Good. And Lally?'

'Mmm?'

They were on the street now, waiting for a taxi to come by. 'I know it's complicated, and maybe you don't want to hear this, but I think your dad would be proud of you. Proud of how much you've achieved these last few years.'

Despite herself, Lally burst into tears. Estelle wept too, but only a little.

'Your father wasn't always bad. When I met him he was so cheeky. If things had been different somehow . . . I don't know. Just remember that he loved you. *I* love you.'

Lally kissed her mother goodbye. What must 'cheeky' have meant for an American man in the 1970s? Jokes that weren't funny anymore. She thought back to the moment when they'd got the letter from the lawyers about Lally's inheritance.

'You should have half,' Lally had said to her mother matter-of-factly.

'I don't want his money.'

'I'll ask you again in a month, and it's fine if you've changed your mind.'

'I won't.'

The following month, Lally repeated her offer.

'What will you do with it?' Estelle asked.

'I'm going to open my own gallery,' Lally replied. 'Even half of this is enough for me to start somewhere small.'

Estelle hugged her daughter close for a long time, and when she pulled away, she said softly, 'Then take it all and start somewhere big.'

It had taken years for Lally to understand her mother, she thought, staring at Estelle's waving figure, shrinking as the taxi drove away down the street. Estelle's family had told her that to leave would be to betray them, and she did, for her own freedom, and for a man who ended up controlling her. So Estelle had left her family money, then the man she left it for kept her dependent on an allowance from him, and even though his death could have made her rich again, she had rejected it. The difference between Lally and her mother was that Estelle had grown up thinking she'd always be wealthy and miserable, and Lally had grown up thinking she'd have to climb up and reach somewhere to ever get rich and happy.

On her way home she received a message from Farr's team requesting the contract to sign. So strange to have them chasing her after all this time of her chasing them! Clearly, they moved fast once they'd made a decision. She sent them a copy of her standard contract when she got home. Easy peasy. Other emails confirmed that things were shaping up nicely for the Armory Show. She had booked the second-smallest booth size but managed to get a great spot with high foot traffic by volunteering to chair a panel on 'Diversity and representation in the independent gallery scene'. 'I'll tick your box if you tick mine,' she'd said to the producer of the talks and ideas program, and they'd laughed.

The next morning she stretched and yawned like a proud cat, taking her time to get out of bed and shower, planning her redecorating moves. While waiting for the kettle to boil she checked the usual news outlets, and her stomach dropped out of her body: FAMOUS ARTIST CHUCK FARR ACCUSED BY FIVE MODELS.

6

ONCE HIS EGO HAD RECOVERED from the blow, the relation-ship that emerged from the ashes of his crush on Em was one Pat was grateful for. He probably couldn't have handled being friends with her if she'd actually rejected him. That would've made working with her awkward too. The way things ended up was sort of happy-accident perfect. He got all the benefits of speaking to a woman—the emotional insights, the lack of certain types of judgement—but with none of the trickiness or tension that seemed to be there with straight chicks. She helped him at work. They made a great team. He vaguely entertained a pipe dream of her being his personal assistant if he worked his way up high enough at the company. The dream was interrupted by the ping of the elevators sounding in front of him, and Josephine materialising from inside. He stood up straight.

'Good afternoon, Josephine.'

She stepped out of the elevator and stopped beside him, checking the watch face on the slim diamond tennis bracelet that hung a little off her wrist. 'You're off to the Bauers' for your four o'clock then?' she asked.

'Yes,' he replied, sticking an arm out to jam the sensors.

The elevator door shuddered against Pat's hand, and she dismissed him with an approving nod then walked away. He stepped into the elevator and jabbed at the button for the ground floor, then watched as Josephine and Em exchanged a few friendly words at the front desk before the doors closed on him. It must be that she just hated men.

The drive to the Bauers' place gave him mad deja vu. When the cab pulled up in front of that manicured lawn the only thing different was that the Mercedes was now a 6 instead of a 4. The rhythm of the fanning sprinkler was the same, water restrictions more like recommendations in this postcode. Hedges finished at clean right angles. There was a beautiful big leopard tree out the front but none of the usual litter of dried seed pods on the ground underneath. Someone raked this place at least twice a week. Pat wondered if the couple even considered the gardener an 'optional expense' or if they'd hang on to the help until the whole ship was at risk of going down. The pavers led the way, but as he approached the front door he felt uneasy and found himself missing Rory. He'd never been to the Bauers' place alone.

The sound of the doorbell catapulted him back in time. Clearly Sophie had forgotten about having briefly met a teenage Patrick and didn't realise what a rich relief her family had burned into the poor boy's mind. Pat had been invited around to the house one night—possibly out of pity for his situation—to watch the State of Origin. There weren't many boarders left at St Augustine's. Rory was Pat's best mate and an incidental middleman between Pat and the more moneyed kids. The huge house in Mosman had a 'media room' with its own bar fridge and microwave. At half-time Pat had gone to the bathroom and run into a man in a polo shirt and cargo shorts. There was a huge watch on his wrist and a gold ring with a crest on his index finger. The man's single hand was somehow big enough to carry five bottles of beer by their sweating necks.

'G'day, mate,' the man had said to Pat, over-articulating. He was drunk.

'Good afternoon, sir,' Pat replied.

'Sir! Ha.' He snorted. 'You Chris's mate or Dan's mate?'

'Dan's,' Pat said.

The man swayed a bit and looked at Pat's clothes and shoes.

'You're the boarder then?' Gregory asked.

'Yes.'

'Your dad a farmer?'

'Yes.'

A pause.

'You want a beer?'

'Sure.'

Gregory held out his arm and Pat took the beer closest to him, letting the other four clink back together. Someone called Gregory's name. 'You boys have fun,' he said, nodding in the general direction of the media room, and continued out onto the deck.

After taking a piss, Pat looked at himself in the bathroom mirror and took a long drink. Tiny bowls of potpourri sat on the counter, chrome and marble versions of the handpainted kind his mum had in their linoleum bathroom back home. He thought of his parents and how they shit-talked city folk like Gregory and how city folk shit-talked about 'bogans' living 'in the sticks' but loved 'farmers' living 'on the land'. Pat imagined his dad laughing at Gregory's soft hands. A woman's hands, he would've said.

Pat stepped back into the dark, loud media room. It smelled incongruously of both sweat and Lynx Africa.

'Oi, farm cunt! Don't fucking take shit out of our fridge,' Chris yelled at him, spotting the beer and getting up.

'Fuck off, Gregory gave it to me,' Pat called back, taking his seat and kicking his shoes off again.

There was an uproar. Each boy had been allocated two beers for the game night and naturally they'd all necked them before kick-off. Chris had tried to give Pat twenty bucks for his second one, which would have been insulting if it wasn't so funny.

'You bullshitting?' Chris had appeared next to Pat, standing over him. Chris was a senior.

'No, man. I'm not going to steal from your fucking fridge. Your dad gave it to me.'

'Hey, Chris, when does your stepmum get back?' Rory asked, cheek in his voice. 'I reckon if I ask nicely she might—'

The joke would hang forever. Chris had climbed over the chairs between them and launched himself at Rory, their bodies crashing to the beanbags on the ground as the others gathered in a semicircle to watch, yelling.

'Coming!' a woman's voice sang from inside the house, bringing Pat back to the present. The door swung open to reveal Sophie in a red v-neck swimsuit, one knee bent a little against the other, leaning on the doorframe like a calendar girl, as though she was dripping. No, she was actually dripping. There was a towel in her right hand, and droplets of water were trickling from the end of her shoulder-length hair down over her fucking incredible tits.

'Patrick!' she exclaimed, delighted, leaning her head to one side and towelling her hair. 'It's such a beautiful day I just couldn't resist a dip.' She straightened her head again and put the other arm out, taking half a step back. 'Come in, come in.'

'Thank you.' His footsteps echoed on the smooth tiles, and he could see little wet footprints glistening from her approach to the door.

'Can I get you a drink?' she offered, turning to lead the way into the house. That arse was still nice and high. She looked incredible for her age. Did he even know her age, actually?

'Sure,' he replied, thirsty. 'Anything cold would be wonderful, thank you—' Pat just managed to stop himself from calling her 'Mrs Bauer'. He tried to pretend as though he didn't know where the kitchen was and followed a metre behind her.

'Have a seat,' Sophie said, and he took the nearest stool at the kitchen bench. She already had a tumbler there, the remnants of an ice cube melting in the bottom. He watched the curve of her back as she reached up into a cupboard and retrieved a second glass, setting it on the counter between them, then he kept watching as she turned again and retrieved the gin, and the tonic, turning again to get some limes, and then the ice. He was aware that she had been making small talk during this time, and that he'd been answering politely, when she replied, 'That's wonderful,' to something he'd said, as the cubes tinkled against the crystal.

'So,' she said then, handing him his drink, 'shall we get down to business?'

The smile on her face made him excited and nervous. 'Great,' he replied, and took a sip of what was at least half gin, then started pulling documents from his briefcase, laying them on the counter.

Sophie came around to his side and stood close to him. The smell of chlorine on her skin transported him back to adolescence again.

She brushed her elbow against him as he started going down the list of works to give or get estimates for. All he needed from her was a 'here' or 'in storage' or 'unknown'.

'Which one is this?' Sophie asked, leaning across him to inspect a photo.

Pat had to lean away to avoid direct face-to-breast contact.

'Top up?' she offered.

'I suppose I don't need to go back into the office after this,' Pat said, looking at his watch and downing the rest of his glass. It occurred to him then that she must have been the one that phoned the office while he was out at lunch to change their appointment from two pm to four pm.

'Brilliant,' she replied, smiling openly.

'You mentioned the divorce and I don't want to pry, but he's not . . . I mean, are we . . .' Pat was struggling. He rearranged some documents, straightened their edges. 'Are we expecting Gregory to join us this afternoon?'

'Ugh,' she grunted at the mention of his name. 'He's gone to Hong Kong for the week. And I told him he's not allowed to come back here. Not that he'd want to anyway.'

'Oh, great.'

'Greg doesn't know a fucking thing about art or the estate, you know?'

'Sure,' he replied.

'I had a chat with Josephine, a little woman-to-woman.'

'I see,' Pat said cautiously.

'Just to make sure, you know, that the other staff will be discrete. I know you and I have an . . . understanding.'

'Absolutely.' Pat nodded. When had that conversation happened?

Sophie poured them more drinks. Her fingernails were huge and the same red as her swimsuit, and her rings looked like golden weights between her joints, sapphires and rubies and diamonds.

'While I'm here I need to take a look at a couple of the works, to get some details,' Pat said, trying to maintain eye contact.

'Ah!' She straightened up, seeming happy. 'Well, grab your drink and I'll give you the tour. The Warhol?' She pointed back to where Pat knew the second dining room was.

'No, actually, there aren't any questions about the Warhol,' he said, smiling to hide a cringe.

'Then what?' she asked.

'The photos,' he said. 'The two large works of photography. I need to check for potential sun damage and inspect the framing.'

Sophie raised her eyebrows. 'Don't talk to me about sun damage!' she quipped and laughed loudly.

They walked to the media room, and more memories rushed back. He sipped his drink and saw a truncated version of his life, a montage possibly ending with Sophie on her knees. She was standing beside the photograph, her arm against the wall, like a gameshow girl beside a prize. The gin hit. He allowed himself to take her in then, the way she obviously wanted him to. When he met her eyes again she lifted her glass to her open lips and finished her drink, holding his gaze. He finished his own drink too.

'I'll fix us another while you do what you need to.' She waved towards the work and left him.

Pat gave his cheeks a little slap and approached the photo. It was in a fine frame. He had to reach his arms out full-span to grab either side of the work and lift it off the wall. Resting it gently on the ground, bending over it, he saw *Billings Brothers* on the bottom right-hand corner and felt relieved. Best framers in Sydney, meticulous record keepers, and he'd worked with them before. They'd have better information on the work than the owners did, and he'd be able to follow it all up later.

'The other is upstairs,' Sophie called out.

Pat took a deep breath. He felt like 'gotcha' cameras were going to pop out from the bushes at any moment.

She was at the bottom of the stairs holding out another drink for him. He took it and she turned and started up the staircase, and he followed. The cellulite on her thighs begged to be rubbed, to be grabbed and kneaded, smacked a little. He kept a hand on the banister to steady himself. She headed straight down the hall to the master bedroom. The balcony overlooked the pool, large terracotta tiles orange against the brilliant blue water. A big straw hat laid abandoned at its station.

Back in the room, Sophie walked to the edge of the bed and put one knee up on the edge of it, resting her weight like that, looking at the photograph hanging above the bed, just where Rory had described seeing it all those years ago.

'Same framers?' Pat asked, but he knew the answer.

'Yes.'

'Wonderful.' He nodded and smiled.

'So are we finished with the formal proceedings?' She looked over her shoulder at him.

He reckoned he had about three seconds to make a decision, but he also felt maybe that it was already too late. If he left now. it would be a rejection. He thought of Sophie's erratic behaviour, then of Josephine. If he lost this client now, for whatever reason, Josephine would blame him. If this was what 'taking one for the team' looked like, all tanned and wet, then that was okay with him. The three seconds was up. Sophie was now sitting on the edge of the bed, her legs noticeably uncrossed, and he walked over to her. She downed the rest of her drink at an impressive speed and let the heavy crystal drop carelessly onto the thick, white carpet. He went to do the same, but she reached up with her left arm and closed her hand over his on the glass, and with her right hand she started at his belt. She was going to suck his cock while he finished his drink? Pat's brain was melting at the equivalent rate of his erection hardening. He hadn't brought a condom. That thought evaporated as she kneaded the outline of him pushing against his pants. He looked down at the crown of her head and saw a centimetre of grey coming through against the blonde streaks. Sophie tugged his pants down to his knees and he moved right up to the edge of the bed, his shins pushing Sophie's knees apart, and his crotch was so close to her face she'd have to move her whole body to get away from it, but she didn't want to get away from it. The gin swirled around strong in his mouth as she licked the head of him and caressed his balls. He always got nervous when women with big nails touched his balls, but when she put his whole dick in her mouth he saw some of her lipstick coming off her lips and onto his shaft, and he realised then that they hadn't even kissed, that it was straight to this, and that made him want to fuck her really, really hard. He angled his hips more towards her head, just a little, but catching her off guard, and she jerked her head back. Before he could swallow his mouthful to apologise she looked up at him with the craziest fucking expression he'd ever seen, and then plunged his dick into her mouth with such force he felt himself hit her throat, and she made that porn gagging noise and kept going, her forehead brushing his stomach. She grabbed his free hand and put it on the back of her head. She wanted him to fuck her face? Okay. He started to thrust into her, and then she jerked her head back again. It scared the shit out of him—was that not what she'd wanted? But she looked up at him again with those crazy eyes.

'I bought some treats with that clock money. Want a bump?'

Pat laughed with relief and then also with excitement. 'Fuck yeah!' And he finished his drink and dropped his glass over his shoulder onto the floor behind him somewhere, and she let out an excited, high-pitched laugh, jumping up and going to the bedside table, saliva and pre-cum glistening on her cheek. He kicked his pants off and followed her, smacking her arse, hard, and they both laughed again, with the careless volume of a pair of not-married people in an empty mansion. He saw various boxes of condoms in the bedside table along with two baggies. Sophie already had an Amex card and a rolled-up pineapple sitting on the corner of the table—she'd been buzzing before he even arrived. Wild.

Things happened quickly. Her hands were against the glass of the floor-to-ceiling windows as he fucked her from behind. He tried to ask her what she wanted and she just said, 'Don't stop,' and took her right hand off the glass to start touching herself. She had a bleached arsehole, absolutely no bush, and asked him if he wanted to come on her face. He said, 'Sure.'

'Take the rest of that first bag with you,' she said from the bed as he left. She was lighting a cigarette, no ashtray in sight. 'Just leave me the full one in the drawer.'

Every time Pat went back to Queensland he became more sure that the lanes in Sydney were, in fact, slimmer and faster-moving than those in Brisbane. The t-shirts and thongs per capita went up, along with the humidity and UV rating. The sense of urgency and efficiency went down. Friendliness went up. Importance went down. Pat felt like Queensland was where he'd retire and die. The old faithful. He had two nights to spend with the family before leaving on the big New York trip. He couldn't *not* tell his mum he was going overseas, and when she'd found out she insisted he 'stop by', as though it was on his way. She was so proud of him getting this big job, and them sending him on a big trip so soon. He couldn't tell her he was still broke.

Luke was there to collect him from the airport. This was how Pat knew something was up—it was a two-hour drive from the family home. No way his little brother would be coming all that way for nothing.

'Oi!' The call came from the opposite end of the pick-up zone.

Pat grabbed his duffel, jogging over. Luke and Beck were twins, only four years younger than him, but the differences were innumerable. Luke kept his hair at a number-three buzz. The strong-and-silent country thing may have started as an affectation with Luke, a play-act at adulting, but every time Pat visited he saw the act had deepened, crystallised. This was his brother now.

Pat reached the back of the ute and smiled at his brother, dropping his duffel to open his arms for a hug. They embraced with the usual roughness, the old too-hard slaps on each other's shoulders a stand-in for how they'd all screamed 'no homo' as kids.

'How are you?' Pat asked.

'Yeah, all right,' Luke replied, grabbing Pat's duffel with one hand and throwing it into the filthy open tray of the ute in a single fluid motion.

Pat flinched.

'Shit, sorry, you got a laptop in there?'

'No, no, it's fine,' Pat said, moving to the side door. It wouldn't even have occurred to Luke that Pat's R.M. Williams leather goods were for style rather than durability. The first few years Pat came home from Sydney as an adult he'd go to extreme measures to dress down, changing from his boots into his old tennis sneakers. After a while he realised it was futile. As soon as he opened his mouth he announced his allegiance to the city. No point pretending not to be the prodigal son.

'So what lottery did you lose to get the airport shift?' Pat asked, ignoring the orange dirt transferring from the seatbelt to his shirt as he buckled himself in.

Luke was keeping his bright, pale eyes on the road, but Pat needed his sunglasses.

'Is it Mum?'

'No, no.'

'Beck?'

Luke nodded slowly.

'Fuck, what is it?'

The car sailed over a rise and back down. Luke seemed to be chewing around his mouth a bit. Pat's mind was pinballing through the possibilities. Had to be cancer. Hereditary.

'It's probably nothing.'

'What's nothing, Luke?'

'It's her boyfriend.'

'Her boyfriend? What about him?' Pat looked at his brother's profile. A rushing tree line and blaring sky flew by around him like a halo. 'He has cancer?'

'What? No.'

What else bad is there except for cancer? 'Shit, he's hit her?'

'No.' But Pat saw something in Luke's face change. 'I don't think so. Not yet.'

'Fuck!'

'But it's . . . I mean . . .' Luke exhaled and ran his fingers through his hair, then wound his window open, not taking his eyes off the road. 'Aircon's busted, so it'll have to be—what does Dad call it?'

'Luke . . .'

'Manual air conditioning—'

'Luke!'

'Righto. Jesus, we've got the whole drive.'

'You're not sure if he's hit her *yet*? What does that mean?'

'I shouldn't have said that. It's just, I've just started hearing some stuff. I've got a buddy in and out of Perth, Damo, does the same FIFO shifts as Sean sometimes. Damo said to me that he wouldn't let Sean anywhere near his sisters.'

'Are we worried about Tom too?' Pat asked. Their nephew— Beck's son with a long-gone deadbeat—had just started primary school.

'Dunno.'

Pat sighed. 'So basically, we do whatever we can to break them up, but don't let Beck know that's what we're doing or she'll dig her heels in.'

'See, you're good at this stuff.'

They spent the rest of the ride listening to music and talking about Luke's work. His sparky business was going well, and it made Pat feel like he could talk about some of his own work-related successes for the first time in a while. Not that Luke understood the ins and outs, but at least he wasn't hypersensitive, like Beck. Luke had reached a kind of acceptance of the state of things that Beck still scratched up against.

A wedge-tailed eagle took off from the top of a wooden gate post as they rocketed along the winding road between two grazing farms. Pat watched it heading towards a smattering of cattle on a hill. It was dry. The entire landscape—every green—had been mixed with too much grey. The only exception was the occasional outburst of bougainvillea and its lurid magenta, like an opera singer in a pub. They passed up and over the hills around the Wivenhoe Dam. A flock of pelicans sat calmly on the surface of the muddy water.

'Why are you turning right?' Pat asked when they reached the T-junction to the town, noticing Luke was in the wrong lane to go straight to the family home.

'I wanna show you the place I'm looking at. There . . .' Luke leaned forward over the wheel after another minute and pointed past Pat to a beautiful old house.

'It's huge!'

'Ha ha.' Luke straightened up. 'It's a house, Pat.'

'What is that, like, ten bedrooms?'

Luke laughed. 'Can't believe you've got your heart set on a million-dollar rat cage,' he said. It was something their father said. People in the city were in the rat race and lived in overpriced cages.

Pat let it go. 'Well, I'm happy for you.'

Ten minutes later they pulled into the driveway and their mother was at the front door before Luke had even switched off the engine.

'Hello!' she called to them, her arms up wide and open. She wore the same small gold hoops as always, her hair in a low ponytail. Her eyes were bright light blue, the same as Luke's, still not needing glasses. She had no idea her Levi's had gone out of fashion long enough to be back in again. Spaghetti-strap singlet and old cotton bra straps showing.

'Hi, Mum,' they chorused, and Pat went over to her for a hug.

'What, no hug for your mother?' she called to Luke.

'I saw you this morning!' he called back, getting Pat's bag from the tray.

'Oh, I'm so demanding,' she said with an eye roll, and Luke groaned and came over to them and gave his mother a hug, putting his chin on the top of her head. She stood beaming between them, holding each one by an arm, looking up at them, lost in a moment of what Pat presumed was a healthy mixture of irritation and love, then snapped into her bustling mode. 'Lunch is on the table! Come in, come in!'

'Hey!' Beck called to them from the kitchen, walking over.

She and Pat met on the mustard carpet in the living room for a brief hug. Nothing in the house ever changed. Even when his parents had 'upgraded' the old couch for one with electric leg-raising capabilities, they managed to find one the same shape and dark brown as the original.

Beck seemed relaxed.

'Where's Tom?' Pat asked, looking around at knee-height for his nephew. 'I brought him some new Lego.'

'He's staying with a friend in Toogoolawah over the weekend,' Beck replied.

'Oh.' Pat frowned.

'What?' she asked.

Pat shrugged a little. 'I wanted to see him.'

'Well, then, you should've told him. That would be a nice thing for him to hear from his uncle.'

Their mother pushed past them, walking down the hall to the back door and yelling out, 'Lunch!' in the same singsong yet forceful way that always managed to transport Pat straight back to school holidays. 'Rebecca, grab the champers from the spare fridge, would you?'

'Yep,' she replied, heading to the garage where the spare fridge-freezer sat, mostly empty now both boys had moved out.

'Putting your stuff in your old room, Pat,' Luke called out.

'Thanks!'

'Hello, Patrick.' His father appeared and offered Pat his hand.

'Give your son a damn hug, Murray,' his wife ordered.

Pat smiled as he and his dad briefly embraced.

Luke returned at the same time Beck emerged with the bubbly, and the living room was suddenly loud and full of chatter. Pat laughed as his mum slapped Luke's hand away from the crispy potatoes near the roast. Beck handed him a flute. 'Champagne?'

'Yes, please!' Now wasn't the time to mention that Yellowglen was not, in fact, champagne.

'Come on, everyone sit down,' his mum said, 'or it'll get cold!'

'Let's make a toast!' Pat suggested as they took their seats. He wanted to tell them about how well things were going at work.

His father paused in his carving duties. 'Oh, Beck, you haven't got a drink.'

'Nah, I'm good, I'm just gonna have a Coke.'

'What? Come on, have some bubbly,' Pat urged. This wasn't like her, she was normally chomping at the bit to 'get on the piss,' as she said.

'I bought your favourite champers,' their mum added, nudging Beck.

'No, no, I'm right.'

'What's the matter?' Luke said, joking, but a little abruptly.

Beck seemed taken aback. 'I just don't—'

Their mum gasped and dropped the salad servers onto the table, eyes wide and grinning at her daughter like a madwoman. Pat had missed something.

'Huh?' Their dad was still hovering over the lamb with a giant knife.

Beck gave a tiny smile.

'Oh my god!' their mum shrieked, shooting up from the table, screaming like she'd won the lotto.

'Holy shit,' Luke said, his mouth dropping open.

'It's early, you know,' Beck said. 'Maybe just eight or so weeks, so I'm not supposed to say anything yet.' She looked up at their dad, and he put the knife down. Everyone watched in silence as he wiped his hands on a tea towel and walked over to her seat.

'Congratulations, love,' he said, and she scraped her chair back to give him a hug.

Their mum began whooping again, suddenly giving zero fucks about the roast going cold, and then she was in tears, and hugging Beck and their dad, and in the craziness Pat and Luke exchanged a quick look. Pat shook his head, and Luke saw this and gave a curt nod in reply, then they both went over to hug their sister.

'A baby in time for Christmas, then?' Pat said to Beck, holding her by the shoulders, smiling. He turned to his dad. 'You'd better buy a second tree to fit all those extra presents under.'

Lunch began and it was the happiest Pat had seen his family in years. Their mum kept clapping and bringing her little paper serviette to her eyes at random intervals.

'Happy tears!' she announced unnecessarily each time, beaming.

Nobody asked about Sean, and Beck didn't mention anything about him. There was no way to know if that was a good or bad thing. From what Pat could remember, three of Beck's friends already had at least one kid. He'd seen them all out wasted at a hens' night on one of his recent trips home. They'd called out obscene things to him from the verandah of the fancy pub in town, sucking on their penis-shaped straws, before Beck recognised him and told them all to shut the fuck up. One of the bridal party said something about getting his number but Beck shut it down, saying something about Pat not being into 'women like us'.

He definitely couldn't ask her what she was going to do about work. She did the admin and accounts for one of the local landscaping outlets. He didn't imagine a small business like that would be prepared to make any decent leave arrangements.

The family habit was to nap through the hot afternoon after a large lunch, waking in time for leftovers for dinner and more drinking. Pat left them to it and went for a walk. His feet carried him into the centre of the small town, the point at which the shops on either side of the single road going in and out were most concentrated. He sat at the foot of a large eucalyptus, looking across the road to the old antiques centre. It was enough to take it in from the outside. He knew how it would smell and how the giant mounted deer head would stare at him as he climbed the front stairs. There was a coffee cart out front now, though: that was new. Maybe other things had changed too. For a few years when Pat was still at the local primary school the antiques centre had been the only air-conditioned building he could go into without his parents and without any money. They didn't get a library in town until after he'd left. Maybe if he'd spent summer with books, he'd be a lawyer. As it was, the old lady who ran the antiques place let him hang out there as long as he looked like he was 'dusting'. Sometimes she'd give him an icy pole in the afternoon.

He snapped a twig in half and threw the bits onto the hot black tarmac. What the fuck was Beck going to do? She still rented. Was Luke going to help her out? By Pat's estimation Luke was about to bypass their parents in terms of cash and capital. Beck was too proud to ask for help and you had to ask Luke if you wanted something. A young man like Luke was the king of this land. Liked by almost everyone, charging reasonable prices for a useful trade. Luke would be batting keen biddies away every weekend, with those eyes and guns like that. Not to mention that huge house.

Babies. Houses. These things seemed like such colossal decisions with terrifying ramifications. As if you had to pick a side and then you couldn't shift until you died. He'd be flying to New York the following afternoon, in completely over his head, still polishing the actual dust off his boots. But the smallness of Esk was unbearable. The boring certainty of manual labour and dying exhausted. A sad part of him knew it was too late to ever come back home anyway. What room was there in a place like Esk for a man with an art history degree? He thought about Em and sighed. In the city he couldn't even tell which ones were lesbians. In Esk it was obvious when girls liked girls: they were butch. Most of the gay people left anyway. He knew that some of the people in town presumed he was gay, thought he had to be gay to want to work in the art world. Once his mum had been cleaning the house while listening to a Prince CD and his dad had picked it up, inspected the cover, and said, 'Looks like a poof, sounds like a poof.'

A ute shook past and a kelpie on the open back tray gave him a single bark. Nothing like a younger sibling doing something big to kick you in the guts. He'd always just kind of presumed he'd end up with kids, but now it was occurring to him that it wouldn't necessarily just happen. Especially not in the city. He was almost thirty. Where he was born that was old to be without a wife at least. Where he lived now it was absurdly young. What did he have to show for all these years that had passed since he left? Nothing. He'd spent ten years getting it wrong in both places.

7

LALLY TURNED TO GEN. 'DO you think me making money from Joseph dying is a feminist act?' Their favourite vegan Mexican place did awful nachos but excellent frozen margaritas. Gen's new boyfriend, Alex, had found it.

Gen laughed. 'I presume this means drinks are on you.' She raised her glass and Lally signalled to the waitress for another round. 'You thinking about your dad again?'

'I think about my dad whenever I think about how shit men are. And how they don't seem to be getting any better.'

Gen shook her head. 'I've gotta say, I don't understand what Rivera had over you.'

'You mean how did I lobotomise myself enough to sleep with him?'

'Well...'

'Yeah, look, it's easy to shit on him now, but he really was a cliché.'

'You think?'

'But in all the good ways too, you know? When he was working on that last piece it was like he was possessed. Every

74

single thing he saw, everything he heard, was relevant, interesting, potential material. It opened the world up. Sometimes we'd be walking down the street and he'd just run into an antique shop to buy something then spend days researching it.'

'I thought he was broke.'

'He was.'

'So . . .'

'I gave him money,' Lally admitted.

'How much money?'

'Not nearly as much as he ended up giving me,' she said dryly.

'He wasn't, like, clearing you out or anything?'

'No, no. I helped him with money for the work. You know, I'm the one who sent him to figure out the blue light trick and paid for the prototypes at the fabricator's place. I paid for his studio space for a few months at the end, and bought him a 3D printing machine so he could make it look like he'd chopped weird objects in half somehow.'

'Fuck, that was the stuff people were raving about.'

'I know. I'm not saying it was all me. At the time I actually felt a bit bad because he had some different ideas but I convinced him the "fucked ocean" thing was best for the space.'

'Which it was.'

'Yeah, and so I paid for it. And he believed in it. He was a believer.'

'Believed in what?'

'*It.* I dunno. Himself, art. He believed he could carve out a place for himself in the art history journals. It was exhilarating. He made me believe that original art was still being made.' She sighed.

'That you could make an original artist?'

Lally nodded. 'I was jealous of how carefree he was, and how confident. I wanted some of that for myself. I wanted to believe in art again too.'

'You've always believed, Lally—don't let him have that. You opened that gallery because you believed.'

'Mmm.'

'Mmm what?'

'It's hard to explain. Sometimes I can't tell if I love the art or if I just love the hustle. I'm serious: he had a bunch of other ideas. One was huge paintings of extinct animals with that blue—pieces I knew I couldn't fit in my galley—so I convinced him it was a gimmick, that it wasn't "the work" he should be doing.'

'Well, if he was a committed artist and thought he had a great idea, he wouldn't let someone else just tell him not to do it.'

'But he couldn't afford any of these ideas. You know what it's like here.'

'Well, then, it sounds like you were his patron, and when artists take money from patrons they do so with the knowledge that the content or nature of their work might be compromised.' Gen shrugged. 'That's the deal.'

'Then I go to set up our booth at the fucking Armory, and I just see so many artists whose partners are attorneys or bankers or fucking whatevers. Or their parents. I mean, New York is barely liveable for broke people anymore, even in Queens, and what's the point in being here if you're not near the actual city? I mean, when I put it all together, I worry that I'm part of the problem and actually killing art. That the art scene can't support good new art anymore, because it's all about the hustle now, about the system and the acquisitions and the coverage.'

'Are we still talking about Joseph?'

'Oh.' Lally paused. 'No, not really.'

'Had you been thinking about this stuff last year? Before him?'

'Yes.'

'I remember you telling me some variation of this when you were brainstorming how you'd make the Saplings Program work.'

'True.'

'I don't think this is really about him at all.'

'I don't think so either!'

'Well, I'm a bit drunk!'

'Me too!'

They smiled at each other.

'I've gotta ask, though,' Gen said, pulling a hard copy of *New York Magazine* out of her bag, 'you're not still thinking about giving this Chuck Farr guy a slot later this year, are you? Everyone is saying he's rank.'

Lally grimaced. 'You haven't seen his work. For over a decade he's—'

'I don't need to see his work. It's him I have a problem with. It's him that *you* should have a problem with. Do you not have a problem with him?'

'But he'll—'

'Are you serious? It was all over the internet.'

'What he did sucked, yes, but he didn't actually assault anyone.'

'Lally, come on. He said he wouldn't photograph them unless they were naked, and then he fat-shamed the ones who said no.'

'The final artist for the Saplings Program this year is an incredible performance artist from the Bronx.'

'And what, he's going to wash your sins clean?'

'*She*.'

'Oh, come on.'

'Nobody else in Chelsea is showing performance art anymore. You know why? Because you can't fucking sell it, can you? Farr is going to pay for this girl.'

'And you don't gain anything from any of this, of course.'

'I'm not a fucking charity. I can run a fucking business and make hard choices. I'm taking from Farr to give to Hernandez.'

A pause was enforced upon them as the waitress arrived with two new comically large drinks. They smiled and thanked her. A quiet moment passed between them.

'It's not Robin Hood if the rich dickheads don't lose, Lally,' Gen said, a little less heat in her voice. 'If you show Farr, he'll be the one benefiting from you. He'll, like, siphon off your legitimacy. If you put his works in your gallery, it's like you're saying to all those young men that what he did to them doesn't matter.'

Lally groaned. She didn't want to talk about it. There was no way she could cancel Hernandez, but she would struggle to keep paying Leah and platform the unsaleable Bronx artist without a boon like Farr. She should have kept more liquid cash from the MoMA acquisition money instead of sinking it all into her mortgage.

'Hey.' Gen reached out and touched her arm. 'I'm sorry, I didn't mean for that to get heated.'

'It's fine.' Lally shook her head. 'Please know I'm thinking about it. Whatever I decide, it won't be done lightly.'

Gen gave a kind of begrudging smile and lifted her new glass. They both took huge gulps.

Lally had had other friends as a child, but none had stuck like Gen. There were two other girls from Flushing in their friendship circle, Kim and Caitlyn, but for Lally those ties had dissolved when they all went off to different colleges. Social media told her that both women were at big law firms now. The two of them were in different cities but it was like they were living interchangeable lives in the same peplum skirts with equally ostentatious engagement rings. They bought new leggings for spin classes each year and eased their quads on identical foam rollers. Lally predicted they would each have a single child at thirty-eight and a half, returning to work in time to make partner by forty-five, leave to open their own firms then retire shortly before turning sixty, still fit enough to go skiing, and putting the inner-city apartment and coastal weekender in a trust for their sole heir. They were obviously working hard, and using their minds, and had chosen partners for themselves, and lived well, but it all seemed so morbid to Lally.

She decided to walk home after leaving the restaurant. Gen could sometimes be a good sounding board for work decisions, but she underestimated the comparative security of her salaried job. Lally's entire life was on the line with this gallery. It wasn't as simple as 'should' and 'shouldn't'. And Gen saved animals for a fucking living. Nobody could beat that for a lawful good. Sure, everyone wanted the rich dickheads to lose, but you needed power for that. Punching up didn't actually work. Punching up was a myth. If she'd done what the moral absolutists wanted, her gallery wouldn't have survived a year. Obviously, it irked her that Farr had turned out to be a creep. But newsflash: Rivera had been a creep too. How many artists were shit to their wives and girlfriends rather than their models? Did it make a difference if the predatory behaviour took place in the home or the studio? The rules of engagement seemed to be changing fast, but the same men still went ahead and broke them. She'd always interpreted Farr's work as being subversive about power dynamics, bringing a sort of forced humility to these subjects. People wrote about being transfixed by their vulnerability. It was true, various exhibitions had varying levels of sex, but wasn't it infantile to immediately conflate nudity and eroticism? Wasn't that a further subversion of the viewer's expectations—to split the two?

Lally had read and re-read and re-re-read what those five models had said, and the more she read about it the more conflicted she felt. All five men were at least eighteen and knew they were getting involved with an artist who was deeply interested in that package of youth, muscularity, virility, et cetera. Two of them were personal trainers who obviously thought being a Farr subject would help them somehow. Only one of the five actually said he'd been fat-shamed, and that was a guy with a finance podcast, so it was difficult to sympathise. Farr had been an asshole, absolutely, but he'd been called out on it now. He couldn't behave like he did in past decades. He wouldn't be stupid enough to do it again.

An email from France the next morning made her decision for her. Guillaume Brodeur was a hot young Parisian artist credited with making etching cool again. Lally had been in Paris when his first solo exhibition was showing at a tiny place near Porte de Clignancourt and knew immediately there was something special going on. Brodeur was twenty-three then, just over two years ago. Most etchings were small for a reason. His grand landscapes were like large poems. His first show portrayed the countryside in Morocco, where he grew up, and his second solo was full of images of western France, where he lived for five years. They had a kind of eeriness to them, or a sliver of melancholy at least, but you could see from the attention to detail that they were also full of love. The tiny church buildings were specific. The way he did or didn't rub the ink off the large blank places at the tops of the plates created an incredible sense of cumulonimbus clouds—a true marriage of medium and material. For the winter scenes he'd found a way to make a million tiny grooves that you just knew instinctively were snow, but the marks didn't disrupt the composition. What Lally had seen and loved in these works was the refusal to choose between beauty and sorrow. It was a rare thing for such a young artist to have grasped.

Guillaume's next show was scheduled for July and the email was from his manager, Emile. A progress report, as per their contract, with some photos of the works in progress.

'Leah, come here,' Lally said when her assistant walked through the door. She brought up the images and clicked through them. 'Look at this. The new collection is so grim.'

Leah handed Lally her second coffee. 'Do you mean grim bad or grim sad?'

'Well, it's immediately apparent that the content is grim, but with etchings, I mean, you can imagine, it changes the whole tone of the thing. They're so murky you wonder if he even knows how to wipe a plate. It's like he's'—Lally struggled to find a way to say it—'it's like there's no love anymore. He's tipped over from that knife edge into the darkness.'

Lally pushed back from her desk and walked around the space with her hands on her hips, calculating. 'We won't be able to sell these. That means we won't sell anything in the whole month of July. Schedule a call for me with Emile.' She looked over to Leah. Lally still hadn't told her about signing Farr. But there was no way she could cancel him now. He was looking like the only damn artist who would pay the gallery's rent.

8

PAT SET OUT FROM HIS hotel first thing Thursday morning and watched his breath fog and disappear in the cold air, joining a cluster of suited people holding briefcases and coffees. Trundling along West 23rd he saw the bustle of Fifth Avenue ahead, and the wind carried a bark across the road. He realised that Madison Square Park was full of dogs. Crossing over for a closer look, he discovered a dedicated off-leash park surrounded by wrought-iron fencing and tidy hedges. It was impossible that people could take their dogs to a park with such a view. Dogs were a thing of homes and regularity, and the Flatiron Building sunning itself in the morning light was a thing from films and fantasy. The dogs were very New York. If a dog was small it was tiny. If it had curly hair then it was undulating. Someone decided that a single giant Irish wolfhound wasn't enough giant Irish wolfhound and so, naturally, there were two. Some had coats, adding another level of anthropomorphic pageantry.

The dog park turned out to be child's play in terms of coated pageantry. Arriving at the ticket booth to the Armory Show fifteen minutes before the doors opened was like stepping into what Pat imagined Fashion Week was like. It made Sydney Contemporary look like a school fete. When the doors opened the jostling was brusque. Pat let himself be elbowed by a woman in a floor-length fur coat, only to step sideways and bump his head on the trilby of an old man in a pale grey suit with a magenta chinoiserie blouse. The woman in front of him in the ticket line somehow had two haircuts. It was a bob but then also long hair. Like a corporate art mullet.

Pat wasn't meeting Al for another hour, so he began a loop around the first of the three piers. Al was going to introduce him to a dealer, John, who knew a few rich families that had moved to Australia with the change of the last US government. This man was what Pat called a 'time splitter'. John 'split his time' between New York and New Zealand. Al 'split his time' between his mansion and his retreat. He suspected Josephine also 'split her time' between whatever the fuck she wanted and whatever the fuck else she wanted.

The booths were all bright white walls, most of the works hanging, maybe one in three galleries showing something more sculptural. Apart from being completely unpredictable, it was, in a deeper sense, precisely what Pat had expected. No real trends, no discernible movements. Lots of flashy stuff. Fun. He made mental notes of the booths at which people clustered. Over the coming week he would need to make conversation with half-a-dozen people who were genuinely gripped by this plastic stuff. He approached one packed area and immediately understood why. Large and striking oil portraits of a family sat against a long wall. Snippets of conversation told him the artist was trying to reclaim and restate the legacy of certain families that still hadn't recovered from Hurricane Katrina. A high burst of laughter erupted to Pat's left.

'Oh, no, no, they're all sold,' the man explained at a higher volume than was required in such close proximity. 'This is the first day the fair is open *to the public*. Beyoncé and Jay-Z bought the final pieces in this collection last week.'

An unkempt, daggy man in a trucker cap tried to pay the coffee cart with cash before the barista, frustrated, announced that they were card only. Pat looked down, embarrassed, then saw the paint flecks on the man's shoes and the extreme age of his hands fumbling with his wallet. All the people were there to see the art, supposedly, but so few of them were the artists. Artists famously stayed away from fairs. He'd heard these big ones called 'meat markets'.

In one quiet corner there was a large wooden bedframe standing in the centre of the gallery's space, with pedestal fans and old heaters inside it. Standing right next to it you could smell the heaters and hear the gentle drone of the fans. Who was paying for this? Which daughter or son was spending their life and their parents' money making such random shit? Just as he was about to turn away, a memory arrived in his mind. The smell reminded him of Esk in winter, of drying wet socks on the heater's bars until they were crispy and the fabric would crackle as he wiggled his toes inside them. On the verandah outside the dogs would be sleeping huddled together. Everyone wore flannelette pyjamas at the big kitchen table. Nobody wanted to make the freezing dash outside to get the chook eggs, and inevitably their father would do it, always 'for the last time'.

The gallerist for the booth was sitting on a small white plinth, tapping away at a laptop, seeming oblivious to her surrounds. So it had reminded him of his childhood, he conceded, turning away. A million things reminded a million people about their childhoods every day. Art should do more than 'remind'.

He went to the agreed meeting spot, popped a mint in his mouth, and took a seat on a funky couch next to a middle-aged man with perfectly round, thick, white acetate glasses, dressed in a white shirt and blue jeans. Pat noticed a tiny gold aeroplane brooch with what looked like a gemstone set in as the cockpit window pinned to the cuffs of the man's jeans so that they just missed brushing the heel of his sneaker. He had never seen a brooch worn on the cuff of a jean. Truly, people with money found the most fascinating ways to waste it.

'Look at this!' Al appeared and clapped his hands together, walking towards Pat but looking at the man with the ankle brooch, approaching him first and kissing him on each cheek. 'John.'

They smiled at each other warmly.

'Morning, Al,' Pat said, after giving them a moment.

'John, Pat; Pat, John,' Al replied, an arm outstretched towards each man.

'We're going to promenade for a bit, and then John is going to show us some young New Zealand artists whose names we need to remember, and then we'll all have lunch,' Al told Pat, and the three of them set off. It was too awkward to walk three abreast in the bustle, and Pat found himself falling in behind the two men, who clearly had a lot to catch up on. The conversation Pat dipped in and out of was about what had sold and what hadn't, of course. John talked about the fair as though it was its last day, giving a rundown of the notable absences of certain galleries as well as the new arrivals. The main coup was that someone had paid half a million dollars for a video work of people spitting into things, or things spitting onto people, or something.

John explained that they needed to head to the next pier to get to the young-and-new section, so they began the short journey outside. The cold smacked Pat in the face, making his nose run. Re-entering the next building over, and lining up to re-check their coats, he got his arm stuck in his sleeve, distracted by a woman to their left. She was possibly the most striking woman he had ever seen. She was slipping out of her own black jacket, and her face in profile was like an evocation of Diana. Thick, wavy brown hair went down to her waist which, very noticeably, hourglassed up to a pair of excellent tits. She tilted her chin up to loosen a black scarf from her neck, revealing pale, bare shoulder blades. Her lipstick was a dark wine colour, but she wasn't wearing much other make-up as far as Pat could tell. Strong, neat brows framed her face naturally. When she had removed her coat and scarf she stood still and upright, waiting for the line to move. This was not a woman from a magazine. This was a woman from a painting.

'Pat,' Al said, turning to him as they handed their coats over the counter, 'make a time with John to show him those odd pieces of yours. You might find a buyer while you're here—for the Miro, at least.'

'Australians never pay enough for the Spanish,' John said with a dismissive wave of his hand, taking his ticket.

When Pat looked up again the woman was gone.

———

The New Zealanders were good. One young Māori artist was making giant prints of geological strata, blurring the line between landscape and abstract. Some of the textile art was incredible.

'Now they've shown over here they'll start seeing success a lot more quickly back home,' John explained. 'The same thing happens to Australian artists who show here,' he said in Pat's direction.

Al and John stopped to inspect some small homoerotic statuettes at a nearby booth and Pat felt like he was intruding, so he turned around to see what was on the other side of the walkway, and found himself gazing down a narrow corridor at the most glorious, extraordinary sight. The striking woman from before, the one who had seemed so statuesque, was chatting to another woman, and they had burst into laughter. Then the beautiful woman screwed her face up into one of the ugliest, most stupid expressions he'd ever seen, and he realised she was lip-syncing to something he couldn't hear. The dark lips curled up, but only on one side, and she bent her knees and awkwardly left-leaned, with a finger in the air, pretending to reach the falsetto, then the two women doubled over in laughter again. When they eventually stood up, both were wiping tears from under their eyes, and then they checked each other's faces. The second woman made a chef's-kiss hand movement, and they laughed again. They chatted some more, then hugged. It was only when the beautiful woman turned towards Pat to walk down the corridor that his heart began beating again at quadruple speed, as if to catch up. Luckily, she was looking down at her phone in her hands. He quickly inserted himself back into the throng.

'Just going to the loo,' Pat said to Al, who made an embarrassed face and waved him off. In that brief moment of looking away the woman's demeanour had firmed up, she was statuesque again, as though the laughter had been just a mirage. He watched her walk past, her hands now in the pockets of her wide-legged black pants, her posture and gait confident and precise. Just as she was about to disappear from view, he ducked out of his spot and dropped into a steady pace behind her. With an explosion of delight he realised she was heading straight for the bar. But then she didn't. A pack of tourists came between them and he lost her. Had she not been heading to the bar? The place was such a fucking zoo there was a real possibility he wouldn't find her again. He might as well piss. He checked his reflection in the bathroom mirror for a brief moment before making sure his hands were totally dry and exiting the bathroom. This was idiocy. He had work to do and Josephine would be waiting for an email update soon.

When he opened the door of the men's he stepped straight in front of the beautiful woman emerging from the ladies' bathroom. His mouth opened, a kind of delighted but terrified gape.

'Hi,' he said.

'Hi,' she replied, and then, when he didn't speak. 'Your first time?'

'Am I that obvious?'

'Yes.' She smiled.

'I was just about to grab a drink.'

'Oh, me too, actually,' she said, so they made a move out into the crowds. Neither of them tried to speak as they shouldered and elbowed their way to the bar area. His mind was clambering for the best work to reference to launch them into conversation. From what he'd seen of her chatting to her mate down the hallway, he figured she'd be down to earth. A kind of realistic, funny chick.

They leaned against the only free spot at the bar and their elbows touched.

'Did you see the bed with the fans and heaters?' he asked, going for a comedic approach.

'Do you mean Spellman's latest? From Presenhuber?' she replied brightly. 'Of course. Did you love it?'

Pat faltered.

Mercifully, the bartender intervened. 'What can I get for you?'

Pat gestured to the woman, inviting her to order first.

'Vodka soda, please.' She smiled and showed him a card with a number on it.

'That's Gallery Lally?' the bartender asked, tapping her point-of-sale screen.

'Yes, thank you.'

'And for you, sir?'

'The same, thanks,' Pat replied.

'On the gallery account?'

'Yes,' said the woman.

'No!' Pat objected, reaching for his wallet. 'I can pay.'

'No, it's fine,' she insisted, replacing her own card back in her trousers pocket. 'What were you saying about the Spellman?'

'Ah.' Pat shifted his weight to the other foot. 'I don't really get it, to be honest.'

'What don't you get?'

'What is there to get?'

She frowned at him and an awkward silence ensued. He was losing her.

Their drinks arrived.

'What do you do?' she asked.

'I work for Osborne in Sydney,' he replied.

She stiffened a little but then seemed to nod to herself as she took a long drink. 'And you're here for business?'

'Yes,' he replied. 'Connecting with buyers and dealers while they're all in one place.'

'You don't find you have to "get" the art in order to sell it?'

Sheesh. 'Well, I just arrived this morning and haven't read any of their artist's statements,' he said, taking a drink.

She seemed confused by his response. 'So why don't you? Or just take it in yourself?'

'With these modern artists you have to read their essays, or you don't get the point,' Pat said. 'I'm not used to it.'

'That's the same with old art—full of waves of specific symbolism. People commissioning paintings to communicate certain things in certain times, portraits giving small biographies depending on the placement of objects and hands and backdrops. You know all this. It's just that the language in your art is taken to be universal because it's canon.'

'A painting of a person makes a lot more sense than a lot of this stuff.'

'There are layers to every portrait,' she said and gestured around her. 'You have to be educated—either specifically educated in a work, or educated in art history generally—to get the second level of any portrait from any time.'

'I can't even get a first level in cubism.'

The joke did not land.

'Well, now that we've moved past the dawn of daguerreotypes and photography, there's a whole other level of exploration, because portraiture need not only be about likeness.'

'Well, portraits are an easy target,' Pat said. 'What about abstracts? That's where it gets really frustrating.'

'You think old art didn't have abstracts?'

'I never said that. I just think "new art" abstracts only have a second, conceptual level, and so are completely incomprehensible to someone uneducated in the work or the artist. And therefore, I'd say, are elitist.'

'Ha!' she said loudly, and two people behind her glanced towards them. 'You think new art is more elitist than old art? Are you kidding me?'

'Look at him.' Pat nodded towards a man further down the bar. 'His rose gold Rolex matches his rose gold MacBook.'

'And I suppose you look at me and see an elitist too?'

'No, I looked at you and I thought you were beautiful and you were having a lively conversation with another woman, and I wanted to be having a lively conversation with you.'

She didn't like that, but it put a hitch in her argumentative rhythm. She went to put her hands on her hips, faltered, and looked up and around, exasperated. 'So you're just a fucking contrarian? Great, how fucking original: a young white dude who enjoys arguing for the sake of it.' She picked up her drink.

'Definitely not,' he said, sensing she was close to leaving. He softened his tone. 'But I love my art and I will stand by it.'

'Well, I love *my* art and will stand by it,' she said, straightening up and looking him in the eye. She was exactly his height.

'Then please let me help you find people to buy it,' he said, and gave her an award-winning, sure-fire, country-boy smile.

'What on earth makes you think I need your help?' she retorted.

This was a fucking disaster. He'd never had his art-chat game tested like this. Normally, when he asked a girl on a date and suggested a tour through the Art Gallery of New South Wales, she was the one begging to go straight to bed.

'Actually, I guess *I* could use *your* help.' He fiddled with his coaster and shrugged.

'Then why are you doing this thing?' she replied, with a kind of up-and-down sweep of her hand that took in his whole body. 'What thing?'

'You know what thing.'

The bar section was filling with people and the flow of the crowd pushed them together. Close up he noticed the definition of her cupid's bow and the colour in her cheeks. He could feel that his own cheeks were flushed too from having captained such a shipwreck of a pick-up attempt. He pulled at his shirt collar where his tie now felt extremely tight at his neck. Under his suit he was sweating, and the realisation that he couldn't remove his jacket lest he reveal the sweating made it all worse.

She was waiting for a reply, but Pat had nothing. He saw in her eyes the moment she decided to walk away from him, and it filled him with panic.

'Pat!' Al called out from nearby, waving over people's heads.

'John?' the woman said, surprised and happy.

The four of them came into a tight cluster facing each other. Both of the older men kissed the woman on each cheek.

'How wonderful you and Lally found each other already,' Al said to Pat. To the woman he added, 'Pat could be a good intermediary for you in the Asia-Pacific, given your portfolio—and the fact that he's the only person at Osborne who isn't ancient like us.'

Pat grinned at her, not believing his luck.

'You've heard all about Lally's incredible gallery, I presume?' Al said to Pat.

Pat shook his head. 'She didn't tell me.'

'He didn't ask,' she corrected.

Al laughed them both off and hooked his arm through John's. 'Well, we're going to go find something to eat, and you're no longer invited, Pat.' He looked from Pat to Lally and said, 'You two should get dinner. I'm serious.'

Pat waited until the other men had left then pounced. 'Dinner?'

She took her sweet time deciding how to answer, clearly not caring that it was obvious.

'I'd love to hear about your gallery,' he followed up.

She sighed. 'You know people back in Australia who would pay real money for new art?'

'Absolutely,' he half-lied. Al must have known something he didn't.

'Artists these days are asking such important questions, it pains me when their work sells for less than some oil by some dead guy.'

'They were grappling with some pretty important questions in the 1800s,' he countered, unable to help himself.

'Sure, but we've answered them.'

He raised his eyebrows.

'Well, okay, we haven't answered all of them, but they're old questions.'

'I don't think the convergence between art and science is an old question. I think modern art is devalued because our society sees the disciplines as a binary in a way they didn't used to. Perhaps if people spent more time looking at *The Heart of the Andes* in the Met, they'd go to the East Village and spend more on their local indie photographer.'

'So, let's agree that everyone should spend more time looking at art'—she was smiling—'but that my exciting new art should sell for as much as your boring old canon.'

'Oof.' Pat grimaced. 'But surely you want this challenging new art with all its important questions in public galleries where people can see it, instead of hidden away in musty old private collections?'

'Touché,' she said, nodding and sipping her drink. 'I suppose I would like both.'

He laughed. 'So we agree that what we want is more art, everywhere—'

'For more money.'

'—for more money, and all the time.'

'And all the time, yes.' She held up her glass to toast, and they held eye contact for a second too long when they each drank.

'Dinner, then.'

They were discussing their respective days when their appetisers were served.

'Your soup, sir,' the waiter said as he placed a dish in front of Pat. It had three sparse bright green cubes on it, a few sprouts and big thin salt flakes.

Pat had no clue what was going on until he looked up and saw the waiter was also holding a carafe, and as he poured the soup into the shallow-lipped dish, the salt flakes melted and the cubes were like buildings being washed away by a great pea-coloured tsunami.

'Ha.' Pat grinned and looked at Lally. 'What a shame your sourdough was baked before it arrived at the table.'

She laughed.

'My friend runs a great bakery, actually, back in Sydney.'

'Do most of your friends do other kinds of work?' she asked.

'You mean not-art?'

'Yes. There's art, and then there's everything else.'

'I have a colleague at Osborne who has become a friend, I suppose, and a couple of people I still see from undergrad.' Pat thought of Rory and the other boys from school. 'But, I mean,

I'm not sure. I guess not. What's a friend, right?' He gave a short laugh. This seemed like a crap thing to say, but she was nodding.

'Yeah, I guess we're at that quality-over-quantity stage with people in our lives,' she said easily, grabbing the wine menu. 'Do you talk to your non-art friends about art?'

'Honestly?'

This made her pause and look back at him. 'Yes, honestly.'

He thought about university and how his mates would pay out his arts degree but then beg him to introduce them to the girls from his tutorials. 'Most of them just kind of decide if they like it or not. Maybe they'll wonder if they could do it themselves. End of conversation.'

'We all do that, right? We make a decision in the first five seconds, then we use our degrees and our reading and our connections to spend the next fifteen minutes coming up with reasons to justify it.'

'That's pretty cynical.'

Lally smiled. 'Do you disagree?'

'No, I guess not.' Pat softened his delivery. 'But the fifteen minutes is the fun part, right? And then sometimes you can hear other people's fifteen minutes and it changes your mind. Or you read the written version of the fifteen minutes and it changes your mind.'

'You read art criticism?'

'Well . . .' He winced.

She laughed. 'I don't know many people who do. I get *Artforum* and just flip through the pages to see if any of my artists are in it, or if anyone I know has written something.' She attracted the waiter's attention with a minimal gesture. 'And then I check to see who's advertising, see what companies have money and think art people are their people.'

The waiter returned with a bottle of red, and he and Lally spent forever doing the uncorking and swirling around and tasting and nodding thing. The two of them sat in silence as the waiter then filled both their glasses, and when he finally left the silence continued.

'Pat,' Lally said bluntly, 'you haven't actually asked me anything about myself. Do you want me to just sit here and smile?'

'Well, fuck.' This was horrific. 'Of course I want to know more about you.'

'Like what?'

'I dunno—everything,' he said.

She just sighed.

'Okay, okay.' He held his hands up in a gesture of defeat. 'Maybe this is a cultural difference. In Australia on a date you just kind of chat and talk shit, and you both pretend it's not a date, and you get drunk and see what happens.'

'Oh.'

'Yeah, and then you ride kangaroos home if you've had too much to drink.'

Lally just opened and closed her mouth, but it was funny, he knew it was funny.

'I do have questions, absolutely,' he said, sensing maybe he could bring her around. 'Please tell me about your gallery.'

'I like talking about my gallery. What do want to know about it?'

'Do you run it alone? Did you start it alone? How do you pick what's in there?'

He was listening to her explain the various parts of her job when their main courses arrived. She'd ordered rabbit with mushrooms and broth.

'Is it good?' he asked after they'd each had a few bites.

'Not bad. I was hoping for more enokis, though. I love enokis.'

'There's never as much rabbit as you think there will be,' Pat said.

'No, the enoki mushrooms—these.' She held some up on her fork. It was like a small clump of long white grass with alien bobbles on the end. 'Would you like to try some?'

He didn't. 'Yes, please,' he said, and leaned towards her with his mouth open, delighting in the shock on her face before she tried to hide it, extending her fork across the table. The mushrooms were somehow both chewy but then also crunchy. 'Mmm,' he said, nodding, but then he looked at her smiling and nodding along, and he shook his head, and she laughed and shook her head too.

'Not for you?'

He swallowed. 'Not for me. Would you like to try some of mine?'

'Your steak?' she said, dubious.

'This isn't just steak—it's Jack's Creek Black Angus,' he replied, and cut off a piece, speared it with his fork, and held it towards her. When she leaned forward and opened her mouth her eyes met his, and he felt a stir of arousal as her lips opened and closed. When she leaned back to chew, closing her eyes, he took the opportunity to quickly adjust himself.

'You're right, that is good,' she said after swallowing. She took a sip of wine. 'Especially with this red. Nailed it.'

'Nailed it!' he repeated.

She made a silly face then. Only a fraction of the face he'd glimpsed at the show, but enough to give him hope that the two women were the same person, one hidden somewhere under the other.

'So,' he prompted, 'you were telling me how you decide what to show in your gallery.'

Lally started talking and didn't stop. She explained how she would draw up a shortlist based on gut feelings about the artists and the trajectory of their work, but then have to make a final decision based on commerce.

Pat practised his active listening. 'Do works normally sell?' he asked.

'If I'm doing my job right, yes.'

'And do you have a normal or regular type of customer?'

'Absolutely not.' She tilted her head to the left then the right, thinking. 'It's more like there are a handful of different types of people I will try to entice. So if I'm showing paintings of regular size I can aim for individual buyers—collectors or dealers—but if it's something sculptural, an installation or experimental, I try to position it in a way that will persuade a museum or gallery to acquire it.'

The waiter swept by to collect their plates.

'Do you deal with many artists directly?' he asked. When she didn't answer immediately, he added, 'I spend so much time with art but never get to meet these geniuses, you know?'

She looked down at the dessert menu the waiter had left on the table.

'All mine are dead!' he joked.

After a strangely long pause she said, 'Pat . . .' Her demeanour had changed to something more serious.

'Yes?'

'Do you want to skip dessert?'

The smile she gave him was unambiguous.

He grinned. 'Let me get the bill.'

'No way. I brought us here because they have an excellent wine list and are happy to split bills.'

'Okay, let's split the bill.'

Lally made the signing gesture at the waiter, and Pat had to fight the poor-boy urge to scull the rest of his wine. Instead, he drained his water glass. More than about six standard drinks and he would get nervous about his performance.

'Wonderful, thank you,' Lally said to the waiter, taking both Pat's card and her own from the small silver dish once the transaction was made. 'I'll grab our coats,' she said to Pat, and he watched her curves under her silky black dress, feeling like he was in some kind of New York dream.

He checked his phone while waiting near the door, swiping away all the notifications from home, dismissing any real-world intrusions. Then Lally appeared, looking pained. His chest tightened. Of course all this had been too good to be true.

'What's wrong?' he asked.

She handed him his jacket. 'They can't find my coat.'

'Oh, shit,' he said.

'Oh, shit indeed,' she replied. 'But I don't want to make a scene. I come here all the time, sometimes with clients. And the waiter was apologetic, blah blah blah.' She flapped her hand and turned to look through the front window of the restaurant, and Pat followed her gaze. People walking past seemed to be almost horizontal as they leaned into the wind, their hands clutching at scarfed throats.

'Well, then'—Pat turned to her with a grin, nudging her—'you'll just have to take mine.'

'What!' she laughed.

'What?' he shrugged, faux-earnest, holding it out for her.

'Oh, my hero!' she said as Pat held out his coat and she slipped it on. 'Okay, then you wait here while I hail us a cab.'

'No, I have to come out and stand proudly beside you, freezing, don't you get it?'

'Oh my god, don't!' Lally moved towards the door. 'Stay here.'

'No!' He followed her, and they mock-tussled at the front door before he bumped them both out into the street, laughing. Then he wasn't laughing. 'Holy fuck.' Pat was getting stabbed.

Lally shrieked with laughter. 'I told you!'

'Get us a taxi!'

'I'm trying!' Her hair was blowing across her face.

'Argh!' Pat yelled, only half-joking. All his extremities stung.

'Here!' Lally called out, jumping up and down, swamped in his coat. A grotty yellow taxi pulled into the kerb and she swung the door open, climbing in, and he ran and launched himself in after her. She reached over him and pulled the door closed behind him while giving the driver an address, and then it was hot and heaven. Lally's body was over his, and she lifted the coat open and put his arms around her waist. Who needed seatbelts? He lifted one of her legs and swung it over his knees, burying his face in her neck.

'We're a big pretzel,' he said, giddy.

'We are a big, warm pretzel,' she repeated, moving her face in front of his, and he held her waist as they kissed.

'Where are we going?' he asked.

'My place, five minutes,' she replied.

He moved a hand towards her breast but she stopped him, took his hand and put it in between her thighs. 'Main arteries, much warmer,' she said in his ear.

'Five minutes is forever,' he complained, using his fingers to massage her inner thigh, pushing and kneading her skin through her tights, making incremental movements up her leg, listening for her breath, for sounds to tell him to continue. He felt her flex her pelvis towards his hand. When he used his fingertip to graze the place where the seams of her stockings met, she squeezed his shoulder, urging him closer.

'Let's take a hot shower together,' she whispered.

9

THE TIMING COULDN'T HAVE BEEN better to move a jumble of old backroom stock at a big fair. With the MoMA direct acquisition, Lally had dealers eating out of her hands, competing with each other to snap things up. Her success with Rivera had a halo effect on everyone else in her stable and Leah was handling everything fantastically, really stepping up. When Lally checked her phone on Friday morning and saw she'd sold her last piece she felt like a million fucking bucks for real. Leah had been working the evening viewing and brought it home with some random interior stylist who was collecting pale blue and green pieces for a lifestyle influencer's Tulum weekender. What a world. She was finally making money while she slept. Or, in this instance, while she fucked. Pat was still out cold beside her as she tapped her phone screen silently.

Lally: *There's an Aussie in my bed*
He gave me head for like 20 minutes last night
Gen: *Shit*
Lally: *I know*

He knows about art?
Gen: *Wtf*
Hot?
Lally: *Yes*
Gen: *Fuck!*
Lally: *I know!*
Gen: *What are you doing on your phone*
Idiot
Go for round two
Lally: *That would be round three*
Gen: *Rude*
Lally: *Might be working with him*
I feel like I should keep it clean or something
Keep it professional
Gen: *Are you kidding? Aussies are great for flings*
All fun
Lally: *Yeah?*
Gen: *YEAH*

Lally woke him up by kissing down his chest towards his dick but dodged blow job duty with a swift shift into cowgirl. Ten minutes to climax, thirty minutes to shower, and she was out the door and on her way to the gallery within the hour.

The walk from east to west was always good, the aesthetics changing as she crossed town. It always seemed a little quieter after Fifth, and she took out her headphones to listen for the birds. The sidewalks got cleaner, and while the green nature squares at the bases of the trees on the east side were mostly bare dirt, they gradually became fenced-off tiny gardens with plaques and dedications. Her glorious city had pulled through the worst of the winter. March meant daffodil bulbs were coming up.

When she had time to spare, like today, she would slow her pace near Bleecker Playground. She didn't stop altogether, let alone sit facing the action. That would be a public declaration that she was considering motherhood. And she wasn't, really. It was more a kind of abstract pondering. Like gazing at the never-ending movement of a fire or the view over a cliff, wondering what would happen if you suddenly flung yourself towards it all.

———

The gallery was wondrously quiet, and she made five of her favourite types of calls: telling her early-career and emerging artists that they'd sold a work. Once she'd taken her cut, they'd get anywhere between a month and a year's rent on their studios, and their gratitude was palpable. Two of them even cried, and Lally thought she might cry too. Her youngest, Gavin, a painter from Harlem with no formal education, had sat down on his stool in shock, too affected to realise he'd sat on his palette, covering the seat of his pants with paint. They laughed together for so long then, and she joked about sending someone over to collect the pants and frame them. To a hungry artist there was no greater gift in the world than freedom and means.

Looking forward in her calendar to the second half of the year, she saw one of her reminder flags had turned red: Chuck Farr's people still hadn't replied about a studio visit. She clenched her jaw. For a long time now she'd wanted to give Leah access to the gallery's emails and calendar, but she still didn't know how to tell Leah about Farr's November spot. The controversy was old news now, and the latest men accused of Bad Things had done far worse. The most recent correspondence she had from Farr's people noted that they'd confirmed the models.

Twelve women had signed up. She found the email: *We're thrilled. They're thrilled.* It was a surprise his subjects were women this time. At first Lally was relieved. It meant he wouldn't be trying the same shit again. She wondered if his pivot to women had something to do with the split from his old gallery, but he'd done mixed-gender shows before. It was great she could promote this one as his first fully female-focused body of work.

Nobody would hold Lally personally responsible if Farr harassed his models, but they would hold her responsible if she put the results of some kind of betrayal on the walls of her gallery. If any of the subjects complained the press would blow up. Obviously, that wasn't the kind of controversy she'd ever plan to manufacture. Her normal machinations were all just pyrotechnics—shows of explosions and clashed swords, never real house fires. But these women were agreeing to sit for Farr long after others had made their complaints. They had that information and they'd exercised their agency. It would be patronising to suggest they didn't know what they were doing. If she wanted to keep making calls like the one she'd just made to Gavin, she'd need to sell big names like Farr. That was the obvious way to explain things to Leah. And she really needed to explain things to Leah, because if the situation with Brodeur's murky etchings didn't improve, Lally would need more and more of Leah's direct involvement to share the burden of managing the emergency PR plan she had in her back pocket.

Her phone buzzed.

It was the Australian: *I make good omelettes. You coming back for an afternoon delight?*

She popped some gum in her mouth, deleted all the Farr-related entries from her calendar, and hit the pavement.

It was good having a friendly fuckboi to come home to. Exactly what she needed. He was waiting, ready to go. On the couch? Sure. As he pulled her tight jeans off over her ankles she realised he'd even tidied the place, and it whipped her into a frenzied imagining of what her life would be like if she had a wife at home to cook for her and clean for her and fuck her this good. She was straddling him and put her left hand on his shoulder, using her right to reach down and grab his dick. Then she hovered over the tip of him. He made a humming noise and she pressed her fingers to his Adam's apple to feel it.

'Relax,' she whispered to him, pushing him back into the couch.

He dropped his hands from her breasts and rested them on the tops of her thighs.

'That's it,' she said. 'You wanna just chill out? Let me fuck you?'

'Yes.' He nodded. 'That's exactly what I want.'

'You want this?' She moved down a bit.

He made a noise and nodded some more.

'Say it,' she said.

'Say what?'

'Say you want it.'

'I want it, please.'

'Please what?' she asked, a little louder.

'Please fuck me.'

Open sesame. She sat down fully over him. He closed his eyes and groaned.

'Yeah, that's it,' she said. 'Close your eyes and lie back and just let me fuck you.'

He did as he was told. Her knees sunk down low into the soft couch cushions on either side of him. Maximum friction. She rocked back and forth, taking her time. When she moved her hands to his torso, using it to leverage herself, grinding and grinding, he opened his eyes again.

'Shhh.' She put a finger over his lips, then dragged her fingertips softly from his eyebrows down over his eyelids to close them again. 'I'm fucking you, Pat. And you love it, don't you?'

'Yes.'

'So just let me.'

His arms went soft and she sped up, pushing and pulling on him, getting louder. As soon as she got close she pinched her nipples and the rush arrived. A long one.

'Now you,' she said quietly. 'Whatever you want.'

'Whatever I want?' he echoed.

'Whatever you want.'

He manoeuvred her without speaking, up and to the right, so that she was folded over the side of the couch arm with him standing behind her, taking her ass cheeks in each hand and squeezing them hard. She enjoyed him as he went hard and fast. He slowed momentarily and ran the tip of his thumb gently over her asshole. Her whole body tensed up with the thrill of it, and he shuddered against her. Perfect.

His phone rang shortly after, and Lally listened to him giving a report on his trip to his boss.

'I've gotta get back to my laptop and do some work,' he said, pulling a shirt on.

'I was starting to wonder if you actually had a job.'

He laughed. 'Are you busy later tonight?'

Pat was very obviously trying to play it cool. She felt like she was getting asked out on a date like in the high school movies.

Lally realised, with relief, that she could still distinguish between feeling flattered and being reduced to gratitude.

'No,' she said. 'Why don't you come back over. Make me that omelette.'

10

PAT WOKE TO LALLY ALREADY in the shower. He watched her figure through the semi-sheer curtain but it just stoked the fire of his morning erection so he got up.

'Good morning,' he said, putting his hands on her towel-wrapped waist and kissing her on the lips. When he stepped into the shower and drew the curtain he was finally waking up enough to realise that the next few minutes might determine the rest of their time together. He only had a couple of days left in town and he wanted to spend them with her. His mind darted back to the night before, scanning for details that might indicate how she felt about him. He'd made her come again, he felt pretty sure of that now he'd seen a few versions, but what else? What could he remember from the talking? She was getting ready for the day. He had fifteen, maybe twenty minutes to figure out what they were doing.

'Use whatever you want, and I've put a fresh towel here for you,' she called back in between what sounded like brushes of her teeth. The basin was right next to the shower so the two of them were only separated by the curtain. He would have to be sly about washing his arse and balls if she could see his silhouette too.

'I have a meeting in SoHo in an hour,' she said, 'but then I'm free again all day.'

What an invitation! 'Shall I meet you somewhere?'

'I'd kind of rather chill,' she replied.

He had misunderstood. She wanted him out of her apartment before she left. Of course. He was such a fucking idiot.

'Do you feel like seeing a movie?' she went on. 'There's a new Juliette Binoche.'

'Cool!' he said. He hated Juliette Binoche movies.

'There's a session at one—does that work for you?'

He turned the water off and grabbed the towel. 'Yep.'

Lally wasn't even looking at him, just dabbing something on her lips then rubbing them together and making *puck puck* sounds. She seemed to have this way with all her words and actions, presuming he was interested in her and boldly making invitations, but then it seemed like she wouldn't care if he rejected her offers. Take it or leave it.

He watched as she slipped herself into a slinky, mesh type of material with a full skirt and some snappy, buckly bits at the waist. She looked fantastic. Severe, but fantastic.

He'd been looking down at his laptop, working, when she called from the front door to say she'd be back in about two hours. His role on the trip was turning out to be pretty straight-forward. Some of Al's long-standing clients in Australia had gaps in their collections they wanted filled, or had surplus they wanted moved. Pat's job was to wine-and-dine rich people who already knew whether or not they were buying or selling but wanted someone to make them feel special. Al had bcc'd him into a message to Josephine and Martin about their meetings:

Pat was a fabulous help. Kept Ross distracted talking about the war (which one?) while I convinced Edith to take both the medium-sized Streetons.

Exhaling with relief, he shut his laptop and took in the details of Lally's space properly. It was all very ordered and controlled. Tasteful, but the details gave her away. Three ornate gold-leafed frames around minimalist illustrated versions of nineties rom-com movie posters. A bronze bulldog was a doorstop for the bathroom. Only one of the bedside tables had a lamp. That was a good sign. It must have been some time since the apartment was shared by two people.

Lally's screaming buzzer went off an hour later.

'Pat!' she called through the receiver. 'Get your ass down here, I'm freezing! Let's go to the movies!'

'Okay, just a sec!' He scrambled for his coat and shoved his feet into his shoes, grabbing the spare keys from their dish and bounding down the stairs two at a time.

'You know, all this time I could have been stealing your stuff,' he said when he reached her, landing a light kiss on her lips.

'I took a photo of your passport while you were sleeping,' Lally replied, smiling, then hooked her arm through his, and set them off down the street.

She was chatting about random things, pointing to tree branches she thought made interesting shapes.

He thought he'd better point at something too. 'Dog,' he said, seeing a schnauzer. 'Schnauzer.'

'There's a great park near here—a dog park, I mean. Near StuyTown.' Lally gestured to the left but steered him to the right. 'Here!' They were at the cinema.

'Oh, it's so close,' Pat said.

'Yep!'

111

The movie was like every other Juliette Binoche he'd ever seen. Too long, not sure what was happening, lots of close-ups on the eyes, lots of meal preparation that showed you how a character was feeling based on how aggressively they chopped the 'oh-ber-zheen' for the ratatouille. Towards the end there was a lot of sexual tension building, and Pat fought the urge to look over at Lally. That would have been so obvious. *Hey! Do you feel it too?* he may as well have shouted. Juliette was taking this man's pants off, and opened her mouth against his shoulder, letting her lips drag across his skin, and just off-camera her hands were obviously manoeuvring his cock, because she was putting one leg up onto the side of a chair. Just as the two actors were about to fuck, Lally put her wrist on the armrest between them and, with the tip of her index finger, grazed the top of his knee. He jolted, and looked at her but she stared straight ahead. Juliette was moaning.

They went straight home as soon as the credits began to roll, fucked, fell asleep for an hour or so, then woke up and laughed about it. Now he'd never be able to tell her that he hated Juliette Binoche films.

Lally said she was hungry and that she wanted a drink too, so he ran to the bodega to buy wine while she ordered food to be delivered and set the table. When he got back and opened the front door with the spare keys he called out, 'Ho-ome,' in a singsong way, and she replied, 'Hi, honey!' and kissed him on the cheek, popping her leg.

Over dinner he asked her more about her gallery and the New York scene. Any lingering self-monitoring disappeared when he pushed her for details about acquisitions and strategies. When he asked her open-ended questions and refilled her wineglass she got on a roll.

They cleared the table together, their bodies moving around each other's in familiar, energetic ways as he washed and she dried. Lally found some chocolate and blueberries, and put some jazz on, and they sat on the couch, finishing the second bottle of wine, opening the third. He grabbed her by the waist and pulled her onto his lap, and she kept talking about her next exhibition while he asked questions and put pieces of chocolate on her tongue. He looked up at her, red wine staining the inside of her lips, and tucked her hair behind her ear. She stopped talking.

'What?' he said. 'I'm listening. Why'd you stop?'

'I just realised I've been talking at you for a whole bottle of wine.' She seemed shocked.

'I like it!'

'What do you mean?'

He shrugged. 'I like listening to you talk.' But he could see she wasn't convinced and her mood was shifting. 'And I'm not wearing pants and you're sitting on my lap.'

'Ah.' This made her nod.

'*And* I like listening to you talk,' he repeated emphatically, and this time she smiled, if a little warily.

'I'm having a great time,' she declared.

'Me too,' he said, and they kissed for a while.

'Tell me how you got into art,' Lally said, taking the chocolate from him, swapping roles.

'Well, I'm not actually from Sydney,' he began. 'I mean, I grew up in Esk, which is in regional Queensland, and then when I was twelve I got a scholarship to go to a good boarding school in Sydney. At the end of high school I had decent grades and started law, but I hated it. My girlfriend at the time was doing art history, and I kind of just followed her into it.'

'You followed a girl into eighteenth-century oils?' Lally asked, sceptical.

'Well, I love it now, obviously.' He shrugged. 'Honestly, I'm grateful she was an introduction to it. Most young men I grew up with don't get the opportunity to find a way into art.'

'And yet men are overwhelmingly over-represented at every level of the industry?'

'Yeah, I see that. I just mean that at university there weren't many guys in any of the lectures.'

'Except for the lecturer.'

'Well, none of the guys I knew went into art history. I'm not sure I would've even known what it meant if I didn't live with someone studying it.'

'You lived together?'

'In a share house, yeah. It wasn't that serious. Living in college dorms isn't that common in Australia. We all just share big houses together.'

'Sounds kinky.'

'Mostly it's just dirty.'

Lally laughed.

'So I followed a girl into old art. Something tells me you didn't follow no man into new art.'

'Ha,' she said. 'No, I didn't. I always loved it. My dad was a jerk. He came from this big Catholic family. He had all these plans for the son he was going to have, but he got me instead, and it made me feel good to ruin all his plans by going to art school.' She smiled wryly. 'Once I was there I got really into it. Couldn't pick a medium, started helping friends organise group shows, landed a few internships at galleries. It just snowballed.'

'Did you ever want to be an artist?'

'Not really. I'm too impatient. I like the work I do now because I get to see the new art and the impact of it every couple of months. Most contemporary artists take about two or three years to make their next show's worth of work. It has to be really focused, you know? The good ones have a kind of doggedness. They're meticulous about a topic or a medium. It's like a cat: they just lick, lick, lick. Over the decades, maybe in hindsight, the developments become clearer. And honestly, I have this love–hate thing about how fragile they are.'

'The artists?'

'Yeah. I mean, it makes me feel good to be able to help them show their work properly. With some of the younger ones, I know I've helped forge their careers. When I go visit them in their studio and tell them so-and-so is asking about their stuff, and it's like, well, we don't have patronage anymore, you know?'

'You're the modern-day Medici.'

'Ha, well, some type of mini-Medici conduit, I suppose. And I like it when I can do that, but I certainly wouldn't like to be the artist, to be waiting on and beholden to someone who does what I do now.'

'No control.'

'That's one part of it. The other part is more a feeling of agenda-setting, or maybe taste-making or something. I'm not sure we have a good word for it. I get to pick what I think the important art is. They slave away making it all, and just have to hope and pray someone like me agrees that they're making the right thing. They all believe they are, of course, or they wouldn't be making it, but their egos and their bank accounts are just so exposed. Sometimes it's pathetic.'

'Pathetic?'

'Oh, that sounds mean, I take it back.' She stopped abruptly and looked straight into his eyes. 'Let's eat blueberries in bed.'

He laughed and put his wineglass down. 'Yes, ma'am!'

He grabbed her under her arse and stood up as she wrapped her legs around his waist, concentrating on not knocking into the doorframe as they moved between the two rooms. He lowered her slowly onto the bed, and they laid side by side, comparing their schedules for the following day.

Pat rolled onto his back and Lally popped a blueberry into his mouth, like a scene from a fresco.

'What's that?' she said, and he was filled with immediate self-consciousness, closing his mouth and covering it with his hand. 'Don't panic,' she said, laughing and gently pushing his hand away from his face. 'I just mean have you got some orthodontics or something?'

'Oh,' he said, propping himself up on his elbows. 'I have a permanent retainer behind my teeth, to keep them in place.'

'Wow,' she said, staring at his mouth.

'It's not that exciting.'

'What does "permanent" mean?'

'The usual meaning?'

'Which is?' She was looking at him in a way that made him feel like the question was not about retainers.

'Well, I'll definitely have it for another few years,' he said, and immediately knew this was not the right answer, 'but I think the idea is to have it for as long as possible.'

'But not forever,' she said.

'You mean until I die?' This was all making him nervous. 'I suppose I could have it until I die.' He looked away from her and at nothing in particular. 'I hadn't really thought about it. I just think about it when I get stuff stuck in it, or when it breaks.'

She put the blueberry punnet down on the bedside table and then he knew that some other conversation had just taken place. Was he more drunk than her?

'Can I touch it?' she said, smiling, maybe mischievously.

'Ah, I guess so, although it probably has blueberry in it now.'

'That's okay,' she said, and looked at him expectantly.

He laid down on his back again, tense, though he could not have articulated why. Was the blood rushing to his head or from his head?

She sat up beside his shoulders, looking down at him, over him, put her weight on her left arm, lifted her right hand to her own mouth and put two fingers inside it. He groaned a little, breaking eye contact with her to watch as her fingers emerged again, wet with saliva. She slowly lowered them towards his face, where they hovered for just a moment, and then when she touched his lips he felt a surge of arousal so intense his knees buckled upwards. He couldn't see her fingers anymore so he looked at her eyes again, and she was staring right at him as she pushed her fingertips into his mouth. His heart was bashing away inside his chest and he was rock-hard. He didn't know what would happen next.

She forced his tongue a little further back into his throat, making his breathing—which was now close to panting—audible between them. He felt her fingertips reach to the back of his teeth, touching the retainer, and his whole body froze at the connection, his mind racing and coming up completely blank. He wanted to roll onto her and fuck her immediately, but he stayed absolutely still, knowing somehow he couldn't do that, couldn't break from whatever this thing was that she was doing. Pat grabbed the bedsheets in his fists. He saw Lally's eyes dart down to his erection, and it was like getting slapped when their eyes reconnected again. Then she moved. She swung her leg over him so that her knees were either side of his head. He was in overload. Incapable of language. All sensations. She withdrew the fingers from his mouth and put both her hands on his forehead, as though she was going to run her fingers through his hair, but also pushing, tilting his head back, and when she lowered herself onto his mouth his hands shot to her arse cheeks, helping her grind down onto him. He could still taste blueberries, and now her. Blueberries and Lally.

11

THE SERIOUS BUYERS WERE LONG gone by the last day of the show, but the people-watching was still good. A woman in shabby clothes and filthy sandals with large, bird-shaped resin earrings passed by, and Lally saw she had a real bird of paradise flower spiked into her bun. Only big money could get you a flower like that in March. Pieces with mirrors had crowds in front of them sheepishly waiting for selfie opportunities. The works with words in them were also popular, as was photography with branding or celebrity. This was all to be expected.

Lally's phone vibrated in her pocket. Caller ID displayed a picture of Gen dressed as a 'sexy vet' last Halloween.

'Hey!'

'Can I go over to yours and raid your wardrobe for tonight, or is the Aussie still there?' Gen was pretending to be salty about it.

'Oh, don't be jealous—you know Armory is always a crazy week.'

'Yeah, but normally I get to be in on a bit of the crazy. We're still on for tonight, right?'

'Ah . . .'

'Jesus!'

'I want you there, it's just, he'll be there too, so don't make a big deal out of it, you know? Don't let him know that you know about him at all.'

'But I don't know about him at all. Why are you being weird?'

'Can you pinch some ketamine from the fridge at work?'

Gen laughed. 'Sorry, the residents of the East Village don't keep enough horses these days.'

'Damn. And yes, go around, pick something slutty but rich.'

Leah returned to the booth with two cups of coffee and Lally mouthed a thank you.

'Actually, Gen, I'm coming home early—let's get ready together and pre-drink like it's 2010.'

'Fuck yeah!'

Lally hung up.

Leah smiled. 'I'll see you for bump-out tomorrow, though, right?'

'Of course,' Lally replied, air-kissing her assistant and stepping into the throng, letting herself be carried from booth to booth on the mad river towards the exit. Within a few metres she got stuck behind a beautiful couple pushing a super-luxe pram. HOT MOM was printed on the top of the bassinet. The handle and covering for the body of the pram were all a light tan leather, there were levers made from polished wood, and all the finishings were gold. As though by sheer willpower and enough money the horrors of childbirth could be ameliorated.

She turned a corner and a momentary gap in the crowd revealed a small painting over at Levi's—a couple in each other's arms, a little grubby around the edges. She changed course to get to it. Lally had heard of Fratino, knew his works were selling well, but she hadn't seen one in real life. It was very stylised but also incredibly tender and true. The figure on the right was caressing the face of his lover, his body turned in a strange but believable way, and though the entire act of penetration was set there before her, the nakedness and earnestness of the depiction was what made it so moving. 'Gentle' was the word that came to mind. It made her think of Pat. All that energy. Like a puppy. Pat the puppy. Nothing to fear. Who knew safety could be such a turn-on?

——————

They were down one bottle of champagne and popping the second an hour before they had to leave.

'So what do I need to know about this Australian?' Gen asked.

'Pat.'

'Pat.'

'Pat gives great head.'

'That is a good news story, my friend.'

'But he's leaving tomorrow.'

'So what I'm hearing is one more night of great head?'

Lally hesitated.

'Aha . . .'

'Don't "aha" me.'

'You like him,' Gen teased. Her high school voice.

'He's leaving.'

'Confirmed. You know there's a joke to be made here about him being from down under and going down under. Or him being an expert at down under—'

'Stop!'

'Hang on, I've almost got it.'

'Shut up!'

'Well, I think it's wonderful. There's a direct correlation between men who respect women and men who eat pussy. Undeniable fact. I'm pro-Pat.'

Lally laughed. 'I mean, obviously, I'm pro-Pat.'

'Divine. So what's the problem?'

'I don't know. I'm just—' She faltered. 'I can't. I don't know how to avoid compromising for them. My guts are telling me I need to shut it down before it gets out of control.'

The buzzer went off. Lally got up and went to the door.

'Hello?' she said, holding the receiver in one hand and her champagne in the other.

'Ah, Lally? It's me—Patrick.'

Gen put her flute down and made a kind of rapid tumbling-hands gesture. Lally mouthed, 'What?' and Gen held her fingers in a V shape and flicked her tongue between them.

'Hello?' Pat's voice again.

'Yes, okay, come on up.' Lally hit the buzzer and spun around to Gen. 'We have thirty seconds.'

'Do you want me to go?'

'No, you're the one who wanted him to come up! What are we doing?'

'We're all having a drink before we go to a party together, Lally, sheesh.'

'Well, I just . . .'

'You just what? You have a crush on him?'

'I'm thirty-three, it's not a crush, it's—'

A knock at the door interrupted them.

'Shhh!'

Lally opened the door while Gen tried to repress her giggles.

'Oh,' Pat said, seeing Gen by the table and turning back to Lally. 'I'm sorry—I didn't realise you had company.'

Gen raised her champagne flute. 'Don't be silly! Come save us from the rest of this bottle.'

Pat smiled but looked at Lally for confirmation.

'Oh, yeah, of course,' she said. 'Come on in. I'll get another glass.'

'Great, thanks.'

'G'day, mate,' Gen said. 'I'm Gen.'

'G'day, Gen,' Pat replied with a laugh. 'I'm Pat.' He took the proffered glass and Gen filled it.

'Cheers,' Gen said, holding up her flute, smiling.

'Cheers,' the other two chorused.

Lally made eye contact with Pat, and it was precisely as electric as she had feared it might be. She felt her face flush. She could practically feel her fucking pupils dilate.

'I'm just going to get some shoes and a bag,' she said. 'I'll be back in a moment.'

She went into the bedroom and stood there, taking deep breaths, until the flush was gone. She could hear Gen and Pat chatting about the Armory Show and the weather in New York this time of year. It was all fine. She went back to the living room.

'Where are your shoes?' Pat asked, looking at her feet.

'Oh.' Lally glanced at Gen, who was grinning. When Pat wasn't looking she made the lewd tongue motion again.

'Sorry, Pat,' Gen said. 'You're going to have to catch up with us. We started at about three.'

Lally picked up the bottle and passed it to him, and when he smiled at her again she felt the flush returning to her cheeks.

'Challenge accepted,' he said.

The next two hours fizzed along merrily. Jokes, news, memories. Gen was the perfect bridge, allowing them to get drunk
enough to talk to each other easily, keeping things light and
funny. Pat taught them that the Australian word for 'chug' was
'scull', and then whenever either Pat or Lally started talking
about art, Gen would yell, 'Snob scull!' and they would all have
to empty their flutes and change the topic of conversation. Lally
was learning all kinds of stuff about Pat. She couldn't believe
she'd spent so many hours with him and not realised how good
he was at impressions. His George Bush made them weep with
laughter.

Eventually, they realised they were an hour late for the party—
'Perfect!'—and they all clacked down the stairs together. Pat held
the taxi door open for both of them to climb in the back, and
then climbed in after them, placing his hand on Lally's knee.
Gen placed her hand on Lally's other knee and they all folded
over in hysterics, the cab driver shaking his head. When they
got out uptown Lally paid for the cab and Pat smiled down at
her from the kerb as she got out. She wondered if this was all so
much fun because it made her feel like she was in her twenties
again, before the gallery, or if it was just nice to be with friends,
or if maybe it had something to do with him.

'This isn't as arty as I was expecting,' Gen said when they
entered the gallery and headed towards the bar. Lally looked
around the cavernous space, trying to see it through Gen's eyes.
Each year these things got more fashion, more money, more
clubby. A vodka brand was launching some new product. Nearer
the bar it was elbow to elbow, and Pat put both his hands on her
waist and leaned forward so their whole bodies were touching,
his chest along her back. The pressure from his fingertips went
straight to her knees, shot up the insides of her thighs and made

her clench all her muscles inside. She tipped her head back a few degrees and the right side of his face met the left side of hers. Just then a space opened in front of them at the bar and Lally saw Curtis, who raised a glass to her. Lally pushed Pat's hands away, stepping forward. She shouldn't be so careless. This wasn't some house party. This was industry, this was work. You don't snuggle up to some fucking kangaroo kid at an Armory afterparty.

She ordered three glasses of champagne and picked up two of them, not waiting to see if Pat had grabbed his.

'Cheers!' Lally said, but Gen waited the extra moment for Pat to catch up with them before responding. Gen and Lally locked eyes over the tips of the flutes and it seemed Gen was saying to her: *Really?* Or maybe: *What the fuck?* It caught in Lally's throat a little, and she looked over at Pat, who was watching the crowd, and regarded his profile with such longing and resentment. How could he not realise what he could take from her? That she would lose legitimacy and appeal once coupled? That he could only benefit from having a wife whereas she could only suffer from having a husband? That they could fuck on equal terms but anything more than that would inevitably cost her? Wives and mothers were not art. Nobody wanted to be reminded of domesticity, of mundanity, mediocrity. And weren't all mothers mediocre? All wives eventually mundane? The only way to be a capital-w-Woman in art was never to be seen within the home, never to be seen on a day off, never to be thought of as willing to compromise for anyone or anything.

Pat turned around and looked at her, and must have read something in the expression on her face. 'Is everything okay?'

'Lally gets serious when she's not quite drunk enough,' Gen said, giving Lally a firm shove.

She had no comeback for this because it was true.

Gen's phone went off. She read the message.

'Alex is just around the corner—he says the place he's at is wonderful. Do you mind if I split? This scene feels a little too cokey for me.'

'Yeah, you go. I'll see you soon.'

The women kissed each other's cheeks, and Gen made the tongue-wagging motion again behind Pat's back.

'Can I introduce you to some people I've just spotted?' Pat asked her.

'Sure.' She wasn't sure at all. Did he mean his friends? Like, he wanted her to meet his friends? She was trying to find an excuse to slip away but he was already leading her along and then the people were right there. Their small booth offered a bit of a sound barrier.

'Sarah and Charles are from Osborne's UK offices, both experts in post-war works,' Pat said easily.

Lally shook their hands and smiled, making eye contact as she did.

'And this is Lally, owner and manager of Gallery Lally in Chelsea. Al and I have filled a lot of our clients' gaps thanks to Lally's connections.'

'So lovely to meet you both,' Lally said. 'I thought about showing at the next Frieze, but I'm afraid the British aren't always receptive to new Yanks.'

They laughed, seeming to appreciate the joke, and she settled into the booth. Fairs, gossip about prices, tips for which dealers used rich clients to up the prices of artists' works, who the dealers had in their own collections, restaurants, directorships and appointments to prize committees—they talked on and on while Pat fetched more drinks when they were needed. At some point Charles caught the time on his phone and showed Sarah, and they both groaned and said they should probably go. An early start for something or other. They exchanged cards and cheek kisses with Lally, Pat shook their hands and then they were gone.

'Christ, I'm wasted,' Pat said, blinking.

'Same!' Lally said, but she was buzzing. 'Weren't they fantastic?'

'Yes.' Pat smiled at her and she smiled back. 'My hotel is near here,' he said, but didn't touch her. 'Can you come back to my place?'

'Yeah!' she shouted over the music. 'Yeah, I can!'

The taxi was an overheated twenty minutes of juddering, and by the end of it Lally didn't feel so good. She was dipping in and out of it. Pat had his arm around her waist, helping her walk through the lobby, then hot air was blasting into the super-fast elevator and it was not good. She was in the bathroom vomiting. She was fumbling with the straps on her heels.

'Your toes are bleeding,' Pat was saying, alarmed.

'Oh, yeah, yeah. Always.'

Then a shower spurted on, and she tried to pull him in, but she just got a kiss on the forehead instead. Tried to rub her waterproof mascara off. Futile! Munched on some toothpaste.

'Better?' he said from the doorway. He was hot.

'Much better,' she replied.

'Want to watch a movie?'

'Absolutely.'

She fell asleep as he was clicking through the new release options.

———

The ring of her Monday morning alarm sounded far-off. She got up and followed it, finding her purse hanging on the bathroom door handle. The end of the evening was a blur, but she still had a robe and underwear on. Her college boyfriend had never offered her the same courtesy.

The sun wasn't up over the city skyline yet, but she could see the room clearly. Pat's things, his way of hotel living. A laptop on the desk, all the curtains open, dry-cleaning wrappers at the bottom of the wardrobe, and his figure a lump in the white sheets, an almost-snore. Lally thought back to the night before and dug into her purse, finding the two business cards, thrilled again. She checked her reflection and wiped some dark left-over make-up from under her eyes, then gargled a bit of water and toothpaste quietly. She took off her robe, climbed back into bed and kissed his face. When his eyes opened, sleepy, she touched his cock and watched him wake up, adjusting to the light in the room. Then he looked at her properly with focused eyes, smiling, and the stakes grew higher. She was experiencing some feelings. He kissed her, used his hand to close her hand over him, and then pulled the sheets up over them. They had sex slowly, gently, looking at each other, only changing positions once, so she could be on top to come, but he still held her close to him. When they'd both finished, Lally felt as though she was going to cry and it scared the shit out of her.

'Want some pancakes?' he asked her, grinning.

'What? No.'

'Eggs?'

'What?'

'Muesli?'

'No.'

'Coffee?'

She paused at that.

'Aha. Okay. Coffee for you. And if I order pancakes will you eat some?'

She paused at that too.

'Knew it!'

He called room service with the phone beside the bed, ordering two serves of pancakes and two coffees. His voice was so incredibly chipper. Lally had her robe back on. She had thought that maybe something would happen to make a decision for her about what they were doing with each other. Being in a rented room made things feel different. Their fling wouldn't have felt so intense if they'd been coming back to Pat's hotel instead of her home. But he kissed her again and she wasn't sure. He must have seen something in her face then, because his tone shifted and he sat up straight, pulling his own robe back on.

'Well . . .'

'I guess . . .'

They both groaned. It was agony. She didn't know if Pat was in pain too, or if he just felt awkward. 'You go,' she said.

'I'll be back in May.'

'Oh, cool.' She nodded. 'Did you want to see each other again?'

'Yes? I mean, yeah, it's only, what, two months? That's like, eight or nine weeks,' he said, and it made her feel good to see him pretending he was only just now doing that math.

On the subway home Lally wondered whether or not to send him a bon voyage message, unlocking her phone and opening the app, then closing it and locking her phone again. When was the last time she'd spent an entire subway ride wondering whether or not to message a boy? Pathetic.

It was Sunday, and when she emerged at Union Square there was the man playing love songs on his baby grand piano.

A message from Pat came through just as she put her key in the door. It was a photograph of a blueberry. She laughed. Things with this guy could easily ramp up or peter out. If he was one of those men who couldn't use their words then it'd be all over in a week, but who knew? She couldn't quite typecast him. There was the rural thing—the farm, the boots—but she could also tell it was a bit of a show. He loved old art. Not just the style of it, but the luxury and the prestige. Something about his attitude towards the Armory Show came from a shitty place—maybe arrogance or insecurity, she wasn't sure which. So often they had the same symptoms. Of course she hadn't told him about her money, but she also didn't live particularly frugally. She looked around her apartment and tried to think about how he would have seen it. It was as though she were standing naked before him while he was fully dressed—he'd seen her home but she had no idea what his looked like. How could she think she felt so much for a man whose world she'd never seen? She'd never even been to Australia. This was all completely moronic.

Entering her apartment felt good and bad at once. Their empty bottles and glasses were all over the table, and he had left a scarf over the arm of her couch. She picked it up and smelled it and her chest seized up, that bolt of desire shooting straight up her legs but settling high this time, in her chest. She put an arm out to steady herself.

'Fuck.'

12

'JAMES IS ON LEVEL FIFTEEN,' Rory said, checking his phone. They'd met on the street, both of them holding their jackets over their arms. It was hot for April. 'Let's roll.'

'Anything I need to know?' Pat asked him in the elevator up. It was a fancy new building with a screen displaying the time and temperature, and showing them the view outside as they rose.

'Like what?'

'I dunno.' Pat shrugged. 'I haven't seen some of these guys in ages. Anything changed?'

'I don't know why you get nerves about these guys. I mean, they say some dumb shit sometimes, but they're good guys.'

Pat laughed. 'Sounds like nothing has changed then.'

'Oh, actually, turns out Nathan is gay,' Rory said.

'Okay. I wouldn't have picked that.'

'Yeah, me either.'

'Everyone's fine with that, though, right?'

'Oh, yeah, yeah.' Rory gave a dismissive wave.

'So he'll be there?'

'No. Don't think so.'

'Right.'

The elevator slowed and stopped. An incredible amount of bass was coming from the door to their immediate left.

'Don't need to look up his apartment number.' Rory said and knocked on the door.

'It's open!' someone yelled from inside.

Pat put his jacket back on and walked in behind Rory. It was super cool inside, museum-level chilly. The floor tiles were huge and shiny. A long hallway with some chic pendant lighting led them to an open-plan lounge area that itself opened onto a huge balcony overlooking Sydney Harbour. It was spectacular.

A round of cheers went up at their arrival.

'Rory!' several voices called then, with some surprise but not, Pat thought, displeasure, 'Pat!'

There must have been over a dozen lads there. He and Rory went around slapping shoulders and backs, someone put a cold beer in his hand, and he spotted where the lines of coke were sitting, many done, many still to be done, on the edge of the marble kitchen island, away from the wind coming through the open bifold doors. They had to yell to be heard over the music and the light from the balcony was so bright most of them had their sunnies on. Pat added his jacket to the pile flung over the back of the low, white leather L-shaped couch. Laughter erupted from somewhere new every second minute, and it was like he was right back at only the best bits of uni. Better beers, though, and better coke, and a much better view.

Pat spotted Dan across the balcony and made his move. It was such a rush. The ultimate high. After all those years of bullying and belittling, Pat had fucked Dan's stepmum.

'So what are you up to these days?'

'Pat!' Dan's demeanour brightened at the attention. 'Good to see you, man!' He reached into the bright, shiny suit pocket, revealing a somehow even more impossibly polyester lining, to withdraw a business card. 'Real estate.'

'Thank you,' Pat said, taking the card and nodding, listening to the walking fire hazard jargon on about bubbles and demand. Pat couldn't stand real estate agents. Every single one he'd ever met had fucked him over. They didn't even need degrees. They made stupid money. And they just fucking lied and lied and lied and he fucking hated them.

'I guess you and I sort of do the same thing then,' Dan declared at the end of the pitch.

'What do you mean?'

'Well, you sell paintings and I sell houses. Sometimes at auctions too.'

Pat opened and closed his mouth, choosing to smile instead of trying to come up with a polite reply.

'That's a nice suit,' Dan told him.

'Thank you,' Pat replied.

'I get all mine made in Hong Kong.'

'Cool, cool.'

'You go overseas much?'

'The States, yeah. You?'

'Oh yeah, every year, all over Asia. Do you sell much Asian stuff?'

'What do you mean?'

'I mean art from Asia.'

Pat gave up trying to hide his grin. This guy was such a dumb fuck! 'Yes, sometimes, here and there—we get all sorts of stuff, actually.' How had he tried to explain his job to his toddler nephew? 'Sometimes we get paintings, sometimes rings and necklaces, sometimes furniture and cars—'

'Oh! What kinds of cars?'

This was uncannily like talking to Tom.

'Old Mercedes, old Rolls-Royces, sometimes a Lamborghini or Ferrari.'

'Nice.'

'Yeah.'

'But it would suck to have to sell your Ferrari, right?' Dan shook his head. 'Nobody buys a Ferrari thinking they're ever gonna have to sell it. That's so embarrassing.'

'That's actually really true, Dan, yes. I would imagine that would suck.'

'What do you drive?'

'I don't own a car at the moment—I'm waiting for Teslas to get here,' he lied.

'Oh, sure.' Dan leaned away from him a little, as though concern for the environment might be contagious.

'Fuck!' someone called out. 'It's seven! We gotta go!'

Happy shouts filled the air. The music switched off so abruptly the silence rang in Pat's ears. One of the boys was standing by the pile of jackets putting a baggy into each breast pocket and handing them out.

'This isn't my jacket!' Rory said, laughing.

'Just fucking take one and go!' Pat yelled from the back of the group, and everyone cheered, all the way down the stair-well, bumping into each other, spilling into William Street in mismatched suits. Someone was running towards someone else, leaping, and then there was a piggyback race. Blood surged in his body. He hadn't felt this good in so long. He slapped Rory on the shoulder. 'How good!'

They all stopped in front of the iron gates for a quick breather. Someone passed a pack of cigarettes around and they all took one and lit up, as though they weren't already late. Pat saw a boy in uniform and hat further along the gravel path of the school grounds. The kid was standing near the entrance to the Great Hall, staring at them with an open mouth. He looked so young. Must have been some nerd who volunteered for this kind of stuff.

'Gotta get that service badge!' Pat said to him, flicking the brim of the kid's hat as the group passed through, and they all laughed.

'Look,' someone at the front said. 'We're right on time.'

And they were! People were milling around chatting. There were so many circular tables laid out, Pat couldn't have counted how many seats. He looked to the table closest to him and realised there were name cards on the serviettes on the plates.

'Rory,' he said, 'where are we sitting?'

'I don't fucking know,' his friend giggled. 'This is like a pope's wedding or something.'

It was. Orchids and cursive writing and someone was playing the organ. That organ took him back. A voice came over the sound system. A man Pat didn't recognise was welcoming them, saying something about a seating chart and the entree being served. Someone grabbed Pat's arm. It was one of the boys he hadn't recognised but whom he'd heard someone call Harry.

'Lines in the gents before we have to get settled,' Harry stage-whispered, and Pat followed.

'Get settled' was what the teachers had always said. At the beginning of assembly: 'Get settled, boys!' Back in class after the lunchbreak: 'Come on now, boys, get settled.'

Three of them crowded into a stall and they did their lines off the top of the stainless-steel toilet roll holder.

'We're looking for table eight,' Rory said to him when they emerged, peppy. The plates had some food on them now. Pat hoped it wasn't salmon. It was always salmon at these places. Cold and fishy. Not that he was hungry anyway. 'There.' Rory pointed, and they weaved across the room towards the only table that was empty.

'Oh bummer, we're not sitting together,' Pat said, seeing other names on either side of Rory's.

Rory looked at Pat and laughed, shaking his head, picking up a name card and throwing it into a large potted palm at the side of the room. 'Still such a good boy, Patty.'

Pat laughed then too, and inspected the plates. 'You want fiddly salami bits or fiddly chicken bits?'

The organ stopped and a woman walked to the lectern on the stage at the front of the hall. Pat didn't understand what she was talking about, but he remembered where he'd heard her voice—she'd been the Deputy Principal of Student Wellbeing when he was a student. He sat there quietly, experiencing a cascade of memories. Being in her office once, listening to her talk about his results and his scholarship position. It was silly that he'd got so worked up about all that stuff. Everything had turned out completely fine. Everything would probably go on being completely fine. Ten years had passed and he had friends, he was fit, he worked for a good company, he'd fucked that hot woman in New York, his folks were fine, he had a lease on his own apartment in an Art Deco building. Life was good. He'd worked hard for this. He deserved it.

The woman finished talking. People clapped. A waiter came around and started taking drink orders and someone called, 'Beers all round, I reckon—just come back with beers, thanks, mate!' and that was fine. Things were speeding by joyously.

Dinner was served and none of them ate, and in between they danced for a bit and went outside for smokes, and once it was dark they could have their coke in the garden off their keys and then someone handed Pat his coat and they were at kick-ons at some bar that was down some stairs. More beers. The group shrank to eight or so then swelled again to fifteen and there were more beers and more lines and then they left and went to a pub down the road by the wharves where they let anyone in anytime. Someone in the group claimed an empty table and they had a fake disagreement about whose round it was. Pat came back with the jugs and Rory had the glasses.

'Oof, there's a bit of something,' someone said, nodding towards the bar.

Pat looked up from pouring beers to see a trio of women in tight dresses and heels. They were dancing as they waited for the bartender to get to them. One of them was wearing a white sash that said *Bride to Be*. Hens.

'Shotgun,' Harry called, and the boys pounded the table.

'You can't shotgun all of them!' Rory protested.

'I get the first go,' Harry replied. 'With the brunette.'

Pat looked back to the women, wondering why Harry would pick a brunette, and he saw the bride and the blonde were dancing and laughing while the brunette leaned over the bar to order, her arse towards them. An arse like that was why.

'No way,' someone else said. 'May the best man win.'

'I'll pay a hundred bucks for shotgun with the brunette,' Rory said and slapped the table.

'We've got a hundred here,' Pat said, imitating the auctioneers from work. 'Can I get a one-fifty?' Everyone laughed.

'One-fifty!' one of the boys at the end called, and they were off.

'One-fifty, two hundred,' Pat called, 'two hundred and a round, two hundred and a round and a bag, three hundred!'

Someone won, not Rory, and they all clapped and drank more. It was either Robert or someone else, Pat didn't remember his name, who went over and approached the ladies. Their whole table watched, unable to hear Robert's line across the music and noise of revellers, but the women at the table appeared to freeze for a moment, then he said something—a punchline—and they all burst out laughing, and he used the moment to pull a stool from under the table, sit his arse on it and put his beer on the table.

'He's in!' Pat yelled, and the whole table cheered again, finishing their beers, someone going to get the next round.

'You wanna try and follow him up?' Rory asked Pat, elbowing him, and for a moment he felt like he just might, but then Lally sprung to mind and he shook his head.

'Your loss!' Rory replied, and when the fresh beer arrived he got up and followed Robert or not-Robert to the hens' party. Pat felt around inside his pocket and realised with the terrible sinking feeling that he was out of coke. And the room started to slow down. And the conversation was grinding away. And he looked over and saw Rory already had his hand on some woman's lower back. That was it. Time to call it a night.

He stumbled out onto the street, missing the kerb.

'You right, mate?' the bouncer asked.

'Right as rain, thanks, mate.'

'Don't know if a cab would take you.'

Pat nodded. 'Sounds fair. Walk it off then, shall I?'

'Good luck.'

Pat gave a messy salute and turned towards the streets, holding his jacket scrunched up in his hand, the cool evening breeze hitting the wet patches of his underarms, jacaranda flowers mushy underfoot.

———

A magpie was warbling outside his window. His feet hurt. He looked down and realised he was still wearing his shoes. Blisters guaranteed. His neck hurt too. He was on the couch, not the bed. When he sat up he felt his stomach kick into gear and made it to the toilet bowl just in time. Everything coming up was liquid. Good thing he hadn't paid for the dinner. He managed to get his shoes and pants off and crawled from the toilet to the shower, sitting in the bottom, filling his mouth with water and spitting it out, filling his mouth, swallowing a little, immediately throwing it back up, waiting a while longer, and finally keeping some down as the hot water ran out. He cracked some paracetamol from the foil packet straight into his mouth, peed a frightening colour, and brushed his teeth.

His dead phone started pinging and vibrating when he plugged it in.

Rory had written at eleven: *How'd you pull up? I'm trying to get home from the shithole that is Westmead but it was worth it ;) Look what Harry posted to the group.*

Pat looked down past his knees and pushed at the loose skin on his right toe. That old familiar burning-face feeling. They had a group chat he wasn't in. He wanted to cry. He wanted to delete everything and run away. But to where? He was in his bed in his own home.

In another tab, his work email was showing a dozen unread messages. He opened the one from Sophie. *A pleasure doing business with you. When's our next meeting?*

13

LALLY TRIED A COUPLE OF different locations to put the laptop. At the dining table seemed too formal. On the bed too desperately suggestive. She didn't like how the overhead lights shone down on her face when she was sitting on the couch, so she took the lamp from her bedside table and set it up outside of the view of the webcam. Then she poured herself a glass of wine and sorted some laundry while she waited for the *beep-boop* noises of an incoming call. They'd had two conversations in the month since Pat left. The first was entirely for business reasons—she'd known someone after a Warhol who paid in USD—but at the end of the call he had said he'd liked hearing her voice again, and suggested he call her back after work just for a chat. She'd woken up at five am to talk to him when he got home from work, then had the whole rest of that Tuesday to try to wrangle her emotions down again. Lally was the one who'd suggested they shift to video calls. She wanted to get some context, see some of his life around him. She'd spent some time imagining that he would take her on a little video tour of his place.

About ten minutes past their scheduled time—her five pm Friday, his seven am Saturday—she heard the call come in. Lally walked back to the couch, sat down with her wine in hand, checked the angle and light, then hit the green icon. Pat's face came up huge on her screen.

'Bit early for that, eh?' he said.

'You picked the time,' she replied curtly.

'Huh?'

'You were the one who suggested this time,' she repeated.

'Yeah, I know. I meant the wine. I was joking about it being early for wine, because the birds are still going off here. Doesn't matter.'

'Oh.'

They both started speaking at the same time.

'Anyways—'

'Right—'

Then they both paused. Excruciating.

'How was your day?' he asked.

'Good, actually,' she said, leaning back into the couch and sipping her wine, before telling him how the office space above her gallery was coming up for lease and she was thinking about taking it. She could see he was waking up quickly as she spoke.

'Wow, that sounds fantastic,' he said. He had pillows propping him up and she could see from the top of his bed hair down to the bottom of his pecs. He was still in great shape.

'Thank you. I feel really good about it. It's crazy to still be answering calls from my apartment. I guess this is where I'd always hoped I'd get to when I opened my own gallery.'

'Of course,' he said, adding, 'I'd love to come to one of your openings.'

'Ha!' Lally said loudly. 'Don't you dare turn up. Or if you do, don't talk to people. Or if you do talk to people, then we have to pretend we don't know each other.'

Pat was quiet for a moment.

'Sorry, that came out more aggressive than I intended. I just mean, if you're going to shit on new art—you know, the way you did when we met.'

He frowned. 'Obviously, I wouldn't do that.'

'What do you mean *obviously*?'

'That was different.'

'How?'

'Don't worry about it,' Pat said.

'Okay.'

'But I wouldn't.'

'Okay.' There was another awkward silence and she took a long drink. 'Got any weekend plans?'

'Yeah, I'll go for a jog. See some mates in the afternoon.'

'Great,' she said, embarrassed that she didn't know if she could or should ask about his friends. It felt absurd that they were staying in touch despite how little they knew of each other. 'Are they art friends?' she ventured.

'Nah.' Pat shook his head and got up, placing his phone on his bedside table as he kept talking to her while looking for a shirt. Lally soaked up what detail she could. Navy sheets, a huge window with a wooden frame and bright blue sky beyond, a novel-sized book on the bedside table, a desk with a laptop on it in the background. 'The baker I told you about and a few of them do business stuff . . . ah, one's a lawyer, and a couple are in property.' He returned to the screen, grabbing it and climbing back into bed. 'A mixed bag. Got a bucks' night next weekend for the lawyer, actually.'

'Eugh.' Lally scrunched up her face. 'What does that look like?'

Pat made a raspberry noise and exhaled. 'Drinking, mostly.'

'Strippers?'

'Nah,' he said, then grinned. 'We couldn't afford more than one.'

Lally couldn't tell if he was joking.

'I'm joking,' he said. 'Tim's fiancée would not be at all cool with that.'

'Let's not start talking about sex workers,' Lally said in a way that she felt made her position clear.

'Aaaabsolutely,' he said and laughed a little nervously, running his hand through his hair then over his chin, the way men did when they were feeling their own stubble. 'You changed the posters.' He pointed to the wall behind her. She had just been to her storage facility again.

'I seem to be craving a kind of reset more than usually lately,' she surprised herself by trying to explain, then drained her glass. 'Normally I'll keep things up for six months at least, but I dunno . . .' He waited quietly for her to finish. 'It feels like I'm looking for something, or a bit restless.'

'You seem like one of those moving-goalposts people,' Pat suggested gently. 'You've finally got what you were working towards. So you're not unhappy exactly, but you kind of feel like, what now?'

'Maybe.' She nodded. 'Something like that.'

Lally took her laptop to the kitchen counter and poured herself another wine, and he walked with his phone to the kitchen and put the kettle on. They chatted about the works she'd chosen, and Pat told her about some of the interesting items he'd seen through Osborne in the past week. They talked about work for a bit, comfortably dipping in and out of professional and personal.

It wasn't until Lally saw her phone light up—*Gen calling*—that she realised they'd been talking for an hour.

'Crap,' she said, reaching for her phone. 'I've gotta go.'

'Oh, no worries—me too, actually.'

'Umm . . .' She looked at his face and smiled dumbly.

'Let's do this again sometime,' he said with a shrug.

'Yeah, okay.'

Call ended.

It was like shutting her laptop created a vacuum, scooping her guts out and whisking them away through a silent internet chasm. The room was so quiet. How far away was his next trip? Beginning or end of May? She couldn't ask him without appearing completely pathetic. They weren't even dating. Gen's call went through to voicemail. She looked to the lamp she'd set up for the call and felt stupid and furious. Her heart was beating extremely hard and she was having trouble breathing. Lally bent down and put her head between her knees. Everything was terrible. She got up, fetched the wine from the bench and returned to the couch, drinking straight from the bottle. There wasn't that much left anyway. What was going on? She'd been so happy. She started that call with all her ducks in a row, everything organised and perfect, and then he'd put in zero effort and they just talked in circles and now she felt like shit because . . . what? What the fuck was happening to her?

After the wine Lally listened to Gen's message. She was asking if Lally would be interested in a last-minute double date with her, Alex and Ben.

'Who is this Ben guy?' Lally asked when Gen picked up.

'A family friend.'

'Something wrong with him?'

'What? No.'

'So why don't *you* like him?'

'He sort of feels like a cousin or a brother. Too close, you know?'

'Tonight? What time?'

'In about an hour?'

'Done.'

'Wow, okay. Well, see you there. You know the place? Just on the other side of StuyTown?'

'Yep.'

Lally thought of Pat's pecs while she let Ben fuck her. It worked well with the lights off. Riding him to finish only took a moment and she pinched her own nipples to speed things up. This was good. Fucking other people, making sure the thing with Pat wasn't compromising her at all. She'd be able to reach a sort of equilibrium if she just exercised a little more self-control. He was a good contact, after all. And it was enjoyable and enriching to speak to someone from out of town about art. All the interest in the work but none of the pressure. If she could compartmentalise things with him it could be fine.

'Do you like that?' Ben said in her ear. He was still going at it in missionary.

'Oh yeah,' Lally replied.

'You're a naughty little girl, aren't you?'

Jesus fucking Christ.

'I'll only be at the courts for an hour or so,' Ben said, rummaging through a basket of clean laundry. 'If you wanted to hang out here, we could go for lunch when I get back?'

Lally was feeling pretty hungover and the idea of sleeping for another hour then getting food was appealing, but then she watched him pull a pastel yellow Polo Ralph Lauren shirt out of the basket and tug it over his head.

'Maybe next time.' She tried to sound sweet about it, a little sorry. 'I should get some work done today.'

'It's all work, work, work with you, isn't it, girl?' He came over to the bed to kiss her goodbye, smiling. If she were feeling slightly more energetic she might have flinched. 'Okay, well, I had a great time, and I'll call you.'

'No problem,' she said, smiling. 'You go now, or you'll be late!'

Lally watched him walk out of the bedroom and waited for the front door to open and close before exhaling loudly and slumping back into the pillows. The more she thought about him the more he disgusted her. She got up to take a shower and noticed three, maybe four dozen fresh daffodils in a tall glass vase on the marble counter in the bathroom. They were exquisite, just opening and trimmed to the exact same height. Ben couldn't have chosen them, probably didn't even look at them. He was rich enough for a flower service, she supposed, possibly as an extension of his grocery service. Standing there naked, she pinched one bloom between her thumb and forefinger, slowly crushing it down and rubbing the happy yellow tube until it was mashed and bruised. She thought about her dad yelling at her mum for buying flowers once. She wondered if she'd be more rich now if she'd invested his money in shares or real estate instead of in herself, in the gallery. Not Ben rich. And anyway, it had felt good to do something her dad would have hated with that precious money of his. He was at his most ugly when Estelle spent 'his money'—though, ironically, he wouldn't have had to spend so much on care in his final decade if he hadn't driven her away. Men always thought women cost them money, but really women were saving them money all the time. What if she sucked it up and married money like Ben? Did the courteously discreet affairs thing. Why did it feel like it was always the men who had all the money? They spent it on stupid things anyway. Ben didn't know a fucking thing about taste.

After she'd showered and dressed, she made the bed, even replacing the absurd throw cushions. She washed the wineglass she'd used the night before, dried it and put it back in the cupboard. She buried her used towel deep in the dirty laundry basket then, before she left, she took the flower she'd pinched, wrapped it in toilet paper and flushed it down the toilet. That made her feel better. Everything was as though she'd never been there. None of it happened.

'Yes, thank you,' she replied when the doorman offered to hail her a cab.

You home? Coffee? Bagel? I'm in cab coming from midtown.

Gen replied immediately. *Good timing. Was just about to shower. Come to mine?*

Lally replied with three thumbs up.

———

'Are those last night's clothes?' Gen asked as soon as she opened the door.

'Yeah.'

Gen gave her a look. 'Good time or bad time?'

Lally let out a short, sharp laugh, pushing past Gen to get inside. 'Yes, Mom, fine.'

'Okay, just checking,' Gen said. 'Just being a friend.'

'Hurry up, I'm hungry.' Lally sat down on a kitchen stool.

'Yeah, yeah, me too. I'll be two seconds.'

They raised their voices to talk to each other while Gen show-ered with the bathroom door open. Lally winced as she noticed the steam from the bathroom was drifting over to the framed original *D.A.R.E.* poster she'd given Gen for her thirtieth. She got up and took it off the wall, placing it on the couch.

'So how was last night with Ben? Seems like it ended well.'

'I don't like him.'

Gen laughed. 'He's always been so nice.'

'So why don't you date him?'

Gen laughed loudly. 'I told you, we grew up together. It's kind of familial.'

'Something tells me he'd go there.'

'What?'

'I dunno, rich people do fucked-up stuff like that.'

The water turned off and Gen said, 'Aha.'

'Aha what?'

'That's what you don't like about him? That he's rich?'

'Well, I mean, it's not that I don't like that he's rich, it's like, I mean, it's like . . .'

Gen appeared in the kitchen, pausing on the way to her bedroom. 'What's it like?'

'I just . . .'

'Spit it out.'

'He doesn't care about art.'

Gen pulled a spectacularly comic face.

'I mean, it's more than that—deeper.'

Gen left the room with a loud groan.

'He doesn't think about art at all. He doesn't seem to see it, or see anything. Like, he has no taste—not even bad taste. I mean *no* taste, like the money has just completely stunted any kind of aesthetic development. He is incapable of even stopping and thinking, *Do I like this? Do I hate that? What's good?*'

Gen poked her head through the doorway to her bedroom. 'Do you want to wear my chambray dress?'

'Yes, actually,' Lally replied. A blue garment was thrown at her, and she started changing into it.

'So he has bad taste?' Gen prompted.

'No! Weren't you listening?'

Gen laughed. 'I don't know, I think only liking expensive things is a kind of bad taste.'

Lally paused at this. 'Maybe.'

'And this is his only crime?'

'It's his main crime, I'd say.'

'Right.'

'I'm serious. It's like he doesn't use his eyeballs properly. And it makes me start thinking, you know, about everything he doesn't read, or doesn't watch, and how he makes his hundred daily decisions.'

'Not everybody likes art.'

'Yes, but it's not just art, it's the entire aesthetic world! And if you're rich, there's no excuse. It's, like, a double-triple crime. To have the means to step into this world, to choose the things with which you surround yourself, and to wilfully choose not to . . .' They left the apartment and started walking down the stairs. 'Has he always been like this?'

'I'm not quite seeing this extremeness of bad taste or no taste that you're talking about, but I know he's turned out to be precisely the man I thought he would when we were about twelve. Did he go play tennis this morning?'

'Lol, yes.' Lally shook her head. 'And think of it this way: people who don't realise the way they think about art effects the way they think about beauty are fucking idiots.'

'And Ben doesn't think about art, so he's a fucking idiot?'

'All he knows about beauty is what he's fucking told, which is disgusting, so yes.'

'You mean, like, advertising?'

'Yes! And all the bullshit! If he's incapable of thinking about art for himself then he's probably incapable of thinking about beauty for himself too.'

'I'm sure he thinks you're beautiful—does that count?'

'Well, he said so when we were fucking, but I'm slim and under forty, right? If he can't form a single original opinion then what the fuck would happen when I turn sixty, you know?'

'But what about all the men who know about art and still think sixty-year-old women are ugly?'

Lally paused at this. They were waiting at the lights. 'That's because they're looking at old art,' she said. 'They only want a young ballerina so they can tell themselves they're the Degas.'

'But what about old, old art, like the lady in the lake, when they had nice rolly bellies?'

Lally sighed.

'I'm just saying,' Gen continued, 'that maybe this isn't about art.' The pedestrian light turned green, and they crossed in sync. 'Not everything is about art.'

'Ha ha,' Lally said, two staccato syllables.

'Does this have anything to do with Mr Down Under?'

Lally sighed.

'I knew it.'

'Knew what?'

They reached the glass door of the tiny cafe and it was full of people and dogs. Saturdays were always nuts. 'Do you wanna get them to go and sit in the park?'

'Yeah, sounds good,' Gen replied, eyeballing the queue. 'It's my turn.'

'I might wait out here.'

Lally stood in a strong shaft of sunlight watching the comings and goings of the neighbourhood. Across the thin street there was a small, triangular park with a few benches before the high wrought-iron fence protecting the church grounds. It would have been close to midnight in Sydney. She pulled out her phone and checked her emails. Like a divine bolt, there was a message from him. Just three lines: *Finally got my travel docs approved today. I'll be there in three weeks. Got myself a little apartment a few blocks from yours.*

'Hey, give me a hand, will you?' Gen called, struggling with the coffees and pastries at the door of the cafe.

Lally hit 'send' on a quick reply and rushed over.

'You okay?' Gen asked.

'Yeah, of course.' Lally held the door and took a coffee.

'What happened?'

'What do you mean?'

'Your face, your body—you're all different.'

'Pat's coming in three weeks.'

'Wowie! I knew it! Wait, he just told you then?'

Lally nodded, smiling. 'Sent a message, yeah.'

'What did you say?'

'I said great and we'd talk later.'

'And?'

'And what?'

'Aaand that you're looking forward to seeing him? Or you can't wait?'

'I don't know if we're there yet.'

Gen snorted. 'You're hopeless.'

'Shut up,' Lally said, grabbing the bag of pastries. 'Let's go to the park. And tell me all about Alex now, please, so I don't feel so bad.'

'Okay!' Gen replied, sounding excited.

'In particular,' Lally added, 'I need to know what the catch is. He made us laugh so much last night. And he tipped. And he listened. He seems too good to be true.'

Gen groaned and shook her head.

'What is it? What's he done?' Lally felt her blood pumping.

'It's not like that.'

'We all say it's not like that.'

'No, Lally, just listen.' Gen sighed. 'He is great. I asked him a couple of times, you know, how come you're still single? How come you don't use the apps and stuff?'

'And?'

'Don't laugh.'

Lally made a little cross gesture over her heart.

'He can't use dating apps or be online much because his image is on the internet in a weird way.'

'Excuse me?'

Gen sighed. 'I think it's easier if I just tell you the story—but it's a secret, okay?'

'He's in a porno?'

'No. When he was in college he needed money, right?'

'He's in a porno.'

Gen laughed. 'No! Stop! Just listen to me!'

'Okay, okay!'

'He went to a photo shoot—'

Lally snorted.

'Listen!'

'I am!'

'He went to a photo shoot for a stock photo company. You know, those pictures where people are in corporate attire and sitting around a boardroom table, or standing in front of a computer, or they're making a coffee, or filing papers, like, whatever—stock photos.'

'Okay.'

'And then this stock photo he was in, where he was pretending to be excited about something on a clipboard, got made into a meme.'

'Right . . .'

'Apparently one of the more, I dunno, commonly used memes from a decade ago. Popular with certain communities who shit-post. So, you know, he can't be on the apps, because when people realise it's him he just gets sent this barrage of every meme that's been made with the template of his twenty-year-old goofball face in a short-sleeved business shirt seeming stoked about whatever heinous thing people have patched onto the clipboard.' Gen shook her head and laughed a little.

'So you looked them up?'

'Yeah, I looked them up. Of course I fucking looked them up. I mean, he looks a bit different now. The photo is from early message board days. Some of them are a bit racist, but mostly they're just stupid.'

'Wow.'

'He says it's more of a problem with men. Sometimes they'll think they've met him before, or they'll recognise him or whatever.'

'I just . . . what a twenty-first-century problem.'

'Right?'

'He says being an anaesthetist is good because people don't remember him!'

'Funny! Well, he is seeming pretty great otherwise.'

'Yeah, he is.' Gen squeezed Lally's arm. 'I feel almost giddy about him.'

'If this meme thing is the catch, then I reckon that's about as good as it gets.'

'I know. I think I'm falling in love with him.'

'What!' Lally stopped walking, and Gen stopped a step after her, then they started shoving each other's shoulders, giggling.

The next morning Lally hung up from a call with Emile feeling a glimmer of hope about what they might do with Brodeur's murky etchings.

'Thanks for coming in early,' Lally said, meeting Leah at the gallery before it opened.

'No problem.'

'Well, I pushed Emile for something we could use, you know? Why did this happen? What am I supposed to do with this?'

'And?'

'Remember how I told you these new works were too gloomy? Well, it turns out the boy's mother was arrested for some altercation in a labour strike—you know how they are with that stuff in France—and she broke her wrist in prison, and now she can't even get the cleaning work she was paid so little to do in the first place.'

'Fuck!'

'I know. So here's what we have to work with. Thank god the pieces are still the agreed-upon size and number. We're not worried about logistics, it's ten works, already framed, each about a metre wide, and they'll arrive on time.'

Leah nodded.

'But what he's been making—I mean, it's why people don't like etchings anymore. The monochromatic murkiness. He has a couple of lines about them being a vision of the future, I don't know, some kind of post-apocalyptic thing, but we're going to need to spin that and really work the devastated-migrant-son angle instead.'

'Right.'

'I'll be frank with you, Leah. I want these works to sell, of course, but Guillaume actually needs this money more than we do right now. You and I are going to roll up our sleeves and do the dirty work of selling so that he gets to imagine his artistry is pure and somehow miraculously also commercially viable, so then he can pay his mom's bills. Do you get me?'

Leah looked shocked, but she nodded again.

'I'm about to show you something and I need you to swear that it'll stay between us. I trust you, Leah, but I wouldn't even make this the subject of an NDA. Honestly, it's a bit more intuitive than that.'

'Okay.'

Lally pulled a scrappy sheet of paper out of her bag. It was originally a printed sheet of a twelve-point list, but now it was covered in handwritten notes from different times in different pens, phone numbers all over it, a post-it in the corner. 'This is what we do when we realise we have a shitshow on our hands.'

'Okay,' Leah repeated.

'There are nine steps. We basically need to create discord around the show, whip up debate. It's a combination of simple and not-so-simple things. A simple thing is to make the media preview a week before opening instead of the night before, to allow space for dissent to breathe and grow. The not-so-simple part is finding and paying the plants.'

'The plants?'

'The plants. Step four.' Lally tapped the sheet. 'I don't pay them with money. The last two times—and I've only ever had to do this twice—they wanted connections, opportunities, guarantees of future work. I'm talking about the critics. We just need one who will say they love the show and one to say they loathe it. Dislike isn't enough. It has to be hate. Their pieces go out first, the editors sniff the clicks and commission the responses, and the rest of the circus just start yelling at themselves and each other. By opening night it's a storm.'

Leah picked up the piece of paper gingerly, scanning it. Lally watched her face move from confusion to disdain and then to acceptance. 'Does Brodeur know?' she asked quietly.

'Absolutely not. The artist cannot know. Not even their managers know. The editors don't know. There is me, and the two other people who know. I cannot stress that enough, Leah. *Nobody else can know.* The critics will never speak out because their own reputations would suffer more than mine.'

'These names . . .' Leah said, looking at the four people Lally had made this agreement with in the past. 'I suppose I shouldn't be surprised.'

'And note, all four of those critics are now in much stronger positions than when I gave them these opportunities.'

'Is that how you sell it to them?'

'Yes.'

They sat in silence while Leah read the whole sheet of paper. Lally tried to act like she wasn't waiting for a response.

'We do this dirty work, Guillaume gets paid,' Lally reminded her gently.

Leah exhaled loudly. 'Okay,' she said, looking up. 'Shall we split up these tasks?'

Lally smiled with relief and clapped her hands louder than she meant to, the sound making them both start. They went out together for more coffee then closed the curtains to the gallery and started the planning and research, looking for new critics who were clearly hungry but not too principled. Ideally, they'd have published in smaller places and this would be their chance to go big. What did the gallery have to offer them in return? Exclusives?

'I've had an idea,' Lally said. 'Can you put together two copies of a confidential dossier with key points of information about the strike Brodeur's mother was involved in? The plants can pad their articles with political content. It'll help rile everyone up.'

By midday they had names and dates, contacts and a schedule.

'Leah,' Lally said, looking her in the eye, 'I feel much better about this already. I couldn't have just anyone in this role. Thank you for your work and your discretion.'

14

'NERVOUS FLYER?' THE FLIGHT ATTENDANT asked, crouching down to be on eye level with Pat.

'What?'

She nodded towards his hands, gripping the armrests tightly.

'I won't tell anyone,' she said with a smile, then stood up again and put another drink on his table. 'Our little secret.'

He wasn't afraid of flying. He was shitting his pants about landing. Specifically, about landing at JFK, and then getting a cab, and then his feet taking him closer and closer to seeing Lally again. He'd had to get a haircut the week before and it wasn't the best. Should he bring her flowers? Should he refrain from initiating sex too soon lest she think she was just his international booty call? She didn't seem too sensitive about that stuff. Trying to catalogue his successes and mistakes with her was impossible. There was no pattern. Lally was affectionate at random times—not when he did something impressive or offered to pay for things. Compliments occasionally landed, but she was such a cynic that deploying too many was dangerous. He'd put an alert function on her name and the gallery's name after the Armory Show, so he'd been sent all the positive press about her line-up for the rest of the year. Once he'd received a notification but it was a picture of her in the social pages of some paper, and she was with a man he didn't know, and he'd felt a surge of something more complex than jealousy. It wasn't like he didn't want her fucking other people, although he definitely didn't want her fucking other people. It was more like he didn't want her to have this whole other life going on that he had no part in. Perhaps he could slip away and nothing would change for her. Maybe he was the international booty call.

The hull rattled around him and he closed his eyes and took deep breaths. This was like the plane ride in New Zealand that time he went skydiving. Same sick feeling.

The little studio he'd reserved in the East Village was just the thing. Only a couple of blocks from her place. The boyfriend experience. He dumped his bags, shoved the keys into his pocket and ventured up to the roof. A cemetery of antennas spread out, cigarette butts like confetti between it all. But when he raised his gaze and took in the neighbourhood, and Stuyvesant Park, and the sounds of the city, and the light of the sun setting, the rainbow tip of the Chrysler Building poking through the high-rise vista, he was thrilled all over again. There was a single wrought-iron chair over to one side. Maybe he would sit on it, and Lally would come and sit on his lap, and he would hug her. Or something, whatever.

Time to rip the band-aid off.

I reckon I can see the top of your building from the top of my building. He scrolled up a little, through their final exchange before he'd left Australia. It was like panning for gold, trying not to get your hopes up in case you were wrong about seeing something sparkle in the sand. *I'm starving—want to get dinner?* He decided he'd let the messages sit there for thirty minutes before reassessing the situation. Back inside, he put some music on and unpacked his small suitcase, sipping on a beer he'd found in the fridge. Outside his window, people were walking their dogs. He could've burst into song when his phone went off.

Wonderful! I'm walking home now. Meet me at my place in 20?

Wonderful, wonderful, wonderful.

Wonderful, he replied.

Flowers would absolutely be the wrong vibe. He knew this, but couldn't put his finger on why. Something about it formalising things, or maybe even taking them a step back into 'courtship' mode. They had moved past that. They had moved past that a long time ago, actually. Back when he first stayed overnight at her place. It was as though they'd been friends as children and had reconnected years on. The weeks of sporadic chatting had had the effect of strengthening the non-physical facets of their relationship. The question now was whether they'd be able to add the sex back into the recipe without spoiling it all.

His stomach went nuts when he crossed the street and saw the red awning out the front of her building. Not from hunger—this wasn't even close to a feeling of hunger. This was the part of the skydiving birthday experience where you were standing with your toes over the edge of the plane's open door, and someone was yelling a countdown in your ear, and your whole being was filled with the single question: *What the fuck am I doing?*

'Pat!'

He was up near 11th when he heard her calling. He spun around and saw her waving, and he was grinning widely, and then he saw her start walking a little faster towards him, and so he started walking towards her, faster, and then she let out a little laugh and sort of skipped, and so he dropped the wine bottle onto a high pile of trash without even looking and started running, and she swung her handbag over her shoulder and was running too, and his mind was full of her face and her laugh, and she lifted her arms up and jumped towards him and he caught her, he caught her with his whole body, his arms around her torso, and they were spinning around and she was pressing her face against his face and they were both laughing. When he bent his knees to put her down she kept her hands on the sides of his head, and they kissed. A great big long kiss. Terminal velocity.

'I've just spoken to the landlords and inspected the space,' she said when they separated. 'I might be taking the floor above for an office.' Her eyes were wild. 'I can't wait to tell you all about it!'

'Fantastic!' he replied, letting her take his hand, their arms swinging as they walked to her building's front door. With his free hand he scooped up the wine bottle from where he'd dropped it.

As soon as they were inside her apartment she started taking his clothes off, and once they were on the bed she got on top straight away and came quickly. What a relief. He tried to spoon her after but she was too excited. She wanted to drink and talk about the gallery expansion, so he fought off the post-nut, jet-lag fatigue.

The smell of the place was the same. A question arose in his mind, the question of what other men may have been there between his visits. He tried to dismiss it, and also tried not to let himself think 'home', but the next morning he got out of bed before she did, and ground the coffee beans, and put the espresso pot on the stove, and peed with the door ajar.

———

During the day he absorbed everything he could at Osborne's New York's new 'institute'. It was a rapidly developing revenue stream for the company in America, offering classes and diploma-type certifications in art-adjacent business roles. The idea was what had sold Josephine on another New York trip so soon. A reconnaissance mission. He'd raised it with her during a video call on his first visit and he remembered her eyes had lit up like a pokie machine at the thought of a similar operation running out of Sydney. All the middle-class Aussie families who wouldn't spend big money on actual art but were aspirational enough to spend that kind of money on their kids' 'education'. With a smile like Pat's on the front of the brochure, Josephine said, he might just 'earn his keep'. She'd approved a five-day trip and he promised to return and get straight back to work on the Bauer account. An email from her reminded him Sophie was 'waiting' to hear from him with an update 'in person'. He pushed the cringey feeling out of his mind.

He'd pictured the institute being full of the worst kind of rich kids, but people were mostly friendly. Mercenary, but friendly. He stuffed his briefcase with the course plans and promotional materials, shook hands with two or three of the lecturers, and sat in for the end of a 'market analysis' tutorial that was a couple of years out of date but otherwise decent.

At six o'clock he went straight back to Lally's, letting himself in with the spare key she'd given him. She was there already, pacing around the living room on a work call. He quietly drew two wineglasses out of the dishwasher and cracked a red. When she'd wrapped up the call he took the phone from her hand and replaced it with a glass.

'Mmm, thank you,' she said, kissing him.

'M'DJ,' he said, tipping an invisible hat and handing her own phone back to her, newly connected to her speaker system.

She laughed and took it from him, and he went to the full laundry basket on her dining table. 'All right, let's fold!' When he'd woken up at her place for the second morning in a row Pat knew he'd have to up his helping-around-the-house game. He took the basket into the bedroom and a moment later some chill groove mix started playing. Lally put her glass down and grooved over to him. He reached into the warm basket and pulled out the bedsheet, handing her two corners. As he took the other two, he slid across the floor away from her, the sheet tenting up between them. When they had the sheet in a narrow band, Lally slut-dropped to grab the bottom of it and bring it up into a square. They laughed and kissed.

'It smells good,' he said, holding one of her dresses up to his face before retrieving a coathanger for it.

The way she looked at him then, with a gentle smile, slowing her actions, he knew he was getting somewhere.

A *bing-bong* noise came through the speakers, interrupting them, and her manner changed immediately.

'Email,' she said, dropping the socks she'd been pairing.

'Leave it, it's Monday!' he said, resenting the intrusion. 'You told me none of the galleries are open on Monday.'

'It'll bother me if I don't just see what it is. I'll be right back.' She left the room.

Pat kept folding shirts and pairing socks. He made a little pile of his trunks, and a little pile of her undies. She had a real mixture of undies. This was a good sign. Sometimes she seemed so well established in her ways, there was a kind of inaccessibility about her, or just a firmness he couldn't get past. He touched the big old baggy blue cotton ones, and the tiny lace g-string, and the three black Calvin Klein pairs. Some of these were professional, and some of these were the undies of a woman who made people laugh with funny music impressions. He was getting closer to the secret bit, he knew it.

'That's more than a quick check!' he called out to her, and went into the lounge.

Lally was on her knees beside the dining table, gripping the edge of it, banging her forehead against it softly.

Pat crossed the room fast, crouching down beside her, clasping one of her hands, putting her arm around his shoulder and taking her weight onto him as he stood up.

'Couch,' he said quietly, and she murmured in response.

Against his body he could feel her breathing like a tiny marsupial, fast and light. Once he got her down onto the couch she wouldn't look at him. Wasn't saying anything.

He held her hand. 'Was it the email?'

The phone was on the floor, incongruously capable of purring out the sexy beats while clearly having given this woman an anxiety attack. Pat was sure someone had died. His immediate response to this—and he was not proud of it—was frustration. He had to go back to Sydney in a few more days. Now wasn't a good time for her to have to attend a funeral.

'Lally,' he said, 'is everyone okay? Do you want me to take you somewhere?'

'No.'

He waited to see if she would clarify, but she didn't.

'No what?'

'No, I don't want to go anywhere.'

'Okay.'

'I just got some bad news.'

'I'm sorry to hear that.'

'They . . .' Lally frowned, and her breaths started coming faster again. 'They want to make a movie or a series or something.' She rubbed her eyes. 'HBO. About Joseph Rivera.'

Pat was struggling to keep up. 'Rivera? Didn't he die?'

Lally released a loud groan.

'Sorry. He was one of your artists?'

She held her head in her hands, looking down, not responding.

'You must have been close,' he said gently. 'I'm sorry for your loss.'

Still no response.

'Isn't it a good thing? Are they wanting to make a documentary about his works, or his practice? It could be a wonderful way to honour his legacy.'

Lally started bawling, then, an angry kind of sobbing. He went to put his arm around her, but a terrible noise came out of her throat and she pulled away. This hurt him. Something was happening that he didn't understand.

He sat with her until the worst of it had passed then said, 'Let's get some air.'

'I don't want to be around people,' she said, wiping her face.

'At my place you can get onto the roof. It's empty. Let's go there.'

Lally nodded.

He gathered some sneakers and a cardigan from her bedroom and brought them to her on the couch.

'Thank you,' she said quietly. Then, 'Sunglasses, please.'

They held hands walking east towards his place, past the bars and bodegas. She leaned on him a little when they had to stop at the lights. When they reached his building and started up the six flights they both paused at the third floor, and it was as though the blood pumping was helping her. He saw some colour returning to her face and kissed her on the cheek, and she smiled at him.

Up on the roof it was chilly but not freezing. He pointed down at the dog park, describing about some of the dog interactions he'd seen from their vantage point. She reached out and took his hand. Even more interestingly, when they turned in the other direction they discovered they could see into the apartments of people who clearly thought their fifth- and six-floor positions safeguarded them against such intrusions.

'This is juicy,' Lally said as they began pointing things out to each other and laughing.

There was a bedroom with a tripod sitting patiently yet suggestively in a corner, and a bathroom in which the shower seemed to be storage for boxes and boxes of plush toys. Lots of people were putting things where they weren't supposed to be.

'Oh boy,' Pat said, spotting it before Lally. 'You're gonna get mad at this.'

'What?'

He pointed, and knew she'd seen it when she groaned dramatically and buried her head in his shoulder. 'No!' she said, like she was wounded. 'What have I done to deserve this?'

An easel in one room was displaying a painfully average rendering of a frangipani on a magenta background.

He laughed, looking down at this funny, beautiful woman. She'd bounced back.

'What're you smiling at?' Lally asked, tilting her head towards him.

He didn't say anything, just put his arm around her and leaned back against the wall, pulling her in between his legs to hold her closer.

'Average art makes you hot?' she said.

'That's not average art, that is bad art,' he said into her neck, his hands on her waist.

'Ooh.' She ran a hand through the hair on the back of his head. 'Talk dirty to me.'

'I prefer acrylics to oils,' Pat whispered in her ear, and she squealed, smacking his shoulder, pretending to pull away.

He brought her in close again, breathing on her neck, and she cringed, ticklish. 'It'll all come together once it's framed,' he whispered.

She doubled over giggling.

He tried another: 'You can't separate the art from the artist.'

Now she gasped. He thought he saw real shock on her face for a moment, and she wasn't struggling away from him but he still held her tightly, grinning.

'Pat,' she said, looking straight into his eyes. Her expression changed, and then she kissed him on the cheek, burying her face into his neck. 'Let's go away, out of the city.'

'Yes, let's,' he said, and his heart knew it was spring.

He'd bumped his meetings back a day and was in a rental Merc heading 'upstate' before he could even think of Josephine. Lally said there was a garden show in a giant greenhouse and a famously good farm-to-table restaurant.

The flowers were beautiful, and the sun was high in the sky when he spotted a community hall advertising an art show and insisted they stop.

They walked between the rows of temporarily erected walls, sometimes side by side. After about fifteen minutes, though, Pat caught up to Lally and saw that her expression had hardened.

He moved to stand beside her in front of a poorly rendered horse. The artist had struggled with the perspective, badly truncating the long nose directed towards the viewer. The effect was pretty funny. A regular horse body, a nice green paddock, and a freaky, bug-eyed, pug-like short face with some teeth bared in a grimace.

'*Majestic Mare*,' Pat said quietly, leaning in to read the didactics, then looking to Lally with a smile when he straightened. Jokes were a safe way to test the waters.

Lally scoffed. 'I fucking hate average art,' she said, not bothering to lower her voice. 'It makes me furious.'

'Lally.' Pat looked around, hoping no one else had heard her.

'What?' she said loudly, hands on her hips.

'That's so mean.'

She waved her hand at *Majestic Mare*. 'People are busy. It's so arrogant that someone thought this was worth my time or anyone else's time.'

'Jesus, Lally, they're just painting.'

'No, they're exhibiting.'

'They're trying to share their hobbies, create some community.'

She looked at him with a disgusted expression. 'That is so incredibly patronising.' She shook her head at him and turned to walk away.

'You're the one saying their art is bad.'

She whipped around. 'That is not what I said. I said it was average.'

'People have spent hours on these works'—she spread her arms out, getting louder—'and then they have put their names on their works, estimated their prices, hung them and promoted a show. They are behaving like artists and I will judge and treat them as such.'

'You just said it was making you mad.'

'It does, because the work is average and therefore they're arrogant.'

'Lally, this is a community hall.'

'And you think great art can't come from a community hall? That's what's patronising.'

'Oh, come on.'

'No. You think there are two categories of artist and there isn't. There's no binary, just a spectrum. It's like you think anyone who isn't one of your grand old masters is just "experimenting". When you talk about modern art it's like you think there is "art" and then there is "modern art", which is a variation, some kind of "other", but it's not. It is all art, and it all deserves our criticism and attention. You dismissed these people before you'd even seen their works. I'm the one who walked into this gallery with an open mind about what I might find here.'

'Okay,' he said, turning and walking away to wait in the foyer of the building. It didn't matter if she had a point, he just wished they could have a chill afternoon.

'Are you sulking?' She appeared beside him, put her arm through his, and they headed for the exit. 'I happen to love and often defend truly bad art. It's just average art I can't stand.' Her tone was quieter but he could tell she was still worked up.

'Don't you just feel like maybe not everything has to be great? Or greatly bad? Most people are just . . .' He paused. 'I dunno. Not everything has to be the best or the worst all the time. It can't be. There're too many people and most of us are kind of average most of the time.'

They stepped outside, both raising their hands to shield their eyes from the light.

'No,' she replied. 'The best way to counter this huge history of so many of us being shut out is to believe in, or at least stay optimistic about, everyone's potential. I think most people do and overcome and make extreme things more frequently than any of us talk about.'

Pat was quiet.

'None of us are that different from each other, Pat. There are no average people, there's just a lot of average art.'

'And it makes you mad.'

'And it makes me mad.'

'Okay,' he said, nodding. 'I can get down with that.'

'Great. Let's lunch.' They set off towards the car.

'When was the last time you went to the Frick?' he asked.

'Not since college. Why, is there something on?'

'I want to take you to see the *Comtesse*. It's one of my favourite paintings.'

'One of how many favourites?'

'Oh.' He thought about it. 'Maybe four or five?'

'Is it four or five?

'No. Three.'

'That's better, now I believe you.'

'And two of them are here in New York. And they're going to be your favourite paintings too.'

She snorted and gave him a warning look. 'You don't even know what my favourite paintings are. You don't even know if my favourite pieces of art are paintings.'

'That's true.' He squeezed her hand, 'We may already have the same favourite paintings.'

She rolled her eyes and shook her head.

'Where's your big open mind?' He kissed her head. 'This is going to be so good. Just this one time, don't fight me, okay? You're gonna love it. Trust me.'

15

LALLY STOOD ON THE SUBWAY trying to use the brief window of Pat-being-quiet time to check her emails. Anxiety about her lowered productivity while he was visiting was getting worse. She glanced towards him, standing with one arm holding the rail, the other arm holding his own phone. He was madly clicking and scrolling through the Frick's website, so excited. She longed to feel that way about art again. Maybe this was just what she needed. Needed, but also needed to manage? Her inbox told her Farr was still pushing back the date of her studio visit, and the Brodeur crisis management was ongoing, and the HBO producers wanted meetings. That was the most delicate task. Leah was helping to manage Brodeur, but no facet of the Rivera situation could be delegated or even left to simmer for forty-eight hours. She knew what they were thinking: Basquiat 2.0. The Latinx Kurt Cobain of art. The latest martyr for the postmodern cause. Everyone had expected her to fully support the idea and help facilitate the introductions, to assist them in brainstorming content ideas to 'elevate his legacy'. She'd sucked that dick for MoMA because MoMA paid her, and she put the money back into the gallery, but HBO were just presuming she'd do months of consulting for them out of the goodness of her good little girl heart. Where was his studio? they wanted to know. Was it true that he had lived in a kind of 'edgy artistic commune' recently? Lally snorted. Great new way to spell crack house. They wanted the culmination of the biopic to be the creation of the 'fucked ocean' piece, and surely she could organise meetings with the studios and teams who'd helped 'realise his singular vision'. Surely she would be delighted to do all this for nothing. They'd had the gall to tell her it would be 'great exposure' for Gallery Lally.

On top of their insulting presumptuousness was the risk they'd uncover how the concept of 'fucked ocean' was hers. Or that they might somehow discover emails demonstrating an increasing personal connection between artist and gallerist. One of Rivera's dodgy friends had caught them kissing once. What if he embellished? What if he told the truth? It was delicate and shitty.

She'd almost finished drafting a response to the email when there was a tug at her elbow. She looked down, but it wasn't some child, it was Pat beside her, smiling. The blue tiles of the 72nd Street stop were visible through the window.

They pushed through the crowd to the station exit.

'No phones allowed in the Frick,' Pat said as they waited in the short queue for tickets.

'I know that, Pat.'

He could see she was typing a long email response. How could it not be obvious to him that what she was doing was important? He shrugged, and she felt a pang of guilt for snapping, and put her phone back in her pocket.

'So who are we seeing here?' she asked him. 'A countess?'

'The *Portrait of Comtesse d'Haussonville*,' he elaborated. 'But I won't tell you anything about it until we see it and you get a good look, and then I'll tell you everything.'

They got their tickets and were handed a map to share.

Lally shook her head as she scanned the information on the flipside of the map. Henry Clay Frick had been an industrialist from Pittsburgh in the late 1800s and his house was 'one of New York City's few remaining Gilded Age mansions'. Gilded age indeed.

'Okay, I know you're going to hate this,' Pat said, 'so let's just get it out of the way up front. Wikipedia says he did railroads and steel and busted unions. He and a few of his rich mates were responsible for the flooding of a whole town. They didn't repair a dam properly, had a strategy to hush it up, donated some money to relief, fought off lawsuits. More than two thousand people were killed. A proper report only came out last year.'

Lally looked at Pat in horror, then looked down at the beautiful embossed page declaring that the museum was known for its 'distinguished Old Master paintings'. If Frick was the dick he sounded like, it made her furious to think of how his money shaped the market and perceptions of art in his own time. And still now! How easy it was to buy venerated immortality. How easily a legacy could be created and maintained with the right number of cheques. The interest on the estate would have been enough to fund the museum's maintenance, and they'd never even touch the capital. Dirty money making beautiful, clean, distinguished money, and it all just circle-jerked back to the same tiny, narrow, limited idea of what constituted good art.

'So where is she?' Lally asked, looking at the layout of the mansion. Dining rooms and staircases and a pond in the middle.

'She's normally here,' Pat said, pointing to a corridor, 'but they recommend walking this way'—he drew a wide circuit with his finger—'through the whole house, room by room.'

Lally fought the urge to counter this suggestion, not liking being told what to do by the ghost of an imperialist prick. But she knew she had to perform open-mindedness, at least, so that Pat would listen to her criticisms later.

It shocked her to realise how frequently she wanted to reach for her phone at first, but little by little, with each new painting Pat provided commentary on, for each new piece of old-world trivia, she imagined a little ingot lifting off the crown of her head. How funny it seemed to her then that all her contemporaries—the gallerists and dealers and curators who bitched nonstop about the negative effects of social media on their scene—didn't have the guts to do what the Frick did and just ban the phones. Of course, that was the difference between a museum funded by an enduring estate and a gallery needing to actually sell shit, but still. There was a reverence among the strangers gathered, a kind of peaceful intimacy. Everyone was there to be enriched, not to document or prove or project. And Pat was such a phenomenal guide! His love of art was wedded to a boyish interest in history, and the result was an encyclopaedic knowledge not only of the works themselves but of how they related to military and economic events through time. It was a bit blinkered, sure, but fascinating.

'So hilarious that he put the Thomas Moore and the Cromwell on opposite sides of the fireplace,' he pointed out with what was almost a giggle. 'I reckon he'd always bring guests in here to see who noticed.'

Lally hadn't noticed. She recognised the names from a documentary she'd watched in school, but she certainly couldn't have picked the men from their portraits alone.

'Okay.' Pat was looking through a doorway where they would move from carpet to tiles, and he reached down and took her hand as he stepped through the arch almost officially, as though they were to cross a threshold together. 'Here she is.' And he extended his other hand towards a painting. It felt to Lally as if she were being presented to the painting rather than the other way around.

When she looked up and saw it she was filled with complete and immediate understanding. 'Oh my god,' she said, grinning. 'She's fucking incredible!'

Lally was looking at a young woman in a blue dress leaning against a fireplace. One arm was stretched across her body, resting against the opposite hip, as though her arms had been crossed just a moment ago, but now the other arm was bent up from the elbow, leaning on a mantel, and she had a finger on her chin. Her body was angled away from the viewer, so that she was looking over her shoulder. The finger-on-chin was a pose normally associated with pensive people, but this woman's facial expression made Lally want to gasp. It was flirty and smart and judgey and unimpressed. Her head was tilted at an angle that said to the viewer: *Really?*

'Daughter of a diplomat, granddaughter of famous writer Madame de Staël, mega rich, mid-nineteenth century—' Pat was so excited it was like he was speaking in dot points to get the information across to her.

'What was she like?'

'She was a fucking wildcat,' Pat said, gazing up. 'Super liberal, really outspoken, published a biography of Byron and some memoirs. In one of her memoirs she said she felt that in her twenties she was'—he quoted—'"destined to beguile, to attract, to seduce, and in the final reckoning, to cause suffering in all those who sought their happiness in her".' Pat snickered and shook his head. 'Fully saucy.'

'And the artist?'

'Ingres. He didn't want to take the assignment, apparently. Had to restart the painting a bunch of times. Took him three years plus. There are tons of drawings where you can see him struggling to prepare for the actual painting. They all have this stare, though. In the end, when he finally presented it people lost their minds they loved it so much. A politician insisted he must be in love with her to paint her in this way.'

'How is she fully dressed and proper-looking, yet so, I dunno, provocative?'

'I know, right?'

'It's so charged.'

'It's like she's looking at you, and there's nobody else in the room, and you're probably not her husband.'

Lally laughed at this. 'How liberal are we talking here? Did she have women lovers too?'

Pat shrugged. 'Probably, right? They lived in Paris. She loved the opera—wrote about it all the time. That's why there are opera glasses on the mantel.' He gestured loosely with his hand. 'She was a pianist, knew Chopin, was famous for reading every new book. She was like this nexus for intellect. Father, husband, son, brother all members of the French Academy. Her great-nephew won a Nobel Prize for science. Her son was a politician and essayist . . .' Pat trailed off. 'Imagine what it would have been like growing up with that much money. All the possibilities at your fingertips. If you were a little bit good at something—you know, showed an aptitude for anything—you'd have an uncle who was too, and boom, you're getting private lessons and an audition with the orchestra.

'Also, this is anatomically impossible,' Pat added as an afterthought.

'What?'

'The way her arms are positioned, and what you can see in the mirror behind her, it's inaccurate.'

'Oh.'

'But he had to paint it wrong to get it right.'

'Yes.' Lally felt herself nodding. 'It's perfect.'

They spent another ten minutes in front of the painting, joking about how the Comtesse must have been such a pain to paint, and whether or not it was fair for any one person to have so many talents.

'And for the record,' Pat said with his hands on his hips, 'this piece was acquired long after Frick's death.'

Lally considered Pat. He wasn't being negative or trying to pick a fight. He wasn't trying to be antagonistic. He was defending the art he liked. A new train of questions arrived in her then: What kind of man is this? How did this happen? What peculiar trajectory had she been on for the last four months that she was now being given a tour of the Frick by a fit young Australian who gave great head?

'We've gotta go,' he said then, checking his watch. 'It's already three and I need to show you *The Heart of the Andes* and it's at The Met.'

Birds sang down the street. A hot dog vendor told them to have a lovely day. Lally just smiled and smiled.

The Met was packed.

'We can't afford to wander,' Pat said, worried. 'Not until after we've found it.'

They got a little lost, turning the map this way and that, fake-arguing, until she saw Pat's face break into a relief as they rounded a corner.

She saw it too. 'It's so big,' she whispered, shaking her head, instinctively stepping backward to try to fit the whole thing in her vision. Right at the back near the disappearing horizon line, a row of snow-capped mountains. Green ranges in front. A grassy expanse in front of that and then, further forward still, a great waterfall surrounded by forest. A blue blossom flowering from a fern on the right. To the left there was a small clearing, and figures standing in front of a cross. They were minute.

'Three metres long . . . To have this feeling for a landscape,' Pat said, gazing up and over the work with both arrival and longing in his voice. 'Isn't it amazing? Look how Church carved his name into a tree instead of signing the painting, and he draws our attention to it with a kind of naturally occurring spotlight on a bright white lily just near it.' Pat had moved nearer the work, pointing. A security guard came closer to them. 'And here, in the other corner, a tiny brown bird is captured mid-flight, and its red breast and the subtle changes in striation of its under-wing feathers are all zoologically accurate.' He turned to Lally and beckoned her forward impatiently.

She looked where he directed, nodding.

'And I love how the people are so tiny, you know? It's the same with Eugene von Guerard's paintings, although his was a German Romanticism thing,' Pat continued. He was on a roll but Lally was genuinely interested and also just enjoyed seeing him like this. All that passion and enthusiasm. 'It reinforces the immensity of the place; reminds you that, yes, you are supposed to feel small in the face of such majesty.'

'Why did Church put people in there at all?' she asked.

'He was travelling all over the globe, inspired by Alexander von Humboldt. It was a time when men really did set sail to the other side of the world and then report back. I think he wanted to convey how tiny we are in the grand scheme of things. When this was first shown—here in New York in 1859—people paid money to see it. It was an attraction. A show in and of itself.'

'Mmm.' Lally took a couple of steps sideways to see a different section of it.

'And I don't know about you,' he said, 'but my eye never rests. He started pointing to different parts. It's not that the composition isn't balanced, or that it's confused. It's more like, he wants you to be startled and then startled again. He wants us to not know where to look—like an extravaganza of nature!'

Pat's voice was getting louder. Lally noticed that an old man had stopped behind them to listen to him speak.

'And just think!' Pat put his hands on his head. 'It's all about to get completely sideswiped by photography. And now people don't paint like this anymore.'

'Because it's been done,' Lally said simply.

'But nothing can ever truly be captured. This isn't spectacular because it's a perfect rendering. You're missing the point.'

Lally opened her mouth to protest but decided to let it slide.

'This is Church's landscape. It's not a photo, it's not supposed to be a hundred per cent accurate. It's supposed to capture the beauty of what he saw, and in doing so reveal a truthful feeling, a testament.'

'But isn't the accuracy important? Isn't that what you were saying, about the age of science and art being so similar? The bird's feathers?'

'Exactly!' he said, thrilled. 'The man is torn! He is trying to do both! His belief that it is possible to do both is the driver! It is that impossible spot on the horizon!'

The old man near them gave a satisfied harumph, and it snapped Pat out of his fervour.

Lally grinned at him. 'So what's your third favourite painting?'

'It's at the Art Gallery of New South Wales,' he replied, turning back to the painting, speaking in a normal voice again and reaching for her hand. 'I'll show you when you come to Sydney.' It was a statement, not a question.

They hadn't spoken about anything like that. But as soon as the words came out of his mouth Lally knew them to be true.

⌐

They were walking along 14th Street hand in hand as the sun was setting when people started pouring out into the street and onto their balconies. She and Pat had been lost in each other, squabbling about framing techniques. At first Lally thought she might be getting a migraine, with the blind spots in her vision, but Pat noticed the colour in the sky first. 'Hey, look,' he said, directing her gaze to the sun in the sky ahead of them, perfectly aligned between the buildings either side of the street.

'Oh, of course,' she said. 'Manhattanhenge—it happens every year.'

People were gathering around them, holding up their phones. A man on a balcony nearby had a camera set on a tripod.

'It's like the sky is on fire,' Pat said almost dreamily. 'Just like a Turner.'

Lally looked around her then, at the huge glass windows ablaze in vermillion, at the smouldering brown bricks, at her own forearm with its little hairs glowing like embers. When they started walking again the sun was blinding them so much they had to go slow. People coming in the opposite direction, a couple together, a dog on a leash, babies in prams, only became visible to them once they were right up close. She looked at Pat, and he smiled back at her, both of them bathed in gold. She just felt so fucking light. So at ease. This was the happiness normally reserved for moments of complete control and achievement. But she didn't know when Pat was coming back to New York, when she would go to Sydney, what they would do in between, what the fuck was going to happen with the HBO stuff and Brodeur and the Farr exhibition . . . Somehow she could just watch these thoughts slip by without them touching this place inside her. Maybe she didn't need to see that far ahead to be okay with what was happening now—what was coming towards her, where she was, who she was with, who she was.

16

AT THE STAFF MEETING PAT volunteered to take on a load of extra appraising work. Partly it was to cover for how dishevelled he knew he looked and partly it was because he hoped he could drown himself in work as a distraction.

'Wonderful,' Josephine said, but with narrowed eyes and her head cocked to the side. 'And come see me in my office tomorrow about the Bauer account.' She always stood at the head of the long table while the rest of them sat in descending order of importance down either side. The exception was Em, who sat at the foot of the table, directly opposite Josephine.

'Why is she so anal about who sits where?' Pat asked Em when they went for a drink after work that evening.

Em shrugged. 'It was like that with my predecessor, Caroline. She was a similar age to Josephine, and she told me that for a long time they were the only two women at Osborne, and they watched each other's backs.'

'That's cool,' Pat said.

'That's not cool, that's awful.'

'Obviously the situation wasn't cool,' Pat corrected himself. 'I mean them being a team was cool.'

Em seemed unconvinced. 'I'm not so sure. I think Josephine plays by the boys' rules and that's what she had to do to get to the top, but now she's there she's not exactly trying to change anything. You know I report to her. So much of the accounts and expensing the seniors think they're sneaking past her, she sees it all. Caroline and Josephine had some kind of spy-handler thing going on that she's getting me to do now too. I gather the intel and send it up.'

'Wow.' Pat was dumbstruck, then immediately realised this information didn't surprise him at all.

'And there are still hardly any women getting hired or promoted, but it's always a woman on the front desk.'

'She seemed pretty pissed when Malcolm offered me a job,' Pat said.

'But you still got the fucking job. You think anything in that building could happen if Josephine really had a problem with it?'

'True.'

'Actually, I wanted to ask you about that.'

'About what?'

Em hesitated, 'I want you to help me—teach me some stuff about your job—so that next time there's an opening for a junior I can apply for it.'

Pat was flattered. He sat up a little straighter. 'Wow, yeah, sure.'

Em snorted. 'Calm down.'

'So where should we start? German Romantics? Baroque?'

'Pat, I know just as much about art history as you. What I need to know is the industry stuff. The who's-who-in-the-zoo stuff.'

'Oh, right.'

'For example, how did you land the Bauer estate? Who helped you move so many works in New York?' She had taken out a notebook and pen and looked at him with a determined face. 'Actually, let's start with how you did get your job, since you reckon Josephine wasn't happy about it.'

Pat shifted uncomfortably. 'Ah . . . okay.'

He told her the Banksy story, but left out the part about it being an old boys' event. Said it was an industry drinks.

'All right. What else? How did you know Sophie Bauer would have so much stuff?'

'Well, me and her stepson went to the same high school and—'

'Fucking hell.'

'Hang on,' he said. 'It wasn't like that.'

She grimaced. 'Surprise me.'

'Sophie didn't recognise me from back then, but I recognised her, and I remembered what kind of pieces had been in their house. It was dumb luck that the walk-in that morning happened to be her.'

'So what I need is a dick, and some luck, and an Emily of my own?'

'Christ.' This was pissing him off.

'Don't get snarky. What the fuck do you have to be snarky about here?'

'You're—'

'I'm asking you for information that will help me. I am sure you have that information.'

'But—'

'I do not believe that you're where you are now entirely on an engine of masculinity and luck, Patrick. There, I've said it—now will you try harder for me, please?'

He was seriously considering getting up and leaving, but when he looked up from his beer he saw how sad and earnest she looked, sitting there with a pen in her hand. He nodded slowly, and tried to think of what he'd learned in the last few months. 'Well, I found out the other week at the senior associates' check-in that Julian doesn't really do any evaluating anymore. His second wife is one of the Inghams women—you know, that dynasty who are millionaires from selling cooked chooks.'

Em laughed. 'Yeah.'

'It's wild. He's barely in the office, but the stuff he brings in . . .' Pat whistled and raised his eyebrows. 'A lot of jewellery and wearables. Seems like they always want different things to wear, you know? So these women buy things, keep them for a year or two, then bring them back to sell through us nice and discreet. I didn't realise how much of our bread-and-butter trade was in wearables.'

'Right.' She was taking notes.

'Maybe that could be an in for you?'

'Oh, because all my mates are dripping in Art Deco Bulgari.'

'Right.'

'What else?'

'Josephine doesn't care so much about single big-ticket items. I mean, unless they're so big they can get us in the *Fin Review*— advertising-you-can't-buy level gear. She cares more about getting families or names to align themselves—she uses that word a lot, "align"—with Osborne. Because you want the estate, not the asset.'

'Right, right, right.' Em's face had brightened. 'This is what I need.'

They went on for one more round of drinks before Pat said he had to go home. Actually, he was late to meet up with the boys at a different pub, then he 'maybe' had a call with Lally.

'Thank you, Pat,' Em said, giving him a hug. 'I really appreciate it.'

At the second pub the boys were commenting on how much less-fun he was these days, and how that was baffling to them considering he'd been gloating about his great open relationship. Pat winced. He wasn't particularly proud of telling them about the hot surf lifesaver he'd nailed the other month, but he also didn't do much to stop their chatter. He'd been trying to find random excuses about why he'd have to get home at odd hours on the weekend, or not get too messed up at night before an early morning, and fell back on blaming work.

'That old biddy is really riding your ass,' Rory said to him, slapping him hard on the back when he left the pub at eight.

'Yeah, she's right up in your butthole,' James added.

Pat paused at the table and gave Rory a look, like, really dude? And Rory looked him straight back in the face, like, yes, really.

He and Lally had made a date for a call—his ten pm, her eight am—agreeing that they'd suffer equally from such an arrangement. *Sounds like modern love*, she'd written, and he was thrilled to see her use the l-word until it occurred to him how resentful it sounded. Lally's sarcasm and dark humour didn't translate to a text-based relationship. He'd had to develop a fair amount of faith to sustain him between their video calls.

He had just got home when a message came through from Lally: *I'm sorry, I have to cancel tonight. There's a situation with an artist. Needs immediate attention. Hope you're well. Xx*

The disappointment was huge. Humiliation. Like a truly shocking comedown. He closed his eyes and saw her waking up in some other man's bed. Getting fucked, fucking him. How stupid of him to think he could rein her in by scheduling a video call for Saturday morning. Then he just felt pissed. He had left the boys, so conspicuously, to get home and wait for her. What a joke. He got another beer from the fridge. It was easier to be angry than embarrassed. Time for *Call of Duty*.

He downed his beer and got another, and as the alcohol was working through his system, he imagined Lally getting hit by a car. Then it occurred to him that if she ever did get hit by a car he wouldn't know. He paused the mission and looked up at the ceiling. He spent so much time thinking about her, and if something happened to her nobody would even think to let him know. He imagined finding out by seeing other people post RIP on the gallery's social media pages. Then he just felt like a fucking fool again. How many hours, aggregate, had they even spent together in real life? She was in New York. She was arrogant and successful—the worst combination for a girl you were trying to lock down. She didn't give a shit about him. Why should he give a shit about her?

He took another large gulp of beer and his phone went off. Same dumb spike. Fucking hell it pissed him off. It was never her.

It was his sister: *Hey, you got a minute?*

He replied that he did and tried to contain his nervousness. He and Beck rarely messaged each other, and certainly not late at night. Images of one of their parents having been bitten by a brown snake flooded Pat's brain as he waited for her next message. Or maybe their mum's breast cancer had returned.

Beck: *Dad finally agreed to get air conditioning*
In time for the baby
Pat: *Holy shit*
Beck: *I know*
Due date late October
Pat: *All good with the baby*
?

Beck: *Yeah all g*

Just FYI also Sean is not gonna be around

Pat started typing a happy reply then deleted it. Was she sad? She wasn't typing anything either. Totally fucking impossible to gauge the situation.

Pat: *I'm here if you need anything*

Beck: *Thanks*

Pat: *What's the plan for work*

Beck: *The shed said I can have a couple of months off*

Pat: *Great*

Beck: *Better off without that deadbeat around*

Like you think the shed is great

He didn't take the bait.

Pat: *Tell mum I'm coming for xmas*

Beck: *You tell her*

Anyways you're coming for October right

?

Uncle

Pat: *Of course*

Wouldn't miss it for the world

Beck: *Okay*

See you then

Love ya

Pat replied that he loved her too, but the message sat unread. He stood up to get another beer and stepped on a bottle cap. 'Fuck!' He leaned against the kitchen counter and held his head in his hands, trying to catch his breath. How could a one-bedroom-basically-studio-apartment in Darlinghurst feel so fucking huge and empty and lonely?

Pat wasn't any less perturbed by the penis-lily photograph outside Josephine's office. He thought maybe he was making it worse, psyching himself out about it every time he was called to that end of the building. Her door was open. Good sign.

'Patrick, come in,' she said, not looking up. 'And close the door.'

Bad sign.

'Good afternoon, Josephine,' he said.

She handed him a large dossier. 'Finalisation documents for the Bauer account.'

'Ah, wonderful.'

'Indeed. We've ended up with almost twice as many pieces as anticipated. Well done.'

'Thank you.'

'I've been on the phone to Sophie, and she's delighted with your performance.'

'Thank—'

'I thought perhaps you could take the rest of the day off and deliver these to her in person. Every separate transfer of title page needs to be initialled so it's probably best we send someone to make sure it's done correctly.'

'Oh, sure,' Pat replied and stood, holding the folder, waiting.

'Is there anything else?' Josephine asked him.

'No.'

'Good afternoon then,' she said with a nod.

'Right. Thank you.'

He closed the door behind him and stood staring at the lily, challenging it. Nothing was the matter. He was killing it. He was handling this account and that real work contract was on the horizon.

Daft Punk was playing in the cab on the way to the Bauer house and it was the cherry on top of Pat's excellent mood. Sophie opened the door dressed in a kaleidoscopic caftan with rhinestones lining the deep v-neck. The house was warm inside, and Fleetwood Mac emanated from somewhere within.

'Pat!' She gave him an enthusiastic kiss on each cheek. 'Come in, come in.'

'Hi, Sophie. I've got all the finalisation documents for initials and signatures.' He tapped his briefcase as he set it down on the counter.

'Good boy,' she said. 'Let's do business first.'

He let the word 'first' go by without comment and pulled a pen from his shirt pocket, handing it to her. Her fingers brushed his and she smiled at him.

'Forty-one initials needed altogether.'

'Sheesh!'

'I know, sorry.'

'Let's burn through it, hey?'

He laid out the pages and pointed to where she should sign, replacing each sheet in the file as it was done.

'Phew,' she said as he clicked his briefcase shut. 'Now, how would you feel about a little celebratory spliff?'

Pat laughed, both from surprise and because it had been years since he'd heard anyone use the word 'spliff'. 'Sure!' he replied, and took off his jacket.

'Yes!' she shouted joyously, then reached for a Tupperware container on top of the fridge and trotted out of the room, her crazy dress billowing behind her.

Pat followed her to the media room, the source of the Fleetwood Mac, closing the door behind him. He felt alarmed that they were going to smoke inside, then he remembered that people who owned their own homes could do whatever the fuck they wanted inside them, and also that he was a man now, not a boy, so he dimmed the lights with the little dial on the wall and kicked his shoes off. There were giant cushions scattered across the floor, and Sophie kneeled down and smacked the cushion beside her. Pat obliged, reclining, and watched as she pulled a seriously fat joint out of the container. They chatted about all kinds of dumb shit as they smoked. Within about ten minutes he was starting to feel it.

'Do you mind if I take these pants off?' he asked.

'Ugh, get them off,' she replied, and they laughed stupidly as she tugged them over his heels and threw them to the side of the room.

'Do you mind if I take this muu-muu off?' she asked.

Pat collapsed into giggles. 'Moo-moo,' he repeated, and then abruptly stopped giggling when he saw she was completely naked underneath. 'Shit,' he mumbled, staring at her body. Everything was warm and soft and easy. She crawled towards him on her hands and knees to close the short distance between them, and he welcomed the memory of being called a 'farm cunt' by this woman's stepson in this very room about a decade earlier. How life came around in the end, hey? How things always turned out great. How you looked back and wished you'd just spent less time stressing.

'Do you mind if I take your shirt off?' she asked, already half done with the buttons.

Pat just lay there watching her breasts hang like panna cottas. Things were getting a little heavy, though. He looked at the roach abandoned in the bowl, and wondered where she got this good shit.

'Where'd you get this stuff?' he asked, blinking.

She made a kind of purring noise in reply, trying to pull his shirt off over his arms.

Pat felt heavy. Good heavy, he reminded himself. Good heavy.

She was at his underpants then. 'Aw,' she said, and he looked down and realised she was expressing disappointment about his lack of erection.

'You're very beautiful,' he said, looking into her face. 'I'm just a bit too high, I think.'

She pouted and grabbed his left hand, placing it on her breast, climbed onto him, and put his right hand on her arse. Then she started touching herself. He tried to focus, squeezing the arse and rubbing the nipple. It was a bit like trying to pat his head and rub his tummy at the same time. All a bit complex.

'Eat me out, Pat,' she said, and fell backward off him.

Pat obliged for as long as he could, his head so heavy, and then she was putting his fingers inside her and also fingering herself and then, to his relief, it seemed like she came.

The next thing Pat knew he was waking up. Sophie was asleep beside him, a blanket covering the lower half of her body. The glass bowl and Tupperware were sitting safely over on the media cabinet and the music was still playing on loop, but quietly. He had no idea how things had ended or how long he'd been out. The only indication of time he had was that he was starving and his mouth was dry and his breath was stinky.

He tiptoed around collecting his pants and shirt. It occurred to him that perhaps he should feel guilty about slipping out on Sophie like this, but mostly he felt something else. Not quite resentment, but a kind of a fear, or a bad gut feeling, about fucking her. Had he even fucked her?

He turned the door handle slowly but it made a slight click.

'See ya,' Sophie grunted from the floor.

He stood by his briefcase in the kitchen, pulling his pants back on, lacing his shoes, buttoning his shirt. It was dark outside. The clock on the fridge showed eleven pm.

On the way home he thought about how normally he didn't have a problem getting it up when he was high. That weed was something else. The whole situation was something else. It didn't feel good when he got back to his empty apartment, all the lights off, freezing.

17

'LALLY,' A MAN CALLED, BUT IT was just the barista letting her know her coffee was ready. Every day a billion tiny shivs jabbing her, then the mortification. That is not him across the park. That is not him calling you. That is not him in your bed.

She followed her usual route, east to west, willing her head to get back in the right space. It was working until she hit Bleecker Park and saw the families. A boy in blue corduroy dungarees whooshed down the slide and his squeal shot across the road as a woman picked him up under the arms. She used to think of these people—these mothers—as so much older than her, but increasingly she was understanding they were not. The universe was offering her an expanding view of professional opportunities while reminding her that her reproductive options were shrinking at an equivalent rate. Ironic. The fertility she'd cultivated at the gallery; her own body's less-loamy soil. Kim had sent her a message about Caitlyn's baby shower. Lally shivered thinking about it. February in Chicago. The slippery slope. Caitlyn was tapping out much sooner than Lally anticipated. The world carried women down this river so swiftly once they acknowledged

195

they might even consider the choice. 'Maybe' became 2.5 in a flash. Plans to 'go back part-time' evaporated into fetid air. The only way to stop the slide was a firm 'no'. Her birthday in a week. Thirty-four. Her mother and Gen were the only ones who knew. What good were birthdays anyway? No, thanks. She knew she should tell Pat, because not telling him would be more strange, but she was still wary, not sure how he felt about the fact their slight age gap was not in the normal direction. These were the loops she got stuck in now. Trains of thought, grooves in her mind she'd slip into, arriving surprised at her destination having obliterated her gum.

'Morning!' Leah opened the glass door for Lally, all fresh and bright and smiling and competent. What a godsend. They set up for their monthly check-in, each taking a stool on opposite sides of the cleared white desk.

'All right,' Lally said, arranging spreadsheets and calendars in front of her. Yes, this was good. She was good at this. Focus on this. Brodeur first. They went through attendance figures and marketing plans, moved on to the financials, then at the end of the hour switched to forecasting and future exhibitions.

'You know you asked me to monitor your individual gallery inbox, to manage Brodeur?' Leah said tentatively.

'Yes,' Lally replied, keeping a relaxed face but scrambling to remember what Leah might be referring to. She'd given Leah access to the account so that while Pat was visiting Lally would be able to put her phone away. A mistake?

'I know we've got Hernandez for December, and I just saw a few emails to and from Chuck Farr's manager and they had November in the subject line, so I wanted to know if that's what's happening?'

'Yes,' Lally repeated. 'It's been in the pipeline for some time now. We were keeping the announcement secret as part of an intense and specific publicity campaign his people suggested, and I forgot to loop you into it all. Add that to my to-do list, would you? I'll forward you the pertinent correspondence and details, get you up to speed.'

'Lally,' Leah said, putting her pen down, 'are you aware of the allegations against Farr?'

'I read the coverage.'

Leah paused, and Lally could see she was confused. 'But . . .' Her eyes darted around.

'I'm listening,' Lally said, suspecting Leah probably wouldn't be able to articulate her complaint.

'I just don't think we should be giving him a platform,' she said quietly.

'Because he's an asshole?'

'Well, yes.'

'You don't think any of the other people we've shown in the past two years have been assholes?'

No reply.

'And the Whitney does another Warhol, and the Met does another Picasso, and people write their think pieces, and everything rolls along.'

'Isn't this different?' Leah asked. 'Aren't *we* different?'

'So we're held to a higher standard than the rest of the industry because we do diversity and representation *better*? The other galleries can do whatever they want and nobody cares but because we care we have to be perfect all the time?'

'We've built a mailing list of people who, I think, wouldn't agree with Farr.'

'What does "wouldn't agree" mean?'

'I'm not sure I agree with his methods?'

'What does that mean, Leah?'

'My friend is in the mailroom at *The New Yorker*, and she said that they had been wanting to do a story for months, but most of the complainants were too afraid to go on record. I just . . . I don't think it's a good look to endorse him.'

'Not a good look? We'll have a line down the street on opening night, you know that. His show here will be all female models—a clean break from the tone of that last series. I'll sell half of the works before the media preview, the other half the morning of opening night. His work is beautiful, challenging and people love buying it. If the world cared so much about ethics and morality in art, they'd pay for the artists in the Saplings Program. But mostly they don't. What people care about is whether they "like" it, and what they think it's going to be "worth", and they like Farr, and they think he's worth their money. The public vote with their cash at every show. This place keeps running because sometimes I give them what they want. Let the noise happen.'

Leah didn't respond.

'Is there anything else you wanted to say about it?' Lally had half-a-dozen comebacks if she did. Leah had been willing to play this dirty game for Brodeur. How could she justify where she drew a line? Didn't her own paycheck come off the back of Rivera's death? They were all mixed up in this business together. But no further argument was necessary. Leah simply shook her head.

'Great. Add that to my to-do list then. And put a weekly reminder in the calendar to keep bugging his people for a studio visit, please—he's being wriggly. We'll cover the marketing and promo plan at our next meeting. And Leah'—Lally put her own pen down now and leaned forward—'I want you to know that you can raise these things with me, and we can have these conversations. I'm not trying to shut you down.'

'Okay.'

'Are you going to be all right working here? On this exhibition?'

'Yes,' Leah replied, making eye contact, sitting up straight.

'Great.' Lally smiled, but when she left the gallery soon after, walking home the way she'd come, she felt uneasy. The emails oversight had been a Pat-induced mistake, but it would look bad to rescind Leah's access now. Accusatory, even. If Lally had had a gig like this straight out of college, she would have said, 'Yes, ma'am; thank you, ma'am; three bags full, ma'am.' How many bullshit 'internships' had she done in her time, for men who did far worse than what Farr had supposedly done? Leah was getting paid. Not a lot, but enough to warrant a little loyalty. Couldn't she big-picture for a moment here? Pat would get it. Lally wanted to talk to him, wanted to bitch and debrief. Gen wasn't an option and that meant she could speak to nobody.

———

'Who's getting married again?' she asked Gen. They were waiting at a large restaurant table for the rest of their party to arrive. Their wider circle of friends—more Gen's than Lally's—were celebrating one of their number getting engaged.

'Oh, stop being a fake grinch,' Gen replied. 'Steph is. You know that, you just don't like her.'

Lally nodded and went quiet, staring into her drink.

'Being performatively anti-romance isn't throwing me off the scent, Lally. I can tell this guy is really tearing you up.'

Lally groaned, rubbing the space between her eyebrows.

Gen laughed.

'It's not funny!'

She shoved Gen in the arm, but Gen laughed on. 'It's hilarious!'

'I am pathetic and ruined.'

'You're just falling in love.'

'No, I'm not.'

'And you're clearly defensive about it.'

'Because it's fucking terrifying.'

'Earth to Lally: love is terrifying.'

'It's never been like this before.'

'I can't believe you're trying to convince yourself this isn't happening.'

'I want him to feel like this too.'

'Yes, you want him to love you.'

'No, I want him to be in pain like this.'

Gen cackled and they both drained their drinks as the bride-to-be arrived.

The three women made a fuss about the ring, chatted about autumn versus spring ceremonies, debated Sardinia versus Croatia for a honeymoon. Lally was watching herself from above, doing this thing, playing this role, speaking in a gushing voice she hated. It was more of a show than when she was on for an opening night. She went to the bathroom and looked at her face in the mirror and saw the envy in it. Not of the convention—fuck, no—but of the ease with which an airhead like Steph seemed to be going through the adult motions. Lally knew it wasn't possible to ever draw a clear line between the two things: between what she truly wanted and what she'd been frightened or pummelled into wanting. Long-distance sucked. The phrase 'white gold with a princess cut' made her want to stab herself in the face.

She and Pat were dipping in and out of work and other topics: movies they'd seen; big bequests they'd heard about; the conservatives in power in their respective supposedly representative democracies. She sipped her coffee and watched him finish two beers, missing the times when they could really get somewhere with their conversations because they'd both been drinking. Sharing secrets was so hard when one of you was sober.

She had waited until the final ten minutes of their call to raise it, not wanting to seem anxious. 'I'm showing Chuck Farr's new work later this year.'

'Oh? I think I know his name from somewhere. What does he do?'

Lally hadn't anticipated this. 'Well, he makes extraordinary portraiture.'

'Nice.'

She was watching the clock while she explained what she liked about his work.

'Hey, this is cool, but I've gotta get going soon, sorry.'

'I know, I know, it's just . . . there have been some criticisms.'

'Of what?'

'Of Farr.'

'Oh.'

'I suppose I just wanted to give you a heads-up.'

'Okay.'

There was a truly awkward pause then. It always felt like a betrayal when that happened. They had such a great rhythm in person. It made her doubt their compatibility when they couldn't translate through the tech, and she worried he felt the same.

'Look, I'm sorry, but I really do have to go,' he said. 'I need to shave before I head out tonight.'

Lally wanted to tell him that he could just shave while they were still talking, that slicing ten minutes off the end of a sixty-minute video call felt significant.

'I miss you,' he said with a tone of finality.

'It's my birthday this weekend,' she blurted out, loathing herself immediately for the desperate disclosure.

'Oh.' His face went blank. 'Why didn't you tell me?'

She couldn't tell what he was thinking. He'd never asked. She shrugged.

'Well, happy birthday for the weekend. I'm sorry there's not much we can do to celebrate it together. I can't—I mean, if I send you something now it won't arrive in time.'

'I know, it's fine.'

'I hope you're spending it with friends?'

'Yeah, yeah, all good. Birthdays get less significant the more of them you have. You'll see.' She forced a laugh. 'Talk to you next week.'

'Talk soon.' Pat smiled and waved.

Lally ended the call and felt like vomiting. She needed to get out of the apartment, needed help. She called her mother. Estelle would have just arrived at the restaurant with a basket full of produce from the farmers' market.

'Mom, can I come over?'

'Of course. What time will you get here?'

'Soon.'

'Are you okay? Do you want to eat?'

'Yes.'

'Well, of course. Okay, do you—'

'I love you, see you soon.'

Lally grabbed an oversized tote and packed her pyjamas and phone charger, left the second half of her coffee on the counter and slammed the door behind her.

The street was noisy. Better. She got another coffee, and hailed a cab.

―――――

The lunch seating at Estelle's was well underway when Lally slunk into the kitchen through the back door. She caught Gary's eye and they nodded to each other in acknowledgement. Flames licked up high against the sides of a pan on a nearby stove. People were calling out to each other. 'Yes, chef!' someone shouted, and Lally spotted her mother holding a clipboard near the floor-to-ceiling spice rack by the back wall.

'Full lunch service?' Gary asked, brushing past her with dirty plates.

'No!' Estelle called, waving. 'I made her favourite soup, it's sitting with the saucier.'

A young man on the other side of the kitchen, presumably the saucier, called out, 'Got it!'

Gary gestured for Lally to sit at the chef's table—a tiny melamine thing at least two decades older than the rest of the kitchen, with stools that could be tucked right under when not in use. Lally couldn't remember a time when they hadn't had it. The table was one of the few things Estelle had taken from the house in Flushing when she left. A bowl was placed in front of Lally. Its contents were slightly cloudy, with chunks of carrot floating around. She had been returning to this meal her entire life. The smell of it, the saltiness, made her eyes water. It was the certainty of the thing. The reminder that she had been in this dark, low place before, and she had returned home to her mother before, and time went on and problems passed, and she survived. Across the kitchen her mother was checking the diameters of strange hunks of meat in a styrofoam box.

'You're the only person she lets eat chicken breast, you know that?' Gary appeared over her shoulder to collect her empty bowl. Estelle had pioneered what they now called 'snout-to-tail' and 'no-waste' food.

'Thank you,' she said, smiling at him.

'A beer, perhaps?' he offered.

She nodded, and as he left she shook her head at the miracle of it. Estelle had once told Lally that she couldn't do what she did without Gary. Where were you supposed to find a Gary? The question, actually, was why she wasn't usually attracted to men like Gary. That was a can of worms. She rubbed her eyes.

'I think the boys can handle the dinner service.' Estelle sat on the stool beside her. 'Why don't we pack up the rest of our lunch and go home and eat?'

'Sounds good.'

They spoke about little things as they walked the six blocks to Estelle and Gary's apartment. At home, they moved straight to the kitchen. Lally retrieved the plates and bowls while Estelle pulled containers of food from her bag. Lasagne, rocket salad, orzo with pesto and beans.

'It's good that you don't have to be in the kitchen all the time,' Lally said, sitting down at the table.

'My hands are starting to go,' Estelle replied, looking down at them. 'I told Gary not to tell anyone. It's embarrassing. Like a surgeon getting the shakes.'

'Oh, Mom, no . . .'

'It's fine,' Estelle said with a wave, picking up her fork. 'David, my sous, is becoming a great chef, and I'm happy to manage and supervise. It's time.'

They served themselves in a comfortable silence.

'Is it something at the gallery?'

Lally sighed. 'Sort of.'

Estelle nodded.

'I thought that money would solve all my problems.'

'Ha.'

'I mean work problems,' Lally tried to explain. 'I thought the challenge would be breaking even then turning a profit. But with that big sale in February, I dunno . . .'

'New problems?'

'New problems.'

'I tried to tell you this when I got the star. Remember? You were pushing and pushing, wanting me to open a second place, a retail range. But more success brings bigger problems. Do you want to be happy?' Her mother was looking at her, concerned.

'Of course.'

Estelle shook her head. 'I mean, is happiness what you're actually going after?'

Lally paused, put a bean in her mouth, chewed.

'People say they just want to be happy, or that the next thing will make them happy once they achieve it. But then they create situations for themselves that make them unhappy.'

Lally kept chewing.

'I know what makes me happy. My restaurant serving good food, earning me a living. Seeing you makes me happy. Going to the community garden on my day off makes me happy. If I had followed success when it came, I might not have these things.' She paused and, in a softer voice, said, 'And Lally?'

'Mmm?'

'Gary makes me happy.'

'Gross.'

'He brings me great happiness.'

'Too much information.'

Estelle shook her head in mock despair. 'Still no man?'

'No, Mom.'

They ate in silence for a while, serving each other final pieces from each dish. 'In that case,' Estelle said, 'I am taking Gary on a holiday for Christmas.'

'Why would my being single change that?'

'I was waiting to book the tickets, to make sure you weren't going to bring someone home.'

'Shouldn't you be more worried about leaving me alone?'

'Ha! You love being alone.'

That was true.

'I thought we could have a Thanksgiving–Christmas mash-up before we leave. And maybe you can spend the holiday with Gen. Remember how you did that years ago and had a blast?'

'Yeah.'

'It's okay, right?'

'Yes, yes, of course.' Lally smiled. 'Go have a holiday. Where will you go?'

'Somewhere warm. An island. Maybe Hawaii.'

'Nice.'

———

Hey, I just found out my folks are going away for xmas this year. Want to spend it together? Also, wanna hang out tonight?

It was a while before Gen replied. *Going to Raleigh for the fam, sorry! And covering at work tonight. Sorry x2!*

That was that then. When Lally got back to her empty apartment and went to squash her tote in the storage space at the top of the wardrobe Pat's scarf fell down onto her face. The smell was faint but still there.

You free? she messaged Ben, adding a wink face.

He didn't reply for over an hour, most of which Lally spent sitting in the bottom of the shower under a stream of too-hot water. When he did finally reply she smiled down at her phone, feeling good, feeling mean. He was so eager. He cancelled his afternoon meeting. He would get some Veuve on the way home. Was she hungry? He could be at his place in an hour or hers in one-point-five.

Lally did her face, put on a short black dress loose enough not to have to remove, fixed her hair and got a cab to his apartment. When he opened the door she was immediately reminded of how little she liked him, and she put on a bit of a show to compensate, turning the lights off and drawing the blinds, drinking quickly, lying about getting wet in the cab over so they could skip the foreplay. He needed so much encouragement, though, to do what she wanted him to, just to fuck her. She egged him on, biting him harder, asking to be smacked, refusing to take off her dress. Finally, when she started talking dirty he began to get the idea. She pushed him over to the side of the bed and got on her knees, presenting herself to him to be taken from behind.

'Harder,' she said again and again. 'Harder!'

He smacked her, but too lightly.

'Pull my hair.'

'Oh, you like that?' he said into her ear, getting into it at last. 'You little slut.'

Lally almost laughed. Even his dirty talk was weak. She wanted to ask him if he'd heard that on his Platinum Amex porn account, but then he was coming, and she was already thinking about how to leave without looking like a crazy person, and whether she'd pour herself a gin or a Scotch. She surprised even herself when she started crying in the cab home. And then, just because the universe was in a bad mood, a voicemail from Emile in that absurd accent.

Hello, Lally. We have a small problem. Guillaume is very upset with me for sharing this information about his mother. He says he has seen some . . . articles? Online. About the, ah, troubles his family has been experiencing. Please call me back when you can. He says he will not speak to press or do any interviews. He will say nothing about his show. We will be there soon, but yes, I am sure, we should speak before then. Okay. Bisous.

18

PAT: *YEAH I'M HERE*
What's up?
Lally: *I've booked flights for Sydney Contemporary in September*
Pat: *Wow*
Lally: *Good wow?*
Pat: *Of course!*
Great wow!
Lally: *For work, of course, but I'm sure we'll get time together too*
Pat: *I could take a couple of days off*
Lally: *No no don't do that*

Pat stared at their exchange. This again! The huge offer, but with the take-it-or-leave-it tone. She was driving him mad. Midnight his time meant ten am Lally time. Maybe she was up and free.

Wanna actually chat? he typed.

Sure, she responded. *Give me 5.*

He climbed into bed with his mobile and headphones, propping himself up with pillows. When the call connected they started talking, easily, about Sydney.

'I think you'll like it here,' Pat said. 'It's a smaller version of New York in terms of attracting creatives. People who want to make it. Ambition and drive and all that.'

'Yeah?'

'Do you think that's the New York special sauce?'

Lally paused to think. 'Some people move to these places to be seen and others come to see. Obviously, art is huge here, and I don't just mean visual art, I mean theatre and fashion and literature—'

'Art in the big sense.'

'Exactly. And some people want to "make it", whatever that means to them, but it mostly means being literally seen in one way or another, having their name in lights or just being acknowledged by other people in their industry—popularity, fame, whatever. A few of them want to be seen in the deeper sense. As in understood, human connection, et cetera.'

'What about you?' he asked.

'I don't like the feeling of being watched, or observed, I guess, but I still really like being in among things. I like the stimulation, the challenges, but I like feeling kind of invisible while I'm doing it.'

'Disappearing in the crowd.'

'Yeah.'

'Except the crowd is in a gallery with your name on the sign?'

She looked shocked, rather than hurt. 'Ouch, Pat. You think it was attention-seeking to give the gallery my name?'

He shrugged.

'Don't challenge me and then shrug. If you're going to present an argument you need to be prepared to articulate it.'

'Okay—why did you give your gallery your name if you don't want to be seen?'

'Because people need to know I back myself and my selections completely. I only have four hundred square feet. There can be no place for pondering the validity of what is on my walls. That space is me. I put my name to those artists.'

'All right,' he said, accepting the explanation she had clearly rehearsed more for herself than anyone else.

'Honestly, it's been hard getting people to take me seriously.'

'Because you're a woman?'

'Well yeah, duh, and because I'm young. Sometimes the young thing is like the nail in the coffin. The old people have all the wealth and the power here, and they're mostly white dudes, sure, but there is a bit of a mixture of people with power in the art world here. The biggest unifier is that they're all old and they're terrified that my success implies they should retire or die. Surely Osborne is even worse?'

'Yes and no. They're all a lot older than me, yes, but I think it's different because a lot of the art we deal with is old too. Like, my bosses don't need to keep up with new movements and emerging ideas. The stuff we each specialise in is kind of static in concept. There's less for them to be insecure about.'

'But our understandings of those artists is really shifting now. The way people talk about Gauguin now is completely different even from five or ten years ago.'

'But not to most of the people buying and selling those artists' paintings. They're, like, the opposite of the kind of people who give a shit about Picasso fucking teenage girls.'

'That's true. It sounds like they suck, though. Do you even like them?'

'I've found the antiques scene pretty welcoming.'

Lally snorted.

'What?' he asked.

'Pat, you're a straight white dude—you'd find a KKK rally welcoming.'

'Fucking hell,' he said, annoyed. 'I meant warm.'

'Yeah, warm and welcoming.'

'Well, what do you want me to say?'

'Just admit it's funny when someone like you expresses gratitude for being "included" in art.'

'Sure, okay, I get that, but you also use this same attitude to just dismiss all the art I deal with.'

'That's a huge generalisation.'

'When I show you old art you presume it's invalid, and I have to work hard to get you to take it seriously.'

'You do the same thing with my art!'

'No, I don't! I take your art seriously,' he insisted. 'I believe it's valid . . . I just take some time to decide what I think about it, if I like it or not.'

'That's what I do.'

'No, it's not. You look at the artist's biography, and if they were a man or rich or European, you dismiss the work like it must have been easy for them.'

'Well . . .'

'Well, what? You actually think Dali's work was easy?'

'No—Christ. I just think Dorothea Tanning's art is equally amazing, and yet she was paid less money for her work during her lifetime, and her work is consistently valued less now by companies like the one you work for.'

They both fell silent. Pat had learned from experiences that when feminists talked about feminism he should just shut the fuck up. But he'd never been in a relationship with a full-on feminist before. Would he have to just shut the fuck up forever now?

'Say something,' she pushed.

'I agree, my workplace is very conservative.' He paused, choosing his words. 'I will try to be more aware of it and try not to contribute to it.'

'Pat, you sound like an HR training module! Try harder. I need to know you'll have my back when I'm over there.'

He grimaced and nodded.

'Let's talk about something else,' she said. 'How are your folks?'

He groaned.

'That good, huh?'

'I find it hard to—' He stopped and started again. 'There's such a huge difference between my family and my colleagues and my friends here in Sydney. My sister is going to have this second baby and she just doesn't have any money, and my brother makes good money from his trade and he finished high school, but only just, and he's a terrible reader. Sometimes when I go home and see my parents' house, or I speak to any of them on the phone, I feel bad for them. Then I get stuck in this loop where I feel guilty and shit about pitying them . . .' He trailed off, realising he was rambling, not wanting to talk about this stuff anymore. 'It's fucked.'

'That does sound pretty fucked.'

'Speaking of pity, I haven't told you about this weird client of ours, Sophie.'

'What a segue.'

'We've just wrapped it all up, the whole account—assets being sold off nice and quiet because of a mortifying divorce. She'll have plenty of money but it'll still run out eventually, and sooner rather than later with her, I reckon. We're talking about a woman who's used to swimming in pools of money, is barely happy with that, and now she's only got buckets of money.'

'Cry me a river.'

'She's pretty lonely, by the looks of it. It's sad. She's sad.'

'And you want me to pity a rich white lady?'

He laughed. 'No, I don't. I suppose she's a cautionary tale.'

'Of what?'

'Better to be broke and loved?'

Lally smiled. 'So wouldn't that mean your sister is better off where she is? Broke but with your folks and loving her kids? Sounds better than Sad Sophie.'

'Hmm, best of all, I suppose, is being both rich and loved.'

The l-word hung in the space between his face and the screen, in the pixels representing her eyes and mouth, and in the salty air over the ocean between them. A panic was rising in him that she was expecting him to say it. If she said it first he would have to say it in reply. Was he ready for that? What was she thinking about? Was it this? These fears all tumbled over each other to disguise the real fear, the big one: that he did love her and she didn't love him back.

'Anyway,' she said, looking at her phone, 'I have to go in a few minutes. Can we talk about my trip?'

'Arrangements, yeah, great,' he replied, pulling out his own phone.

'I land two days before the fair opens to the public.'

'Then you unpack your suitcase at my place, I steal your passport, and you stay here forever.'

'Cute,' she replied. 'I'm getting a hotel room. This is a work trip. I need to have a base.'

'Why don't you just stay here with me? My place can be your base.'

Lally shook her head. 'You can stay in my hotel room as much as you want. It's close to the fair and we can have room service—it'll be fun.'

'All right.' Pat dropped it.

'I'm really looking forward to seeing you,' she said.

'Same,' he replied.

He wanted to say he missed her, but the words just didn't come out.

19

'I ALMOST CAN'T BELIEVE IT,' Leah said to Lally as they cleared the gallery's desk. 'They were falling over themselves to say yes. I barely needed to offer them anything.'

'Freelancing is grim these days,' Lally said, shrugging. 'And Guillaume is a great story.'

'I've got the media night scheduled for Tuesday, all key attendees personally notified and confirmed. The bump-in this weekend is also reconfirmed.'

'You're a star,' Lally said.

A knock announced Emile's arrival. He wore a white linen shirt and looked like a man from an ad for watches, folding his sunglasses and wiping his brow with a small handkerchief, which he then returned to the pocket of his chinos.

'Welcome, welcome,' Lally said, ushering him into the air conditioning.

They kissed thrice.

Emile put his hands on his hips. 'I am sorry, Lally. I have tried to coax him out of this shell, but he will not have it. I have never seen him like this.'

There was a lull. 'Do I need to cancel the interviews we have scheduled for tomorrow?' Leah asked.

'No!' Lally and Emile answered at the same time.

'And the media preview? Is he just going to not speak at all?'

Lally and Emile exchanged the faintest conspiratorial smile. Emile nodded.

'What if he just doesn't speak?' said Lally. 'But it's deliberate. What if—'

'What if it is a protest?' Emile finished.

Lally nodded. Yes, he got it.

'And a little poetic too, no?' Emile gestured to the walls. 'He has spoken with his works.'

'Absolutely he has.'

Leah was looking back and forth between them.

'So, we go ahead as planned,' Lally explained to Leah. 'We tell only the two people we've agreed on, so they can work with it, and nobody else. Do you understand?'

'Yes.'

Guillaume Brodeur was one of the sharpest dressers Lally had ever met. Black suit, crisp white shirt, black tie. It was an evolution from the man she'd met just a couple of years ago. He seemed older too, and more assured. Her gallery was a comfortable space for him. He did not smile at the press gathered, but he wasn't rude either. He wasn't performatively mute—he said 'thank you' to a glass of water, for example—but he acted as if the critics were addressing their questions to someone sitting just to the left of him. For a moment, a ripple of confusion went around the room. Then Lally watched the magic unfurl.

'Why the same format as the past two shows but such a different tone?' someone asked.

No reply.

The crowd whispered among themselves.

'Is it something to do with showing in America for the first time?' someone else tried.

Nothing. He uncrossed and recrossed his legs.

'Can you hear us?' the first questioner asked again, genuinely unsure.

'Yes,' Guillaume replied simply, and a little shock went through the group.

'And why aren't you answering?'

Again nothing.

The first of the two plants piped up, a young Iranian–American woman Lally had been watching for a while. 'Artists don't need to explain themselves to us.'

Dissent fluttered through the group. 'We're at media preview,' someone muttered, frustrated.

'Perhaps the artist's refusal to speak about his work is simply a refusal to take responsibility for how it affects us,' the plant reasserted.

'Is this a protest?' the second plant called out from the back of the pack. He was a jock with an uncle at *Vulture*. Lally didn't particularly like or trust him, but the plants had to come from opposite ends of the spectrum. They wouldn't even know each other's identities until they sorted through the articles in the aftermath and tried to guess.

Guillaume smiled then for the first time, and the room broke into chatter. The formalities dissolved immediately, people turning to each other and speaking, the volume growing louder. A few people still tried to call out questions, but they were ignored. Journalists returned their focus to the works, describing their thoughts and feelings to each other in a way Lally hadn't seen before. She walked over to where Emile was standing on the other side of the room.

'All good?' she said, knowing it was.

He smiled. 'Very.'

———

The hot takes went out later that evening, right on time. Three major publications followed suit the following afternoon. Lally's phone was ringing nonstop with people asking to be added to the opening night guest list. Leah sent through an email at the end of the day with a dozen URLs of blogs and social media posts. Jerry Saltz chimed in and the gallery's accounts spiked with thousands of new followers. Emile sent her a message saying that Madame Brodeur had been contacted for an interview with the *Times* about her accident and arrest. Lally managed to catch about three hours of fitful sleep before opening night. They'd need to double the usual number of catering staff. Probably best to hire security too. After the first evening they'd stopped trying to moderate the social media posts—the dissenters were occasionally nasty and the defenders would leap in to scream back at them. Lally hated it all. Hated how much attention this show was getting, and it wasn't even close to being the artist's best work, not even remotely the strongest show of the year. She ignored a couple of messages from Pat complimenting her on the news he'd seen from Sydney, the hype around her gallery and the show. How could he not see what she did in these murky pieces? He was a fool like the rest of them.

The opening night itself passed in a blur. Lally attended for the first hour then made a strategic exit, realising too many people were asking her questions that she wasn't sure she could lie convincingly in response to. The next morning she tried to go through the regular motions—the pot of coffee, sitting at the table—but the peacefulness wouldn't come. She was fried. Maybe she was hungry? It was incredibly hot too. She walked to Tompkins Square for a bagel, wearing a wide-brimmed hat and large sunglasses, and her phone rang as she was crossing the street towards the park.

'Leah, how are you? I'm fucking exhausted.'

'Yes, same, but this should cheer you up.'

'Hmm?'

'I just got a call from the office of France's Minister of Trade, or whatever his title is.'

'Right . . .' Lally's heart started to beat faster.

'He's made an offer for the entire collection, with an extra few thousand—euros, that is—if we let him have every piece. Says they can go in the government's offices. A reminder for the incoming minster.'

Lally stopped walking abruptly and someone behind bumped into her and swore. 'I didn't think they would sell,' she said.

'Me either.'

'Well, do it, obviously.'

'Should we check with Emile?'

'No, I'll deal with him later. I'm sure it won't be a problem.'

'Okay, great . . .' Leah paused. 'So the plan worked.'

'Sure did.'

They spoke about logistics for a few minutes and then hung up, and as sweet relief washed over her Lally noticed her vision was starting to blur. 'Oh, no,' she said aloud. 'No, no, no.' She was too far away from home. It was going to be a big one. She hadn't brought her handbag with her, not even any aspirin. When she waved her right hand in front of her face it completely disappeared in and out of blind spots. Could she call an ambulance? They wouldn't come. And she hadn't been in a hospital since her dad died. No. Her mother? No, that would take too long. She tried Gen, but as the call was ringing through to voicemail Lally felt the numbness engulf the front-right part of her brain, the strangest sensation, as if a gentle brush were running over the inside of her skull, painting it with the numbing stuff dentists used. Gen's voicemail message was in a different language now. The tiny remnant of logical thought in Lally's mind knew it was too late.

'Gen. Lally. I'm scared. Bagel Square bench. Please help.' She started crying quietly. 'Can't see. Don't know home. Please.'

A passer-by slowed their pace to look at her as they passed, but then went on.

Lally could feel that her mouth was wide open but she couldn't close it. 'Please, Gen, please. Please.' As she tried to breathe the pain arrived, and she lay down on the bench, weeping, clutching the brim of her hat, shielding her eyes from the sunlight that was now stabbing her brain through her eyelids. The pain danced across her head before settling on that same right side. The nausea came next, and she turned her head to the side, preparing for the vomiting. She burped, crying still, as her phone vibrated. The glass face of it was sweaty in her hand, and when she looked at it all the lights were so confusing. The words had letters missing. She dropped it on her chest. 'No!' Scrambling to pick it up, mashing at the green light.

'Lally?'

'Hhnngg.' She put it against her face.

'Lally?'

'Help,' she cried quietly.

'Migraine?'

The word was an abstract to her.

'Where are you?'

Impossible to form words to answer.

'Tompkins Square Bagels?'

Lally turned her face away just in time to vomit on the bench.

'Oh god. Lally, listen to me: Tompkins Square, yes or no?'

'Yes.'

'I'm coming, okay? Stay there. I'm coming.'

'Please.'

'I'm coming now. I'll be there in ten minutes.'

'Don't go.'

'I have to hang up now.'

'No!' she tried to plead, but the pain exploded and she fell silent, trapped by it.

The phone went dead and she vomited again, the exertion making the swelling in her head even worse. Through her left eye, through the gap in the bench, she saw her own sick in a little pool on the gravel and a pair of shoes slowing near her. She made a gurgling noise, an absurd hope, but they moved away again. She drew her knees up to her chest and began to rock, sweating. Time stretched on, impossible to judge with such a chunk of her brain incapacitated. There was a brief relief from the sickness immediately after the vomiting, but then it came again, and she felt it dribble down the side of her chin as she blinked and scrunched her eyes shut. Far away her phone was doing something, but Lally was in another place now. The pain place. The place she was terrified would go on forever.

'Lally!' She heard the call but did not recognise her name.

Footsteps running, crunching on the gravel, skidding to a stop. Someone took her hat from her and she cried out, the sunlight unbearable.

'I know, I know,' the voice said, and a scarf was being wrapped around her eyes. Fingers were wiping her chin and cheek. A wafer of something under her tongue. 'She's drenched, yes. Bring a water bottle, yes.' This was not addressed to Lally, and in some distant part of her she felt relief that she would not be expected to answer. Her phone was taken from her. This was a relief too. It had been so confusing.

'Lally, it's Gen.' The figure crouched beside her.

'Gen,' Lally repeated dumbly.

'Yes. Alex will be here soon and we're taking you home.'

Lally cried and made a little fist, touching it to her forehead.

'I know, sweetie, I know.'

Lally felt a hand clasp hers. Waves of pain followed waves of numbness and nausea, then she vomited again, which brought a few moments of relief, then back down again into the dark place she went. By the time a second person arrived, and she had to walk, it felt impossible. She shook her head when a water bottle touched her lips, then began crying again because the motion hurt so much. After a long time she heard a familiar sound—a particular door opening—and then swearing from the people, and then Lally was being carried, carried up the steps, put down at a landing, carried up some more steps. It hurt her head, to be picked up and put down, to jolt with each step, but to be held by someone hushed the fear inside her: the fear that she was stuck, alone, in the wrong dimension.

The smell of her own apartment reached her. The cool cushions of her own couch. Curtains being pulled along the rail. Voices reached her ears.

'I have to get back to the surgery.'

'It's fine, I can stay with her until you finish. What do I need to know?'

'Vomiting every fifteen minutes or so unless she can sleep. Keep trying with the water. Light sensitivity, obviously. A cool cloth on the forehead seems to help. These are her pills. I'll see if I can bring something back from the vet.'

'Can I have some too?'

'Ha ha, no.' A kissing sound. 'Okay, see you in a bit.'

'No,' Lally cried. 'Please.'

'She'll be back, and I am here,' the man said.

Lally opened her eyes. The room was bearable. She saw his face, and knew it somehow, but did not know its name, just that it was a man, and she felt there was still some vomit on her chin, and the thought of this made her need to vomit again.

'Bucket,' she managed, and vomited as soon as it arrived. The man wiped her mouth.

Lally was slipping away now. Her shoes were removed from her feet, and the cold air on her toes was a small mercy. Sleep wasn't the right word for what followed, but when she came to, she recognised Gen's face, and said, 'Yes,' as Gen kneeled beside her, injected something into her arm, then said, 'Yes,' again as she placed another wafer under Lally's tongue. She opened her eyes properly and grabbed Gen's retreating hand.

'Delivered,' Lally managed to say, willing Gen to understand.

'You're welcome,' Gen replied, smiling.

The two people sat at the table talking in low voices and Lally lay on the couch, feeling the pain recede like a tide as the exhaustion set in, and she let herself be carried away.

———

It was late in the night when she woke up. Gen and Alex were curled up in her bed. Lally was unsteady on her feet, but managed to shuffle into the kitchen without waking them, pouring herself a glass of water. The first sip was sweet, and she was parched, but she knew to pace herself. When she stood in the doorway to her bedroom, watching Gen and Alex sleep, their chests rising and falling in unison, a realisation arrived in her. She felt it and knew it before her mind could turn it into specific words. The migraines were growing more frequent this side of thirty. Her refusal to acknowledge them, her absurd denial of this colossal weakness in herself, was not a solution. The confusion they created in her mind was far more frightening than the pain. She forgot her name, didn't know how to take care of herself or get home. Gen had a person now. Lally did not. If Gen had to take care of some children that could arrive anytime, Lally would still be on the bench whimpering as day turned to night, and someone would steal her bag or rape her or kick the shit out of her. She thought of her father dying alone. What was strategic about that? What was so cost-effective about being on your own? How was work so lucrative and alluring if this was how it manifested in the body? No, this was the truth she'd brought back from the dark place. Independence had always been an illusion.

20

IN THE LIFT ON THE way up to his office Pat checked himself out in the shiny chrome doors, mentally planning what would happen now the Bauer account was done and he was on a proper contract. He'd have to start sticking his neck out more, bring in more families, estates, find a niche or two. Perhaps it was time to call Malcolm and ask for a catch-up drink, see if he would throw Pat a bone. The doors opened, revealing his two greatest fears, combining into his new single greatest fear: Josephine and Sophie in conversation.

'Patrick!' Sophie said, and his stomach clenched.

'Sophie, what a pleasant surprise.' He smiled, and extended his hand to shake hers then watched, horrified, as she playfully slapped it away and leaned in to kiss him on the cheek, her hand lingering on his shoulder. He smelled something, a perfume, that catapulted him back to the Bauers' media room. What the fuck was going on? 'I didn't realise you were coming in today.' He couldn't bring himself to look at Josephine.

'There's been an incident. Gregory has gone. His passports are gone. His assistant has been fired so we can't get to him or track him.' Sophie said all this as though she were reading it in the gossip pages, as though it were being done to someone else and she was laughing about it.

'And,' Josephine added, 'our records show he accessed the joint firm–client trust account and drained it of the money made from sales of their estate so far.'

'Oh!' Pat was taken aback. 'I'm not sure what to say.' He really wasn't. 'I'm sorry for your loss?'

Sophie shrieked with laughter, hitting his arm. 'Oh, Pat, you're too good.'

Josephine glared at him. 'Sophie is in a delicate situation, with the separation still being processed and Gregory seemingly uncontactable.'

'But that dickhead must have been in a rush, because we've got plenty more things we can sell.' She seemed delighted. 'I decided we can just keep working together, and this time we'll put the money in a separate account so Greg can't get it. Fuck him if he wants to come after me—the lawyers can fight it out. But I doubt he'll be back. Not anytime soon.'

'Wow.' Pat was speechless.

'You say "thank you", Patrick,' Josephine schooled him.

'Of course—thank you.'

Josephine continued, 'We're delighted you're happy with our service, Sophie, and thrilled to keep working for you and your estate.'

'Of course, of course. Pat's been a star. I've got to head now. Just thought I'd pop in on my way to an inspection for a place at Vaucluse.'

'Lovely!' Josephine cooed.

They walked to the elevators. Pat followed, listening to them discuss real estate, agreeing that north-facing was the only option for apartments, as though this were the first time such a consensus had ever been reached.

'You'll be hearing from me, Patrick!' Sophie said, waving as the doors slid closed.

He and Josephine stood side by side, watching for the light above the doors to prove the elevator had left the floor, then turned to each other.

'Dear god,' she said, 'I'd picked her to be the one to up and bolt, not him, wouldn't you say?'

Pat shrugged. 'I don't think I understand what's happening.'

Josephine scoffed impatiently and walked away from him down the corridor. 'Get Emily to explain it to you,' she called over her shoulder.

Pat went over to Em, who'd been watching the scene unfold from the front desk.

'This is gonna be fucking juicy,' she said, opening the folder Josephine had left with her. The documents revealed it all. Gregory had made multiple withdrawals over several days, each of ninety-six thousand dollars, so that mutual approval from all trustees wasn't required. The money was transferred to a number of different accounts in various countries.

Em flipped to the back of the folder, showing Pat pages of images. There was a lot of traditional stuff this time: men's watches, war memorabilia and antiques. Pat stared in astonishment. He thought they'd already sold their key pieces, but it turned out there was so much more.

'She must be clearing out the stuff Gregory was going to hold on to,' Pat said.

'No jewellery,' Em noted, nodding. 'You're off probation now, right? So you'll be on track for a big commission if you can move all this.'

'Mmm.' He was seeing dollar signs in his mind's eye, but also a field of red flags.

'And it'll mean a few more months working with Sophie.' She looked at him, one eyebrow raised.

He mulled for a moment. 'Do you wanna get a drink after work?'

'Sure.'

When they were settled at a table with their drinks Pat tried to verbalise what had been niggling at him. 'Do you think there are any kind of, I dunno, client relationship no-nos?'

Em, who was squeezing a lime into her vodka soda, looked up. 'What do you mean? Like, expensing things?'

'No, no, nothing like that,' he replied. 'I mean as in having relationships with clients.'

'Oh . . .' She shrugged. 'I think part of what makes the business successful is what a huge grey zone that is.'

'Sure.'

'And that is why it's so much harder for women to crack the code and get into the scene.'

'Sure.'

'I mean, golfing buddies, business buddies, fuck buddies—it's all a conflict of interest, it's all a mixture of business and pleasure. This is art. It's in everyone's interest to avoid making those kinds of distinctions.'

'Sure.'

'Why?' she asked.

'No reason,' Pat replied, trying to come across as nonchalant and failing.

'Tell me.'

He exhaled. 'I slept with Sophie.'

Em sipped her drink. She didn't seem surprised.

'Sophie from the Bauer account,' he specified.

'I knew who you meant,' she said.

'Well, yeah. She initiated it, definitely, I was just going along for the ride really.' He winced. 'Sorry—unfortunate choice of words. I just mean, I didn't go there to seduce her or anything. And she's fine. She seems fine. It's more, I'm not totally sure what to do. I'm not sure where this leaves me.'

'Well, what do you want? And what are you worried about or afraid of?'

'Honestly, I didn't feel great about it.'

Em put her hand on the table, like she was reaching out. 'Pat,' she said, with a strange softness in her voice, 'did you feel pressured to sleep with Sophie?'

'Huh?' He forced a laugh. Drank some beer.

'Do you think Josephine knew this would happen? Or that it would be'—Em faltered—'strategic?'

'Fuck, that's a bit much, Em.' He tried to shrug it off, but her hand reaching towards him across the table was making things feel super intense. 'You're making me fucking uncomfortable with this reaching-out bullshit.'

'Sorry.' She withdrew the arm.

'I shouldn't have told you.'

'Yes, you should have. I mean, I'm glad you did.'

'I'm not. This isn't some half-cocked psych session.'

'I didn't mean to—'

'Great. Let's move on.'

She was quiet for a moment, staring down at her drink, stirring it with her straw. 'Do you ever feel like you want to find a different company to work for?' she asked.

He made a scoffing sound. 'I thought you wanted to learn the ropes so you could get in with them?'

'You still say "them".'

'Huh?'

'Get in with "them", you said, not "us", even though you're on a contract now.' She was still being so serious. 'You don't think you're one of them?'

He sighed. 'I dunno. Not yet. I figure another few years and maybe the gap will close.'

'What gap? The age gap? The money gap?'

'Both, I guess. Maybe also some trust. Josephine doesn't trust me yet.'

'Do you think it would be different somewhere else?' she asked.

'I don't know. Probably not. Could be worse.'

21

'THE FEELING YOU WANT TO cultivate with social media and the gallery,' Lally explained to Leah during their handover, both of them hunched over Lally's phone, 'is that everybody wants the pictures they've seen online, but they're all too embarrassed to pose for them once they get here.'

Leah laughed.

'I'm serious! Look at the pictures we get tagged in. They're either idiot tourists wearing velcro amphibian sandals, or they're the kind of person who has other people take their photos for them.'

'And we remove the amphibians from the feed.'

'Yes, we do.' Lally put her phone away. 'Now, I'm going to see what I find at the show itself, and maybe stick around Sydney for an extra week or so if I need to keep looking.' She felt herself explaining more than was necessary, justifying the length of the trip. 'I don't want to come back without two or three artists for the second half of next year.'

'Sure.'

'Okay, great. The only other thing I have on my list here to cover with you is that MacDonald's piece on Gavin for *New York* magazine is coming along, and we need to make sure they get one last phone call, if MacDonald wants it. Can you just keep an eye on that for me?'

'Of course.'

'Wonderful, thank you.'

'You know MacDonald gave a guest lecture in my final year?' Leah said.

'Oh? How was it?'

'Well, he said he felt his job was to "skewer pretension".' Leah gave it air quotes with her fingers. 'And I was really impressed by that, you know, undergrad and all, so I went back to his most recent dozen pieces—I was going to put them together for my end-of-term—and I could barely understand any of them, and I found three repeated metaphors. Obviously even he didn't think anyone would actually read them all.'

'Incredible.'

'Tobi spoke too, but I liked him.'

'What did he say?'

'He said: "Criticism can act upon art. It's not just some passive towel with which art can be wiped down. It can be a gun pointed at art."'

Lally nodded slowly. 'That's something.'

'I think so.'

'Do you want to be a critic?' Lally asked Leah.

'Maybe. But I'm not sure anyone reads criticism anymore.'

'What would you say to an artist who told you they were worried nobody cared about art anymore? You need to do it because you love it or it won't work, you know that.'

'I do like feeling as though I could . . . I don't know . . . push the work. And I like living in a time—now—when we ask questions of artists. Questions about legitimacy and deserving and accountability.'

An awkward silence arose between them. Leah was either grappling inwardly or prodding outwardly, perhaps both, but Lally would not cower. If Leah could actually articulate a new concern, raise a valid new question about Farr, Lally would hear it.

Leah did not.

'Why don't you start doing some of our press releases? Kuo went from *Artforum* editor to curator at MoMA. If you're good enough at two different roles you don't really need to choose. You could even do the opposite, from gallery into publication, if you wanted. Once I'm dead and no longer need you, of course.' Lally smiled at her.

'Krasinski says the language of praise has been co-opted by the press release, making it harder to write convincingly positively about art.'

'What do you say?'

'I'd like to try writing a catalogue essay. Hernandez's in December. And put my name on it.'

Lally stopped and looked to Leah's hands to see if the tremble was there, but she had them clasped in front of her this time.

'That's not an option, I'm sorry.' Lally frowned. 'It's not a good look. It would reflect poorly on Hernandez, suggesting we couldn't find or didn't want to pay someone out-of-house to do it.' Leah began to protest but Lally cut her off. 'I'm not finished. I'll do you one better. Schedule me a phone call with Wendy from PPOW when I get home. Find two or three shows of theirs that are at least six months away, I'll tell her you're good, she'll give you a shot.'

Leah beamed. 'Thank you!'

'Yeah, yeah.' Lally waved away her gratitude. 'Just remember what I said about not leaving me until I'm dead!'

As her assistant gathered her things to leave for the day, Lally thought about how people's absolutes became relative under pressure. Even Leah, the eternally politically correct, had doors she wanted opened.

The final person who needed convincing was Gen. Lally still hadn't found a way to tell Gen.

She checked her suitcase and found a bar. An extra three hundred dollars was a small price to pay for a flexi-ticket for the return journey. She hadn't told Pat this, of course, in case she'd misjudged things or in case he was weird when she arrived, but Sydney Contemporary only went for four days and Lally had prepared Leah to cover her for two weeks or even three. When had she last taken even a week off? It would have been the middle of the night in Sydney, but she sent Pat a message when she was in line for boarding, just in case.

Taking off, see you soon.

When the plane landed for the LAX layover and she turned her phone back on she saw he'd sent a dozen messages. Offering again to pick her up from the airport, which she had refused, as it would be smack bang in the middle of his work day. Links to booths he thought she might like, and a place they could go for dinner.

Lally was buzzing the whole second leg.

Walking from baggage collection out the sliding doors to the taxi rank was an electric shock. The sun in Sydney was so bright. A different colour, a different intensity, than anywhere she'd been in Europe or the Americas. It occurred to her that she should put sunglasses on, or look away, but the blue was extraordinary. In the back of a cab on the way to her hotel she saw a dozen pink-and-grey birds launch themselves into the air from a tall grey tree, and she laughed with delight.

At the hotel she forced herself to stay up long enough to unpack her suitcase and hang the dress she'd brought specifically for that evening. Then she set an alarm for four pm, giving herself an hour in which to wake up and shower and get ready before they met in the bar downstairs. Lally had imagined the moment he would walk in and say her name. She would be leaning against the bar, and she would turn around to face him, like in a movie, and he would think she was beautiful.

A phone rang like a banshee from right beside her head. It had cut her right as she'd hit REM sleep.

'Fuck,' she said aloud, fumbling for the receiver. 'Hello?'

'Good afternoon, I'm sorry to disturb you, but there's a gentleman here who says you're expecting him. Of course we can't give him your room number without—'

'What time is it?'

'Ah, it's just past three o'clock.'

'What's his name?'

'Just a moment, please.' She heard the concierge's hand move over the mouthpiece of the phone, then he was back: 'Patrick.'

'Pat!' she said. 'Yes, yes, that's fine. Send him up.'

Lally scrambled out of bed and looked in the mirror. Would it be better or worse for her to wash her face? She reapplied her deodorant, pulled on a clean shirt, and was about to change underwear when she heard his knock. Too late. She opened the door and he was standing there, grinning.

'Come in,' she said, her voice sounding a bit strange.

'I hope it's okay that I'm early.'

'Sure,' she replied, closing the door and turning to face him. 'I just don't have pants on.'

'And then he was crossing the distance between them. He was smelling her hair, kissing her neck.

'I need a shower,' she said.

'Nope,' he repeated, and stepped back to sit on the edge of the bed, bringing her body down with his. She put her legs on either side of him and pushed herself against his lap. It was overwhelming to be together again at last. Lally felt desperate to catch them up, to bring their bodies up to speed, to get their physical in sync with their intellectual.

'We don't—' he started to say.

She pulled back to look at him, amused. 'Pat,' she said and made a face that would convey how incredibly unnecessary his attempt at restraint was, and then she kissed him softly, and he softened his grip on her too, bringing his hands to her shoulders, and then she started undoing his belt.

The sex itself lasted for about a minute, the two of them on the side of the bed just like that, both with their clothes still on. She came almost immediately, possibly the fastest she ever had, being on top of him, having worked herself into a frenzy through the second flight, and the familiar smell of him having gone straight up her legs. He had moved as though to lay them down on the bed after she'd orgasmed, but she just held him tight there with her thighs, lifting herself off his lap a little more, bouncing a little more, until she could see how close he was, and then she'd just said his name into his ear and he'd come. They sat holding each other for longer than the actual sex had lasted. His hair was freshly cut and she ran her fingers over a spiky bit at his neck.

After some time she spoke. 'Now,' she said, 'I really do need to shower.'

They stayed in bed for an hour, chatting and kissing, then decided to order room service instead of going downstairs to the bar. Pat found a way to put some music on through the TV menu, and on their third round of drinks, at about seven, she realised they'd missed the beginning of the VIP preview night of the fair.

'Shit,' Lally said.

'Do you want to go?' Pat asked.

'Not really.'

'Me either.' They clinked glasses. 'However, I do have to work tomorrow,' he added, 'and I do not have a change of clothes.'

'Why didn't you bring an overnight bag?'

He laughed. 'How smooth that would've looked. *Hi, person I haven't seen in months. Wanna fuck?*'

'Hi, person I haven't seen in months,' she said to him, finishing her drink and setting it down on the bedside table. 'Wanna fuck?'

He put his drink down too. 'Come to my place,' he said.

'But—'

'You can keep your room here or not, whatever. Just bring what you need for tonight and come with me to my place. I want to sleep with you again.'

'Yeah,' she said after a moment. 'Yeah, okay.'

Pat's apartment was a bit better than the bachelor's pad Lally had expected to be disgusted by. When she went to throw a tissue in the bin she saw rubber gloves, a dirty sponge and an empty bottle of surface spray inside. Cute.

'Lucky you're from New York,' he said, sitting on the two-seater couch and taking his shoes off, 'because my place is tiny. My folks would lose their shit if they knew how much I paid in rent to live here.'

'I didn't tell my mom exactly how much my apartment cost,' Lally replied, deliberately neglecting to mention that she was actually paying a mortgage. 'Although the rent for her restaurant space has gotten a lot higher in the last five years. Rapid gentrification.'

'It's so cool that your mum runs her own place.'

'Yeah, I think so.'

'My mum had to go back to work for a while when everything went bad with the farm, but it embarrassed my dad. She was a checkout chick at the supermarket in town, and he said to her that every time she rang up someone's groceries they'd be thinking about how Murray couldn't support his own family.'

'Fuck,' Lally said, but gently. 'I suppose small towns can be hard like that.'

'Mmm.' Pat just nodded, putting his shoes away.

'My dad was also weird about my mom working after I was born,' she said. 'And by weird, I mean he wouldn't let her.'

Pat didn't say anything in reply but looked at her with an open expression.

She exhaled loudly and shrugged, kicking her own shoes off by the door.

He stood up and gave her a peck on the forehead. 'I'm going to take a shower. Make yourself at home.'

The door behind him opened to a tiny black-and-white-tiled bathroom, half of which was taken up with an old tub. A very loud exhaust fan rattled to life, and he pulled his shirt off and dropped it on the floor.

'No art?' Lally asked.

'Landlord says no nails in the walls. Dickhead.'

Lally went through to the bedroom, recognising the door-frame and bedhead from their video calls. A small wooden box sat alone on top of his underwear drawer and she resisted the urge to peek inside. Condoms? Cufflinks? Did normal twenty-eight-year-olds still smoke weed? Back in the living room there was a gaming console under the television. His place gave her that young-happy feeling again. She heard the shower stop and Pat emerged, drying his head roughly and throwing the towel over the top of the bathroom door.

'What are you looking at?' he said with a grin, putting his hands on his hips, stark naked.

Lally woke to a pair of birds screeching as though they were killing each other. Pat was still asleep, his cheek smooshed up against his forearm, a little drool at the corner of his mouth. She knew where his apartment was on a map in relation to the city centre and her hotel room, but she was itching to get outside and walk around, to scope out the neighbourhood. Watching her own neighbourhoods change so radically over a couple of decades had lit a glowing ember of interest in real estate, which grew into a great flame once she bought her own apartment. Capital changed everything, and only special things could change capital. Was this the rich area? How long since it had been gentrified? Was it recently? Or so long ago that it was now fully commercial and residential? Prices of apartments in Manhattan were still higher than Sydney, but not by much. If she'd done her basic calculations correctly, and presuming Pat had about thirty grand in savings as he approached the big three-zero, he'd still need another five years of solid squirrelling before being close to affording a deposit on a two-bedroom place in this neighbourhood. Maybe he was hiding something, like she was.

She'd read that there were pockets of galleries all over the city, but didn't know which were the best. Sydney Contemporary would be a better first stop. That was the best thing about these fairs in other cities—you could window-shop, get a good idea of how a gallerist wanted you to receive their work. She'd start making notes on a map after a walk-through. A picture would emerge.

'You think New York traffic is bad,' Pat said, launching out of bed when his alarm went off. 'It takes me thirty minutes on the bus just to get from here to the other side of the city. You want a coffee?'

'Yes, please,' she said, moving to get up.

'Nah, you stay there.'

'Okay.' She took his pillow and put it behind hers, sitting up in bed. He knocked about in the kitchen, coming in and out of her view from the bedroom door. He had an Italian espresso pot for the stove and had a shower in the sixty seconds it took to start bubbling. When Pat brought her a cup and kissed her again they smiled at each other. Lally sipped on the coffee as he rambled on about what he was evaluating at work. Deceased estates with the occasional valuable find. 'Grunt work,' Pat called it. She spoke loudly enough for him to hear her plans for the day as he shaved over the bathroom sink.

'Okay,' he said, sitting down on the side of the bed, 'spare set of keys for you on the hook by the door.'

'See you at six,' she said.

'See you at six.'

They kissed again and he was gone.

She took her cup to the sink and rinsed it, looking out the tiny window to some treetops and the street. Very leafy. She judged the rather sparse contents of his fridge, and the two-in-one shampoo/conditioner in the shower. Truly, she was on the upside-down part of the earth now. As she took her keys from the hook, she felt a kind of trill of happiness rise up inside her along with their tinkle.

A cab took her to the fair venue. Its scale was impressive—an old railway workshop with enormous ceilings, light streaming in through skylights and huge steel-framed windows. So much light, she marvelled, everywhere all the time. The coffee was excellent. Everybody was smiling. Their cash was rainbow-coloured.

She took her time inside, not introducing herself to anyone yet, just looking. She recognised most of the gallery names from her research, and was surprised by the calibre—both high and low—of a couple of others. The 3D works stood out to her. The textiles and sculptures were incredibly bold, some of it quite exciting. Sculpture, of course, was trickier to move, commercially speaking. There seemed to be a huge amount of photo-realism, which bored her, but of course people gathered in front of it. Lally stopped to see what everyone was gawking at in one stall, and found it was just a pencil drawing of a line of tins of beers she didn't recognise. Perhaps she was missing some provincial symbolism.

There was one person she wanted to say hello to. Lally consulted her map, turning left, then heard his laugh before she even saw him. Clark Joyce had started his gallery in Sydney in the nineties and expanded with a place in Brooklyn around the same time Gallery Lally opened. She had been emailing him a little, and he'd been generous with his perspectives on the very specific split between the two cities. It was a conversation she hadn't told anyone she had been having—especially not Pat. She wasn't even being totally honest with herself about the logistics and rationality of such an extension. But she'd cancelled the plan to rent the office space above her gallery in favour of this half-baked, harebrained scheme.

Clark spotted her, smiled and waved. She watched him interrupt the man he was talking with and then the other man turned and smiled as well. Lally smiled back at them. Everybody smiling.

'Clark,' Lally said as she reached them, and they kissed on the cheek.

'Lally,' he replied warmly. 'Before you tell me what on earth you're doing here, I'd like to introduce you to Harry Moran, the director of this menagerie.'

'Ah,' Lally said, and there was more smiling as they shook hands. 'Lovely to meet you, and congratulations.' She gestured to the bright, busy space around her. 'This is wonderful.'

'Thank you very much,' Harry replied. 'And welcome.'

'Lally's on the up-and-up,' Clark said.

'Oh, come on now,' she said. 'Stop it.'

'It's true. Direct acquisition from MoMA in what—your third year?'

'Wow,' Harry said. 'I remember now, the big installation. Congratulations.'

'Although tragic circumstances, of course,' Clark added.

'Of course,' Lally murmured.

'Of course,' Harry echoed.

'So, what are you doing down under?' Clark asked. 'This isn't something to do with our emails, is it? Are you serious about opening a place here?'

'No, no. Well, maybe.' She wasn't ready to talk about it out loud. It was still just a frightening, exhilarating mirage on the horizon. 'I've got a few spots free on next year's calendar year and thought I'd come see if I can poach some of your fresh young blood.'

'Ah!' Harry was delighted at this. 'Here's my card. If there's anything I can do to help, I'm at your disposal.'

He drifted off and Lally stayed chatting to Clark about suburbs and spaces and comparing government funding initiatives. She hung around for a performance piece—unfortunately sexy—then ducked back to the hotel to shower and check her emails. After dealing with her correspondence, she made some notes about what she'd seen so far. There was one particularly strong Asia-specific gallery, but much of the rest had been overwhelmingly white, and it showed. A homogeneity of vision, a low bar for standard mediums like paintings and photography, mediocrity in general. The silver lining was that this made the stronger examples easier to spot. She'd taken a few cards and made note of a few names. It had been far from a waste of a time. And she could see clearly where there were gaps in the Sydney scene that someone—possibly her—could fill.

By five thirty Lally was heading back to the fair when a message came in from Pat. He'd arrived early and was waiting for her. She went straight to meet him at the bar and they stood leaning against it, heads together conspiratorially, bodies all alongside each other. It was a how-was-your-day, what-did-you-get-up-to conversation, the kind they'd had so many times before but so rarely in the same room. Now she knew he could feel it too. A desire to be in contact. The mind could be as aspirational as it pleased, could frolic along realising the purity of its intentions, but the body could never lie, could never be denied, could never move above its station.

They finished their first drinks like this, then ordered another round and turned to people-watch. This was the type of function Lally normally attended alone, acting relaxed but actually working the room. It was fun to be there with Pat.

'Oh, there's the fair director,' he said excitedly. 'The bald guy.'

Lally smiled. 'Harry? Yes, I met him today.'

Pat shook his head. 'Can't you at least pretend once in a while that I'm telling you something you don't already know?'

She laughed and kissed his cheek. 'Is there anyone you want to say hello to while we're here, any networking you need to do?'

'Nah, I'm only here because of you.'

Lally looked around. She was tempted to follow up on a few of the promising connections she'd made, but felt like she shouldn't leave Pat by himself. 'Do you wanna just go then?'

'Yeah!' He seemed delighted.

They finished their drinks and made their way through the crowd.

Pat was holding the glass door open for her when someone called their names. Al was approaching from outside, just arriving.

'Well, well, well,' he said. 'How terribly unsurprising to see you two here together.'

'Hi, Al,' Pat said, shaking his hand.

'Al!' Lally hugged him and kissed his cheek. 'It's so lovely to see you again.'

'Are you really leaving? I hear it doesn't get fun at these things for at least another two hours.'

Lally considered capitulating. It seemed ridiculous to have come all this way only to blow off her professional opportunities.

'We just wanted to catch up with each other,' Pat explained, taking Lally's hand.

She looked down at their joined hands, then up at his face.

'Fine!' said Al, pretending to be hurt.

'I'm in town for a week or so,' Lally called over her shoulder as Pat pulled her away. 'I'll email you.'

Al was already inside, waving his hand in the air, dissolving into the crowd.

'Dinner? Drinks? My place?' Pat was leading her towards a line of taxis.

Lally let him decide. Let herself be carried away from work, in the car to wherever his place was, whatever food he picked moving into her mouth, whatever beers were these going down her throat, whatever shirt this was to sleep in, whenever it just so happened they called it a night. Relinquishing.

'You should have just stayed here with me,' he said as they brushed their teeth before bed, their elbows knocking in the cramped space but turning it into a joke. She didn't reply, mumbling nothing really, with a mouth full of toothpaste. 'And did you tell Al you're staying for at least a week? Do you know how long you'll be here for?'

Lally looked at Pat's face in the mirror. It was looking at her in real life. She leaned down and spat into the basin. 'I'm not sure yet. It sort of depends on whether I can find the artists I want, and then how hard it is to . . .' She trailed off as she met his gaze in the mirror.

'Well, how long can you stay?' he asked.

'I mean, I've cleared two weeks . . .'

'Two weeks!' he shouted. Pat dropped his toothbrush into the holder, took hers from her hand and dropped it into the sink, then pushed her out of the bathroom and into the living room, putting his arms around her. 'Two weeks!'

She laughed as he spun her around.

'Fourteen days!'

He pulled her down onto the couch. 'You have to check out of that hotel,' he said, gathering her legs up and draping them over his lap. 'I don't want to see that place ever again.'

She laughed. They really must be drunk. Were they?

Pat babbled on, 'I'll make a space in the wardrobe for your clothes and you'll be here when I get home from work and we can have dinner together at night and maybe take a little trip somewhere this weekend . . .'

Eventually he ran out of steam and they went to bed. He was asleep within minutes—Lally could hear his breathing even out, and she lay there trapped underneath his arm looking at the tiny blue flashing light of her phone, plugged in on the ground beside the bed, an anxiety-laden beacon alerting her to unread emails. If she was serious about this relationship she'd have to find a way to work while with him. He felt like a holiday. Like paragliding. How many more days could she ignore the ground rushing up?

22

AT THE FAIR PAT TRIED to keep his promise not to make any
public displays of affection. It made things exciting and funny.
They played professionals, speaking in overly formal language,
nodding, discussing 'the market'. He told a joke that made her
laugh a little and he felt pretty chuffed about it. Then someone—
a woman—was calling his name. Over Lally's shoulder he saw
Sophie coming towards them, waving to him. His guts sank
down low.

'What's the matter?' Lally asked him.

He didn't have a chance to reply.

'Patrick!' Sophie said his name again as she reached them,
sidling up to him and kissing his cheek. 'You left your scarf at
my place. Was that deliberate?'

He just smiled and cleared his throat, trying to repress
his panic.

Sophie turned to Lally. 'Hi, I'm Sophie. Pat went to school
with my son and now he's selling my ex-husband's man-trinkets.'

Pat's mind was reeling. Sophie knew who he was?
Remembered him?

'Well?' Sophie nudged his arm.

'What?' he replied, looking between the two women, stuck. He saw something come across Lally's face.

'Are you going to introduce us?' Sophie persisted.

'Right, sure, this is—'

'Lally, just visiting from the States. I'm just going to slip away to the ladies' room, leave you two to catch up, solve that scarf mystery. Nice to meet you, Sophie.'

'Oh, bye, then,' Sophie replied, and turned to Pat with a confused expression. 'What was that about?'

He shrugged. 'Uh, about the scarf . . .'

She laughed then, and started describing a work she'd just seen that she wanted to buy. He was maintaining eye contact and trying to nod at the right times, but his mind was galloping away. How would he find Lally? How much explaining would be required?

Sophie spotted someone she knew across the room and called to them, kissed Pat's cheek again and was gone.

What terrible timing. What incredibly, phenomenally, shitty bad luck. Sophie had talked for about two minutes. Why couldn't she have bullshitted to someone else for those two minutes? Why did she have to come ruin things for him with those two minutes?

Lally reappeared wearing deep red lipstick and her posture was stiff and upright. When she saw him watching she turned away and walked off in a different direction. Heading to the bar? He followed. She was doing the boiling thing, though, he could see it in her shoulders, in her hands. He knew exactly what was happening inside her head. She was chastising herself for coming all this way, wasting the time and money. When she glanced down at her sleeves—purple—he saw the muscles in her neck tighten, and it was obvious she was regretting not wearing her blacks. Lally was a portrait he'd studied so closely he could read her symbology. Or some of it, at least. What he wasn't able to do was approach her. No opening line felt sufficient to convey his feelings, until the statements that occurred to him—'I love you more than anything', 'I'll do whatever you want'—became too grand. Hollow with performance. When so much of their life together had been lived onscreen it was impossible to eradicate that aspect—that twinge of television, that framing, a postcard reproduction an insult to something original. How had he reached through all that when they first met? She had seemed so different in those first few days. He understood only now how much easier everything was when the idea of strings or stakes was an impossibility. He remembered how he'd followed her at the Armory Show, had seen the laughing woman in the corridor, a side of her she concealed beneath so many layers. If he hadn't caught that glimpse, like a divine X-ray, he probably couldn't have stuck it out with her long enough to crack that carapace. Was he glad he had? She could be so demanding, so cold, so judgemental and ready to discard people.

Lally reached the bar and ordered a drink, and Pat saw a man standing nearby clock her and check his watch. Jealousy bloomed. Maybe she would flirt with him in revenge. How did their arrangement cover that? Was their relationship open, but only when they were in different cities? Certainly he wouldn't have thought he could fuck anyone else when he was in New York, but they had never really discussed the rules. She never brought it up so he presumed she was happy with their arrangement, whatever it was.

The man finished his drink and caught the attention of the bartender, signalling another for himself and, holding up his card, pointing to Lally. Pat smiled. She'd fucking hate that.

His phone vibrated in his pocket. Work emails and a text from Sophie telling him about a big dinner happening that night. When he looked up again Lally was gone.

He tried to call her but it rang out. He was about to go home when his fear started swirling into anger. Lally was the one who obviously liked their relationship being open. Now she was cut about him having slept with someone else? And it was an older woman—she should've liked that! She was always bitching about men not dating women their own age. Fuck this. He checked the time. It was early afternoon. Rory would be finishing work soon. He'd get it.

'Fucking Americans,' Pat said. 'Have you noticed how loud they are? And they never listen when you speak, they're just waiting for you to take a breath so that they can jump in.'

'You all right, mate?' Rory paused his work to look up at Pat, his eyebrows raised.

Pat grunted.

A clanging gas bottle hitting the ground meant Rory would be flambéing the tops of twenty-four ginger and cardamom tarts then sprinkling them with crushed pistachios. 'What are you actually cut about?' he asked, picking up the small blowtorch.

'Whether we're exclusive or not, I guess,' Pat said. He found it a lot easier to talk about stuff with Rory while he was busy working. 'What the fuck we're doing. We talk like we're properly together but then when we're apart there are no actual rules.'

'Well, it sounds like a pretty fucking good set-up,' Rory said, sprinkling pistachios into the molten sugar. 'You get a girlfriend, and you also get to have sex with other women. Do you have weird restrictions, like when men date hookers? Like no kissing on the mouth?'

'What? No. It's not like that.'

'Then what's it like?'

'I don't know. I thought it would be good too, but then you realise it's so much harder for a dude to get laid than a chick. For every time I strike out, she's never striking out. And I just find myself wondering if maybe she's getting the better deal here.'

'So you want to fuck other people but you don't want her to fuck other people?' He was halfway through and the bakery smelled like a fairy floss machine.

'No, maybe I just don't want her to fuck too many other guys?'

Rory laughed. 'Or any rich guys.'

'Yeah.'

'Or any huge, baller, Black guys?'

Pat laughed. 'Yeah, exactly. You know—she can have one or two other sexual partners but they have to be scrawny broke dudes with small dicks.' He sighed and leaned back against the wall. 'When you and Mikayla were together was the monogamy always worth it? Did you want have sex with other women?'

'Well, those are two separate questions. It's different when it's non-optional. You're in a situation where you'd have to be the one who says, "*Lock it down, only monogamy.*" With Mikki, or I guess any normal relationship, it's the opposite. If you go to the girl and say, "*I want an open relationship,*" you better be fucking sure it's worth the risk, because she's going to flip and it could ruin everything. So normally it's, like, monogamy or nothing.

And sure, you meet people sometimes and you think, *I'd love to fuck her*, but if you're a good boy you don't and it passes, and if you're lucky you've got a good girlfriend and that's life.'

'But if you could have had what you did with Mikayla but make it open, would you?'

Rory fired up his blowtorch again and began on a second tray. 'I don't know. When things are good you just don't find yourself looking elsewhere. But mainly I'd hate the idea of another guy fucking her. I'd probably hate that enough to renounce my own appetites.'

'But how do people think that could possibly last for, like, five decades?'

'Beats me. Also, your situation is a different kettle of fish because of the long-distance thing. For you right now it's open or celibacy.'

Pat groaned and rubbed his eyes. The sweet smell was making him hungry and he hadn't had a decent feed in hours. 'Can I have a pie?'

"Course, mate.'

Pat grabbed a serviette from the small pile at the counter and went to the hot box, standing in front of it, looking at his reflection in the glass. 'What if we live together and she still wants it open?'

'What if you live together and she wants to lock it down?'

'I think that's what I'd prefer, to be honest.' He selected a classic and went back to his stool, poking a hole in the top of the pastry, beefy steam jetting out.

'So you want to live together and be monogamous?' Rory asked.

Pat looked up at him, a bit helpless. 'Yeah, I guess so.'

'Sounds like you're in love, mate,' Rory said.

Pat felt sick. He looked down at his pie with a rush of regret, suddenly not sure if he could stomach food at all. The kitchen felt hot. Too many smells. He was light-headed.

'Are you okay?' Rory asked, pausing to look down at Pat.

'What if she doesn't love me back?'

Rory nodded, seriously considering the question. 'I guess that's the biggest risk of all.' He spread his arms out like wings. 'And the greatest adventure of all!' he declared in a boom of song, firing the blowtorch into the air.

'Fuck you!' Pat said.

'Fuck me!' The song continued with Rory sweeping an arc of sugar into the air, spinning around on the spot.

'Shut up!'

'Pat's in love!'

'I said shut up!' Pat threw the pie down onto the floor, hard. It landed with a heavy splat, gravy fanning out like licks of Pollock.

Rory burst into laughter.

'I'm so fucked,' Pat said.

Rory put a hand on Pat's shoulder. 'You'll be right, mate. Happens to the best of us.'

'I have to go to her.' Pat bolted up to his feet. 'I have to see her before she leaves.'

'Yeah, sounds like you do.'

Pat grabbed his wallet and keys, moving fast for the exit.

'I'll just clean this up, shall I?' Rory called out after him, but Pat was out the door.

Lally had left too much stuff at his apartment. If she was going to leave the city she'd have to at least stop by. He started jogging towards home and managed to find a bus heading in the right direction. How long had he wasted at the bakery? She could have been in and gone by now. When the bus pulled in at his stop he leaped down the stairs and ran.

The front door to his apartment was open.

'Lally?'

She appeared in the bedroom doorway and he hurried over to her. She was putting things in a bag.

'Hey,' he said.

'Hey,' she replied, doing up the zip on a little pouch of cosmetics.

'Please don't be mad.'

'Mad?' She stopped what she was doing and looked at him like he was an idiot.

'About me sleeping with Sophie. I thought . . . I mean . . .' He gestured between the two of them. 'I thought you wanted to keep things casual, at least when we're apart. I'm really not sure.'

'I don't care that you slept with someone else, Pat.'

'What?'

'I'm a bit weirded out, and really disappointed.'

He groaned. 'I'm so confused.'

'The way you spoke about that woman to me was with such disdain. That was Sad Sophie, right? You mocked and belittled her. You said she was a lonely old idiot lady. It's disturbing that you would think so and also sleep with her. Did you sleep with her before or after you told me all that mean stuff? Actually, I don't want to know—I don't know which is worse.'

'It was a mistake. Please don't go.'

'What was a mistake?'

'Sleeping with her.'

'You don't get it.'

'What, you've never fucked anyone from your work?'

'Yeah, I did, actually, and then he died.'

Pat froze. What the fuck was she talking about? Did she mean that Rivera guy, or had she slept with someone else since then? Was that why she was getting so emotional?

She looked down at her bag but didn't move.

'I'm sorry,' he said quietly, and sat down on the side of the bed, between her and the door. 'Do you want to talk about it?'

'Fuck, no,' Lally replied, but she didn't leave.

He felt like he had nothing to lose at this point, so decided just to blurt it out. 'I want us to be together. Properly.'

'What does that mean?' she asked, without looking at him.

'I mean we don't see other people, and I was thinking maybe you could come meet my family at Christmas.' Pat surprised himself with that last bit.

'Wow.'

'Is that a good wow?'

She sighed. 'Are you sure that's what you really want?'

'Yes. That's why I said it. You're the one who hasn't replied.'

'Okay.'

'Okay what?' He reached for her hand, and Lally didn't pull away.

'It's September now,' she said. 'Do you think you can last another two months?' She still wouldn't look at him.

'What's that supposed to mean?' he countered. 'I'm the one asking you.'

She seemed defeated rather than happy. 'You're right. Sure.'

'Sure what? Lally, you have to tell me what you want. What we're doing.'

She sighed. 'What, we'd be boyfriend and girlfriend?'

'Yeah.'

'Pat, it's been a long time since I had a boyfriend.'

'Okay.'

She was silent.

'Do you want to come meet my family at Christmas?'

'I'll have to check with my mom, but that could be nice.'

'I know it's a bit intense, but I don't want to spend Christmas apart, and we would only have to be with my folks for a few days and then we could spend the rest of the time together in Sydney.'

'A few days?'

'It's a pretty cool trip. You could see some kangaroos.'

'Wouldn't you rather come to New York, have a white Christmas? And I've just been here.'

He shook his head. 'I've gotta go home for Christmas, I'll have a new niece or nephew. And I only get back there once or twice a year. My mum would kill me if I missed Christmas. They just got air conditioning too.'

'So you've told them about me?'

He hesitated. 'Well, I will now, obviously.'

She nodded and they sat together quietly. 'What do we do now?' she asked after a while.

'I'm exhausted,' Pat said, and he lay back on the bed. 'Let's have a nap.'

She lay back too, and he pulled the doona over them, knocking her bag to the floor. She made a move for it, but he pulled her in close, keeping her in place.

'You can unpack again later,' he said, giving her a gentle kiss.

'Okay,' Lally replied, and kissed him back, and he fell asleep.

23

CHUCK FARR'S STUDIO WAS AT the north end of Hudson Square with views of the water. The building looked deceptively old and decrepit, but inside there was a comprehensive security-focused front desk and ultramodern double-sided elevators. She'd had to show ID just to be told what level to go to. Stepping from the elevator straight into an open-plan space made her realise that Farr must occupy half of the entire floor. Lally couldn't begin to imagine what this would have cost. The floors were polished concrete. Over to the left was the classic white-sheet set-up with a tripod sitting expectantly, a table with a laptop open beside it, and a range of lights and umbrella-shaped reflectors stacked against the wall to the side. It was slightly overcast, but Lally could easily imagine how exhilarating the light off the water would be when the sun came out. There was a kitchenette along the far wall, and in a corner she could see, half-obscured by tall curtains, a huge low couch. Lally remembered the accusations she'd read in the industry forums. One man had described a 'day bed' but she couldn't see one.

'Lally,' a voice said almost lazily, shocking her. He had been leaning on a windowsill to the far right, and now pushed himself off and made his way over to her. She'd never met Farr's agent in person, but she recognised him from the general air of arrogance he exuded, even via email.

'Eric.' She smiled and extended her hand for him to shake, but he gave her a look and pulled her in for a hug. Lally stiffened in the embrace but kept smiling. 'Will Chuck be joining us?'

'Oh, he might come over if he feels like it,' Eric replied casually, not elaborating.

'Sure.' She tried to match his flippant tone, not wanting to lose face.

'He's happy for me to handle your little check-up.' Eric turned away from her as he said this, communicating clearly how unnecessary he and his client found the exercise. This frustrated her. She'd loosened all kinds of knots for Farr, and adhering to even this one tiny protocol was apparently beneath him.

'Well, you're undoubtedly very busy,' she replied, with a nod to the quiet, empty space. 'I'm sure this won't take long.'

'Mmm.' He made a distracted noise, as though he wasn't even listening to her, and started tapping the keys of the laptop.

'I trust you received our correspondence about the media preview night?'

He hadn't confirmed and Lally didn't want to have to remind him it was part of the contract. Somehow that would feel desperate.

'Sure, sure,' he replied, still not looking at her.

She walked over to look at the screen.

'So as you know, all twelve sitters are currently acting students,' he said.

She did not. They hadn't even replied to her request for basic information about the work so she could plan press kits.

'And of course it's Chuck, so it's portraiture,' he continued, clicking through files. 'But what you don't know,' he said, standing up straight and looking at her, 'is that Chuck decided to make them audiovisual works.'

Lally's chest seized up. He was watching her to see how she'd respond, she knew. She tried to keep her facial muscles relaxed, tried to breathe through her nose. The opening night was just weeks away. Her mind reeled at the logistics. The loss of anticipated income.

'Oh, don't stress,' Eric said with a little chuckle. 'We'll bring the screens and do all the hanging.'

'When?'

'The morning before the media preview.'

'Okay.'

'As you can imagine, Chuck has a set idea of how he wants things done, standards and so on. He would need complete control.'

'Sure.' She wasn't going to bite.

'Here's Jasmine,' Eric said then, and hit the space bar.

Lally looked at the screen. A young woman of about eighteen, maybe twenty max, South Asian probably, sat on a stool in front of the white backdrop. She was thin, wearing a black singlet and shorts, no bra by the looks of it, and bare feet at the end of her long, crossed legs. For about two seconds Lally thought it was a still, and then Farr's voice came out through the speakers, rough, directorial, but undeniably performative.

'Yeah, baby,' he said from behind the camera, and the woman smiled.

Lally's guts clenched. She could hear Farr's shutter going, and see the woman looking towards him, just slightly to the left of the video lens.

'Turn your head a little to the right,' his voice scratched out sweetly.

She did so.

'Open your mouth a little . . . yes, yes, yeah,' he went on. 'We've gotta get those lips.'

The clip continued like this for several minutes. The woman didn't make a sound. Lally's unease was growing, but she couldn't deny it was mesmerising to watch. The stillness of the subject, yet the tweaks every few seconds. Her following his directions, devastatingly eager to please him. Somehow, as a viewer, Lally knew the woman was performing for Farr and his camera, but also not for the video she was watching now. It gave everything an illicit vibe. All the beauty of a woman who knows she's on show, but still somehow the voyeurism.

'Move your stool over here,' he said then, and there was a pause in the shutter noises. 'Come towards me.'

Of course, the woman did so.

Farr continued to give specific directions—'a bit to the left, a bit closer'—which were clearly designed to put her in frame for the video rather than his camera.

Now the video frame was tight around her, an inch of space above the spout of her ponytail, cutting off at the exact spot where her waist came in beneath the slight curve of her breasts. Seeing her up close was both harder to watch and even more riveting. The video was picking up the way her eyes crinkled at the corners when he complimented her and the flicker of concentration on her forehead when she made an adjustment to follow his demands.

Next he told her to get rid of the stool and stand up, and for another few minutes this woman did as she was told, bending her body, facing left right up down as Farr pleased.

At the ten-minute mark, when Lally was thinking it might be getting a bit monotonous, Farr said, 'Let's get on the floor,' and adrenaline flooded through her. 'No smiling now,' he directed.

There was sitting, and lying down, and putting her hands exactly where he told her to. Then, just as it was about to become overtly sexual, Lally's entire body tense with dread, he piped up, 'We've got it!' and the woman's face broke into a gut-wrenchingly genuine smile.

'Come over here—let me show you how beautiful you are,' Farr said, and she moved up close to the camera again, every excruciating second of her pathetic gratitude laid bare on her face, caught in motion. She opened her mouth to say something but just before anything could come out the video shut off. Lally blinked at her own reflection in the newly black screen.

She righted herself slowly and realised she had been clutching her handbag to her chest and that her lower back was sore. Eric was standing right behind her. Had he been there that whole time as she was bent over watching? It was undeniable that something intellectually riveting had just occurred, but there was a different type of excitement coursing through her too. She didn't know what to say.

Eric smirked. 'Do you need to see all eleven others?' he asked and made a show of checking his watch.

She didn't have time, even if she had wanted to. She was due to meet Leah back at the gallery.

'They're all like this?' Lally asked.

'Yes. Each a video portrait of one person, the title of each work their first name.' He was affecting boredom again.

'Well . . .' She exhaled.

He started walking back towards the elevator doors and Lally followed.

'So?' Eric pivoted to face her.

'So what?'

'What do you think of the work?' He asked it slowly, like he was speaking to a child.

'I see the references to early video art, but this is something else, I know. Playing with the endurance element of the sitting portrait, I see that too. The gaze is . . .' She didn't want to say 'pornographic', but it was the elephant.

'Charged, isn't it?' he said, almost cheekily, and pushed the button to call the elevator.

'Yes,' she agreed. 'Charged.'

They stood in silence listening to the hum of the elevator approaching, and when it arrived he hugged her again. When she raised her arms to return his embrace she realised with a rush of shame that she had been sweating. As the metal doors were about to close she heard a voice come from the curtained area at the back of the studio. It was Farr's voice. She recognised it from the video.

'Finally,' the bodiless voice said.

Lally gasped, she couldn't help it, the elevator doors shutting the second after she saw the curtains rippling and Eric moving towards them. She leaned against the cold steel as she plummeted back to earth.

Stepping out onto the sidewalk again was like emerging from an incongruously high-up nightmare. Her heart was still thumping away as she shielded her eyes and gazed up at the building, looking pointlessly for some kind of confirmation that the last twenty minutes had really happened. It would be cutting it close, time-wise, to walk back to the gallery, but she was desperate for the fresh air. Besides, she needed some extra time to figure out how the hell to explain the work to Leah.

She tried to think about what she'd seen calmly, rationally. It was true that the artists who most excited her were the ones who rewrote the rules of mediums or genres. Was this a new level of authorship, a new level of the craft of videography? Or was it a different, not-okay type of rule-breaking? Lally was incapable of deluding herself enough to think it was totally fine. Perhaps her discomfort was more to do with Eric and that space. It was certainly possible that once these videos were in her own gallery, on her nice white walls, they would feel more official, less . . . Less what? Less cruel? Rivera filming her while they were fucking was cruel. But that was different. That was a private act between two people, twisted into something else by one person using a camera. These women were already up for the camera. The camera was part of the agreement between the two parties. These women wanted the exposure. It looked like they had a good time making the art that would expose them. They'd signed the forms. Was there a clear line between presuming agency and victim-blaming? Were they even victims in any way? They'd signed up knowing they wouldn't have control over how the artist's ultimate vision was realised. Lally had never signed up for anything like that with Rivera.

She cursed herself for letting Farr have the November spot without confirming the medium in the contract. She would never let one of the artists from the Saplings Program lock in with only 'portraiture' as the designated delivery. How had she let that slip? What fucking lobotomy had she given herself? When she remembered that she'd confirmed via email when Pat had been visiting a rage rose up in her. It was too late now. Cancelling would be catastrophic to both her finances and the gallery's image. This was what it looked like, suffering through the compromises Pat was costing her professional life. The gallery was both a teething child and an ageing parent—it needed constant care and maintenance. It required vigilance. This Farr situation was a direct result of her lack of attention to detail. But then again, what was the 'situation'? Everyone knew the man was rude. People would read the pre-show press for the same reason they'd line up down the street: because he pushed the envelope and made exciting work. Exciting good, exciting bad—that differentiation was significantly less important to a young gallery than the fact that it was exciting rather than boring. She hadn't risked everything to open up a safe, friendly gallery selling pretty pictures. Joseph's art had been all about human waste and the environment, he'd never even put people into it, and he'd still been a cunt.

A movement to Lally's left caught her eye. A group of six people at a table inside the restaurant she was passing erupted into laughter. Her stomach started churning. It was Leah. Leah was saying something and making them laugh again, and all the people she was with were like her. People of colour. Two more Asian women, a guy with an afro, and two others with dark skin whose faces she couldn't see. Not a single white person at their table of six. Lally hid behind a bus stop nearby and pulled out her phone, pretending to look at it but watching them. All six of them. They were creatives too, she could tell. Maybe even queer. Were they talking about art? Were they talking about her? Comparing notes about whose boss was the biggest Karen? Coming up with secret urban handshakes? The group laughed again at something Leah had said. Since when was Leah that funny? Lally hadn't even heard of this restaurant. Some kind of

Jewish cafeteria. So that's what was cool now? Leah turned her head towards the window and fear of discovery startled Lally into movement. She strode on, perturbed. Hadn't she done enough to champion marginalised voices? Hadn't she made the diversity pie chart to show she represented artists of varied cultural and linguistic backgrounds?

Unsurprisingly, Leah was still suspicious of Farr's exhibition, even though Lally had sanitised the nerve-racking effect of the moving images. 'The main problem, from the perspective of the gallery,' Lally said, 'is that we can't sell video art to regular buyers or collectors. I'm going to have to try to pull another direct acquisition out of my hat.'

'Would they do that?' Leah asked, astonished. 'They would buy his work?'

Lally laughed. 'Make a list of all the mediums and majors who already have one or more of his works, and a list of those who don't. It'll come up at about the half-half mark.'

'Wow.'

Lally tried to choose her next words carefully, but the image of Leah laughing with her secret arty friends infected her inflection. 'You think they won't buy his work because he's mean?'

Leah looked hurt but didn't reply.

'And all twelve of these women chose this. Who are we to say they don't know what they're doing? Is that where we're at now? So perpetually victimised that any agency is impossible? The subversive aspect of Farr's work is its strength. He's left his old gallery, run by a man, and the bad news article came out, and his new work is full of women and being shown at a gallery run by a woman. There are plenty of ways to demonstrate this as an evolution of his work.' She wanted people to feel that same subversive spirit was a strength at her own gallery too. And poaching a major name was a big move for Gallery Lally. This could be seen as an evolution for both of them.

Leah just sighed and nodded.

Lally got back to her quiet apartment and flicked the light on. Was Pat's apartment empty? Was he with Sophie again? Maybe blow jobs felt better if the blower's lips were eighty per cent filler. She put on some Coltrane and poured herself a wine. Thinking of Sophie's blatant thirst reminded her of the sound of Farr's voice, of his direction and Jasmine's pandering. It wasn't the spectre of bad sex that haunted Lally when she thought of the video. It was Jasmine's gratitude right at the end. Precisely the state she was terrified of being reduced to. Somewhere deep in her gut she knew she'd forever be haunted by that moment when she'd almost forgiven Joseph for filming her. That seam of weakness had to be filled or crushed. It could never, ever resurface.

God, she was mad. All these men were all her problems! All her problems were them! If there really was more to life than art, more than her work, how was she supposed to know where to start, or how to know if she'd ever 'make it'? On some level she'd always known that she would have her own gallery eventually—the early inheritance just meant it happened in her thirties instead of her forties or fifties. In artworks and in the industry, compromise was obvious to her. You just had to ask yourself, is this a deviation from the vision? But in love, what? Should she picture her life as a vision, and exercise caution when love made her deviate? What if she had a vision for a family and it was the work that caused her to deviate? They could never be balanced. One would always cost the other. This whole shitshow could have been the universe sending her a sign, but was that the interpretation of a coward or a lovestruck fool?

Gen never taxed Lally, never cost her time. Gen was an enrichment. Gen made happiness happier, brought insight to conversation. With Pat it was different. When she and Pat were in the same city it was like someone else took control of her body and she vaulted into a black hole of sleep-ins and takeout. It wasn't even just the hours he'd been taking up lately. The real fear was what would happen if they did make a life together. She didn't know a single gallerist who had a happy marriage, or any artist managers whose children didn't resent those adopted artist babies. The industry—the world—sniffed out compromise and shamed it. Lally did it to other people all the time. Would a family of her own be an enrichment or a duty? And what if the family meant her and one other person, compared to her and a person plus a baby? Would these things become the new vision from which art would have to steal hours? Pat nipped at her heels even from the other side of the planet. Would it be possible, ever, to be a good person in life as well as a great person in art? Both seemed to require every ounce of her energy at all times. Neither came naturally.

24

PAT FINISHED HIS COFFEE AND threw the takeaway cup into the full rubbish bin in the kitchen. That wouldn't be in the frame and was therefore a problem for later. Time to get this show on the road. His laptop was set up on a pile of old textbooks in front of the TV, and he opened the camera app. If he closed the door to his bedroom he wouldn't have to sort out that laundry basket of clothes. The couch looked a bit sad so he banged on the pillows. Sunlight streamed in through the one window in the tiny lounge area. He walked over and pulled the light-blocking curtains shut and turned on the old standing lamp in the corner. Then he set a knife and fork down on the cleared coffee table, fetched a bottle of wine and changed into a clean shirt. It felt a bit stupid to be stuck inside on such a beautiful day, buttoning a shirt up to the neck. He could have been at the beach, tanning, admiring others tanning.

His frustration was replaced with nerves when their call connected and he saw her face. Deep red lipstick, black around her eyes. He preferred her face normal, but it boosted his confidence to see she'd gone to some effort for him too.

'Good evening,' he said.

She smiled. 'I appreciate this. Date night hits different when it's actually, you know, night-time.'

'I don't know what you're talking about.' He made a show of swirling the red wine in his glass, taking a big gulp of it. She released a short and small laugh, and he relaxed a little. 'How was your day?'

Lally launched into what she had going on at work, and he sort of tuned in and out, listening sometimes, nodding, mostly just watching her face, both glad to see it and disappointed that it wasn't really there with him. She was talking about some crazy-sounding performance artist she was trying to work with, or had started to work with. The red wine was hitting him nicely in between the eyes.

'And what about you?' she asked. 'What's going on with your work?'

'I'm trying to wrap up the second phase of this Bauer account,' he began, immediately regretting it.

'So you got your scarf back?' she responded dryly.

'Ah, no,' he replied, sitting forward, rubbing his hands down the length of his jeans. 'I actually haven't seen that woman—'

'Sophie.'

'Yes. I haven't seen her since the fair and'—he faltered—'I won't see her again.'

'Okay,' Lally said with a shrug.

'Ever,' he added.

She just stared at him down the camera lens. 'Do you wanna see my boobs?'

He didn't know what to say. He felt a bit stung, maybe dismissed, but it was an invitation for more, obviously, which he couldn't, and wouldn't, decline.

'Pat . . .' This was gentler. She lowered her chin, looked up at him. 'Do you wanna see your girlfriend's boobs?'

He smiled. 'Yeah.'

She turned her laptop around so that the couch was in vision rather than the kitchen, and he heard the sound of her chair being pushed back, the clink of her wineglass being set down on the marble table. He saw her body appear in front of the camera again, watched her adjust the tilt of the laptop's lid then pull her black silk slip up and over her head, dropping it by her feet. She wasn't wearing a bra, just one of the plain black Calvin Klein g-strings he remembered from doing her laundry. Watching her run her fingers through her hair, slowly, slowly, then moving her hands up and down her body, her hands grazing her own nipples, he instinctively leaned back into the couch and undid his belt buckle.

'Pat?' she asked.

'Mmm?'

'Let me see you.'

He felt nervous about that.

'Pat?' she said again.

'Mmm?'

'Are you hard for me?'

'Yeah,' he replied.

'I wanna see how hard my boyfriend is.'

He took another huge mouthful of wine, then pushed his hips up off the couch to slide his jeans down to his knees, pulling his erection from under the band of his undies and pushing them down too.

'Show me,' she insisted, sitting on her couch with her legs apart and moving one of her own hands down to the front of the little scrap of black cotton covering her.

He stroked himself two, three, four times, making sure he was at maximum, before tilting his own camera down a bit.

She made a good sound, said 'Yeah'—then bent over and picked up a box of matches.

Pat's mind started to race. What the fuck was she doing? Oh, she was lighting a candle. Okay.

'Bend over,' he said.

'Is that a request or a demand?' She took another match from the box and lit it, then blew it out, flicking it towards him, towards the laptop.

'Request,' he said. 'I want to see my girlfriend's arse.'

Lally laughed then, and dropped the matches. Turning from the camera she lifted her left knee up and onto the couch, then bent over. His eyes travelled up and down the thin black line between her cheeks, bouncing left and right, left and right between them, pulling on himself as slowly as he could bear to. Then he saw her own right hand appear in the space between her legs, and he couldn't help it, he tightened his grip on himself as he watched her fingers rubbing on the fabric. Fuck, this was so hot. She was so hot. And she'd said yes to not fucking other guys. So she was finally all his. This arse, those tits, that cunt, all his and only his. Jesus fucking Christ. Goddamn, it was painful not being able to feel her. He would have given anything, anything in the whole world, to smack that cheek. To pull that g-string to one side. If he were there, maybe he'd start fucking her with it still on.

She turned to the camera. 'Tell me how you wanna fuck your girlfriend.'

He groaned.

'On the couch?'

'Yes.'

She lay down on her back, keeping one foot on the floor, and lifted the other leg, resting her ankle on the top of the couch, so the camera was pointed directly between her legs. He couldn't believe what he was seeing. Her hand went down inside the fabric, and he was mesmerised by this, watching the outline of her fingers moving in fast little circles. His back arched. He was too close.

'Tell me, Pat,' she urged, 'what do you wanna do with your girlfriend?'

'Put my fingers inside her.'

She did this. 'She's wet.'

'Yeah?'

'You know she's wet,' Lally said. 'Then what?'

'Then I suck on her nipples.'

Her free hand reached to one, pinching it, and she closed her eyes and tilted her head back.

'Don't you wanna be inside her?'

'Fuck, yes.'

'So what are you gonna do?'

'I'm gonna push her knees up.'

Lally obliged with one leg.

'Right up.'

She went further. He was so close.

'Then I'm going all in at once.'

She moaned again. Her hand was going so fast.

'And I'm pushing down on her legs, pushing them down as I fuck her, so she's all bent up, so her pussy is right there open, and my hands are there behind her knees, pushing, pinning them down, and I'm fucking her so hard.'

'Do you wanna come inside her?'

'Yes.'

'Do you wanna come inside your girlfriend, Pat?'

'Say my name again.'

She opened her eyes and watched him. 'Patrick,' she pleaded.

'Again.'

'Patrick, don't you wanna come inside your girlfriend? She wants you to.' Lally put her fingers deep inside herself. 'Feels good, Pat—it feels so good to come inside this pussy.'

'Again!' This was it.

'She loves it, Pat.'

He groaned and felt the surge, grabbing the paper serviette from the coffee table just in time, the cum soaking through it quickly. Puffed, he fell back into the couch.

'I'm close too,' she said, and he sat up again, blinking. She'd brought her knees down again, but one of them was a little bent to the side, and he could still see her hand at work.

'Keep going,' he said.

'Tell me,' she said, closing her eyes, turning her head away from the camera, 'tell me you wanna fuck me in the ass.'

'Holy shit.'

'Tell me!'

'I wanna fuck you in—'

She came. He could see it, the wave of it coming over her, the strange noise she made, the breathing fast then slow, seconds going by, and then the moment of stillness, followed by the exhale and slump. She stayed like that for a moment then took her hand out of her undies. Pat put the serviette down on the coffee table and pulled up his own pants. What would they do now? In real life they'd just lie there in dozy, companionable silence. He watched her reach down and grab the crumpled black dress, pulling it on inside out, walking out of the frame towards the kitchen. He listened to the faint sound of the tap running and tilted his camera back up.

'So,' she said, spinning her laptop back around, chirpy, sitting down at the table, 'where were we?'

⌐

His phone buzzed: *LUKE is calling.*

Pat reached for it. 'Hello?' It was two in the morning.

'Get your arse up here, Pat—Beck's in labour!'

'What?'

'Your sister is having a baby, remember?' Luke laughed. His voice was strange, distant, lots of background noise. 'I'm in the car on the way to the hospital. What do I tell Mum? Are you coming?'

'Fuck.'

'Yes, fuck! What do I tell Mum?'

'I'll check the flights now and text you.'

'Hurry up!'

25

FARR'S TECH CREW WERE FINALLY finished. The three young men crouched around their toolboxes, gathering the bubble wrap and level strings they'd left scattered around while working.

'Oh, just leave that,' Eric said to them, waving his hand. 'You've been wonderful, boys, as always. Thank you.'

Eric had been there the whole time, but Farr was yet to grace the gallery with his presence.

'Are you going to grab a coffee anytime soon?' Eric asked. He was standing in the middle of the space, pivoting slowly, looking between the giant screens now hanging on the walls.

'Are you talking to me?' Lally replied, leaning on her desk and grabbing her phone. She wasn't going to let him try his power-moves bullshit in her own gallery.

Eric turned to look at her. 'Yes,' he replied. 'I thought you had an assistant here.'

'Leah is the assistant manager, and we fetch our own coffees. I can recommend Blue Bottle next door.' Lally smiled.

He crossed his arms. 'You were the one chasing Mr Farr for this exhibition slot, and now we're here it seems you're upset about something.'

'Well, I'm yet to actually meet Mr Farr, but I'm very much looking forward to it,' she replied. It wasn't until the words came out of her mouth that she realised why Eric was getting to her. He had all the ego one would expect from a major artist—except he wasn't the artist. He was some kind of hybrid manager-assistant-mouthpiece. All the arrogance and none of the genius to forgive it. Characters like him were not uncommon in the business, but she'd never met one who acted as though he hated her, rather than wanting something from her.

'Everybody wants to meet Mr Farr,' he said dismissively.

'I'm counting on it.'

There was a knock at the glass door. They had the thick curtains pulled for the install so she couldn't see who was there. Lally stood up, smoothed her dress, and went to look.

Chuck Farr was standing outside. He was wearing a black coat that was plainly not warm enough for November, one hand shoved deep into a pocket and the other clasping the neck of the jacket closed. For a brief moment Lally was tempted to just step away from the glass slowly and let him shiver a while longer, enjoying his discomfort, but she couldn't do that. He did resemble his photo. The eyes were deep-set into the skull, a strong jawline, clear and surprisingly tanned skin. He was tall, but not quite as tall as Eric, thank god. She breathed out, like a sniper, then pulled the trigger.

'Mr Farr,' she said warmly, swinging the glass door open. 'Come in.'

'Thank you.' He said it kindly enough as he moved past her, but as though she were a waitress or steward. Lally extended her hand to introduce herself formally, but he shrugged his coat off and went to hand it to her. When she narrowed her eyes he paused and said, 'Ha! I'm kidding,' then walked over to the coat rack behind her desk, helping himself to a hanger. Lally walked over to join Eric and together they watched as Farr inspected the hanging.

'Good, good, good, yes.' He pointed to one screen, and then another. He sounded excited. 'Perfect, and the lighting goes dim. Yes, yes, yes, all great.' Only then did he come over to greet Lally. 'It's all looking great, thanks.' He was thanking her as though she had hung the screens herself. This was not a partnership.

'Shall we?' he said to Eric, who nodded and pulled out a small tablet.

Lally saw an application open, one she didn't recognise, and a blueprint of her space appeared on the screen. It was not a comfortable feeling, seeing her gallery in his hands like this. Slim red rectangles, numbered, sat along the walls of the schematics, corresponding to the screens in the space. Without a word the three of them turned towards #1, immediately to the left of the gallery doors. Eric tapped the tablet and the red rectangle turned green. The screen on the wall came alive. The white backdrop with the stool. Lally had been trying to put this imagery to the back of her mind since she her visit to Farr's studio, but like all great art, it had lodged itself in her psyche. She took a deep breath in and exhaled silently.

The young woman standing beside the stool was not Jasmine. This was a blonde. Scandinavian perhaps, again very thin, her hair middle-parted and braided in a way that made Lally even more uncomfortable for how obviously youthful it made her look. Farr took the tablet from Eric then, and turned clockwise to #2, tapping the screen quite hard. Jasmine sprung up. The screens on the walls had in-built speakers and even with only two videos running the effect was a kind of overlapping murmur. Farr activated the following two videos in quick succession with a gleeful sound, like a child opening a present, then tap-tap-tap-tap-tap-tap-tap-tapped the other eight as fast as he could, and the three of them turned a full circle together, watching woman after woman jump from limbo into the space, materialising before them in all their eager glory. It was completely overwhelming. The noise was now a discord of lenses shuttering, Farr's saccharine voice, and the occasional dragging of a stool. Lally heard a giggle behind her, and as she turned to see which woman it had come from she felt slightly nauseated. The heating was turned up too high, perhaps, or she hadn't eaten enough today. Twelve beautiful young women—girls?—surrounded her, each of them looking slightly off-camera, most of them quite still, only moving to make minor adjustments to their bodies. They could have been life drawing models, or part of a tableau. Lally had exhibited countless nudes. What was different about this? Something. The work was filling up her sinuses. It was inescapable. She was struggling to find words to respond, unable to articulate how painfully sensory this was, aware of her heart beating hard in her chest, and she was sweating again too. Where was the eye supposed to travel to? Her attention was wholly on one particularly still woman, but then her peripheral vision would catch a minute movement somewhere else—hair being tucked behind an ear—and she would pinball to a different screen. The mind did travel: they're beautiful, they know how beautiful they are, they're adored, he's in control, he wants to fuck them, I want to fuck them, orgy maybe, sexual but no nipples are showing, captured youth, just like ads, a buffet, did they get paid, is this art, I wish I looked like that, different from a photo, how long does it go for, bored, turned on, can't look away, confused. Lally wondered if there was some respite to be found in the idea that all these women were in it together, but the white space between each screen excluded any sense of solidarity. They were in framed silos. There was also the matter of how devastatingly silent they all were. It would be like suggesting calendar girls of separate months were in-it-together.

Lally tore her eyes away from the works and looked to Farr. They made eye contact and he smiled, hit the button to lock the screen of the tablet, and passed it to Eric. Horrified, straining to maintain a serene face, Lally watched as Eric slipped the tablet into a case, zipped it up and put the case into a satchel. He then retrieved both men's coats from the rack and returned to hand Farr his.

'Don't look so panicked, Lally,' Eric said patronisingly. 'The videos are all on loops. The system shuts down for an hour between five and six in the morning, then reboots itself. You can call me if anything goes wrong, but it won't.'

'Well, then, I suppose—'

He cut her off. 'We'll see you back here at six for the preview.'

Farr put his jacket on and smiled at Lally, extending his hand for her to shake. What else could she do? She smiled back at him and shook his hand. She watched Eric loop the strap of the satchel over his shoulder and they took the tablet and they left her. Alone in a room with these twelve women not quite looking at her, with Farr's voice saying, *Beautiful, yes, perfect,* from three hundred and sixty degrees, and the shutter sounding like an irregular audio strobe light. It would be impossible to work at the gallery desk for the next three weeks. A wave of anxiety was rolling in towards her.

'No,' she said aloud, cautioning herself. 'Work.'

Okay, work. It was just after midday. The press preview opened at six. Cleaners were arriving at four and Leah with the caterers at five. She had to go home and change and do her face.

That left just over two hours to plan how the fuck she would articulate her response to the work. She didn't have to fawn over it, didn't have to say it was 'good'. What people wanted to hear from her was why she chose it. She hadn't fucking chosen it, though, had she?

'Stop being a child,' she said aloud and closed her eyes. She just had to remember her history, her references, everything she'd learned in the past decade. How did the work stretch a medium or genre, how did it take the art a step further?

She opened her eyes again walked over to her desk, sat down, and began to take notes. The baseline, of course, was the Warholian ability to make the viewer uncomfortable about revelling in the sex and celebrity—viewers wanted this sex but also resented the women for wanting the celebrity, enjoying a feeling of superiority while nevertheless continuing to watch them. The work was accusatory. Did the viewer respect these women by presuming their agency? Did the fact they were clothed make a difference? Then the gaze. Going deeper into how frustrating it was that none of them ever actually looked at the camera—at the viewer. The viewers were unacknowledged admirers. Were grateful. The only person in control was the artist, and he remained unseen yet omnipresent, working between the viewer and the subject. Was it right to give him thanks and praise?

The statement emerged quite organically once Lally let it. She spoke it to herself, finessing the language, honing her delivery. At home she rehearsed it more as she pulled on her stockings and curled her eyelashes, looping long ruby earrings through her lobes and walking into the invisible cloud of perfume she sprayed into the air.

'It makes you uncomfortable, of course. But it challenges you to articulate why.'

The cleaners were clearly uneasy. They gave her apologetic nods as they left. Why were they feeling sorry? she wondered. Sorry to have seen it? A kind of broad-spectrum embarrassment for the state of society? The catering staff were similarly on edge.

'Would it be possible to turn the audio off, or just down a bit, while we're setting up, so my staff can hear each other?' Maria asked politely.

Which was worse? Saying she didn't want to, or that she couldn't?

'I'm sorry, Maria'—Lally chose to reply with the truth—'but the artist took the controls with him this afternoon.' As though she'd ever get them back.

Lally had been bracing herself for Leah's arrival. Fully anticipating some initial reproach, yes, but she was also genuinely curious to hear the language Leah would use to enunciate a response. To a friend you could simply say it creeped you out or gave you a bad vibe, but formal language was required in this setting. If Leah was serious about wanting to move into art criticism this was an excellent show to practise with. Complaining of how something made you feel was difficult to do without reverting to melodrama or vagueness.

Leah pushed through the glass doors and curtain, and Lally watched her response. The screen to Leah's right emitted some noise, probably Farr saying something, and Leah's head snapped straight to it, then her whole body froze. She took two slow steps towards the screen, regarding it cautiously, the way you might approach a rattlesnake enclosure. Then she clutched her bag to her chest unconsciously, just as Lally had done in Farr's studio the other day. This made Lally mad. Why were they all so trembly? Why couldn't they respond with a shout, a point—shame! Then Leah took the inevitable steps backward and opened her senses to the other eleven screens and sources of sound, and her mouth dropped open.

'Whatever you want to say about the work,' Lally observed, walking over to stand beside her assistant, 'this is the first exhibition we've shown here that has made your jaw drop like that.'

'But . . .' Leah just shook her head.

'It's uncomfortable, isn't it?'

Leah closed her mouth and nodded.

'Just to clarify,' Lally said, 'I am very interested to hear your thoughts on this. My position at the moment is that I do not need to "like" work to show it in my gallery. I do think he has achieved something. We're struggling to find words for it, and you know that's often a good sign.'

'I'm not struggling to find words for it,' Leah said. 'It's fucking disgusting.'

Lally stayed silent.

Leah turned to face her. 'And I don't think it needs more than those two words.'

She walked away, first hanging her jacket up, then putting her handbag in the lockable drawer in the desk, before going over to Maria. Lally knew Leah was doing her job, going through the checklist, but she could also tell that through her body language she was trying to communicate to Maria that she didn't approve.

Lally sighed. Leah's response was disappointing. Juvenile and impatient. It was easy to hate the work, easy to dismiss it, harder to justify why.

In an unusual move, Lally made the first ten media arrivals wait outside before she let them enter the space together. They went through ten simultaneous journeys: first shocked, then dumbstruck, and finally turning to Lally herself imploringly. How pathetic that they couldn't make their own minds up. It was literally their job to articulate their responses. Within ten minutes of arriving most people were on their phones. The show was under embargo for a few more hours, but Lally guessed the critics and journalists were messaging their editors begging for a firm spot or an increased word count, insisting that this exhibition had to be covered.

The room was warm with bodies by the time Farr and his small entourage arrived. Eric had his satchel. It was now an object of painful focus for Lally. She watched as Farr handed Leah his coat, and Lally kept watching as Farr watched Leah turn around to hang it up. Lally loathed the small stab of envy she felt at this. The hurt she'd felt on stumbling across Leah and her friends at lunch returned. Lally was a decade too old to be the subject of Farr's interest. What a wounding relief.

Eric walked to the end of the long wall of the gallery and began to hold court, and when he beckoned Farr over to join him the small crowd clapped. The first three or four questions were about the artist's ideas and intentions. His answers were infuriatingly ambiguous. The group fell quiet, seeming both confused and frustrated.

'Do they know they're being recorded?' a man asked. It was an accusatory question, but it was easy to see why someone felt it needed to be asked. That feeling of voyeurism was so pervasive, the slightly off-camera point of focus of the young women's eager eyes.

'They do now,' he replied.

A ripple went through the crowd. Lally was aware of Leah watching her, but she also knew the journalists would be alert for any sign of discomposure, so she kept her face blank. Her pulse was like a galloping horse in her ears.

'We called them all individually this morning,' Farr replied, sounding frustrated.

'And?' the same man called out.

'What do you mean "and"?' Farr shot back. 'These women all look beautiful.' He held an arm out then let it fall. 'They want to be on screens. They answered my ad and asked for this opportunity.'

More silence.

'Nobody *withdrew* their *consent*, if that's what you mean.' He was mocking them.

The group had received their answer, but they were not mollified.

Farr continued, 'This is a reallocation of resources. Jasmine told me this will be her third year of auditioning for the Victoria's Secret show. You think she's going to be upset about appearing fully clothed in a piece of video art for a high-calibre contemporary gallery? My shots of Kate and Naomi are in the National Portrait Gallery.'

Touché.

After a few tense seconds a different man called out, 'Can you talk about this first extension into moving images? This stillness, perhaps?'

It was obvious Farr liked this question. 'Look at Caroline,' he said, gesturing to the brunette on his right. 'She barely moves.

It's the anxiety of stasis in a world much more comfortable with constant movement.' A scratching of pens on paper. 'But what you should also be asking is why is video so different from photography if she is not moving? What are we afraid of in this moment? Why do we like paintings and photographs of beautiful young women, but we bitch and whine at seeing them in videos? None of you would be fidgeting if these were prints. Who the fuck made those rules?'

More scratching.

There were a couple more questions, and Farr responded to both by telling the journalist what they should have asked and answering that question instead. After that, understandably, there were no more questions.

Farr and Eric left. Lally watched with sadness and anxiety as the satchel and tablet left with them.

'Not a single question from a woman,' Leah whispered to Lally as the group began to disperse. She was right. 'And look at how quickly they're leaving,' she added, nodding towards the door.

It was true. Those who remained were mostly men.

'But why?' Lally whispered back. 'Obviously they don't like it, or don't like him. That's fine. But surely they go to shows all the time where they don't like the artist or the work, and they don't just leave immediately.'

'It's exhausting being here surrounded by it, Lally—you know it is.'

'Isn't there something in that? That endurance element? That discomfort? Abramovic? What is he showing us that we do not like? What specifically?'

'Him, himself,' Leah replied, irritated. 'Supposedly I'm looking at twelve women, but actually all I see is him. His gaze. His money. His lens. His control. I couldn't get a clearer picture of him if these were self-portraits.'

Lally put on a show for the rest of the allocated media call time then started actively winding things down, fetching people's coats for them. Normally she let the journos and reviewers linger and drink, greasing their wheels, but for about twenty minutes there was a group of twelve people—all men—watching the videos, and it wasn't fun to stand around wondering what they were thinking.

Lally pulled the curtains, turned the overhead lights off and locked up, pausing at the door to let the cold air in. The sound was still on, the screens spitting out bright white light, the twelve women trapped inside.

When she got home she couldn't help but feel as though she'd left them back there, alone in the dark, mute, told again and again on an endless loop how beautiful they were. She drank too much to try to knock herself out but slept poorly and woke at four in the morning then lay awake until five, when she knew the screens would be off for an hour. Only then did she sleep soundly.

26

PAT PUT THE PLATES OUT and the slices of bread on top of them while Luke and their dad ripped into a pair of cooked chooks, piling hunks of flesh and bone in a big bowl. Their mum rinsed the iceberg lettuce and retrieved blunt knives for the butter and mayonnaise. Kel was always in a better mood when she'd had a night off from the cooking. He and Luke would pretend to fight over the drumsticks. Murray would offer them the parson's nose and then eat it himself, licking his gnarly fingers, satisfied. For about twenty minutes Pat would be able to rose-tint the scene, pretend he hadn't missed the baby being born. Pretend he didn't have to get back to Sydney within twenty-four hours because the Bauer account 'needed his personal attention', apparently. At least Beck and her baby girl were fine. That was what he should have been thinking about.

'You want to come stay at my place?' Luke offered when he and Pat were clearing up.

'Nah, I'll just crash here. I've had too many beers.'

Murray had left to drive Tom to visit the hospital again because Kel, in her excitement, had drunk two glasses of white wine. Luke and Pat hugged, and Luke kissed his mum on the cheek and hugged her too before heading out the front door. Pat wiped his hands on the tea towel and hung it over the rail on the front of the old oven.

'What about you, Patty?' his mum said, embracing him. She was such a lightweight.

'What about me, Mum?' he replied, feigning ignorance.

'You know what.' She put on a jokey, pleading voice. 'Have you got a girlfriend yet? You can't leave it too long. It's much more fun to have children when you're young enough to play with them.'

'I've got to get the job and house stuff sorted first,' he said, sighing, and wriggled out of her arms to pour himself a glass from the warm bottle of chardonnay on the dining table.

'Pffft.' She plonked onto a chair. 'If you wait till you can afford a baby you'll never have a baby.' She took a sip from the glass and patted the seat next to her.

Pat obliged.

'You don't think things would have been easier for you and Dad if you'd waited a bit, had a bit more money?'

She sighed and shrugged. 'The early years are fine. Little kids don't know if you're rich or not.'

Pat stayed quiet, had another sip of wine instead of speaking. He felt he had always known, from his earliest possible memories, that his mother was stressed about money.

'And anyway,' she continued, 'even the best-laid plans can blow up in your face. We thought we would be rich by the time you were all in school.'

'And then the farm,' Pat said.

'And then the farm,' she echoed. It was history now. The drought, the overextension, the miscalculations, the crash in '08, the double mortgage, the offer from the overseas investor, losing the huge property and big house, moving to this shitty place in town. 'It would have been nice to give the twins a bit of a better go,' she said regretfully.

'You mean sending them to boarding school too?'

'I don't know.' She ran her finger over an old stain in the wood grain of the table. 'For a long time your dad thought that at least one of you would take over the farm—probably Luke, because he seemed more interested. So what was the use of a diploma, or whatever, you know? He used to have all these sayings about learning on the job.'

'What about Beck?' Pat asked.

'Oh, you know your father,' she replied, brushing the question aside. 'The girl was my job.'

'And?'

'And what?' She hadn't liked that question. 'I took that volunteer spot at the library so that she'd be around the books. You don't remember that? I was always checking her homework and going to the parent–teacher nights. They all said she was bright, same as they did with you, and they started getting her excited about what she could be when she grew up. Then your dad went and lost everything. And this was when the accounts were in his name, you know. I went to the bank with questions—Mrs McInnerney was the teller back then—and she just laughed at me. "Ask your husband," she said. Well, wasn't she delighted when we had to go in and sign all that paperwork after selling the property. God, that was so humiliating.'

'Losing the property?'

'No, that scene in the bank! "Ask your husband." You don't know what it's like, feeling like you don't even have any say over this home you're supposed to keep nice. And then whoosh!' She flung her arms up. 'It was all gone.'

Pat had never heard any of this. He'd never heard her talk about those years. They weren't allowed to bring it up with their dad or even mention it when he was in earshot.

Kel had another sip of wine and sighed loudly. 'And yes, of course, losing the property was humiliating too,' she went on, 'but a lot of people were hurting then. This was when there was still a bit of community around here, at least. I'm not sure if I really believed the twins would be fine at the local school, or if I just hoped they would be. It was such an awful time. You know, we started keeping the chooks because we needed the eggs. You boys just ate and ate and ate. I remember thinking those yolks were like gold dollars disappearing down your throats.'

'I do remember eating a lot of eggs,' Pat said.

'Eggs and eggs and eggs. And then, you know, your father and I had to make the decision about you and your school. God, that was awful. We could really have used the money. But, then, you had almost graduated, and if we brought you home where would you finish school? It seemed cruel to take you away, even though all you ever did was complain about the place. Plus they always say it's bad for teenagers to be uprooted, and we'd had so much change already—'

'But I was on a scholarship,' Pat interrupted. 'Wasn't I on a scholarship?'

'You were on a half scholarship,' she said. 'The school covered your tuition fees, but we had to pay for the accommodation and all your books and supplies and uniforms, and I'm telling you, at that place, all that stuff ended up just as much as the teachers cost.'

'Oh.' Pat rubbed his face. 'I thought the scholarship had covered everything.'

'That's why we bought the twins that damn dog.' Kel took another sip. 'They weren't dumb. They knew something was up. We'd gone broke, but you still came home on the holidays from a place where your name was embroidered on every pair of socks.'

'I was so jealous of them getting that dog.'

She scoffed gently and put a hand on his arm. 'You kids all just wanted what the other one had. That's what kids are like. It's natural. And now look. You're rich, and you can get yourself a dog.'

'Luke's richer than I am.'

'Well, then that's on you. You sold us on that school as much as they did. Said it would set you up for life. Every Christmas a dozen fancy new words for "upward mobility", as though it just hadn't occurred to us. At least we didn't live near your snotty friends. Picture your father having to coach a footy team and the other dads being there—those bankers who kept their jobs while we lost everything. Can you imagine?'

Pat wondered where Gregory Bauer was right at that moment. All that money he'd disappeared with. He thought about what that money would buy in Esk.

'But anyway, that's all done and dusted.'

'Why are you telling me all this now?' Pat asked.

'Grandkids,' she replied. 'They make you realise it's all so short, it all goes by so quick. And also that you're old. When you think you're going to die, things become a little clearer.' His mum smiled at him and squeezed his hand. 'I just want you to be happy. You've always complicated everything. Sometimes it seems like you make it all hard for yourself. The really important things are actually the simplest.'

His head throbbed the next morning. Cheap white wine was such a killer. He folded the blankets and left them at one end of the couch, taking a quick shower and gathering his gear. His phone was showing emails from Sophie. It made him feel sick.

His mum kissed him goodbye and stood at the front door, holding her cuppa in one hand, waving with the other, as he backed the hire car out onto the street. He detoured past Beck's place on the way out of town. It was such a dump. Car in the driveway rusty. One of the two bedroom windows had a flyscreen missing. Pat turned the radio on, hoping for a distraction. The conversation with his mum had left him with terrible feelings and more questions he'd probably never ask. As the sun came up it challenged the tinted windows so much he was squinting for the whole second half of the drive. Why did it always have to feel like this? Every time he came back he got scrunched up and chucked around. Why was he always surprised and re-surprised by how they lived? Why didn't he ever remember how extreme the heat and the light were? Again and again it was such a rude shock to see how old his mother looked. To see how young Beck looked. To find the town stuck in the past, the bakery's vanilla slice still cheap and too sweet. How come the steaks weren't as good when there were cows in the paddock outside? At the servo he sensed people staring at him, sniffing him out. It was difficult. Uncomfortable. At least up until now he'd had some sense that his own brilliance had been his passport out of there—that his scholarship was responsible for the splitting and shifting of his life trajectory from his siblings'. Now he knew that was only a half-truth. Was a half-truth a lie? God, it was so fucking exhausting, not knowing whether or not he even respected himself.

27

'FUCK,' SHE SAID INTO THE mirror at eight in the morning. She looked like shit. Huge bags under her eyes and dry skin. She knew her email inbox would be full of journalists seeking clarification on components of the exhibition for their copy, so she sat down to attend to that before starting her routine. There were more than she was anticipating. This was good. It meant that they all intended to give the show some kind of coverage, but the questions were overwhelmingly addressed to her. That had never happened before. It was ironic that the only time she'd been addressed directly like this, the only time people cared so much about her insights, was with this particular show, by a male artist. How did this show fit into Lally's strong year? How did she feel about helping Farr move into a new medium? Were the themes of his work something she had personal opinions about? It was infuriating. She imagined Leah sipping a coffee, checking the sent messages to read Lally's replies.

Opening nights usually made her nervous in a good way. This was different. It felt like anticipating surgery. She just wanted it to be over.

At exactly seven on opening night everything was in place. The servers were standing behind their table with the glasses set out. Leah was in the corner by the curtains, ready to pull the cord to draw them back as Lally opened the doors to the guests waiting outside. The socials photographer was standing to her left. Normally there would be music playing, but it was inappropriate to add another audio element to the experience of a work which was audiovisual.

'All right, everyone,' she said. 'Let's go.'

Leah began to pull the curtains open, revealing a huge crowd outside—the biggest Lally had ever seen. It made her chest explode with excitement. They spilled inside as she opened the double doors. There would be no way to keep them closed or keep the place properly heated, she realised immediately. They'd have to rely on the mass of bodies keeping each other warm.

Wave after wave of people kept coming, until they were at capacity and there was still a line down the street. Word must have got out. Voices started to rise in volume, and it occurred to Lally that perhaps she should have booked extra security. Too late now.

Within ten minutes some people were arguing and others were laughing. She was keeping an eye on the models too. One in particular, a redhead named Fleur, on her third flute already, leaned against the glass at the front of the space. She was a bit of a star, actually. Lally could see it immediately. She had a beautiful Southern accent and was about as lithe and pale as they came. In the video her hair was tumbling to her waist but now she sported an incredibly flattering pixie cut. Beneath her big fur coat she wore only a lace slip, and she got caught trying to smoke inside. She posed for photo after photo in front of her video, sometimes mimicking the pose on screen.

Tearing her eyes away from Fleur, Lally saw through the window that Curtis was trapped outside, so she hurried out to usher him in. They could barely get near the screens on the wall, which was a bit of a relief. He started up with the questions about her 'intentions' around putting on this show. She regurgitated a couple of the lines she'd practised, helped him find the Guggenheim crowd, then retreated.

When Lally spotted Jasmine her heart sank a little. Illogically, Lally felt particularly attached to her. Responsible somehow. The memory of her in the video, terrifyingly vulnerable, had been haunting Lally. But was that Jasmine's father there with her? Christ almighty, how awkward. Lally went over and introduced herself.

'This show is fucking sick!' Jasmine called over the noise in a Bronx accent. 'Sweet space too,' she added.

'Thank you,' Lally replied, revising her assessment of the young woman.

'This is my friend Ravi,' Jasmine said, and the man beside her shook Lally's hand.

'I tutor a bunch of these chicks,' Ravi said to Lally.

'Oh,' Lally replied, nodding.

'Could've warned you about Fleur,' he said, looking over Lally's shoulder.

She turned to follow his gaze and saw Fleur's head tipped back in laughter, some of her champagne sloshing onto her hand. She sucked it off her skin and licked her glossy red lips.

About an hour into the event, Lally found Leah for a quick check-in. Which curators had come, which hadn't, who to look after.

'It's lucky so many of these people smoke,' Lally said. 'Gives the line outside a chance to move.'

'I think the bar have cut off Fleur, but it looks like her mates are just passing more drinks to her.'

'I can't kick her out,' Lally said, just as their group erupted into squeals again, all crowded around someone's phone.

'Bit of a different crowd, hey?' Leah said.

'Yeah,' Lally agreed, looking over just in time to see Ravi's hand slip inside Jasmine's coat at ass level. Lally's heart seized but then she saw Jasmine laugh and kiss his cheek, and yet again she tried to climb down from her high horse. Some tutor.

'Hey, isn't that Eric?' Leah said, pointing towards the drinks table.

Lally spotted the crown of Eric's head floating a couple of inches above the crowd and a sense of dread shot through her as she realised Farr was by his side and they were heading towards the exit.

'Looks like they're leaving,' she said.

It was incredibly rude of them to have come and gone without making an effort to talk to her, but she wasn't surprised. She couldn't make a fuss about it. Farr would find that much too gratifying. She had to keep pushing down the urge to foil him somehow, remembering that his success and hers were now inextricably connected.

Lally was about to ask Leah if she'd seen Curtis leave when the lights flickered. She and Leah looked at each other, alarmed. The crowd hushed and a stillness fell over the room, even the servers pausing in their pouring. They all remained frozen for a few seconds, but when nothing further happened the movement and chatter increased again.

'Everybody's on edge,' Leah said.

'Tell me about it,' Lally replied, finishing her own flute.

'Hey, what's going on with Caroline?' Leah pointed subtly across the room.

'Isn't she just a bit drunk?'

'No, I mean in the video.'

Lally looked at it. It did seem to have changed. Caroline's body was moving in a way Lally hadn't seen in the first hundred loops.

'Is that a different video?' Lally asked Leah.

They both stared at it, puzzled.

'What the fuck is happening to Tanya—Tanya's video, I mean?' Leah didn't point this time.

Lally saw it too. Tanya had been largely still in her video, but now it showed her dancing, the casual kind of bop you might do when a song you liked started playing in the supermarket.

Then a young woman's voice shouted, 'Hey!' and Leah and Lally looked over to see the video of Fleur blowing a kiss to the camera before dropping to the floor.

'What the fuck?' Lally said.

Someone was pushing through the crowd towards them. It was Fleur, wild-eyed. 'That's not my video,' she said to Lally. She was right up close, clearly trying not to make a scene, though she already had.

'Leah,' Lally said, 'can you give Fleur a hand, maybe get her some water and—'

'No, I'm serious,' Fleur interrupted. 'I never did that.'

'Lally.' Leah tugged at Lally's sleeve urgently. 'We need to do something.'

Lally looked up and saw it. The women in the videos were now rubbing their hands up and down their bodies. Jasmine had started tweaking one of her nipples through her singlet. Maeve was now straddling the stool, grinding against her hand, which was planted between her legs.

'Hey!' a man called angrily. 'What's going on?' But then someone else wolf-whistled and the crowd cheered, laughed, getting rowdy.

Lally's mind was racing. Had Farr really fucked all these women? Was this a big, elaborate ploy to show off? Was this some kind of extra component of performance art—was it possible that they were all being recorded in the gallery right at this moment?

'Please!' Fleur seized Lally's arm. 'Why won't you listen to me?'

Lally looked at Fleur's video again. She was sucking on the end of a tendril of hair and her hand had moved beneath her dress. Standing in the centre of the screen, Fleur was masturbating.

'But he called you yesterday to tell you about this.' Lally shook her head, furious at having been left out of the loop about the work on her own walls.

Caroline was coming towards them now, a furious look on her face. The Caroline in the video was writhing on the floor, pulling at her miniskirt.

The crowd was getting wild. There were at least thirty phones out, recording the videos.

'Stop filming!' Fleur screamed at a group in front of her video.

Everyone in the room turned to look, embarrassed for her, a dangerous and tense energy flowing between them all. Fleur swayed a little, now suddenly speechless, the camera phones of the crowd aimed at her. Outside the clear walls to the gallery an entire crowd was looking in, some of them tapping at the glass, a sea of little flashing lights recording.

Caroline reached Fleur's side. 'This isn't right!' she pleaded.

'Looks all right to me!' a man yelled back to applause.

'Shut the fuck up!' Fleur screamed, her voice breaking.

The crowd pulled away from her, jeering, still recording.

Lally was about to step in when all at once the videos synced up. It was impossible not to look. All twelve women stood up straight, looked at the camera, and simultaneously began pulling their tops off.

'No!' someone cried from the corner. It was Jasmine. 'No, no, no.'

Ravi, her tutor, was laughing hysterically.

Fleur lurched towards Lally and started smacking her arm. Skirts and shorts were being taken off now too. Fingers were being hooked into the edges of underpants.

'I don't have the controls!' Lally kept saying, but Fleur wouldn't listen.

Leah pushed through the crowd roughly, the mayhem still rising. A woman was shrieking, 'Turn it off!' while others were cheering, 'Take it off!' Leah reached the far side of the room, where the master source of electricity for the space was located, and Lally saw her reach down and yank the power board out of the wall. One by one, the screens snapped to black.

Some faces in the crowd were tear-streaked, others shocked, many delighted. Countless people had their phones up, each of them with their own recordings. Fleur's friends carried her away back into the crowd and Caroline disappeared into the night outside. The removal of the audio track had inspired a complete silence in the gathering. Leah turned the house lights back up to full brightness and, to Lally's horror, everyone turned to face her. She stood there, flute in hand, alone.

'All right, everybody out!' she yelled, but it was mayhem.

'No!' Leah reached her, breathless, panicking. 'You can't let them all leave with that footage.'

'I can't tell people what to do with their own phones.' Lally shook her head, giving firm looks to stragglers but trying to remain professional. 'It would just make things worse. Start trying to call Eric. Something tells me he has no intention of picking up.'

People were lingering outside the gallery doors. Some of them were still recording.

'Draw the curtains, Leah.'

She found Fleur on the sidewalk, sputtering incoherently to a significantly diminished group of her friends.

'It wasn't me, that wasn't me, I didn't do that,' she kept repeating.

'Can someone take her home, please?' Lally asked.

'Yeah, I will,' one said, and moved to take Fleur's arm, but Fleur pulled away.

'You fucking bitch!' she screamed, turning on Lally. 'Why didn't you stop it? I told you!' She dissolved into tears. 'I told you, I told you.' Her friends closed in around her and she let herself be carried away.

Lally turned back to the gallery to see this, too, had been recorded. Her stomach sank.

'Is this all part of the show?' someone called to her, and before she could answer more people were shouting questions at her, some hurling accusations. The single security guard had to clear a path for her to return to the gallery.

Inside was like the eye of a storm. Noise and banging on the front glass, and the awareness of the hurricane taking off on the internet all around them.

'I can't get Eric,' Leah said, shaking her head.

'*Fuck*. What the *fuck* just happened!' She slammed her hand on her desk.

'Chuck Farr just happened,' Leah replied, stony serious, looking Lally straight in the eye.

Lally put on a show of going into damage control. She found Maria and apologised to her staff, telling them they could either stay and clean up now, or go home and finish cleaning tomorrow. She was surprised when they all started taking their aprons off. It was like a desertion.

'We need to release a statement immediately,' Lally called to Leah, walking over to the desk and turning on the computer.

Leah was standing still, scrolling through her phone.

'And I need you to get me the contact details of all the models, and do whatever you can to get me an appointment with my lawyer first thing tomorrow morning.'

No response.

Lally looked up. 'Leah!'

Leah put her phone in her pocket and looked down at the ground.

'Leah, what's the matter with you? We don't have time for this!'

Leah walked over to the desk and retrieved her handbag from the locked drawer.

'What are you doing?' Lally demanded.

Her assistant reached up and took her coat from its hanger.

'Are you kidding me? You've got to be fucking kidding me. Are you—'

'Lally . . .' Leah said quietly and paused, but then she just shook her head. 'I'll call you.' She turned and walked towards the doors.

'Call me when?' Lally asked, pleading now.

But Leah just knocked on the glass door and waited for the security guard to open it. Then she stepped out into the crowd and was gone.

The floors were sticky with spilled champagne and the lights were stark and it was all silent. Lally felt panic swelling in her chest. 'No,' she said aloud to the empty space. She couldn't afford panic. That was not possible right now. Not an option.

Returning to her computer she saw it wasn't even nine o'clock yet. People would still be turning up at the gallery, wondering what the hell was going on. She had to issue a statement. But what kind? An explanation? She didn't know what the fuck had just happened.

It took twenty minutes to hit the main points: Lally and the entire media preview audience were told the day before that all the subjects had consented to the works; Lally did not have control of the screens; Farr's studio could not be contacted; apologies for any distress caused; show and gallery closed until further notice.

She opened half-a-dozen internet browser tabs to post the statement across all the channels but it was like a hellscape flashing in front of her face. Grainy footage of the videos of the women was everywhere. Photos of Fleur screaming at Lally, and Lally coming across as a haughty ice witch. A group of people cheering, *Take it off!* was already featured across several forums and groups and pages. The gallery's social media accounts were chaos, people screaming at her and Farr and the women and each other.

It was too late to control any of it. She went to the back end of her own website and altered the layout of the home page, uploading the statement as a block of text, removing the inquiries form. She put the same text on all the other platforms

303

and switched tasks, sending an urgent email to her lawyer. How would she contact the women? They were all aspiring something-or-others, so they'd be online, but she'd have to find them one by one. Fucking hell. Could that wait until tomorrow? Emails were flowing in already. Perhaps they would reach out to her when they couldn't get Farr. Would they be able to get Farr?

There wasn't even time to ask the bigger questions. Why did they all strip and touch themselves for his photos? And weren't they worried when he called them the morning before to say he was actually going to use the videos? There was a lingering possibility that this was all part of a publicity stunt, but Fleur's devastation had seemed too genuine for that. Then again, these were acting students. Maybe it was all a project. They were trying to go viral. Lally sighed and put her head in her hands. Nothing made any sense.

A knock on the glass disturbed her.

'Ma'am?' The security guard poked his head in. 'There's a lady here, says she's your friend.'

'Lally, it's me!' Gen called.

'Yes, let her in, please.'

Gen hurried through the door. 'What is going on?' she said, pulling off her gloves and hat. Alex was with her.

'Is the crowd still outside?' Lally asked, standing up to greet them.

'No, what crowd?' Gen asked.

'Thank god it's so cold out there.' Lally exhaled. 'There's been a . . .' A what? She was going to say 'an accident', but it wasn't. This felt more like an attack. 'Farr put videos on the screens that the girls—Jesus Christ, I don't know—that they didn't think he would? That they didn't know he'd filmed? I don't know which particular level of bullshit we're talking about here. Everything was fine for an hour or so. The videos I was telling you about were playing, the ones from the preview. Weird and a bit creepy, sure, but nothing fucked up at all. Then Farr swings by the show, and the next thing you know the videos are of the women touching themselves and taking their clothes off.'

'Oh my god.' Gen's hand went to her mouth.

'Yeah. Fucking pandemonium. People recording, some of the girls screaming and losing their minds. We pulled the plug, literally'—she pointed to the power board sitting innocently on the floor—'and kicked everyone out, but of course enough of them made their own recordings. It's a mess.'

'Oh my god,' Gen repeated.

Alex stood beside her, shocked into silence.

'Are the girls okay?' Gen asked.

'I don't know,' Lally replied. 'I don't have their contact details. I sent one home in a cab because she was so wasted and hysterical.'

'You have to find them,' Gen said.

'I know!' Lally replied, exhausted. 'I've emailed my lawyer and put out a statement—'

'An apology?'

'Yes.' Lally fought off a feeling of defensiveness. 'And I said that I didn't know about any of it and that I haven't been able to reach Farr.'

'Where's your assistant?' Alex asked.

'She left.'

'She did what?' he asked, but Gen nodded.

'Why are you nodding at that?' Lally asked her.

'If this is as big and bad as I think it is, she's going to distance herself from you,' Gen said. 'She's, like, twenty. No way is she going to go down with this white lady's non-PC ship.'

Lally groaned. She had not been ready to hear that particular fear articulated so clearly. She pushed her fingernails into her palms. 'Will you leave me too?'

Gen scoffed. 'I feel like a huge fucking I-told-you-so is in order,' Gen said, 'but I'm not going to leave you. God, Lally. This is going to be long and hard. It's probably not going to feel fair, and you're going to have to pace yourself in dealing with it.'

'Maybe you should call one of those emergency PR firms?' Alex suggested.

'Sometimes I feel like those are an admission of guilt, though, don't you?' Lally replied. 'I don't even understand what happened—and I definitely didn't do anything wrong.'

28

PAT COULDN'T STOP THINKING ABOUT what he'd seen that morning on his way into the building. Em and a man had got out of a cab and then kissed on the lips before going their separate ways. It was a married peck. A see-you-later-for-dinner peck. The man looked to be in his thirties, navy suit, nice briefcase, thick hair, Ray-Bans. Pat didn't know where to place the feelings this brought out in him. He was wounded, of course—but because it meant Em had lied? Because she'd rejected him? Because he'd thought they were friends, but it seemed he didn't know anything about her? He was supposed to be with Lally properly now, and he was happy to be, so why should he care about this other chick dating some other dude?

Bringing his focus back to the task at hand, he kept scrolling through recent sales of vintage fishing gear, trying to make sense of the wildly varying listed prices. It wasn't as boring as he thought it was going to be. One of the reels Gregory had kept in his study was the same model that had been used in an old James Bond film, and it had sold for over ten thousand dollars a decade ago. He'd started with fishing sites and magazines, before realising that Gregory probably didn't actually fish and would have picked up this stuff some other way, and that's when he started getting somewhere—forums about what tackle Hemingway preferred and all that shit. It was a good job for a Friday at the end of a long week.

Pat caught some movement out of the corner of his eye, looked up, and was startled to see Josephine entering his office, closing the door behind her. He stood up and reached for the list he'd been working down, smoothing his tie.

'Sit down,' she said, and he did, but she remained standing.

'One of these reels is easily worth ten grand,' he said, pointing to his list. 'I want to check the other miscellany before we risk losing any special pieces in a bulk lot.'

'Do you remember what I told you about items and estates?' she asked.

'Ah . . .'

'An item can be worth a lot of money, but—'

'The real value is the estate, the client. Yes.'

She stood there, as if waiting for him to add something further.

'Is there some problem with the Bauer account?' he asked.

'You tell me.'

'I was under the impression this second lot of items was good news, that we'd sealed the deal with them?' Everything came out as a question.

'Managing an estate is like managing any relationship, Patrick.'

He hated it when she said his name like that.

'You don't just get it then forget it. It takes maintenance. You must maintain it.'

'Okay, sure, yes.'

'So why is Sophie calling me instead of you? I gave you this permanent position on the understanding you could handle the work. I can delegate work to you, Patrick, but you cannot palm off work on me. Do you understand how much more my hours are worth than yours? Every single phone call I have to take from one of your people is taking time away from one of mine—and mine eat yours for breakfast. Do you understand that?'

'Yes.'

'I can't believe I have to say this to you, like you're a child, but apparently you are, so here we are—this is your only warning.'

'I understand that.'

'Do you?'

'Yes.'

'Because the Bauer account is your lifeline. Sophie Bauer is your bread and butter and the air you breathe.'

'Yes. I wasn't aware she'd called you. I certainly haven't missed any calls from her.' Twisting around in his guts, he had some sense he knew what was going on. Had a feeling that he knew precisely why Sophie had called Josephine, but there was absolutely no way he could find the words for that feeling.

'She said you're acting strange.'

He felt frozen. Paralysed. Was he supposed to tell Josephine about them fucking? How could he do that without sounding completely unprofessional? She would hate that. She could fire him for that.

'All I can think is that—and I mean I'm only guessing—like, I don't even know or think it was this—but she wanted to have dinner—to talk about the pieces, you know—and I suggested lunch instead. She was wanting to meet in the evening, or at her place, and I suggested we meet during business hours, or at the office.'

Josephine crossed her arms. 'You don't want to get in a taxi for your client?'

'It's not—'

'You have a problem with working after five pm now and then?'

'Absolutely not, no, I'm fine with that.'

'So?'

Impossible situation. 'So, I will fix this.'

'If Sophie calls me once more *I* will fix this.'

'I understand, yes.'

'Give me that list.'

Pat's arm shot out. Josephine took the pages and read through them silently, her stance softening, she nodded once or twice. A minute ticked by, Pat waiting silently.

Finally she spoke. 'You've already gone to Alison about the watches?'

'Yes.'

'Good, good. And all this cartography business. We don't have anyone in-house with that kind of expertise, but I know someone at the museum who owes me a favour. Would you like me to call in that favour?'

'That would be fantastic, thank you.'

She gave him a look. 'You like this fishing paraphernalia?'

'Ah . . .'

'Take your time with it, start learning. This isn't the first estate I've seen where the men collect the fishing crap as well as the hunting oils. It could be a useful niche for you. You know, with the jewellery, Alison gets two or three big pieces a year, and we publicise those, but the steady flow of income comes from the small-to-medium pieces. She's one of our most valuable people.'

'Absolutely, sure. I understand.'

'Good, good.' She handed the pages back to him, smiling. 'Whatever you were doing when you first took on the Bauer account, just keep doing it. And let me know when it's done.'

'Can do.'

'That's a good man,' she said with a nod, and left, leaving the door open behind her.

Pat stood still, listening for the sound of Josephine's footsteps disappearing down the corridor. Then he slumped back into his chair and ran his hands through his hair, again and again and again.

'You all right?'

Pat sat up with a jolt.

It was Em, leaning through his open doorway.

He groaned in reply.

'You want company or you want to be alone?' she asked.

'Actually, I think I need your help,' he said.

'What's new?'

He looked up at her. 'But we can't talk about it here.'

She glanced down the corridor in the direction Josephine had gone then looked back at him. 'You wanna buy me a drink after work?'

'Yeah, great.'

'Anytime.'

She disappeared and he slumped again, pulling his mobile out of his pocket for a distraction. It was chock-a-block full of notifications, all featuring Lally's name and the name of her gallery. He started to read the attached articles, unable to make sense of what he was reading. Some people seemed to be saying that nude models had been abused or violated in the gallery, some were saying they didn't consent to their nudes being shared, some were saying Lally was responsible and others were asking why Chuck Farr was still being exhibited, especially at a so-called progressive gallery run by a woman. Pat was fifteen minutes into reading when he realised the situation was still unfolding. He switched across from the news stories to the social media platforms and found an absolute shitshow. He didn't know what to text Lally or if he even should. Would it look like he was keeping too close an eye on her? He scrolled through the comments and this time saw a photo of her amid a crowd. The image was taken with a powerful flash, lighting up Lally's unmistakable brows and her hair in her clip, one hand covering her face and eyes, the other clutching her phone, her legs mid-stride. In the shadows around her a stylish crowd appeared to be in varying states of distress. Some angry, some crying, a few pointing. One person appeared to be yelling at her. It was almost midnight there. He should definitely send her a message. This was getting nasty and weird.

Hey, he typed, *I'm not sure I totally understand the situation but call me anytime. I hope you're all right.*

He waited for ten minutes but there was no reply.

———

A few agonising hours later and he and Em were sitting in the pub near their office.

'I don't know how to say it.' He fumbled with the wet coaster, peeling the cardboard at the edges.

'Is it about Sophie Bauer?'

'Yeah.'

'Take your time.'

Pat took a long drink. 'I tried to set some professional boundaries.' He turned the coaster over and over. 'She said dinner, I'd say lunch, she said home, I'd say the office.'

Em nodded. 'That sounds like a good idea, if a bit late.'

'Too late, apparently.' He couldn't look Em in the eye. 'Sophie was . . .' What was she? 'Disappointed, I guess.'

'Oh.'

'She called Josephine.'

'Oh.'

He looked up at Em. Her eyes were wide. 'Yeah,' he said, 'so Josephine said to me, basically, that if Sophie calls her again, that's it, I'm done.'

'Jesus.'

'Yeah.'

'I mean, I'm doing good work.' He could hear the whine in his voice and he loathed how he sounded. 'I'm pricing this stuff, I'm finding buyers, I'm being discreet. It's, like, a really good start for me in this role, except for . . .' He trailed off.

'Except for Sophie wanting to have sex with you.'

'The first time, sure, it was like a happy accident or something—you know, a nice bonus, whatever. But it changed. And now Lally and I are getting serious.'

'I didn't realise that.'

'Yeah.'

'Serious like if you slept with Sophie it would be cheating?'

'Yes.' It was easier to explain it this way. Using his exclusivity with Lally gave him more of an angle on why his position on Sophie had changed. He was in a relationship now. It was a better out. A nice-guy reason.

Em nodded slowly. 'And you think you'll be fired if you don't give Sophie what she wants?'

'That seemed to be implicit in what Josephine was saying.'

'Sounds pretty explicit to me. She said that you were done if you don't fuck Sophie again?'

'Well, no, she didn't say it like that. She told me to, like, go back to my previous client-management techniques.'

Em sighed. 'You don't really have grounds for any kind of formal complaint.'

'No shit, Sherlock. I'm also not keen on exiting Osborne within twelve months. Nobody else would take me.'

'Josephine has her enemies. Maybe one of the smaller rival groups would give you a go?'

'There's no way. They may not like her, but she's smart. If she rejects me, I'm damaged goods. Nobody wants sloppy seconds.'

'True. Also, you'd need to be ready for this to go public if Sophie were to complain in any way. People won't really get it. You slept with her and then you changed your mind . . .'

'Fucking hell.'

'It's what they'll say, that's all I'm telling you. It's different—'

'It's different because I'm the man?'

'It is different. Some things about it are the same and some are different. That's it.'

'Em, if some old man was doing this to you I would be a bit more sympathetic.'

'Old men have tried to do this to me my whole life, Pat. And when old men do this to young women it's very rare that we're ever into it, even the first time. When old men do this to me they don't give a fuck whether I'm into it or not, and some-times they prefer it when I'm not. So yes, some things are the same, but some things are very different.'

'So I should just shut up then?'

'You asked me to come here and listen.'

'And don't I regret that.'

'I came here and listened, Pat, and I'd be happy to try to help you get out of this mess that you got yourself into, but fucking hell, I'm not going to sit here and listen to you try to chalk things up as some reverse-sexism crap.' She got up to leave.

Pat finished his beer.

'So that's it?' Em looked down at him as she slung her bag over her shoulder.

'I saw you kissing a man.'

She stared at him. 'You've got to be fucking kidding me.'

He shrugged. 'You lied.'

'Yeah, I did. I was hoping to have one workplace where I didn't have to deal with this shit.' She gestured between them. 'One where I could be a human fucking being instead of a woman. But no. I reject you, and so my two options are lesbian or bitch.'

'You're sure being a bitch right now.'

She stared him down and Pat looked into his empty pint glass.

'Well, for the record,' she said loudly, 'I'm bi, and you're a piece of shit.'

'Whatever.'

He watched her leave, then he reached for her undrunk vodka, pulling the ice out of the glass with his fingers and then drinking the whole thing down in one go. God, it was disgusting. He didn't know why girls drank that shit. Through the tinted windows of the pub he saw Em stomp around the corner of the building and out of sight.

What did they all want from him? Too much. Too fucking much. Pat got off his bar stool, pushing through the door of the pub, sliding his sunnies down to cover his eyes, the early evening still bright, and began the walk home. He tried an exercise he'd read about online. He took all the things making him unhappy—Josephine, Sophie, Em—and he put their names on little pieces of paper, and put them in a box that would go on a shelf. Actually, he put them inside a ball. He put them inside a nice hard, shiny new footy, and then he kicked it right over the intersection he was waiting at towards the far horizon. He lifted his hand to his brow, gazing up at the end of the sunset, watching all his problems fade into the distance.

The feeling didn't last. On his way home he'd stopped in at a little park surrounded by terrace houses. Beautiful places with jasmine and wisteria climbing the wrought-iron fences, white shutters on the windows and small backyards. He could work every day for fifty years on a junior associate wage and never come close to affording one of them. Life was pointless and unfair. Everything would be hard and he'd be a useless sack of shit forever. He wanted Lally to hold him, to kiss his head. It was lucky she wasn't there, actually. He wanted to tell her all the things making him so sad and anxious, but he couldn't explain any of it. Couldn't explain Sophie and therefore couldn't explain Em or Josephine. What was his plan? What was he working towards?

To his right, he heard the clicking of a dog's claws on bitumen and the tinkle of a tag hitting a collar. A wiry-coated Jack Russell strained at the end of a leash, excited to get to the shrubs and trees in the park, an open mouth panting and grinning. Its fat tail went straight up in the air like a chubby periscope. That was the dream, and Pat had a choice to make. Step towards it, or away from it? The Jack Russell started taking a shit, and its owner was unrolling a little plastic baggy from a pouch. Every good thing had its crap side, he supposed. Not much he could do about that. The shits didn't go away if you just tried to hold them in.

He pulled his phone out. Still no reply from Lally, still no idea what the fuck that was all about. He found Sophie's number and dialled.

'Pat!' she trilled, picking up on the second ring. 'To what do I owe the honour?'

'Hi, Sophie,' he replied, attempting bright but risking deranged. 'I thought we could go through those documents together at your place this weekend, if you're still free?'

'Oh, sure, wonderful. Come by Saturday night?'

'Perfect. See you then.'

29

LALLY DIDN'T SLEEP. SHE HAD tried Leah and Eric at least
a dozen times each until midnight. When she got home she
wanted to call her mother, or Pat, even though it was late, but
the screen wouldn't stop pinging with horrific notifications.
The vitriol was getting worse. Every platform. Screenshots from
platforms Lally hadn't even heard of, wasn't on, being sent to
her via email. What was she supposed to do, have two phones
from now on? At some time in the wee hours Pat had sent her
another message but she didn't open it. What good would it
do, having his . . . what? His moral support? She'd gotten this
far without crutches. It was always the same with men—the
more you let them in, the more they took from you, the more
mistakes you made. There was a magnet on her mother's fridge:
*It starts when you sink in his arms, and ends with your arms in
the sink.* No, better to keep him apart from this for as long as
possible. He was the weekend thing. The holiday guy.

Overnight the online swamp got rank. On the left they
were scrambling for the moral high ground, climbing over each
other to summit the 'top comments' thread with lectures about

anti-capitalist intersectionality. People who believed the women had known they were being recorded went in to defend them as sex-positive sex workers, saying that by cancelling the show the gallery and media were being hypocritical about when they did and didn't want to make money from women's work and bodies. Someone found a flattering interview *T Magazine* had run about Gallery Lally in its first year and shared it with an all-caps rant that accused her of being just another pick-me girlboss. On the right, incels and neckbeards doubled down to new depths, promising to find and hack the women's accounts and see if their private nudes matched the ones Farr had shared. They knew where these women went to acting classes, knew where they went for their morning coffees. They would be followed. An ex-boyfriend of one of them had come out of the woodwork claiming he had 'better nudes' and linking to his podcast. *Don't forget to like and subscribe!*

It would have been great to be able to avoid the whole mess, but while Lally was still searching for answers she couldn't afford to ignore anything. The comments and shares and posts and threads all contradicted each other. Some repeated the idea that Farr had done everything without consent—a convenient position that was inaccurate but allowed them a slightly more elevated soapbox. The disgusting male contingent seemed to draw no distinction between women performing in pornographic films, women taking intimate images for their partners, and women posing in a photographer's studio for portraits. All sluts. All dumb bitches. All fair game. The most frustrating thing of all, so obvious and undeniable, was that people were commenting on Gallery Lally's accounts, sharing images from her space, asking what she had done, what she was doing. There was this overwhelming acceptance that of course Farr had done this. There had always been and would always be men like him. He was somehow an inevitability, but it was Lally who was the aberration. They knew why Farr would want to do this, but couldn't fathom why Lally would let him.

She showered and dressed. In the mirror a widow stared back. Whatever steely resolve she'd bolstered herself with was rapidly failing. She was briefly invigorated by the cold air on the walk to the gallery, but once she got there she realised she was still alone, and the place was still dirty, and although the screens were black and silent they still emitted the same haunted feeling she'd had before. Lally waited until nine to call Leah, but it went straight to voicemail. Half the catering staff returned at ten to clean up and clear out. Lally tried to act friendly and normal but gave it up after about five minutes when she realised they just wanted to get out of there. When she popped out to get a coffee she suspected the barista was watching her over the top of his coffee machine. Her muscle-memory response was to get her phone out and look busy, but of course it just screamed at her with a new influx of abhorrent notifications.

The non-art news outlets started to pick up on the story, and after that her cell was ringing nonstop. Voicemails hitting four, ten, twenty-two. Every journalist she'd ever given her number to was trying to reach her for comment. Lally sat at the computer and made a list of the names of the sites and papers, and decided which one to give an interview to. It was painful work and her body pumped with resentment and a deep sense of injustice. She chose the *New York Times* because of its credibility and because it could go online immediately. She had given the head arts journalist there, Rob, a scoop a little while back. He might go easy on her.

Rob picked up on the first ring. She reiterated the points she'd posted on her website and socials the night before.

'This is all in your statement,' he said to her, unimpressed.

'Well, what more can I say?'

'Did you think Farr would do something like this?'

'Obviously, I never would have hung his works if I thought he would do something like this.'

'Were you aware of the anonymous harassment allegations made against him twelve months ago?'

'Yes.'

'So you didn't believe them?'

'I didn't say that.'

'So you did believe them?'

'I . . .' She faltered. 'Farr said he had consent forms signed by every sitter.'

'But that was after you programmed him.'

'Yes.'

'So you didn't believe the allegations?'

'I don't know what to say other than how sorry I am.'

She did know what she wanted to say: that she wouldn't be able to work in this business or make any money if she refused to work with dickheads. That people had continued to buy Farr's work after those allegations were aired, maybe even more greedily. That they were all in this sticky web together and it just so happened to be her head on the block now, but glasshouses and stones and fuck them all.

'I've got a call with an expert in this stuff scheduled for eleven,' he said.

'An expert in what stuff?'

'Deep fakes.'

'What?'

'You haven't spoken to any of the women?'

'I haven't been able to find their numbers. Nobody from Farr's studio is taking my calls.'

'I've spoken to three now. They all back each other up. At no time did any of them remove their clothing or perform any of the sexual motions in those clips. Farr created them.'

'Holy shit.'

'So I can confirm that you didn't know?'

'Yes!' she replied. 'I mean, I really can't stress this enough—I had no idea.'

'One woman, Ms James, said she alerted you to the videos being fakes and you did not acknowledge her or act on this.'

'Ms James?'

'Fleur James.'

'Oh.' She knew she couldn't tell him Fleur had been wasted. 'It was chaos. This all happened within minutes and everyone was very confused.'

'Ms James said she knew immediately that the images were doctored, and alerted you to that fact.'

'Well, I suppose I would say that there was a lot of confusion, and I believe we did act quickly in turning off the screens and closing the gallery, and I'm sorry if it wasn't fast enough.' Lally rubbed the space between her eyebrows forcefully. 'Have you been able to contact anyone from Farr's studio?' she asked him.

'We received an email from them attaching the release forms the women signed. They're very open-ended, allowing for any type of editing of the images, not being subject to sitter approval and so on, but they'll still sue.'

She sighed. Fucking contracts.

'You didn't hear this from me, Lally, but they're talking about suing you as well.'

'*What?*'

'You can't be that surprised.'

'Well, I am,' she shot back.

He had a few other background and fact-checking questions, and they said goodbye amicably. When Lally hung up she looked at her phone and saw a text from Hernandez. She was pulling out of the December spot and had issued a public statement about not wanting to work with galleries or individuals who didn't respect women and blah blah fucking blah.

'Goddamn it!' Lally yelled.

Someone tapped on the glass and she sat upright again, staying completely still until the shadow cast against the bottom of the curtains went away. She put her forehead on the glass tabletop and tried to focus on its coolness. Deep breaths.

Pat had sent her several messages but it had frightened her how much she wanted to call him, lean on him. She missed him so much. She knew it was worse like this. Feeling like she had a person but not having that person, not there with her, not the way she wanted or needed. It made her want to rip him out of her life. This half-half wasn't working. He was offering himself as a crutch, but he felt like a wound.

She went to her lawyer's office and explained the situation. The last time she'd had anything significant to do with him was on the morning they dealt with her father's estate. She'd spent the afternoon at the wake, cleaning underneath her fingernails with the corners of his 200gsm business card. This time when the lawyer said he'd get started on things she was significantly less optimistic about the outcome. Initial consult six hundred dollars. Lally just shrugged in reply to the receptionist and asked for it to be charged to the company. At this point in time it wasn't an optional expense. She was already stressed about not making a commission from Farr's works, but she would have been truly fucked if she had banked on being able to sell anything from Hernandez's show.

As she walked home from the meeting the sun came out, and with a brief glimmer of relief Lally realised that for two whole months there'd be nothing showing in the gallery. Then her phone went off in her pocket again and the darkness came rushing back in. She hoped it was Leah messaging, but it was not. It was Gen, inviting her to join 'us' for dinner—that meant Gen and Alex. Lally liked Alex, but she didn't want to be around anyone other than Gen. She just wanted her friend to come over to her house, the way it was before. Why couldn't it all go back to how it was before?

———

She woke up from a terrible nightmare to someone knocking at her front door.

'Lally, it's me—Gen!'

Lally stumbled over to the door and opened it.

'My god, have you been smoking in here?'

'Yes.'

'And drinking too, clearly. Alone.' Gen pushed past her into the living room.

'What's new?'

'It's ten pm.'

Lally didn't know if she'd slept for four hours or twenty-eight. Couldn't have been twenty-eight. She must just be drunk.

'I cancelled on Alex and picked up some pizza,' Gen said, setting the box on the table.

Lally didn't move.

'Have at least one slice,' Gen urged, going to the kitchen for plates.

When one had gone down another three swiftly followed. Lally felt like she was coming to.

Gen was smiling and shaking her head, one hand on her hip. 'You are so predictable.'

'Yes, but you love me?' Lally replied.

'Yes, but I love you.' Gen reached out to tuck some hair behind Lally's ear. 'Speaking of which, I got a call from Pat. He's worried about you. Says you're not reading his messages.'

Lally wiped her mouth with the back of her hand. 'What can he do?'

Gen was silent.

'And besides, I have you.'

Gen sighed. 'I think you'll feel better if you call him. I know you talk about not knowing where your relationship is going, but he is your friend too. I know he is. And he speaks your language. Why don't you just read his messages tomorrow?'

Lally rolled her eyes, took another piece of pizza, and retrieved the second half-bottle of red from beside her bed. 'Wine?' she asked, returning to the kitchen and taking two glasses out of the cabinet.

'You been swigging that?'

'What, you worried you'll get girl germs?'

'Touché,' Gen said, taking a glass. 'Alex is defending you, you know,' she added. 'Don't be afraid of being around him.'

'Defending me against who?'

Gen just gave her a look.

'Okay, okay. I don't want to know.'

'I read the *Times* article. What did you think of it?'

'I guess it doesn't matter what I think anymore.'

'Come on.'

'Well, don't you think these sitters are complicit too?' Lally asked. 'Weren't they helping Farr by working with him? The *Times* make it sound like he kidnapped a dozen sexy babies.'

'But they're young wannabes, they had no power in that interaction.' Gen was gentle but firm. 'And Farr has a pattern of targeting people downwards like that, exerting pressure.'

'But the first incidents were harassment, like generic he's-a-creep stuff. So these twelve women would have seen those things too, right? And they still went along for a portrait shoot. Is it impossible to be at all complicit if you're the one with less power?'

Gen shrugged. 'It just doesn't feel right.'

'I know it doesn't feel right, but I'm trying to get one single fucking person to articulate why!'

'I suppose all I'll say is—' Gen paused, obviously choosing her words carefully '—there are a lot of confusing ways to do the wrong thing, but I think most of us know when we can do the right thing. And working with Farr isn't—or wasn't—the right thing. For any of you, but in different ways.'

Lally took another slice of pizza and got another bottle of wine down from the rack.

When she woke up the next day her fingers were still greasy. There was a wine-coloured stain on the pillow where she'd dribbled. Looking out the window, she wondered what would happen if she didn't get up. How many hours would go by until she just decayed, or until Gen got the cops to break the door down. It was strange to not want to check her phone. To in fact be a bit afraid of it. It made her feel disconnected, alone. Ironic, given that she couldn't get people to stop contacting her and tagging her and 'alerting' her.

Eventually, she took a shower. Without her phone by her side Lally had a distorted idea of time passing. She didn't own a watch, and didn't have a clock in the house. Why would she? She was always working, always on a device, always knew what time it was. Now the morning—or was it early afternoon?—stretched out in front of her like a funhouse mirror.

Once she was dressed she picked the phone up, doing her best to dismiss all the irrelevant information, keeping an eye out for correspondence from any of the women, or her lawyer, or Gen, or Leah. The most concerning development was Olivia Hernandez announcing she was going to live broadcast an interview series with each of the models in turn. The project would allow them to 'reclaim' their narratives, returning their 'voices' to them, making the camera a 'safe object' again. If Hernandez broadcast one a week it would drag on for months. Would the attention on it steadily increase or decrease? Would Lally be the target or would Farr? It could be terrible. There was no way of knowing.

There were more messages from Pat. Her heart tugged towards them when she saw his name. She was about to open their chat screen when the phone started ringing. It was Leah.

She picked up too quickly. 'Leah.'

'Hi, Lally. Are you all right?'

That was fucking rich, coming from someone who had abandoned her, but sure. 'Not really.'

'I'm sorry to hear that.'

That sounded funny to Lally, the way Leah had just said that.

'I'm calling to tell you a few things, and I would appreciate if you would let me speak for a couple of minutes, and then I'd be happy to hear your reply.'

Lally almost snorted. 'Sure.'

What came out was clearly rehearsed, possibly even being read out. That Leah had tried to warn Lally about Farr from the beginning, that Lally should have thought of the women first that night and the following morning and they were upset she hadn't contacted them immediately, that Leah had helped her build a specific type of trust at the gallery . . . On it went.

'I've accepted an offer of employment from PPOW,' Leah finished, 'and as my contract with you was as a casual employee, I am not obliged to give notice of my departure. In any case, I know the gallery will now be empty until the new year, so I trust this is not an inconvenient time for you to try to fill the position.'

Lally leaned her back against the wall behind her.

'Are you there, Lally?'

'Yes. I mean, I would really love for you to take a little time and think about this.'

'I already have,' Leah replied, firm. Perhaps forty-eight hours was a long time these days. Sure felt like it.

'I want to thank you for the very valuable time I spent with you. I learned a lot. Please feel free to come by PPOW and see me here whenever you want.'

See me *here*. So she was already there. Her new colleagues were probably listening.

'Thank you for calling, Leah, and best wishes.' She forced the words then hung up, sliding down the wall until she was sitting on the carpet.

Alone again. A distinct degree more alone than before. Betrayed, even. One extra shovel of dirt heaped on top of her that she'd have to somehow dig herself out from under. It was all so heavy.

She opened the chat screen with Pat. Messages from him full of kindness and concern filled screen after screen, breaks of a few hours before trying again, some gentle, some firm, missed video call requests. *I think you came across well in this*, with a link to the *Times* piece. The last message had been sent two hours earlier: *If you don't want me to contact you anymore that's fine, but I'm just worried you're not seeing these?* She hit the video call button and clutched the phone in both hands, willing him to pick up, but it rang and rang. At just the moment she almost broke down, abandoned again, the *beep-boop* noise rang out and suddenly there he was, filling the screen, rubbing his eyes and turning his bedside lamp on, wincing when the light flooded the room.

'Lally?' he said, looking at her, and when she saw his face she opened her mouth to speak but a cry came out instead, and tears starting falling down her face, falling and falling.

'Shit,' he said. 'Hey, hey, I'm here, Lally. I'm here.'

She didn't even know what to say, just shook her head, her crying getting louder, her chin wet.

He balanced his phone on the windowsill and sat on the edge of his bed just looking at her, waiting.

'I don't know what to do!' she sobbed, wiping snot from her nose with the back of her hand. 'Everyone hates me. I've ruined it all.'

'No, not everyone hates you. This is . . . this is a bad thing. It's a bad time. But it's temporary.'

She rested her own phone on the edge of the bedframe, pulling her knees up to her chin. 'Leah quit and hung me out to dry, and she has all these friends and connections I didn't know about. I thought . . . I don't know . . . I thought she looked up to me,' Lally heard herself whining. 'This was everything! The gallery. My reputation. Everything is gone.' She could feel her eyes swelling with the sudden rush of tears, the force of them.

'It's not. You are still you, and you're amazing.'

She shook her head.

'I'm not sure how to comfort you, or say it's not a big deal, without sounding like I don't care about the accusations against Farr,' Pat said.

Lally rubbed her eyes till she saw static behind the lids. The crying wouldn't stop.

'But I know you, and you can do anything.'

'It hurts.'

'Okay. It's okay to feel hurt. Lots of people care about you, though. Gen cares about you, your mum cares about you, I care about you.'

She cried on and on.

'Lally, I love you.'

A wave crashed over her. 'I love you too.'

'I don't know why you didn't want to talk to me before, but it doesn't matter. Just talk to me from now on, okay?'

'Can we talk every day?'

'Absolutely. But maybe not at four in the morning.'

'Sorry.'

'It's okay. I'm glad you called. But why don't we make a regular time? At least until you're in less of a . . . situation.'

'Situation,' she repeated.

'Is there any update on the situation?' he asked.

Her mind pinballed between all the moving parts, all of them terrible, insurmountable. 'Can we talk about something else?'

'Yeah, of course, totally. I'm looking forward to you coming back in December.'

'Me too.'

'And you know, it's only a few weeks away, so you just have to get through a little bit more, and then you'll be here, and you can relax.'

She nodded, wiping her nose again.

'What do you normally do for Christmas?' he asked.

'Ah, normally I'd go to Mom's place and spend it with her and Gary, and sometimes Gary's daughter from his first marriage is there too, but they're going away this year. Gen and I have spent Christmas together a couple of times, but she's going to visit her folks in North Carolina this year. She's taking Alex to meet them. Everyone is coupling up.'

He nodded.

'I'm going to see Mom in the first week of December, before they leave.'

'That's good.'

Lally nodded. The crying was easing.

'Does your mum know about this stuff?'

'Yeah. But I haven't spoken to her yet.'

'Why not?'

Lally sighed. 'I don't know. I spent all Dad's money on the gallery. If it's not successful, or if I mess this up, it's . . . I don't know how to explain it. She gave up so much for me, for me to have opportunities she didn't. It's a lot of pressure. If I fail at this then it's like I'm spitting in her face. It was bad enough that I wanted to go to art school. Then to put all the money into this one basket. There's only one of me, you know? I don't have any siblings to take the pressure off.'

'But she loves you.'

'Yeah, but that doesn't mean I want to talk to her about being a fuck-up.'

'You're not a fuck-up.'

'Well, I sure fucked up.'

He was silent.

'I should let you go,' she said.

'No, it's fine.'

'No, no, you go back to sleep. Call me when you get home from work. No, that won't work. Call me before you go to bed.'

'All right. Well . . .' He paused.

'I love you,' she said.

'Yeah, I love you too,' he replied with a sleepy smile.

'Sweet dreams.'

The snot on her sleeve was thick. Aching, she heaved herself up off the carpet and headed to the bathroom, shedding her clothes on the way. She stood in front of the mirror and met her own gaze. Oily hair, bloodshot eyes with heavy bags underneath, patches of red skin at the sides of her nose, chapped lips and fine lines. This was what he'd been looking at when he said he loved her. She had been brought low. Her worst failure was the most public thing that had ever happened to her, and still he loved her. No boy had told her he loved her in a long, long time. Just the bad one in college, and before that? She didn't count the one in senior high who said it, who she then slept with, who then told everyone and also dumped her shortly after. Her dad had said he loved her all the time, but he also said he loved Estelle, so his words didn't mean shit.

This was it. Pat was it. It couldn't have come at a worse time. It couldn't have come at a better time.

———

Within another forty-eight hours two more young women had come forward with historic allegations against Farr, causing the story to flare up again. Farr was rumoured to have left New

York. A group of angry art students were camping outside his building waiting to pounce and hadn't seen anyone go in or out. It occurred to Lally while she was reading this news that she hadn't been back to the gallery. She shivered at the memory of how many people must have tried to peek in the last time she was there. Seeing a photo of the students with their spray-painted signs made her decide to swing by and check nobody had vandalised the place. Big rainproof jacket, beanie, large sunglasses. She looked at herself in the mirror on the way out and thought of Pat again. Just a simple toast-and-butter kind of missing. She wished he was there with her, that was all.

Her phone pinged with a message from Gen. The first Hernandez interview was live already. Jesus, these kids moved fast. It was bad news because it would keep the controversy boiling up, but it was good news if it all happened fast and ripped the bad-PR bandaid off.

There are a lot of questions about how much you knew, Gen wrote. *You should consider doing an interview with Hernandez yourself. Position yourself alongside them rather than against them.*

It was drizzling outside. Lally stood underneath the red awning at the base of her building. The sharp corner of someone's umbrella hit her shoulder as they passed, and she just watched them walk away. Hailing a cab was an option. So was ordering a car. But really, what did she have to lose? If she caught pneumonia and went to hospital then maybe they'd at least give her something to help her sleep.

Nobody had graffitied the front of the gallery. No students were protesting. She stood across the street, drenched, looking at it from far away. Rain was slicking down the glass, the frosted logo looking good when the curtains were drawn closed behind the glass. They would stay closed until late January, and even then it was always difficult to get people to go out until around March. Both the early-year slots were confirmed with the artists. Thankfully neither of them were locals. She had assured them that the news was classic New York-centric gossip which would have died down by Christmas. Lally stood in the rain, which was coming down harder now, replaying those conversations. Replaying the conversation with Leah. Replaying how wasted and incoherent Fleur had been and what she should have done differently. Thinking of the emails she'd received from Al and Curtis, both variations on a this-too-shall-pass theme. A cab slowed down in front of her and she waved it on, then crossed the road and stood closer to the double doors.

What would pass? The controversy? Sure it would. Lally felt maybe she had a bigger problem, though. At some point in time, her love of art had morphed into a love of her gallery, which had morphed into a love of seeing the gallery succeed, which had morphed into a love of being seen to be successful. The snake ate its own tail: the more successful she appeared the better art she could platform and sell, the more she could help artists and herself, the more she could elevate the status of the gallery, the more money she made, the more she could expand, the more emerging artists she could turn into superstars, the more more more more more. Some cogs inside her were turning. It had something to do with the money, something to do with her father, with Rivera, with Farr, something about what she was trying to prove in this part of town. Prove to these men. She had wanted to beat them at their own game. Use their own money and work to get herself a spot up on the podium. But when she got it all, it didn't feel like winning. It had felt empty all year. She had wanted to give a spot to an artist like Hernandez but the equation was impossible. Broke and morally perfect or imperfect and actually helping? Money was the clearest indicator of worth, an undeniable metric of success, but you weren't supposed to chase money, despite longevity in business also meaning longer in which to do good. She'd gone into the profession thinking she had her own metrics, her own definitions. Had she, or had they changed? In this industry—in any industry?—there was no way to be successful without using people. She was using the artists. Selling them. Selling their images. Selling her own story. Selling her story to herself. But she couldn't see a way out. Dump the whole dream and join a commune? Dump the whole dream and pop out some babies? Every time she got to this place—the 'just quit' place—she couldn't help but feel that to do so would be giving in. Giving them what they wanted. 'Suck it up or leave,' they'd said when things at art school got hard, not acknowledging that they were only making it hard for some of the students. They would always try to push women out. The most effective way to do it was to make her think she was choosing to leave. Complain? Punished. Climb too high, despite them all? Punished. Attributes and attitudes that were rewarded in Farr and Rivera, that made them mavericks. Lally was supposed to be grateful. Always, eternally, grateful. Success wasn't the retribution she'd imagined.

A group of young women hurrying past erupted into laughter, and Lally glared at them shrieking and hooting, remembering back to the group of friends she hadn't realised Leah had. Gen was seeing more of Alex. That was normal. After the honeymoon phase she and Gen would get back into their groove of hanging out all the time. Unless they didn't. Her mom was always in her corner, but Estelle was ageing. Being 'single' had suited Lally when these other people were there for her, and when she didn't need the approval of strangers because she was undeniably a 'success'. It wasn't that simple anymore. Love had changed everything. Failure too. Glass she thought had set cold was somehow being re-blown, and it was hurting her heart to be so turned and turned and turned.

Her phone was ringing. Caller ID displayed *HBO Dudebro*. A messaged pinged through. *You have one new voicemail.*

She mashed the buttons through her glove and smacked the little device against her frozen right ear, plugging her left with her free hand, to listen.

'*Lally, hi, it's Seth. I hope you're well. I'm here in the meeting room with the boys and, look, I didn't want to leave this as a message, but we've been trying you for a couple of days and can't get through.*' He took a breath. '*We won't be going ahead with the Rivera project. I know, I know, I'm so sorry to do this over the phone. It's just, honestly, it's not the right climate, we feel, with everything that's been happening with the situation . . .*' He went on but Lally was just sort of mentally flat-lining with jubilation. How could one accurately capture the irony of this situation? It was like a giant cunt of a meteor had been plummeting towards her, and then another giant cunt of a meteor had come out of nowhere and knocked it off its collision course.

Maybe there was a God. Maybe God never gave us more dickheads than we could handle.

30

EVERY MINUTE THAT TICKED BY waiting for the cab to arrive was like stepping slowly towards the edge of the cliff. He couldn't stop compulsively checking his phone every minute or two, hoping for some nutso miracle that meant Sophie would cancel. It wasn't until he was in the car on the way to Mosman—running late—that his phone vibrated.

It was a message from Lally.

Lally: *Hey*

Pat's heart and stomach twisted in on each other.

Pat: *Hey. Isn't it super early there?*

Lally: *Yeah, my alarm just went off. I was having a dream about Christmas*

Pat: *Nice*

Lally: *We were unwrapping some presents and then there was a dog? I'm not sure. It was shaking snow on us*

Ha

Pat: *Random*

Lally: *What are you up to?*

Pat stared at her question. What was he up to?

Pat: *Just in a cab to see*—He stopped typing. 'A friend' wasn't technically a lie, but it sounded deliberately vague—*Rory.* A lie was safer.

Lally: *Oh nice. What are you doing?*

Pat: *Beers*

Lally: *Well, I'll leave you to it then. I miss you*

Pat: *I miss you too*

Lally: *Xxx*

Pat: *Wait, can I see you?*

There was no immediate reply. Then a graphic was loading. It was a short video of her, mostly her face, on those huge fluffy white pillows, a soft morning light streaming in, her hair all messed up and bare-faced. She waved at the camera and though he had the sound turned off he could see her mouth silently: 'I love you.'

I love you too, he typed.

'This it?' The cab driver's gruff voice slapped Pat back to the real world. They were idling in front of that lawn, that path, that car parked in the driveway.

'Yeah, thanks, mate,' Pat said, putting his phone away. 'Can I get a receipt, please?'

The driver just nodded, giving him a suspicious look in the rear-vision mirror before looking out the window at the Bauer house. 'Some business.'

'Thanks,' Pat replied, sliding across the ripped vinyl bench seat and slamming the door behind him.

The cab took off and left him with the quiet hum of the suburbs. The warm night. The little cluster of bugs hanging around under the streetlight. He put his hands in his pockets and stood there, looking at the house. Unfortunately, no miracle had manifested on the ride over. If he fucked this up with Sophie and lost his job, would he then lose Lally too? Would she stick around if he couldn't find other work? Was cheating on Lally that much worse than lying to Lally? Wasn't cheating just a type of lying?

'Pat?' a voice called from high up somewhere. 'Is that you?'

It was Sophie. She was on a balcony at the side of the house wearing a short dress and she had a glass of wine in her hand. 'What are you doing standing out there? Come in!'

He pulled a hand out of his pocket to wave but she'd already disappeared inside. Pat was experiencing some kind of fight-or-flight response. Frozen on the spot, wanting to run.

The front door opened and he walked towards her.

'Are you all right?' she said, holding the door open with her hip, a glass of wine in each hand. She handed Pat one when he reached her.

'Thanks,' he said, leaning in to kiss her on the cheek.

'What's going on?' Sophie asked, closing the front door behind them, leading the way to the lounge area. That Norah Jones song from that movie was playing. She perched on the edge of the couch and patted the seat beside her, crossing her legs towards him, one arm draped along the back of the couch. He sat down, holding the glass in both hands between his legs, looking down at it.

'What's the matter?' she asked gently.

'Ah, it's . . . I have to tell you something.'

'Oh god.' She put a hand to her chest.

'I'm . . . I mean . . . I have . . .'

'What? You have what?'

'A girlfriend!' he announced, louder than he'd intended, finally raising his head to look at her.

She paused for a moment, her mouth still open, then burst into laughter. She laughed and laughed. 'I thought you were going to say you had an STD!' Then she laughed some more and slapped her leg, and slapped his.

Pat took a gulp of wine.

'Oh, Pattie, Pattie,' she said, calming down. 'Good for you! Cheers!' She held her glass out.

He clinked it with his, and they both drank.

'She's—' he began, but Sophie cut him off.

'Oh, you don't have to tell me, I don't want to know.' She was smiling, but firm. 'We had a nice time, and we can still finish off all this work together, right? We're big kids.'

'Absolutely, of course.'

'Wonderful!' She got up from the couch and walked towards the kitchen, still talking. 'Tell me you're getting good money for all that fishing shit! You know the moron didn't even fish?' She reappeared with the rest of the bottle of wine.

'Actually,' Pat said, 'it turns out a lot of it is collectible. They're pieces from film sets.'

She snorted, refilling her glass then his. 'Trust Gregory to be that basic. So how quickly can we move it all? It's costing me to pay for his fucking storage units out there at Waterloo, and I spoke to our lawyers today and they said every account we know about has been completely inactive since he left, so it seems he's gone for good. At this point in time I wouldn't even mind if you wanted to auction them off. I don't care if the whole world sees how stupid he was.' She scoffed. 'Collecting things he didn't know how to use.'

'An auction would be a great way to do it,' Pat said. 'We could select all the items with cinema credibility and bill it that way. Those types of things can really draw a crowd, sometimes get a bit of press even, if there's a special piece or two.' He was getting excited now.

'And is there? A special piece?'

'He has the Walther PP prop gun from *Dr No*.'

'How much is that worth?'

'Six figures, I think. If two people want it, easily two hundred grand. People go mad for Sean Connery memorabilia.'

'Excellent work, Pat!' She patted him on the shoulder. 'This'll be a nice little bonus for you!'

'Thanks,' he said, smiling, brightening. Things had gone so quickly from dire to excellent. 'Actually I think for Christmas my girlfriend is going—'

She laughed a little, cutting him off again, 'I don't want to know, Pat.'

'Right,' he nodded, shutting up.

'I hate that word "memorabilia",' she said. 'So tacky. I find . . . what do you call it'—she clicked her fingers, looking for the word—'when you're looking backward?'

'Nostalgia?'

'Nostalgia! I find it so sad. Especially in a man. Especially in men of a certain age. Don't ever get nostalgic, Pat.' She sighed and ran her red-nailed fingers through his hair. 'No baldness in your family, I'm guessing?'

'Lucky me.'

'Indeed! Always play to your strengths. Now, shall we talk about what an auction would look like? Do you think we can get it done before Christmas? I want to go skiing. Do you think people would buy this stuff as Christmas presents?'

'Yes and yes,' he replied. 'I can fast-track the photography and get the items uploaded to the website this week. I've already prepared and identified the key pieces.'

They finished the bottle of wine and finished making the plans. Pat was giddy with relief. Josephine would be beyond thrilled. They'd make so much more money this way.

When Sophie stood up and walked him to the door they were chatting like friends. At the front door she kissed him on the cheek then didn't wait for his cab to arrive before closing it. Business.

He stood in the warm night air, in the same spot where the cab had dropped him off a couple of hours earlier, shaking his head at his luck. The evening could so easily have gone so differently. What a fucking fluke.

31

THEY GOT OUT OF THE cab and Lally turned around, shaking her head. 'I can't do this.' She couldn't breathe. The sweat was soaking into the underarms of her silk blouse. Her tights were cutting into her gut. People were going to laugh at her. She would be shamed. Further denigrated. Humiliated.

'Yes, you can.'

'I'm going to be sick.'

'Well, be sick here in this trash can and I'll wipe your face and you'll chew some gum and then we'll do this.'

Lally looked Gen in the face. Such luck. To have someone stick by her through all this. To have that person be the precise combination of caring and zero-fucks she needed. Lally turned back towards Broadway, PPOW a block away.

'The first one was always going to be the worst,' Gen said, plucking non-existent lint off the shoulder of Lally's coat. 'We rock up, we shake hands, we keep our chins up and our shoulders back, and we leave after fifteen minutes.'

'Ten,' Lally pleaded.

'Fine, ten.'

'How many times do I need to do this?'

'I'd estimate five to eight before the puking feeling begins to subside.'

Lally grimaced. She wanted to rub her eyes and chew her lips but she'd only just done her face for the night, so she ravaged her cuticles instead. 'I've done harder things, right?'

'There's my girl!'

There was a cluster of people smoking and stamping their feet outside the gallery's glass front, but no line. A show this late in the year was always going to have a small opening.

Lally spotted Leah just inside the front door and had to hold her hands in fists inside her pockets to stop the ferocity of the picking. For a brief moment Lally feared Leah might not even let them in.

'Lally?' Leah said loudly.

The room hushed and people turned. Lally recognised plenty of the faces. Faces that previously would have broken into smiles at her arrival but were now a mixture of shock and pity.

'Leah,' Lally said pleasantly. She and Gen had rehearsed this. 'Congratulations on the great exhibition copy and your new position here. Strong work. I'm thrilled for you.'

Leah's own hand must have extended on auto-pilot, because the young woman didn't have a verbal reply. Lally saw an opening and went in for a cheek kiss, which Leah, clearly stunned, accepted. Then Lally felt a gentle nudge behind her from Gen, so they went further into the space, as planned, with their chins up.

'Yes, please,' Gen said to a passing waiter, accepting two flutes and passing one to Lally.

'Thank you,' Lally said as the noise levels began to rise again around them. She recognised three-quarters of the people in the room, but the strategy was not to 'push' her first re-appearance by putting anyone on the spot. PPOW's owners would be here somewhere but they would no doubt avoid her.

'You're doing great,' Gen whispered to her, and they began their loop, sipping their champagne. 'Eight minutes left.'

People were moving out of their way as they neared each work. 'Everyone is avoiding me,' Lally whispered.

Gen shrugged and smiled, pretending to point to a spot on the landscape in front of them. 'We knew that was going to happen.'

Lally's face burned. 'We should go.'

'Not yet. You're going to breathe for another four minutes, you're going to finish this drink, and then we're getting fresh air and martinis.'

One hundred years later, they gave their empty flutes to the waiter and made a swift exit. Leah was no longer on the door and the space had filled quickly.

She and Gen hurried across Canal Street to the bar.

'I think I should cancel the interview with Hernandez tomorrow,' Lally said, looking down at her bleeding thumbnail.

'You can't do that. Do you need me to come with you to her studio?'

Lally sighed. 'No, thank you.'

'Are you sure? You nearly freaked in there.'

'I know.'

Lally got off at Tremont station with barely any memory of the ride uptown. She followed Hernandez's directions to a semi-industrial sublet on the second floor of a place opposite a car yard.

'Come in,' Hernandez called through a propped-open door.

Lally fought her rising panic. All her career she'd tried to stay off camera. To keep her face hidden. To be an elusive, mysterious, not-online presence. Years of effort in subtly side-stepping certain types of media requests. And after all that work and effort, here she was, her face about to be broadcast live online for the invisible sneering masses to get their scalp.

It was supposed to be an interview between her and Hernandez alone, but as Lally pushed the door open she saw half-a-dozen women she recognised immediately. The models. In various positions of crossed arms and furrowed brows. Jasmine was the only one who offered Lally a miniscule nod of acknowledgement.

Hernandez stepped forward from the group and Lally was struck anew by how tall the artist was. How much her intense physical presence brought to her performance work. It was intimidating to see such a young woman so very . . . what? Confident? Assured? Embodied? What a damn shame she'd refused to show at Gallery Lally. Hernandez would have filled that whole space.

'I floated the idea with all twelve, and these women accepted my invitation,' she explained.

Lally nodded slowly, realising she had been ambushed. How ironic.

'They've got questions for you. We're going live in a few minutes. Do you need to use the bathroom?'

'No, thank you,' Lally replied.

Hernandez directed her to a stool that forced Lally to perch awkwardly. A camera was pointed at her.

'Could I have a glass of water, please?' Lally asked.

Fleur raised an eyebrow, but Hernandez nodded and left the room. Lally set her handbag down on the floor beside her and looked inside it to the now-useless list of talking points she'd stayed up all night studying. When she looked up again she realised she was alone in the room with six gorgeous, hurting, pissed-off young women. It was cinematic, no denying it. The townsfolk would get their ritual burning. The beautiful women would stand together to throw rotting fruit at the witch.

Over the hour-long livestream Lally lost count of how many times she explained how she also had no control, also had no idea, also couldn't believe what had happened.

'I am sorry,' Lally said. Again and again and again. 'I am sorry.'

When she finally stumbled back outside into the light she made it around the corner and into a filthy alley in time to lean against the wall, burping. She heaved and the water she'd sipped came back up. She heaved again and this time it was the morning's coffee stinging her throat, dribbling down her chin. Hunched over, spitting, she finally let the tears come.

Thanksgiving with her mom and Gary was nice. They'd prepared a mini Christmas feast for Lally's sake and exchanged gifts. Gary had bought Estelle a pair of golden earrings. Emerald studs.

'I know they're small, but this way you can wear them in the kitchen,' he said.

Her mother said nothing but smiled at him for a long time, reaching out to put her palm on his cheek. Lally felt she was interrupting something intimate, but she was grateful too. People thought Estelle was such a hard woman. Lally knew Estelle would never stop worrying about her performance as a wife. It had been too heavily ingrained in her since birth by one family, then pushed to breaking point by another. She could run and jump towards a new vision for herself, but the bungee cord tethering her to her upbringing would always pull her back. It was incredible that Estelle had found a man who bought her jewellery she could wear to work. He knew her. Saw she needed to be reassured that she was a good wife but didn't want to do any of the shit that usually went along with it. She wanted to work hard, make good money and come home to someone who was kind to her. He understood.

Estelle hadn't been overly enthusiastic when Lally announced she would be spending Christmas with Pat's family in Australia. 'You're going out into the middle of nowhere? Into the outback? Haven't you read about the girls that get taken there?'

'I don't think his family live in the actual outback,' Lally had replied. 'Esk isn't far from Brisbane. And I'll have my phone the whole time. Besides, Pat works for Osborne. It's not like he's some random. Gen has met him.'

Estelle narrowed her eyes. 'What kind of drunk is he?'

'Silly,' Lally assured her.

'Good.'

It was risky for Lally, wellbeing-wise, that she didn't have any work, and was essentially alone in New York in the lead-up to Christmas. Planning activities each day was the only option to stave off despondency and doom-scrolling. She went ice-skating in Central Park and laughed at the children falling down, lapping them with her arms behind her back. Sometimes she went past the gallery just to collect the mail that got shoved under the doors. Shopping for gifts for Pat's family was something to focus on at least.

Her suitcase was ready beside the door on Wednesday but her flight didn't leave until Friday. There was nobody left in the city to make her pretend she was embarrassed about this. Gen sent her messages from Raleigh every other day, and Lally responded to them immediately. She intended to spend the day before her departure finally sorting through her emails. Normally she liked keeping the inbox to only actionable content, but it was full of hundreds of read and unread emails from the Farr fallout. Her hands were shaking and her stomach was churning after about an hour. It was still too soon. She started drinking at eleven am and fantasised about just deleting everything. An exhilarating temptation. What a great fuck-you to all the people who didn't know her yet had spent hours puking their loathing through their keyboards. She couldn't quite bring herself to do it, but the drink at least emboldened her to start deleting messages unread when the subject line indicated vitriolic content. It halved her inbox. That would do.

Nobody had heard from Farr. A young hotshot law firm was representing nine of the twelve women pro bono. Lally's own lawyer called to tell her that the women didn't intend to take legal action against Lally at this stage but reserved their right to do so.

'Cool.' She hung up and rested her forehead on the table in front of her.

She saw him first, standing alone in the crowd at Brisbane airport's arrivals gate, and the wave crashed over her again.

'You smell so good,' she said, pressing her face into his chest.

He loaded Lally's suitcase into the car while she adjusted to the heat and light, cranking the air conditioner to maximum.

'Ready to roll?' he asked, getting into the driver's seat.

'Yep.'

'We'll stop in about an hour for a break, then it's another thirty minutes.'

'Any country sweethearts I should be worried about?'

He smiled. 'No.'

'It's okay if there are.'

'If any girls I knew are still around they'll be married with babies by now.'

'Like Beck,' Lally said matter-of-factly, but regretted it immediately.

'Yeah,' Pat replied, and they rode in silence for a bit.

'I didn't mean . . . I mean, I'm sorry if that was inappropriate,' Lally said awkwardly.

Pat exhaled loudly. 'Well, it's true. If she'd gone to uni she probably would have a decent job instead of kids already, but you can't really get to university from the local high school. Well, technically you can, but most people don't. It's more of a . . . I dunno . . . a cultural thing, I guess.'

'This is the family sore spot I should avoid talking about?'

'Yes—Christ almighty, yes. Whatever you do, don't talk about education or career prospects.'

'Or any kinds of women's issues, I presume?' she asked in a slightly mocking tone.

'Well, that's not totally true. The women in my family are definitely headstrong.'

'Headstrong,' Lally said, using her fingers to make air quotes, 'normally means bossy but still not allowed an abortion.'

'That's . . .' Pat hesitated. 'That's about right.'

'Great, I might just shut the fuck up then and speak when spoken to?'

He laughed again. 'Jesus, don't be dramatic! All I'm asking you to do is avoid mentioning literally the most controversial things you can possibly think of.'

She laughed, but he got a bit sullen.

'It's just, I don't feel like I fit here. I . . . This isn't me. I feel like you're psychoanalysing me. I'm nervous you're going to decide things about me because I used to live here. I haven't lived here for a long time.'

'Okay.'

'I don't want this to be my future.'

Lally reached out and put a hand on his thigh. 'Pat . . .' she said, and he looked at her. 'I know what it is to love your family but to want to grow into something different.'

He nodded.

She squeezed a little, and moved her hand up his leg.

His body went stiff in response.

'All good?' she asked.

'Yeah,' he replied, glancing towards her then back to the road. 'But I really, really wish we had some time alone before seeing my folks.'

She smiled. 'Are there cheap motels in Queensland?'

'Yes.' He grinned back. 'Yes, there absolutely are.'

32

PAT ELBOWED LUKE AS THEY watched Tom tear into one of his smaller presents while the adults were still finishing their coffees on Christmas morning.

'Can you imagine what'd happen to us if we did that?'

'You're just jealous,' Beck said from her spot on the floor with Tom, not looking up.

'You bet I am.'

'Come on now,' Kel said, gathering them the way she corralled the chooks, 'let's do this properly.'

Pat shotgunned a seat on the sofa and pulled Lally down next to him.

'What've you got there, Tom?' Luke asked.

'Lego!' The boy thrust the box up into the air, triumphant.

Pat watched his mum sorting through the small pile of presents, getting ready to hand them out. 'Tom has opened his first, so let's find one for our new family members.' She handed a parcel to Beck. 'For Hannah.' The baby was dipping in and out of sleep and gurgling, and Beck opened the wrapping gently to reveal a pale pink blanket with *Hannah* hand-embroidered at the bottom.

'It's beautiful, Mum, thank you.'

'Just like the one you had when you were a baby,' Kel replied, happy.

Pat watched his mum pull out a sandwich-shaped parcel, wrapped in thin green paper with cartoon reindeer all over it, and hand it to Lally. 'And here you are, love—our other new addition.'

'Thank you very much,' Lally replied, accepting the gift with a smile.

Pat tensed. His mum's earrings were dangling snowmen with silver tinsel and tiny LED lights in them. Luke had on his 'Christmas pluggers'. Pat had forgotten to talk to his mum about what she'd get Lally. He had no idea what would be in the parcel. Everyone was watching, waiting for her reaction. She began to peel off the tape.

'Rip it!' Tom yelled.

'Okay,' she said with a laugh, and did, and a colourful piece of material slipped out and onto her lap. Pat held his breath. Lally exclaimed, 'Oh, a Picasso on a scarf—how beautiful!' Smiling with her mouth and eyes, she looked up at Kel. It was frightening to see how well she lied. Lally hugged Kel and thanked her, then looked at Murray. Pat's dad's eyes were fixed on Tom, not smiling, but not frowning either. Whatever.

Pat watched his mum pick up a small box. 'Oh, this one's for me,' she said, surprised, turning towards Murray hopefully.

He just shrugged. 'Nothing to do with me.'

'That one is from American Santa,' Lally said sweetly.

'Oh, how lovely,' Kel replied. She sat down on her chair, pulling slowly on the long red ribbons tied around the box. 'Oh my goodness,' she said, opening the lid and looking inside. Her free hand covered her mouth in shock.

Murray tensed. 'What is it?'

'It's so beautiful,' Kel breathed. She held up a bracelet. Silver and gold, with little round beads on it.

'It's from Pandora,' Lally explained. 'I chose a couple of charms to start you off, but you can go into their store and choose more, or people can buy the charms for you as gifts, and they just thread onto it.'

'I've seen ads for these in *Women's Weekly*,' Kel said, draping it around her wrist, fumbling with the clasp.

'Jewellery?' Pat's dad grunted, more of an accusation than a question. The old man shifted his weight in his chair. Kel put her hand out to show him and he flinched. Everyone was quiet. The baby gurgled.

Kel sighed. 'Murray is just embarrassed because he never buys me jewellery.'

'Didn't realise this family could be bought,' he said, getting up from his chair.

'Oh, come on now,' she tried to say lightly, but she was obviously hurt.

'Where are you going, Dad?' Beck asked.

'Coffee,' he replied over his shoulder.

Lally squeezed Pat's hand, gave him a what-the-fuck look.

Then Tom called out, 'Pops! You already had the coffee! You said coffee then presents!'

The shout made Hannah squirm, the gurgling threatening to turn into crying.

'Go get him,' Beck whispered to Tom, and pushed him in the direction of the kitchen.

They waited a couple of minutes for the old man to return with his cup of coffee, Tom dragging him along by the arm, and the ceremony continued without incident.

'How about some more carols, Luke?' Kel asked after the last present was opened.

'White Christmas' came on and Pat stood up, holding a hand out to Lally, and tipped the bauble on his Christmas hat. 'Dance, m'lady?'

She laughed and rose to her feet, and they held each other and swayed to the old crooner. Over Lally's shoulder Pat saw his dad leave the room. Past them all, he could see out the window to the heat glimmering off the black tarmac of the road in front of the house, easily soaring over forty degrees. He couldn't have brought Lally here unless they'd gotten air conditioning. His dad might have blown up for real without the mercy of its cool. Pat leaned over to his brother and whispered, 'Dance with Mum.'

'Your hand, madame?' Luke said to their mum, who pretended to shrug him off before giving in, delighted.

Strips and scrunched balls of wrapping paper were strewn across the floor, brushing at their ankles as they moved. Beck sat on the couch breastfeeding while Tom started on his Lego, lying on his belly by the tree.

Pat looked down into Lally's eyes.

'Merry Christmas,' she said to him.

'Merry Christmas,' he replied, and kissed her.

After the dancing Pat offered to put Hannah down to sleep. He took the baby in his arms and carried her to the guest room, bouncing and swaying like he'd seen Beck do. The baby was impossibly light. Lighter than the Christmas ham. About as pink, though.

Beck followed him into the room and started rummaging through the baby bag.

'Suits you,' she said when she saw him lowering Hannah into the crib.

'Nah, not sure,' he replied.

'Because she doesn't want to? Or you don't know yet?'

'Don't know yet.'

'City girls.' Beck made a *tsk-tsk* sound. 'They think they know everything until they turn forty-one and then waste all that money they've earned on IVF that won't work, as though nobody warned them they can't actually control Mother fucking Nature.'

Pat didn't respond to this. There was truth there but also defensiveness. Having Lally around challenged some very essential choices Beck had made. Pat knew he wasn't spectacularly observant, but it was obvious that Beck wasn't sure how to take Lally. Not sure what to make of her, how to be around her.

They both watched Hannah sleep for a few moments, then Beck turned on a baby monitor and they left the room, Pat pulling the door closed gently behind them.

In the kitchen, Lally was whipping some cream in a bowl and their mum was very delicately rinsing a punnet of blueberries.

'Jeez, Mum,' Luke said, coming in to get a beer out of the fridge. 'Blueberries are like five bucks a punnet.'

'Oh, shoosh,' she said dismissively. 'We always have blueberries on the pav.'

Pat and his siblings exchanged a look. Lally didn't seem to hear or notice over the whirring noise of the old electric beaters.

Red-and-green paper plates were arranged around the kitchen table, and the towering mound of meringue and fruit and cream was placed proudly in the centre.

Within fifteen minutes it had been demolished.

'Time for your afternoon nap, Tom-tom.' Beck patted her son's head.

He groaned.

'That sounds pretty good, actually,' Luke said with a yawn.

'Why don't we all have a little quiet time?' Pat suggested. 'I'll do the dishes.'

'Sounds lovely.' His mum smiled then stood up, retreating to their parents' bedroom.

'I'll give you a hand,' Lally said to Pat.

'No way,' Beck cut in. 'Cooks don't clean.'

Lally's protest was overcome by a yawn that seemed to catch her by surprise. 'In that case, I'll have a nap too.'

Everyone filtered out and left Pat in the kitchen. As he was clearing the table he saw his dad in the living room. Tom was already dozing on the couch, and Murray was crouched by his side, undoing the velcro on his sandals, slipping the shoes off the boy's small feet. He placed them side by side at the edge of the couch then lifted and moved Tom a little so that he was lying down properly, his head on one of the cushions. Pat couldn't remember his dad ever tucking him in. Envy was blossoming in him until he found a stray blueberry under the edge of the pavlova plate and popped it in his mouth. In America berries had been a regular kind of fruit, not too expensive. If he visited Lally more often he'd have as many berries as he pleased. Blueberries and Lally.

'Need a hand?' His dad appeared at his side, grabbing a pile of dirty cutlery.

'Thanks,' Pat replied. He felt like maybe this was an opportunity, when his dad was clearly feeling relaxed, to have a chat. 'So,' he started, 'what do you think of Lally?'

Murray turned the hot and cold taps on, placing the plug in the bottom of the sink. Pat watched him add a minuscule drip of washing detergent, reach for the old sponge.

'Sure,' he said finally, reaching for a bowl.

'Sure what?' Pat asked, taking more plates from the table and carrying them to the side of the sink.

'Your wife, your life,' his father replied cryptically.

Pat stopped moving, stared at his dad's profile. 'Yes, I know that. I'm asking if you like her, because I think she's great.'

'Well . . .' The old man placed a dripping plate on the drying rack. 'All good people are great, but not all great people are good.'

This was vague and confusing, and felt a bit insulting. 'You don't think Lally is good?'

Murray shrugged. 'You tell me.'

'What don't you like about her?' Pat demanded.

'Never said I didn't like her. I've only known her a couple of days.'

'Well, you don't sound very positive. You don't sound very nice.'

Murray snorted. 'If you want nice, go ask your mother.'

Pat sighed and grabbed the ratty tea towel from its hook. Maybe he was digging for something that wasn't there. Maybe there would never be some kind of aha moment with this man. Maybe it was just too late.

'At least be polite to her while she's here,' Pat said.

'Don't tell me how to behave in my own home.'

'I'm not telling you how to behave, I'm—' Pat stopped. He could see his father's shoulders tensing. 'Sure.'

They finished clearing up in silence and Murray left the kitchen without saying a single other thing.

Pat went to his old room and found Lally sprawled on the bed, a clunky pedestal fan pointed directly at her. She opened her eyes a little and smiled, then closed them again when she saw it was him. He shut the door behind him and took his shorts off, getting into bed beside her in just his t-shirt and underpants. He stared at her. She was so beautiful. She was so not from this place.

'You all right?' she asked quietly, turning onto her side to face him.

'Yeah, why?'

'You seem a little stressed.'

Pat sighed. 'Family.'

She nodded. 'Some you're born with'—she reached out and took his hand—'and some you choose.'

He kissed her. She kissed him back and pulled his hand to her breast. He felt himself easing into this feeling, letting her take him away, everything else disappearing. She sat up and pulled her dress over her head, and then went to the edge of the bed, leaned over to the fan and turned it up to its maximum setting, the whirring and the clicking conveniently loud. Pat sat up then too and moved to the centre of the bed, reaching forward to grab Lally's waist, dragging her back to nestle in his lap. She inhaled sharply when she pushed up against his erection, and touched herself as he unclasped her bra. They moved quickly and quietly, hitting an intimacy-efficiency sweet spot. He squeezed her arse cheeks and she nodded, so he did it again, and he watched her mouth open, her eyes scrunched shut, the riding slowing to a halt, the breathing quickening, then the little pause, and the slump. He turned them both over into missionary and groaned quietly into the pillow. It felt so good. If only he could go back a decade, to the Pat in this bedroom who was so insecure, tell him not to worry, that he'd be fucking a hot rich American chick who loved him. Without warning she raised her legs and wrapped them around his torso, and he came as quietly as he could, the fan still clicking and whirring, cooling the sweat on their bodies. Lally slipped her dress back on and snuck out to the bathroom, and when she returned he was almost asleep. Her head on his chest was the perfect weight.

———

'Didn't know you could drive a manual,' Beck teased. He'd volunteered to drive her and the kids home on Boxing Day. She couldn't afford to get her old bomb repaired and was borrowing Kel's ancient Corolla to get the kids around.

'Your lawn needs a mow,' Pat replied, pulling into the parallel grooves of dirt that served as her driveway.

'Did you hear that?' Beck said to Tom, unbuckling him from the car seat and putting him over her shoulder, grabbing the baby bag with her other arm. 'Uncle Pat said he's going to mow the lawn for us! Could you get the scooter out of the back?'

'Yeah, easy, where do you want it?'

'Just leave it in the carport.'

She disappeared inside with the kids and Pat did as he was asked. The corrugated-iron roof of the carport had holes in it, and there was a whipper-snipper lying on the ground near a jerry can, alongside a bunch of other junky-looking stuff. He leaned the scooter against a pole and nudged the can with the toe of his sneaker. Empty. He couldn't even see a lawnmower among all the other crap. She probably just borrowed their dad's. Maybe he really would mow their lawn for them when the sun had set. Beck always seemed pissed off at him and he could never find the words to fix it. Perhaps he could do this chore for her and leave on a pleasant vibe.

Inside her place he saw where the carpet was worn near the front door, where the lino was peeling at the edges of the kitchen, and the mismatched chairs around the dining table. No wonder she spent so much more time at the family home. This place was a wreck. When he went to wash his hands in the kitchen sink he saw the tap was dripping.

Beck came into the kitchen.

'Can't Luke fix this for you?' Pat asked, pointing to the dripping tap.

'Landlord pays the water bill,' she replied with a shrug, putting a container of leftovers in the fridge.

'Yeah, but—'

'But what, Pat?' she cut him off, hands on her hips.

'Nothing,' he replied. Nothing at all.

'You know what your problem is?' she started, about to launch into something, when they both heard a noise from outside near the car. They walked to the front door and saw someone running from the carport back to the front gate.

'Fuck!' Beck yelled. 'He's got Tom's scooter!'

Pat burst through the door and leaped down the concrete steps, running around the car and out the front gate. The shithead was wearing knee-length board shorts, flapping along in thongs, carrying the scooter awkwardly in one hand.

'Hey, cunt!' Pat yelled. 'I'm gaining on you!'

The idiot limped faster.

Pat surged forward, catching up with him in the middle of the road, grabbing the man's shoulder and turning him around.

'Fuck off!' the guy screamed, his mouth pocked with dark teeth, and Pat realised this guy was just a teenager, or at least much younger than Pat himself, but he had crazy, bloodshot eyes and scabs all over his face. Pat recoiled, didn't want to touch him, didn't want to be spat on or bled on, but he had to get the scooter back. The guy started screaming then, nonsense and swear words, taking a swing at Pat with the hand not holding the scooter, completely missing, falling to his knees on the hot asphalt. Pat kicked the man's right arm and he cried out and dropped the scooter, screaming that Pat was a 'fucking dog', trying to get back on his feet.

Pat kicked at his shoulder, shoving him face down onto the road. His neck was sunburned red, bloody scabs at the creases there too, and then Pat saw the loser's arse crack over the waistband of his board shorts, and was overcome by a surge of rage and disgust. Pat seized the scooter in his left hand and brought his right fist down onto the side of the filthy cunt's head. The impact rolled him over so he was sprawled on his back, still screaming nonsense. His ratty singlet was up around his armpits, one hand holding the side of his head. Pat moved forward, raising the scooter over his head with both arms.

'Pat!' Beck yelled from the footpath. 'Pat, stop! The cops are coming!'

Pat could hear his blood pumping in ears, feel it in his chest and arms, feel it at his temple. The grub was wriggling on the ground, crying now, shuffling along on his back. 'We can't let him get away!' Pat yelled.

'I know who it is. The cops know too. His folks live up the road. Just leave him.'

'What the fuck?'

Pat lowered the scooter and tried to take deep breaths, retreating to the footpath, watching as the rank idiot got to his hands and knees, pulling himself up on the other side of the road. He turned to look at them and spat, called them dogs one more time, then pulled his pants up and hobbled away.

'Let's get back,' Beck said. 'I've left the kids alone.' She tugged the sleeve of his shirt. 'Come on.'

They walked in silence. Pat carried the scooter in his right hand and noticed his left was shaking. He made it into a fist and let it go, fist and let it go.

'Breathe,' Beck said to him when they reached her place.

They trudged up the steps and through the front door. Beck went straight to the kids' bedrooms and Pat went to the kitchen sink to wash up. He realised he was still holding the scooter and put it down, leaning it against the counter. Water streamed from the faucet, splashing up onto his front. He rubbed the old bar of Imperial Leather all over his hands, all the way up to his wrists, then even further, to his elbows. He'd have a proper shower back at his folks' place. For now, the cool water was good for his red knuckles.

Beck appeared beside him and handed him a small green towel.

'Thanks,' he said.

'Thank *you*,' she replied, 'for getting the scooter back. Tom would've been devastated.'

'No worries. That dickhead steal from you often?'

She turned around, flicking the kettle on, getting two mugs from the drying rack. 'I've heard people say they've had things go missing. Not from inside their homes—just opportunistic stuff.'

Pat dried his arms. 'He was jonesing for something. Meth, ice, whatever they get around here.'

She nodded, putting two heaped teaspoons of sugar into her mug. 'Sugar?'

'Nah. Does Tom walk to school?'

'Of course. It's just up the road.'

'The same road I just chased that guy up?'

'Don't say it like it's a question if you're trying to make a statement.' She turned to him, the kettle behind her starting to boil.

'Okay, here's my question: are the kids okay out here?'

'What the fuck does that mean?'

'It means you've got dickheads on ice nicking shit from your driveway and throwing punches on Boxing Day. Does Tom walk to school by himself?'

'He walks with his friends, Pat. With his *friends*. You wouldn't know what that means, would you?'

'Wow.' He laughed. 'Real mature.'

'I'm serious. Do you have real friends? Or just people you climb up?'

'Fuck off.'

'You fuck off. You're in my house. You're in my town. This is my family.'

'Our family.'

'Hasn't been your family in a long time, though, has it, mate? And now you're starting a rich new family with some woman in America, as far away from us as you can get.'

'Is that what this is about? You're still pissed at me for getting out? You are so fucking transparent.'

She threw a teaspoon at him, hard. It missed and skidded along the kitchen table. 'How fucking dare you, you arrogant fuck. This happens'—she pointed to the scooter—'and all you can fucking think about is how much fucking better your life is than mine?'

'That's not—'

'Shut the fuck up, Pat! You're like a psychopath or something.'

Tom came trundling in, rubbing his eyes. 'Mum?'

Pat moved towards the boy but Beck pushed him out of the way.

'Stay away from my children,' she said, scooping the child up and carrying him back to his room.

'Come on, Beck,' Pat said, trying to placate her, but he could hear the words came out frustrated, like a challenge. She was gone a minute or two and he couldn't think of a way to diffuse the situation without just leaving, then he heard the door to Tom's bedroom close and she came back in, pushing past him into the kitchen.

'I'll bet you think it's basically child abuse for me to raise my kids here, don't you?'

'Where are they going to go to high school?' he asked, wringing the towel in his hands. 'I can get Tom into my school, if you like—there's a list for old boys.'

'I don't want your filthy old boys anywhere near my children. What the fuck don't you get about any of this?'

'What I don't get is why you don't want to help your children get a fucking education and get out of here.'

'That old-boy bullshit with all those priests? Or the fucking wood-panelling and coke and doped-up bimbo wives? Those people are disgusting.'

'Disgusting is that man I just chased down the road.'

Beck shook her head and stepped away from him. The kettle clicked off and she went over to it but just put both her hands on the benchtop beside the cups, leaning against it with her head down.

'Why can't you admit you're jealous?' he demanded. He couldn't stop himself. 'Why can't you admit you hate it here? That's what you used to tell me every Christmas when I came home: how jealous you were. How unfair it was.'

'I was a child, Pat, I didn't know any better.'

'Well, you're being a child now, Beck. You've got two kids and no career and no man. Swallow your goddamn pride and let me help you.'

She turned around and roared at him, 'I don't want your fucking pity and I don't need your fucking help!' She pushed him in the chest. 'Get out!'

'Jesus, Beck.'

'And don't come back!'

Pat put his hands up and backed out of the room, dropping the towel on the floor behind him.

The afternoon heat of the walk back to his folks' place made everything worse. Sweat dripped between his shoulder blades and down his back, and he could feel his ears getting sunburned. Was Beck lying to herself as well, or just to him? Life didn't offer you constantly expanding opportunities. You were born with the potential to pivot any which way, and then one by one avenues were sealed off. Going to university was one of the few things you could do in life to try to wrestle open a few of those closed doors, but kids from Esk didn't seem to make it to university. How could she not see that with no husband, no career, stuck in a tiny backward town, she was condemning her kids to the same thing? He felt angry at his parents too. How could his mum see this happening and not do anything? She was selfish, wanting her grandchildren nearby, happy to throw her own daughter under the bus of an average life just to have them. All those lectures she gave him when he was at school, about opportunities and the difference between a career and a job—she'd never given that talk to her fucking daughter, had she? Hypocrite.

He passed houses with acres of lawn surrounding them. The sheer vastness of the country always shocked him when he came home. All that empty space around each home was both familiar and off-putting. Children in one yard were squealing and putting detergent on a slip-n-slide they'd probably just got from Santa, their bicycles lying abandoned under the carport. Two houses further along a kelpie jumped up from a front step, barking, launching itself up against the fence with a wagging tail and wiggly body. Pat reached over the gate to pet the dog and it licked his hand madly.

'Hey there, beautiful,' he said, grabbing its collar. A bone-shaped tag had a mobile number and *Spot* engraved on it. A classic. Pat tried to remember the names he'd been planning to call his own dog, when he finally got one, but he couldn't access them. He just kept seeing the image of Tom, upset, rubbing his eyes. The image of that crackhead teen's bloodshot eyes. The feeling of Beck's hands on his chest, shoving him away. There was no way to win. You live in the city and you can't afford shit, no dog, tiny place. You live in the country and there's no smart work and you trap your kids there.

His dad was waiting for him in the living room when he got home.

'Where've you been?' the old man asked.

'Just thought I'd take a little walk to get home,' Pat replied.

'Didn't think to come home and help your mother with the cleaning?'

Pat shrugged.

'Nothing to say to me?' Murray said, louder now, maybe getting nasty.

'Sorry, Dad, I'll go find Mum, give her a hand.'

'Got a call from Rebecca while you were out walkabout daydreaming.'

Pat groaned.

'What's that, boy?'

'Nothing.'

'Well, it seems like you had plenty to say to her.' Murray glared at him. 'Did you tell her you didn't think that Tom should go to school here?'

'What? I—'

His dad cut him off, voice getting louder still. 'How do you think that makes your brother feel?'

Pat looked over to Luke, sitting at the kitchen table behind their dad. Luke raised his beer bottle and tapped it with his finger. Pat received the message and sighed. Bad move.

'Am I boring you?'

'No.'

'Why won't you look at me?'

Pat looked up at his father. It was obvious now. The redness of his face, the large gut. Pat walked over to stand beside Luke's chair.

'Where's Lally?' Pat asked his brother in a low voice.

'Out back with Mum,' Luke replied, quick and quiet.

Their dad was almost shouting now, following Pat to the kitchen. 'I didn't break my back in those paddocks to have you go off to the city and come back looking down on me!'

'You sent me there!' Pat protested.

'And you can fucking guarantee I won't make that mistake with my grandchildren.'

'That's not your decision to make, is it?'

'More mine than yours.' The old man jabbed Pat in the chest with his finger. 'You haven't been around. You can't come back here and dish out advice, acting like you know better. What would you even know? Fucking some snob slut—'

'Enough!' Pat yelled.

Luke pushed his chair out and stood up too.

Murray drew himself up tall, pulling his shoulders back. Even after all these years it filled Pat with dread.

Luke raised his hands, approached the old man slowly. 'Come on, Dad.'

'Don't you patronise me, boy!' their father yelled.

Luke shrank away, dissolving behind his older brother.

Pat saw Lally appear in the doorway at the far end of the living room, behind his raging father. She crossed her arms, watching. He looked back to his father. So red in the face. Both hands in fists. What could Pat do? What was he supposed to do? Stand up to his dad and get the shit kicked out of him in front of his girlfriend? Get his little brother and together kick the shit out of their dad, in front of his girlfriend? It had been so long since this last happened, he didn't know if Luke would help this time.

Pat exhaled and stepped forward.

'Pat . . .' Luke pleaded quietly, trying to grab his arm, but Pat pulled away and walked past the pair of them, giving his dad a wide berth as he left the kitchen.

'Where are you—' their dad started, but he was interrupted by a bang.

'What's going on here?' Kel burst through the back screen door, a basket of sheets and towels in her arms.

Everyone stood stock-still. Pat looked at the carpet in front of his feet. All the different browns. A droplet of sweat fell from his brow and landed between his sneakers. Another brown.

'I'm going to the pub,' Murray said finally, grabbing his wallet from the top of the fridge.

'Like hell you are,' Kel shot back. 'It's not even open on Boxing Day, you know that.'

But her husband stormed past her out the screen door, slamming it behind him. The ute engine fired up and they could hear it backing out of the driveway. Luke's shoulders didn't come down from around his ears until the noise had fully faded down the street.

Pat ran his fingers through his hair. His hands were shaking. He ignored his mother's questions—Luke could do some explaining for fucking once—and went over to Lally. She turned and went into their bedroom and he followed.

'I can't stay here, Pat.'

'I don't think—' Pat stopped himself. Maybe his dad *was* dangerous. 'Who fucking knows. I don't know. I want to leave, so if you want to leave too, then it's settled, we leave. I don't know where we'll go, though. Our flights aren't till tomorrow.'

'We can change them. Or we stay the night in a hotel.'

More money, but no other real options. 'Okay.'

He took his t-shirt off, scrunching it up and wiping his neck and underarms with it, then pulled on a clean one and started throwing things into his suitcase. They carried their bags out to the rental car. It was boiling hot inside. Pat opened all the doors then he and Lally returned to the house.

'Mum?' he called.

No reply.

Luke was at the kitchen table, cracking another beer. 'She's gone out looking for Dad,' he said.

'We're leaving.'

'Without saying goodbye to Mum?'

'Well, we can't stay here.'

Luke smiled sadly at Lally. 'It was nice to meet you,' he said with a pathetic sort of wave. 'Sorry it got weird.'

'Don't worry about it,' she replied.

Pat walked over and gave his brother a rough hug. 'Tell Mum goodbye for me.'

They were ten minutes out of town when Lally asked him to pull over.

'Why?' he asked.

'Just pull over.'

'Can you wait until we get to a servo?'

'For fuck's sake, pull over!'

He switched on his indicator and bumped from the tarmac onto the gravel. Lally was rummaging through her handbag.

'You left something behind?'

'No,' she said and cracked a pill into her hand, swallowing it. 'I'm having a migraine. We have to go somewhere dark and quiet. Now, please. It's going to get bad.'

'Shit, okay, well, we're still another half-hour from the next town, where there might be a—'

'Too long!' She started to cry. From her bag she took the Picasso scarf she'd got for Christmas and tied it around her eyes like a blindfold. 'Please, Pat, take me somewhere dark and quiet. *Now.*'

'Okay, fuck, just relax.'

She groaned.

'I'm turning around.' He did a U-turn, heading back in the direction they'd come.

'But your dad?' She reached for his arm, sounding panicky.

'We'll go to Beck's.'

'He can't come over.'

'I won't let him.'

'Okay,' she whimpered, putting her head in her hands.

'Okay.'

Pat sped up, going too fast around bends he knew had killed people. They were back in town in a matter of minutes.

'Okay, we're here,' he said, pulling into Beck's carport. 'You stay there and I'll come round.' He took her handbag and slung it over his own shoulder, then went to her side of the car. Opening her door, he took her hands and led her up the path to Beck's house. She seemed so tiny. Diminished.

'What the fuck?' Beck's voice said from behind the screen door.

'I'm sorry,' Pat said. 'Lally is sick. We need to get her—'

Beck opened the screen for them. 'What is it?'

'Migraine,' Lally gurgled.

'Ah . . . I got them when I was pregnant,' Beck said. 'Come through to my room. I still have the light-blocking curtains.'

They made their way slowly down the hall.

'Bucket,' Lally whispered.

'It's all right,' Beck replied before Pat could. 'We'll get a bucket, we'll get a cool towel, we'll get some good painkillers—it's gonna be all right.'

Pat heard his mother in Beck's voice.

He helped Lally into bed and turned away to go get the bucket and towel, but she wouldn't let go of his hand.

'Don't leave me,' she pleaded.

'You stay,' Beck said. 'I'll get it.'

Lally burped, and he laughed a little.

'No,' she cried, and pulled off the scarf but kept her eyes scrunched shut. 'It's going to get worse. Don't laugh. Please.'

'Bucket,' Beck announced, putting it down beside the bed and leaving again.

'Bucket,' Lally repeated, reaching for it, and Pat passed it to her.

She leaned forward, barely making it over the side of the bed, and started retching into it. Within a few heaves she was bringing up breakfast. Just when she seemed to have finished she was overwhelmed by another wave. She farted as she leaned over to vomit some more. When the wave had passed, she started to cry.

'Hey, hey,' he said softly, tucking her hair behind her ear. 'It's all right.'

Beck returned, handing Pat a roll of paper towel and a wet face washer. 'Thank you,' he mouthed. She just nodded and left again. He tore a square from the roll and wiped Lally's mouth.

'Lie back and let me put this washer on your forehead,' he said. 'It's nice and cool.'

She just kept crying, hiding her face. 'Don't look at me.'

'Hey, hey, it's me—I love you.'

'I'm scared.'

'Don't be scared. I'm here.'

'Don't leave.'

'I won't.'

'Don't let your dad come.'

'He won't come, I won't leave.'

'Pat,' she whispered.

'Yeah?'

But she didn't say anything, just opened one eye to look at him, then took his hand and rolled onto her back. He folded the face washer into a rectangle, and did what he thought his mum would have done, kissing her forehead and then putting the washcloth onto the spot he'd kissed.

33

A COOLNESS CAME ACROSS HER forehead. It didn't stop the pain, but it allowed her a glimpse through it for a moment. It was him, and she knew his face, although she couldn't say his name. He dabbed her forehead. She felt like a baby. A surge of heart. Trust. She wept. For the pain and for the pivot. The clarity that came when she began to emerge into this liminal space, her brain functioning altered. Truths revealed to her, washing over her, changing what she knew and what she wanted. She wanted this. Him, caring for her. Kindness to her. To do kindness. She dipped back down into the other place.

When she woke again, some hours later, her head a little clearer, he was still beside her. What would it look like if her life was governed by something other than her own exacting, never-ending choreography? She looked up at his profile, lit faintly from behind by a sliver of light coming through the curtains. Delivered. She reached for him, and when he smiled at her it was like pushing up from a deep salty ocean into clear, fresh water, and when he said, 'How are you feeling?' it was, finally, air.

'I'm so sorry to have imposed on you like this,' Lally said, hobbling into the kitchen. The sun had set a long time ago.

'Oh, it's fine,' Beck said. She stood up from her seat and got some mugs out.

'No, really, I'm very grateful. I . . .' Lally struggled to explain it. 'They're not just headaches. I get disoriented and it can be dangerous.'

'Yeah, I had them when I was pregnant with Tom.'

'Oh my god.' Lally sat down at the table opposite Beck. 'I can't imagine having one while pregnant.'

'Yeah, but my mum—our mum,' she amended, as Pat joined them in the kitchen, 'said that whenever she was pregnant all her joints got better, not worse.'

'I didn't know that,' Pat piped up.

'Did you ask?'

He mumbled a nothing reply.

'I'm an only child,' Lally said, 'and my mom doesn't like talking about life when my dad was around.'

Beck nodded. 'You wanna put the kettle on, Pat?'

'Sure.'

'Do you mind if I ask,' Lally said, looking at Beck intently, 'was it frightening?'

'What? Giving birth?'

'I mean the whole thing. The pregnancy, and the birth, and being a single mom.' Lally saw Pat stiffen, standing at the counter behind Beck, as he stared down at the kettle.

Beck snorted. 'Well, I didn't plan the single part.' She paused, then went on. 'Three of my friends had already had their first kid before I even got pregnant with Tom, no real complications, so I wasn't that scared, medically or anything. The pain passes, and honestly, there doesn't seem to be much difference for the mums who are single compared to the mums who have FIFO husbands. Except the money, of course. The girls reckon that when their husbands are home it just means they have an extra kid to feed and clean up after.'

'Yikes,' Lally replied.

'And the money difference, well, that's always been more about what you're born with than who you shack up with.'

'So,' Pat said, putting cups in front of each of them, 'if Lally is feeling up to it, we might head off after these.'

'No worries,' Beck said, 'Probably best if Mum and Dad don't know you're still here.'

'I reckon.'

'Are you sure you're all right to go, though?' she asked Lally.

'Yes, thanks.' Lally smiled. 'I'm still a little shaky, but better now it's dark.'

'Just tell me if you want to pull over or stop,' Pat said, helping her with her seatbelt and closing her door for her. They waved to Beck and she waved back.

'Pat,' she said, turning her head towards him as he pulled away from the kerb, 'I want us to live together.'

'I want us to live together too.'

They rode in silence for a while. She had decided to wait for him to speak first and watched his hands grip and release the steering wheel.

'I would like to live with you,' he said. 'I can move to New York. If that's what you were thinking. If that's what you want too.'

'I think that's a wonderful idea.'

He smiled at her quickly before turning back to the road.

'I was thinking about it while you were sick. Being back here, hoping for Christmas to do something, I dunno, positive. But it just made everything worse. And because of your dad . . . I know I can't ask you to be around my dad.'

'Do you want to be around your dad?'

'No. But I'll miss Mum, I guess. The flights are expensive.'

'I own my apartment.'

'What?' He glanced at her in shock. 'So you have a mortgage?'

'Barely. About fifty grand still owing. I'll have it paid off by the end of next year.'

'But,' he shook his head, 'your place must be worth millions.'

'It is.'

'You're a millionaire?'

'No. I have an asset worth over a million. Capital, not cash.'

'I . . . I don't know what to say. Why didn't you tell me?'

'Plenty of reasons. Would it sound like I was bragging? Would you get the wrong impression and think I was from a wealthy family? Would it make you nervous about any disparity?'

'Okay, yeah, sure.'

'And then, I suppose, just whether or not you really liked me.'

'Well, I do really like you,' he confirmed.

'I really like you too.'

'Actually, I love you.'

'I love you too.' She grinned. 'Gallery Lally can sponsor your visa. I can support you until you find an equivalent position. Probably better paid too. I don't know what your exit terms with Osborne are, though.'

'Just the standard two weeks' notice. But as a courtesy I should do a client handover. I was thinking of this last night too. I know the perfect person to take over my job.'

'Great, it's settled then.'

'There is one thing,' he said, tentative.

She was instantly nervous. 'What is it?'

He took a deep breath in. 'If you own your place that means we can have a dog. I want a dog.'

'A dog? That's your condition?' she laughed, even though it hurt her head.

'That's my condition.'

'Okay,' Lally said, closing her eyes, resting her head back. 'Okay.'

34

PAT WAS HAVING A BEER, sitting at the dining table going through their mail while Lally sipped a gin and tonic. 'Check it out,' he said to Lally, holding up a colourful brochure. 'The program for next year's Armory.'

Lally's phone rang and she answered it. 'Hey, Gen, what's up? When are we meeting you guys?'

'Well, actually,' Gen said, 'I was wondering if we could just come over to your place instead, have a night in?'

'Oh, thank god! I've been trying to explain to Pat that New Year's Eve in New York is actually hell. He doesn't believe me, but now he's outnumbered.'

Gen and Alex arrived an hour later with bags of food and drink.

'What's all this?' Lally asked as she let them in.

She kissed them each on the cheek, and Alex extended a hand to Pat.

'Nice to meet you, Pat,' he said, and the men shook hands.

'You too,' Pat replied. Then he frowned. 'Have we met before?'

'I don't think so.' Alex smiled and produced two bottles of champagne.

'Are you sure? I could swear I know your face from somewhere.'

'So how come you changed your mind about going out?' Lally asked Alex, interrupting Pat.

'Ah, well . . .' He looked to Gen.

Gen joined them standing around the table. 'We have some news.'

'Holy shit,' Lally said.

'Yeah.' Alex was grinning, staring at Gen in a sort of manic wonderment.

'About two months, we think,' Gen said.

Lally screamed, and the women hugged. The men hugged. They all hugged each other.

'So I said to Alex, you three can all toast tonight, and then after this he's not allowed to drink in front of me.'

Everyone laughed.

Lally got the flutes.

'How about some sparkling apple juice, Gen?' Pat asked her, holding the bottle like a fancy waiter would.

'Hmm, what vintage?'

Alex popped the cork.

'A toast,' Lally announced, as the four of them held up their glasses. 'To two beautiful, smart, wonderful people, making a third person. A baby born in 2020. I've got a good feeling about this.'

'Cheers!' they all sang out.

Pat started asking Gen and Alex about dogs.

'We are not getting an Irish wolfhound!' Lally yelled across the table.

Hours passed and they put some frozen pizzas in the oven.

'What are you going to do for work?' Alex asked Pat.

'I've got some contacts at Osborne's Academy here,' Pat replied, 'and if that doesn't come through I can always wait tables at Estelle's.'

Lally gave him a teasing nudge.

When midnight was close they crowded around one of the windows to catch the corner of the highest fireworks.

The countdown played on the television behind them, and the four friends hugged and kissed.

'I've got a good feeling about this year,' Pat said out loud to the group.

Alex put his hand on Gen's belly. 'Us too. 2020 has a ring to it, doesn't it?'

Lally kissed Pat. 'It's finally gonna be good and easy. No more video calls.'

'I've got a girlfriend and I'm about to get a dog,' Pat replied with a grin. 'I'm living the dream.'

AUTHOR'S NOTE

I KNOW SEVERAL MEN CALLED Patrick. I have borrowed names from some works of art, artists and institutions, and have created many others. My family live near Esk but these are not my parents. If you believe you recognise yourself in these pages then I'm sorry but you are mistaken. I've written a lot of non-fiction; if I wanted to write about *you* I would.

ACKNOWLEDGEMENTS

THANK YOU TO MY FAMILY for being the rock-solid foundation I could always return to throughout the five years of making this work. And a special thank you to Mum for letting me skip school to work with you at Lee's Visual Art Supplies. Formative!

To my agent Grace Heifetz: I deeply value our friendship and with every book I am more grateful we found each other in 2016. To my publisher Jane Palfreyman: you are still my number one badass motherfucker. To my publicist Isabelle O'Brien: thank you for your savvy hard work, and I am so incredibly excited to tour this with you! To my cover designer Sandy Cull: we had tears in our eyes and goosebumps on our arms when we saw what you had created; I cannot imagine a better way for this work to be presented to the world. For the various stages of editing and behind-the-scenes mastery at Allen & Unwin, I am immensely grateful to Ali Lavau, Genevieve Buzo, Christa Munns, Jennifer Thurgate and Sarah Barrett.

The album *Lux Prima* by Karen O and Danger Mouse was released in March 2019 when I was in New York researching, and it became the soundtrack to the story and characters developing in my mind. I listened to those nine songs on loop every time I worked on this book, and only when I was working on this book, such that they became a place I could return to and be immediately inserted back into Pat and Lally's world. We don't always know what other art our art will catalyse. I'd like to thank Karen O and Danger Mouse for the excellent record I've spent five years of my life listening to.

A long time ago David McGuinness and the kind people at Bourke Street Bakery put up with me nosing around in their space before dawn. I'm always moved when people give up their time with no expectation of anything in return. Please know how much those mornings helped me; thank you.

Over the years I have been honoured with several grants and residencies. I'd specifically like to acknowledge the support of the Copyright Agency x UTS Writer-in-Residence position I received in 2020. It was vital as I established myself here in Sydney and worked on this novel.

Vincent, this book is for you. Growing up together has been such a joy! And growing old together will be a privilege.